HEART'S MASTER

ELIZABETH SCHECHTER

Clasp Editions

the romance imprint of

Circlet Press, Inc.

Cambridge, MA

Cover images:
man on throne © Sergey Velikanov | Dreamstime.com
man in rope © Andrei Vishnyakov | Dreamstime.com

First paperback printing Decemb er2016
ISBN 978-1-61390-172-4

Published by Clasp Editions,
an imprint of Circlet Press, Inc.
39 Hurlbut Street
Cambridge, MA 02138

www.circlet.com

Contents

To M & J, for their infinite patience when I was on deadline.

To the crew at ERWA, who read the initial manuscript and pronounced it good.

To Dan and Janet, who read the final manuscript and pronounced it better.

And to Jen. What a long, strange trip it's been!

Chapter One
One Step Forward

I sleep really hard. Hard enough that my mother used to say I'd sleep through the Second Coming. I'd regularly sleep through my alarms, until Mom got me one of those alarm clocks that actually shakes the bed. She had it set to the highest setting, the one that the manual affectionately called "Earthquake Mode." And even then, I still sometimes slept through it.

Like I said, I'm a really heavy sleeper; which was the excuse I was going to offer if I was called on the fact that I was over an hour late to work. My boss had seen me napping between shows before, so she knew how I slept. It just wasn't the whole truth. I had, indeed, overslept, but that wasn't the whole reason I was late. Still, it was a good excuse, one that I really thought would have gotten past all of Maureen's bullshit detectors. It might have, too, if it hadn't been for one thing: Maureen coming into my dressing room without knocking, and while I still had my shirt off so that I could inspect the damage that my lover Joey had done to me.

"Your call was for noon, Steven," she said as she came in, and did she ever sound pissed. "The curtain goes up in less than an hour. You've barely got time to warm-up and get into makeup. What in the name of God's labia majora did you do to your wrists?" Her voice spiraled up on the last sentence, and I sighed and held my arms out in front of me for her to inspect.

Stupid, Stevie, really stupid, I scolded myself as she took my hands and peered at the bruises encircling my wrists. What the hell was I thinking? I owed Maureen way too much to try and bullshit her. Never mind the fact that she'd probably have seen right through me. She'd taken a huge chance on me, given me a place in the company when all she knew about me was that I was a friend of a friend, and that I was a shiny new college graduate with a theater degree. Six years later, she was a friend in truth, and one of the two people I had in my life that I could really consider family. She studied my wrists, then looked into my eyes for a moment before saying, "My office. Now."

Obediently, I followed her, closing the door behind us and taking the seat that she waved me towards. The office was quiet, an unusual occurrence. "Where's the Nat-monster?" I asked, looking around for Maureen's two-year-old daughter. "She napping?"

"Natalie woke up with a cold, so she's home with the nanny," Maureen answered, filling a mug up with water from the hot-pot on the table. She dropped a tea bag into the water, then raised another mug and arched an elegant eyebrow.

"None for me, thanks. If she's sick, do you still need me to babysit tomorrow?" I had long ago offered to be the emergency stand-in babysitter for Mo's daughter. This was going to be the first time she'd taken me up on the offer, and I was looking forward to it; I liked the little rug-rat, and we got along fine.

"No. We'll be ordering in. But thanks for the offer," Maureen smiled. She sat down across from me and just looked at me for a long moment. I hated it when Maureen gave me that Mom Look, the one that felt like it looked into the bottom of my soul. She didn't do it often, but when she did, I knew I didn't have any secrets left. She narrowed her eyes for a moment, then shook her head. "Joey did that?" she asked as she nodded towards my wrists.

I grimaced and mumbled, "Yeah."

"And that's why you're late?" She leaned back in her chair, her eyes narrowed.

"Yeah..." Before I realized what I was doing, I told her the whole thing—how I'd gone to bed the night before without letting Joey fuck me, and how he'd gotten his revenge by chaining me up before I was awake, and keeping me that way until long after he'd gotten himself off. I left out the part about the spiked cock-ring that Joey had told me was my new collar. Thankfully, he always hid the keys in the same place, or I'd be in deep shit; there was no *way* I'd have been able to dance with that thing on my junk.

I rubbed the back of my neck, kneading the knots there as I spoke. "... And when I got to the bus-stop, I found out he'd emptied my wallet. I ran the whole way..."

She held one hand up and interrupted me, "Steven, stop there. Just... stop. Do you realize that you are sitting here, very calmly telling me that Joey *raped* you this morning?"

"What?" I gasped and sat up straight in my chair. "Mo, that's not..."

"Did he ask you if you wanted to have sex this morning?" she asked.

"Well... no, but..."

"Did you agree to any of what he did to you?" she continued.

"No, but..."

She leaned forward and looked into my eyes, "Steven, would you have thrown your safe-word this morning if he hadn't gagged you?"

That one stopped me. "I didn't tell you he gagged me..."

"You still have tape on your face," Maureen said softly, tapping her cheek. I touched the corresponding spot on my own face, felt something sticky and winced. "Baby, I've been a Mistress a lot longer than your little wanna-be dom..."

"Mo, that's more info than I needed..." I said weakly, scrubbing at my cheek, trying to get rid of fibers that would not let go.

"Deal. And answer me. Would you?"

I nodded slowly, "Yeah. I would have." I let my hand fall into my lap, feeling defeated.

"And he's done this to you before?" She didn't wait for my nod. "Baby..."

"Mo, can I sleep on your floor?" I blurted out, interrupting her and surprising myself. I hadn't known I was going to ask that until the words fell out of my mouth. "I'll help around the house, babysit, whatever you want, but I need to get out of there. He's started going too far, and I don't like where this is heading."

"I don't like where it already went. But you're right. You need to be out of there. Now." She looked at me again, then nodded. "You can stay with me on one condition."

"What?"

"Tomorrow, you're sitting down with Cheryl," Maureen said flatly. "And we will be calling the police."

"Cheryl... the lady who lives across the street from you, the one who makes those really good brownies?" I asked. When Maureen nodded, I frowned. "Okay, I understand calling the cops. But why talk to Cheryl?"

"She's a rape counselor."

I didn't have an answer. The only thing I could think of to say was "Oh."

"Steven, how long has this been going on?" Maureen asked gently.

"The bondage thing?" I asked, running my fingers through my hair, then clenching my hands in my lap to keep them from shaking. "Only about six months, I think."

"I meant the abuse," Maureen said softly.

I felt sick and cold, and I didn't understand how we'd gotten to this point in the conversation. I mean... rape? Was it possible to be raped without realizing that it was happening? I hadn't thought so, but now... now I was thinking about how many times he had ignored me when I told him no. How many times he'd gagged me so I couldn't say no. "I don't know. A... a few weeks, maybe? Maybe a month?" I said, hearing my voice wobble. Maybe I did need to talk to that counselor. "Mo, I..."

"I know, Baby. I know. Will he be at the wrap party tonight?"

I shook my head. "I don't know. He knows about it, but I don't know if he's coming. He's working tomorrow, so he'll want to get to bed early. I figured I could put up with anything for one more night, and then pack up and be gone before he got home."

"You're sure you want to go back there?" she asked. When I nodded, she sighed, "I'll be over with the truck and a couple of the stage hands. What time?"

"He leaves for work at eight thirty."

"I'll be there at nine. Hopefully, he won't get the bright idea to chain you up so you can't run off. But just in case he does, I'll bring bolt cutters."

"Thanks, Mo," I relaxed slightly and looked down at my bruised wrists. "I really did love him. And I thought he loved me. I... how could he do this to me?"

"He's a prick, honey."

"But I loved him." It sounded so lame, but it was true.

"You love them all, honey. You love them, and they break your heart." Maureen sighed, sounding just like someone who had nursed me through a broken heart before. She came around the desk, sat down next to me and took my hand, studying me for a moment. Then she nodded, as if she'd made up her mind about something. "I'm going to introduce you to someone. I think you'll like him..."

"Mo, I think I need to be celibate for a while after this."

She sniffed. "I didn't say I was shoving you into bed with someone, Steven. I'm just introducing you to someone. A nice guy, for a change. And not yet. Not until we get you back on your feet." She looked at me and smiled, her expression softening. "Unless you've changed your mind? Or are you still not interested?"

I laughed and squeezed her hand. "Still don't do girls, Mo. If I did, you'd be first."

"I'd take better care of you, I can tell you that. Well, at least I'll be able to take care of you while you're staying with me. Go on and warm up. Unless you want Kyle to take the matinee?"

I shook my head, "No. I need to work. I need to not think for a while." I stood up, and my stomach decided to let me know I had been ignoring it. Maureen looked shocked.

"Was that you?"

I looked at her, embarrassed. "Yeah."

"Thank goodness. I thought that we somehow had gotten a rabid tiger in here. When did you last eat?"

"Dinner last night. I was going to grab something on the way in, but I told you, he emptied my wallet..."

"Bastard. He'd better not show his face around the stage door tonight. There's a pizza in the freezer, Baby. Help yourself. Don't overdo it, though." She glanced at the clock and made a face. "Go on. We've got a full house for both shows."

The matinee was good, just what I needed so that I didn't have to think about Joey and what he'd done to me. What he might still do, tonight; Maureen had put the idea of Joey taking me hostage into my head, and my way-too fertile imagination ran with it. But apparently, I sublimate really well—two curtain calls and a standing ovation for a matinee was a new record for me. Maureen, bless her mothering instincts and seemingly bottomless pockets, made sure I had money to eat between shows, and I went on that night with more fire than I'd thought I'd ever possess, ending the night with four curtain calls and another standing "O." A heady ending to a crappy day. I finally got off-stage after the fourth curtain call, and was about to head to my dressing room when one of the stage-hands called me over, "Hey, Steve. C'mere."

"What's up, John?" I said, going over to where he was lingering by the curtain.

"Take a look. First row, on the aisle closest to us." He twitched the curtain out of the way, and I saw the man he must have meant. Older guy, nice looking, expensive suit, looked like a businessman. Then he pulled a notebook out of his jacket and I revised my assumption to reviewer. Which was odd. Who reviews on the last night?

"He was there for the matinee, too," John said, letting the curtain fall back.

"Interesting. Did you tell Mo?"

"Yeah. But he looked like he was watching you. So I thought you'd like to know."

I grinned. "Thanks, John. See you at the party?"

"You bet!"

I headed off to my dressing room to catch a shower and change, and ran into Maureen on my way out. She linked her arm into mine and laughed as we headed towards the stage door. "You, my dear, should break up more often. You were hot tonight."

"Thanks, I think. What do you think of the guy in the audience?"

"No idea. Doesn't matter, really. Shall we?" She tugged my arm and we left the theater. I glanced around as we walked out into the humid August evening. Joey wasn't there, but the suit from the front row was. He perked up as we came out, coming towards us. "Miss Hobart? Mr. Ahearn? Could you spare a moment?" I looked at Maureen, who shrugged and stopped. The man smiled at both of us and handed us each a business card. I glanced down at mine, reading "Gerald Taylor, Casting Director." My jaw dropped, and I looked up at him. He was looking back at me, and he nodded once. "I assume you know Max Fleishman?" he asked.

"The theater reviewer with the newspaper?" Maureen asked.

"Yes. Max called me because he knew I was going to need a triple threat. He wanted me to take a look at a young man who had impressed him." Taylor folded his arms over his chest, "I was quite impressed, too. Mr. Ahearn, would you be interested in coming to New York?"

I coughed, "What?" For a minute, I thought he was joking. I looked at Maureen, who looked as stunned as I was.

"Which show?" she asked slowly. Mr. Taylor leaned towards her and whispered in her ear; her eyes went wide and she looked up at me. "Oh, Steve. You did it. You made it!"

I was so stunned that I didn't understand what she meant at first. Did what? Made what? Then Mr. Taylor told me for which show he was casting director, and which role he wanted me to take over. I don't think it really hit me just what he was offering me until Maureen pinched me. Then I got it—this man had come to Baltimore to see me! And he was offering me my wildest dreams on a plate! Broadway...

"I... holy shit... I..." I stammered and looked at Maureen, who was practically dancing in place in her excitement. "Mo, I can't afford to move to New York!"

"If that's the only reason you'd say no, don't say no," Mr. Taylor said. "I'll put you up in a hotel myself until you get situated. Or help you find an apartment. I just need you in New York by Friday at the latest."

Friday. It was Saturday now, so I'd have a few days to think... and my mouth ran away with me. "Would Wednesday be good?" I asked, and heard Maureen's delighted squeal.

Taylor laughed, too. "Wednesday will be great. I'll have my office overnight the script to you first thing Monday, so that you can start learning your lines. You going to drive or take the bus?"

"I'll be putting him on the train myself, Mr. Taylor," Maureen said before I could get a word out.

"Call me Matt, please. And just let me know the schedule and I'll meet you at Penn Station with a contract," he said as he held out his hand. "Welcome to Broadway, Steven."

I looked at Maureen, feeling my face nearly ready to crack from the goofy grin I hadn't realized I was wearing. Her grin was probably just as wide as mine; I nodded and took Matt's hand, shaking it and sealing the agreement. "Thank you," I finally remembered to say.

"No, Steven. Thank you," he answered. "Now, you two were on your way somewhere. I'll let you go..."

"Wrap party," I blurted out. "You're welcome to come, if you like?"

"Of course!" Maureen agreed. "You have to be there when we tell the others."

Matt shook his head. "That's very nice of you both, but I can't. I need to be back in New York tonight, so I have a train to catch. I'll see you on Wednesday, Steven."

"Can we drop you anywhere, at least?" Maureen asked.

"I've already called a cab. Don't worry about me. Go enjoy yourselves." Matt waved and headed out towards the street. When he was gone, I looked at Maureen and said, "Did that really just happen?"

"You mean, did you really just get your break?" Maureen asked. "Yes. Yes, you did." She squealed and threw her arms around my neck, hugging me tightly. "You did it! You're going to Broadway!"

I hugged her back and then, completely on impulse, kissed her. It was supposed to be a friendly thing, something to celebrate my incredible good fortune. It didn't end up that way—Maureen laced her fingers into my hair and took control of the kiss, and all I could do was put my arms around her and go along for the ride. She kissed really well for a girl, but I couldn't get past the differences. She was tall enough, but she was... I don't know. Too soft. Too rounded. Not enough muscles. Not... well, not a guy.

She let me go, and I could see the heat in her eyes when she smiled up at me. "Never knew you were that good a kisser, Baby."

"I could say the same for you," I answered, letting my arms fall.

"Still not interested?" she teased gently.

"Still no," I answered, feeling a little self-conscious. "Sorry."

She turned towards the street, linked her arm into mine again and tugged me along with her. "Just my luck," she grumbled. "Gorgeous, great kisser, fantastic voice, body to die for, and you're completely gay. I just can't win."

I had to grin at the frustration in her voice. "Well, you could always take it out on Nick when you get home," I suggested. I was expecting her to laugh or to tell an off-color joke. I wasn't expecting the silence. "Mo?"

"I didn't want to bring it up. Not tonight. Especially not now," she said quietly.

"What?" I asked softly. Maureen had been with her boyfriend Nick for longer than I'd known her, with a wedding in the works for some time next year. For some reason, I'd never actually met the guy. Maureen described him as a bit of an introvert. They didn't even live together; he had his own place out in the suburbs. From everything I'd heard, he seemed like a good sort, and I was happy for Maureen. Hopefully, I was the only one having relationship problems.

"Nothing. Or maybe something. I don't know. Do me a favor and don't mention to him that I said anything tonight?"

"He's coming?" I was shocked. Nick never came out to the theater parties, which was the main reason why I'd never met him.

Mo smiled broadly at me. "He'll be making an exception tonight. He's coming to your celebration party. You drive, and I'll call him from the car. Who else do you want there?"

I gave her a few names and numbers, and she made calls the entire way to the little restaurant where we usually had our wrap parties. They had a private room in the back, which was crammed full of the rest of the company and the stage-hands, some of them already eating, all of them drinking. It was pretty true that a good performance made for a rowdy wrap-party, and this was no exception. The room was already too warm for comfort, and the noise was deafening; Maureen had to climb onto a chair and shout to get them all to shut up long enough to hear her.

"All right. I have good news and bad news!" she called out once she had their attention. "The bad news first. Steven is leaving us. Tonight is his last night with the company." Groans and cat-calls, with some of the stage hands shouting out ribald insults until Maureen waved them quiet again. Her eyes were sparkling when she pulled me up onto another chair. "The good news... is that he's leaving because he's been offered a role on Broadway!"

It was like the entire room exploded. People were shouting and cheering, and I don't think I'd ever been hugged that many times before, or by that many people. By mutual assent, the wrap party turned into a going away party, and the alcohol started to flow like water. Maureen and I grabbed a table in the corner, and she stood guard over me so that I could eat in between congratulations and hugs.

I was just finishing another drink—my fourth or fifth—and I was feeling nicely squiffed when I saw the stranger coming towards us through the crowd. Tall, broad shoulders, long brown hair pulled back in a tail, early thirties at the most—this guy looked like he belonged on the cover of a romance novel. And he was heading towards us.

"Maureen, you shouldn't have..." I murmured, leaning back and enjoying the view. She looked at me, then looked up, saw him and smiled.

"Nick!" she called out, waving. My jaw hit the floor.

"Nick?" I repeated. "That's Nick? *Your* Nick?"

She grinned at me and stood up, hugging the stranger and kissing him lightly. "Nick, this is Steven Ahearn, the man of the evening. Steven, I'd like for you to meet Nicolai Vikentiyevich Rozhenko."

I stood up and wiped my hand on my jeans before accepting his handshake, trying not to be dazzled by a pair of amazingly blue eyes. "It's nice to meet you," I said. "I've heard a lot of good things about you."

"As have I," he answered, and I heard a hint of an accent in his voice. Eastern European, Russian, something like that. Sexy as hell. "Maureen tells me that you're leaving, though."

I smiled broadly, "My big break. I still can't believe it..."

"Who the hell let him in here?" Maureen murmured, her anger plain in her voice. I turned to look and cursed softly. Joey, all six-foot-one of him, shoving his way through the crowd and leaving an angry, muttering trail of actors and stage hands behind him. I heard Nick's voice, speaking in French, and Maureen answering in the same language. Then Nick was in front of me, standing between me and Joey.

"What do you want?" he demanded.

Joey stopped and stared at him, then asked, "Who the hell are you? For your information, I was invited. And you're standing between me and my boy, so get the hell out of my way."

I felt my temper flaring. His *boy*? Since when? Even from where I was standing, I could smell the alcohol on Joey. I knew he was a mean drunk—it was the main reason that I refused to let him keep hard liquor in the house. I knew where my money had gone now, and I was not looking forward to telling him that I was leaving him. But I also wasn't going to let anyone else get hurt because of me. "It's okay, Nick," I said, stepping out from behind my new defender.

Nick looked at me, his eyes narrowed. "Steven? You're sure about this?"

"Yeah. I'm fine." I met Nick's eyes and nodded once, then tipped my head ever so slightly to the side, towards the side door that had been propped open in the hopes of getting a breath of cooler air into the too warm room. Hopefully, Nick would get the message that I wanted him to follow us. "C'mon, Joey. We need to talk." I turned without waiting for Joey's answer and headed for the door, and nearly jumped out of my skin when a hard hand closed around the back of my neck. I winced as Joey's fingers dug in, but he held on tight and shoved me forward, out the door and into the alley.

"You're very full of yourself tonight, slave," Joey snarled at me as we walked out into the cold night air.

I stopped and twisted, breaking his hold and stopping just out of his reach, "Enough of that shit, Joey. I'm not your boy, I'm not your slave, and I'm not your whore. I'm done with your little power trip bondage games."

Joey looked at me like I was talking in another language. "What?" he sputtered. "You just wait until I get you home..."

"I'm not going home with you, Joey," I interrupted. "I'm moving out."

"Out?" he echoed. "What are you talking about?"

"Out of the apartment. We're done, Joey. You went too far this morning, and I'm not putting up with your shit anymore. Go find yourself someone else to abuse." I decided that I didn't want him to know about my good fortune, or where I was going, so I deliberately didn't mention New York. Instead, I started to go past him, back inside to my party. I was expecting Joey to turn, to stalk off the way he always did when he was angry. I was not expecting him to grab me and slam me back against the wall, hard enough to knock the wind out of me and bounce my head off the bricks.

Before I could recover, he pinned me in place, his hands locked around my upper arms, his chest hard against mine.

"Let me go!" I snarled through clenched teeth. He laughed, leaning in and kissing me roughly. I tried to push him back, but he was bigger and heavier than I was. He shifted, pressing harder against me, his thigh hard against my crotch.

"Who's being abused now, slave?" he crooned as he pulled back, his breath hot and stinking in my face. Under the alcohol, I could smell something else, something harsh, and I could see now that his eyes were glazed. He must have taken something. Suddenly, I was afraid. Drugs? When had he started using drugs? How had I not noticed? Shit, what had he gotten in to? "Tell me you don't like this..." he rubbed his hip hard against my crotch, then stopped and looked down, his eyes narrowing. "Wait a minute...." He shifted, catching me around the throat with one hand, holding me painfully tight and leaving me gasping for breath while he pawed at me with his other hand. "Where's your collar, slave?" he asked, sounding annoyed. "I told you that was supposed to stay on. So where is it?"

His fingers around my throat grew tighter, and I heard him laugh again as I struggled to breath. "Oh, yeah. I like this. There's your punishment, slave. I'm gonna choke you out and fuck you until you wake up. And that's only the beginning..."

No, that was the end—I grabbed Joey's wrist in both hands to try and keep him from killing me outright, braced myself, and slammed my knee up between his legs. Never, ever give a dancer a chance to kick you in the crotch; he went down like a dropped brick, gagging and puking. I left him rolling in the trash and staggered back towards the door, taking long, shaking breaths and feeling the ache of incipient bruises on my throat and my arms. I wasn't surprised to see Nick standing in the doorway waiting for me. However, I was surprised to see the baseball bat in his right hand. Where had *that* come from?

"Are you all right?" Nick asked.

I nodded and grimaced. "You should see the other guy," I quipped. Nick grinned.

"Where is he?"

"Trying to pry his nuts out of his sinuses, I think. Let's get out of here." I brushed past him and into the restaurant, only to find Maureen waiting for me just inside the door.

"Baby?"

"He didn't take the break-up well," I said, slumping into a chair. I felt Maureen's fingers on my chin as she tipped my head back.

"I can see that," she murmured. "The bruises are already coming up. I think we should get your things tonight."

"And call the police?" Nick asked.

"That will be tomorrow," I said. "I'm not ready for that. And I need a drink before I do anything."

I saw the two of them look at each other, then Nick took my arm and hauled me out of the chair. "Come on," he said. "I know a place." As we walked out through the crowd of people, I noticed that the bat was gone, and I wondered briefly what Nick had done with it.

The place turned out to be a vodka bar in Federal Hill. About half of the party moved with us, and for a while, I forgot about the break-up, about Joey and his violence, and about the fact that tomorrow I'd be talking to police about what he'd done to me. Nick decided that I needed to learn how to properly drink vodka, and I proceeded to get very, very drunk. I vaguely remembered Maureen telling me that we were going to go to my place to get some of my things, and then she and Nick were pouring me into the backseat of their car. After that, I didn't remember anything until the truck hit us.

Chapter Two
Endure the Darkness

I'm told that the first time I woke up in the hospital, I woke up
screaming, and they ended up having to strap me down and sedate
me before I did any more damage to myself. I don't remember
that at all. I just remember that the second time I woke up, Mary
was there waiting for me. Mary was the sister I wished I'd had, the
only one from my old life in Boston who'd stood by me after I'd
come out of the closet. She'd taken me in after my father kicked
me out of the family, she'd moved me into her tiny apartment in
Baltimore, and she'd introduced me to her friend Maureen, who
happened to run a theater company. It made sense that they'd
called Mary—she was listed on the cards in my wallet as my emergency contact, and she'd apparently expanded on that and somehow managed to convince the hospital that I was her brother and
that she was my only family.

I opened my eyes to darkness, closed them again and licked
my cracked, dry lips. It was about the only thing I could do—I
could feel heavy straps on my wrists and ankles. For a minute, I
thought this was one of Joey's twisted wake-up calls, then I dismissed that idea. This place smelled too clean to be our apartment—Joey was a slob.

"Stevie?" Mary. I'd recognize her voice anywhere. I licked my
lips again and tried to speak.

"...Mare?"

I heard her sob, once, then her hand was in mine, "Stevie,
honey, we thought we'd lost you."

I frowned, trying to think, to understand what she was talking
about. It didn't seem to matter how hard I tried, though. My brain
didn't want to work, and all I could remember was screaming and
blood. "...What... what happened?"

There was a long pause while something cool and wet passed over my lips; water dribbled into my mouth and seemed to evaporate almost instantly. "There was a truck, Stevie," Mary said quietly. "It ran the red light on North and Mount Royal. The police said it was doing nearly seventy, and the driver was drunk. The car... it rolled. They had to cut you all out." She stopped and her hand in mine started to shake. "Stevie, Mo's dead."

I blinked, irritated by the darkness and wishing that Mary would turn on the lights. Then what she said hit me, really hit me, and I moaned. "Mo? No... Mary, no..."

"They tried to save her," Mary said in a broken voice. "She died on the operating table. The funeral was four..." Her voice trailed off, and I knew that she'd said something she hadn't meant to say. Four what?

"Mare?" I asked.

She hesitated only a moment, "Four weeks ago. Stevie, you've been in a coma almost six weeks." Six weeks. There was something about that number. Something important... "I talked to Mr. Taylor," Mary continued, and more water dribbled over my lips. "He told me to tell you he wishes you the best, and that when you're back on your feet, he wants to hear from you. He was really upset."

Taylor. Matt Taylor. The casting director. That was it. I was supposed to start on Broadway in six weeks. But now... With a start, I remembered that there had been someone else in the car, "Nicolai?"

"He's fine, Stevie. He had a concussion, and he's got a broken arm, and bruised ribs. He's taking Maureen's death pretty hard. And he's missing Natalie something awful."

"Why? What happened to Natalie?" I asked.

"Mo's mother took Natalie home with her after the funeral. Since Nick was hurt, and with everything to do with the arrangements, it just seemed to make sense."

I tried to shift and found that I couldn't move at all, and it wasn't just the restraints—there was something holding my head still, some kind of bizarre constriction around my throat, and another from my armpits to my hips. My left leg felt itchy, tight and heavy. And I still couldn't see a damn thing. "And me?" I asked. "How bad?"

"Stevie, maybe you should wait for the doctor..."

"Mare, how bad?" I repeated. She sighed and ran down the list: Whiplash, severe concussion, broken ribs, broken back, fractured skull, and a badly broken left ankle. That last one almost did me in—it was like a death sentence. I was never going to dance again.

"That's it," Mary said when she was done. "All in all, you were lucky. You didn't do too much damage to your spine, so with some therapy, you'll walk again."

"Lucky," I repeated. "Right. Lucky." I swallowed, feeling like there was sand in my throat. Between that and the darkness, things were just irritating enough that I snapped, "Mary, why in hell are we sitting in the dark?"

"What?" Mary sounded confused.

"It's dark in here," I repeated. "Mary, turn on the lights."

Mary didn't say anything. I heard a click, and a few minutes later, I heard someone come in, "Is there a problem?"

"Doctor, Steven wants to know why it's so dark," Mary said slowly.

I could hear the doctor breathing as he walked around me. When he touched my face, I jumped, as much as the medieval torture devices they had me strapped into would allow. As he examined me, I slowly realized that there was something wrong. Something... wait. Mary had been giving me water. And now the doctor was examining me! That meant they could see. Which meant that it wasn't dark in the room.

"Oh my God," I whispered. "I can't see."

He patted my shoulder. "It's probably just temporary. You took a bad blow to the head. We'll run some more tests. I wouldn't worry."

Did you ever notice that when a doctor tells you not to worry, the immediate response is that you start to worry *more?* And then, of course, there was another thing to worry about. Tests... God, who was paying for this? I was an actor, for pity's sake. An out-of-work actor, now. I didn't have insurance, let alone a reasonable line of credit. I didn't have even have family to turn to for help. When the doctor was gone, I asked Mary, and got a surprising answer that raised more questions than it answered.

"I don't think you're going to have to worry about money for a while. Nick has a really good lawyer and the trucking company has very good insurance."

"What does that mean?"

"All your medical bills are being taken care of by insurance, and anything that needs to be paid for now that they aren't covering is coming from Nick. Which isn't much. He's very nice, Stevie. You'll like him. He's been here every day to check on you." She patted my hand. "I forgot to ask the doctor about the restraints, and if he could take them off. I'm going to go and find him before he disappears. I'll be right back." Before she left, she tucked the call button into my hand; once she was gone, I let it drop.

Broken back. Broken ankle. Blind, for the love of God. Everything I had was gone, all my dreams... My father would have said this was my punishment, that God was punishing me for my sins. Maybe he was right. But why in hell did my punishment have to hurt Maureen? I pulled on the restraints, frustrated, hurting, and completely devastated. I could feel tears sliding down my skin, into my ears, and back over my scalp. Which told me that they'd cut off my hair, too. For some reason, that little bit of vanity was what it took to undo me completely. If I'd been able to, I probably would have slit my wrists right then and there. But I was tied down; I couldn't move and I was alone.

I just wasn't as alone as I thought. I wasn't expecting someone to wipe tears from my face, or a deep, gentle voice to say "Steven, stop fighting it. You'll hurt yourself. Calm down."

I stopped, and tried to place the familiar, accented voice. And failed. "Who's there?"

"It's Nicolai. I'm sorry. I didn't mean to startle you. I came in as Mary left. Should I go?" His hand moved away, and I wanted to turn towards him, grab for him, make him stop.

"No. No, please. Don't go," my voice cracked as the words tumbled out. "Don't leave me alone!"

Immediately, I felt something tugging on my wrist. Then the restraint fell away, and a hand closed around mine. "You're not alone. I'm here, and Mary is here. You will not be alone."

I clung to his hand like a drowning man, "I... I'm sorry. About Maureen. Nick, I..."

"It is not your fault. We would have had to drive that way to get home even if you weren't in the car," he said as he squeezed my hand, hard. "Steven, I don't blame you at all."

Maybe he didn't, but I did. "Mary said you were hurt, too."

"Simple fracture, and a few bruises. Nothing of note. I was very lucky. Have they told you what's to come?"

"No. Not yet."

He made a rude noise. "And the doctor was here a few minutes ago, wasn't he? I've been dealing with him when Mary isn't here. Try and remember that I'm your cousin, all right? This doctor... I don't think very highly of him, but he is the best available. You're going to be here for a while, Steven. A few more weeks, at least, until your ankle heals enough for you to stand and you are on your feet again. Then you'll move to a rehab center. After that, Mary and I decided that you should come and stay with me. Until you know what you want to do next. If that's all right with you, that is. It might be for the best; my home is almost all on one level, so you won't have to deal with stairs."

I couldn't have heard him right. "With you? Wait... why can't I go back to the apartment with Joey?" As I said the words, I remembered why not, and realized that I really didn't have anywhere else to go. "Never mind. I remember now. But... has anyone seen him? Does he know what happened?"

"I really don't think he cares," Mary answered, her heels click-ing on the floor as she came back into the room. "The nurse is coming to get rid of the straps. Stevie, I have some of your things. The stuff that bastard didn't trash."

"He trashed my things?"

Mary sighed and rested her hand on my arm. "Anything he couldn't sell. Stevie, he sold your drum kit. And the rest of the collection, too."

"My drums? All of my drums?" I echoed, stunned. I kept think-ing that things couldn't possibly get any worse, but the universe just has to keep proving me wrong. Never mind the collection; those were just drums I'd bought for myself. My mother had given me the drum kit when I'd turned sixteen and started playing in my father's bar band. Joey knew how important they were to me. "No!"

"I'm sorry, Stevie. I know what they meant to you. I went by to get your address book for your parent's phone number..."

"You called them?" I cut her off. "What..." I stopped, trying not to get my hopes up. "What did they say?"

"I talked to your mother. She was really upset. I'll call her tonight and let her know you're awake. I don't know about your father, though. I didn't talk to him, and your mom didn't say. I don't know if she's going to come or not." She patted my hand. "Anyway, I let myself in with the key you gave me, and I caught Joey pitching your clothes in the trash. He said it didn't matter, that you were going to die, and he didn't need your junk. He wouldn't tell me who he sold the drums to, or I'd have tried to get them back. As it was, I almost strangled him."

"You should have," Nick muttered, adding something in another language, something that I heard as "pissed duck."

"Probably, but I didn't. And... he's got a new fling. Or maybe I should say a new boy. The bastard." She sniffed once, then continued, "I don't have the room for you now. Do you remember me telling you I was seeing someone? Max is living with me now. And I have three flights of stairs. Nick's place will be better for you, until you're on your feet again and you know where you want to go from there."

Having them make the decisions about what was going to happen in my life was both comforting and uncomfortable; I wasn't sure if I liked it. But at the same time, not having to think about everything helped. Having someplace to go, and someone who was willing to help, that was what I needed to hear. I tried to nod, and winced, "How long do I have to be like this? All strapped down, I mean."

"The traction will be another week or so. The doctor is very pleased with how you're healing. You will need to wear the brace for several months, I think. At least, that's how I understood it." Nick squeezed my hand again. "And we will be here with you every day. So you will not be alone."

Not being alone helped more than I wanted to admit. If I was awake, one or both of them was with me, and very often I woke up from a nap to hear the rapid, soft tapping of the keys on Nick's laptop, or the quiet, metallic clicking of Mary's knitting needles. They settled into a pattern, with Nick spending most of the day with me, and Mary joining us for dinner after she got out of work. That meant that when Joey showed up early one afternoon just before I was released to the rehab center, Nick was the only one with me.

The cast had come off my leg, and I had started physical therapy that week. It was hard and painful, and by the time I was done, I was exhausted. I remember that I was fading in and out of sleep when I heard Nick curse and the sound of his chair screeching against the tile. "What are you doing here?" he demanded.

I heard Joey's voice, bitingly cold as he answered, "I came to see him. And I could ask the same thing about you. Feeling responsible?"

I rubbed one hand over my face and blinked, trying to wake up. "Nick? Is that Joey?"

"Yes," he answered, and I could hear the anger in his voice. "If you want him thrown out, I'd be happy—"

"No, let me talk to him," I found the bed controls and raised the head of the bed so that I was almost in a sitting position. "Why don't you go get a cup of coffee or something?"

Nick paused before asking, "Are you sure?"

"It's okay, Nick." He patted my leg as he left, and I waited until I couldn't hear his footsteps any more before turning towards where I'd heard Joey last and asking, "Why did you come?"

"What do you mean? I..."

"I mean why did you come?" I repeated. "Don't try and tell me you're here for a tearful reunion. The last time I saw you, I kicked your nuts into next week. I could still have your ass thrown in jail for what you did to me. Oh, and I know about your new boy. And then there's the fact that you haven't been here once in the entire time I've been here. So why the fuck did you come here today?"

I heard him stammer, and then clear his throat, "Baby, I'm sorry. I've been busy..."

"Bullshit. Did you think Mary wasn't going to tell me how you gave me up for dead and tried to trash my things? Or that you sold my drums?"

"I needed to make the rent..."

I ignored his protest, too angry to let him try to explain, and knowing he'd just try to lie to me. "And before that, you didn't want me except for when you wanted to fuck. I think I have a good reason to ask you why you came. And don't tell me that you love me. I don't buy that any more. If you loved me, you wouldn't have hurt me. You would have listened to me when I said no." He hemmed and hawed for a few minutes, and I just listened to him founder before finally asking again, "Are you going to tell me why you came? If you're not, you can leave."

"I wanted to see you!"

I snorted, hurt far beyond what I thought I would be. "Try again, Joey."

"Stevie, I... I'm sorry. I was wrong. I was wrong about everything. I never should have treated you like that." I heard him pacing, heard his rough breathing. He hummed softly, then sighed. "Look, I'm sorry. I'm really sorry. I was stupid and I want you back.

The other guy... he's gone. I kicked him out. So when you get out of the hospital, you can come home. I mean, if... you forgive me?" He took my hand, squeezing my fingers tightly, rubbing the back of my hand with his thumb. He sounded very sincere, almost enough to make me listen, until I heard Nick clear his throat from the door. Joey dropped my hand as if something had burned him.

"You saw the news, didn't you?" Nick asked quietly. I heard Joey sputter before Nick continued, "The television is on the waiting room. They are reporting that the truck driver is being charged with vehicular homicide and aggravated assault. The trucking company will probably settle out of court now, and the insurance company will be paying everything we ask. I'm surprised my lawyer didn't call me. Steven, you're going to be a very wealthy man." His voice was flat, and I found out much later that he had also received a large settlement... and so had Maureen's estate.

At the moment, I didn't care. Except that I finally understood what had brought Joey to the hospital. He'd been lying to me, trying to get me back under his thumb. My brain shied away from what that could have turned out like, if I'd believed him. "You're here because of the money?" I asked, unable to keep the hurt out of my voice.

"No! No. Stevie, I'm here because of you. I want you back."

"Tell me the truth, Joey," I said quietly. "For once."

"Stevie, I never lied to you," he protested. I folded my arms over my chest, and just waited. After a long moment, broken only by the ever-present hospital noise, he sighed. "Okay. The truth. He really is gone. I... I screwed up, and he dumped me. The way you did. And he moved out already. I can't afford the apartment. Not by myself. And... Well, I miss you. I was an idiot."

"And more so if you think that he'll come crawling back to you after what you did to him," Nick growled.

"Nick, cut it out," I started to say, only to be cut off by Joey.

"Well, I'll be damned... you didn't waste any time, did you?" He sounded shocked, and I wasn't sure who he was talking to, me or Nick. He didn't say anything else to either of us; he just left,

leaving me sitting there, confused. What had just happened?
"What was that all about?" I asked, and got no answer. "Nick?"
No answer, until finally Nick cleared his throat. The bed
creaked as he sat down on the edge and rested his hand on my
thigh. "He's right about one thing. He is an idiot. I doubt he ever
really cared about you at all, *Styopa.*"
I blinked, the odd name and the weight of his hand both
immediately distracting from thinking about what else Joey might
have been lying to me about. "What did you call me?"
"*Styopa.* It is... well, a nickname. A diminutive."
I arched an eyebrow. "The Russian equivalent of Stevie?"
"Yes. If you don't like it, I will stop."
"No. It's all right." I reached out and covered his hand with
mine. "I like it." I found myself smiling, warmed by the implica-
tions of him tagging me with a nickname. A small part of my mind
wondered just why he'd started thinking of affectionate diminu-
tives for my name in the first place, and when, and wondered what
the diminutive for Nicolai would be in Russian. Then Nick turned
his hand and laced his fingers into mine—I felt oddly warm, and
coherent thought flew right out the window.
"He is an idiot to have done this to you," Nick repeated quietly.
"You deserve so much better."
That afternoon was the beginning of the change in our
relationship. I didn't realize it at the time, but from that point until
the day that they wheeled me out of the rehab center and put me
into Nick's car for the trip to his house, Nick was at my side. It felt
as if he was there every minute of every day, helping me with
rehab, learning all about the after-care procedures he'd need to
help me, learning to help me live again. The only time he was gone
was the week he spent in Pennsylvania with his daughter, a trip he
came back from moody and silent, and that he refused to tell me
anything at all about.
I really didn't understand just how much everything had
changed between us until I walked for the first time into Nick's
sprawling ranch house. He led me on what he called the grand

tour, telling me where everything was, helping me to get comfortable with the new space. Then he brought me into the great room and sat me down on the couch.

"You're welcome to stay with me as long as you like," Nick said as he sat down next to me. "I have plenty of room."

"Thank you," I said, but I was really only paying him half my attention. I was tired, and not at all comfortable. Usually, when I sat down, it was more of a boneless slump, but now I was strapped into a clam-shell back-brace and I could only sit ram-rod straight. Thankfully, I no longer had to wear the neck-brace, or I'd have felt like I was being strangled. As it was, I just felt like I couldn't breathe most of the time.

"We have the initial interview tomorrow for your seeing-eye dog," Nick reminded me. I nodded and let my head fall back against the cushions, letting myself zone out and listening to Nick talk about the guide dogs and how it would help to have one. Good thing I liked dogs. Good thing Nick liked dogs, too. "We'll be staying on their campus for four weeks to learn how to work with your dog, once they choose one for you."

"How did you get them to agree to that?" I asked. "When you read the brochure to me, I got the impression that I had to go alone."

"I know the administrator of this school. I assured her that I would not interfere in your training, but that you are still recovering from back surgery and you still need assistance. She was very helpful. And in return, I promised to do some work for her."

That reminded me of something. "Nick, you know you still haven't told me what it is that you do."

"I haven't?" he asked. He laughed, a nice, deep sound. "I program assistance technology. I know the administrator of the seeing-eye dog school because that is the school where my father's last dog came from."

"Your father was blind?"

"From birth," he answered. "I grew up around guide-dogs, and I can read Braille in three languages."

"You speak three languages?" I was impressed. I didn't know anyone who really spoke more than one.

"Four, actually. I read Braille in three."

"What languages?" I asked, curious.

"Georgian, Russian, French, and English. Oh, and I can curse in Armenian. I can read Braille in Russian, French, and English. My father was a French professor at a university in T'Bilisi..."

"Where is that?" I interrupted.

"It was in the Soviet Union," Nick answered, then hummed softly. "Now, it is the capital of the Republic of Georgia. We left T'-Bilisi after my mother died, which wasn't long after the Soviet Union dissolved. We were lucky; we left only about a month before the civil war in Georgia started. We lived in Paris for a few years, then my father was offered a position teaching Russian and French at Georgetown, and we moved to the United States. My father is the reason I started doing assistance programming to begin with. My first coding project was to make a screen-reader that could read in Russian and French, so I wouldn't have to read his research to him anymore."

"That sounds challenging," I said.

"You have no idea," he said, laughing. "Your therapists know about that, by the way. They cleared me to teach you to read Braille. We will start that whenever you like. I still have my father's books packed away in the storage unit. We'll go get them whenever you're ready."

"Cool," I said, starting to fade out again.

"Tomorrow, we'll go to Mary's and get what she salvaged of your things. Once we know what you have, we can go shopping for what you need."

"All right."

"I would very much like it if you would share my bed tonight."

Now I was awake! "What did you just say?" I gasped.

"You heard me, I think," Nick replied, and I felt his hand, warm on the back of my neck. "I do not want to make you uncomfortable, *Styopa*. I find you very attractive. But I don't want you to think that this is the price for you staying here. If you say no, that's the end of it."

I felt my mouth watering at the thought of having Nick in my bed. He thought I was attractive? Me? "I... I didn't know you were bi. Nick, I... I haven't been cleared yet..."

"Just to sleep, *Styopa*. Anything else can come later, when you're ready for it," Nick answered, his fingertips trailing over the nape of my neck and making it very hard for me to concentrate. "I should tell you... That night, Maureen told you she was going to introduce you to someone. Do you remember?"

"I remember. But, how did you know about that?"

"She was going to introduce you to me. Our relationship... we were probably going to be ending it. Canceling the wedding. She was hoping that you and I might connect."

"You were?" I remembered Maureen's comment, about not telling Nick that she'd hinted about something being wrong. "Can I ask why?"

He paused. "We... wanted different things. She was going to tell everyone after the show wrapped. We were already working out custody and child support, so it would be a clean break."

I was having a very hard time thinking. All I seemed to be able to concentrate on was the feel of his fingers on my skin. I blinked, shaking my head slightly. "I didn't know. Nick, I..." I paused and bit my lip, then asked, "Are you sure? I mean... I've kinda got a lot of baggage right now."

"What's the line from that show? Oh, yes, '*I'm looking for baggage that goes with mine*,'" he said, making me laugh. He laughed with me, then rested his hand on my shoulder. "Steven, I was interested in you even before I met you, just based on what Maureen had told me about you. When I saw you, I knew I wanted to know you better. Then..." He stopped, and I knew he was thinking about Maureen. So was I. Was it somehow disloyal of me, with her only a few months gone? Should I be wanting her boyfriend this badly? Or be so turned on that he was admitting to wanting me? My God, what would she have said?

"Steven?" Nick's voice was soft, and much closer than before. I hadn't even noticed him moving, but now I could feel his thigh pressing against mine. If I could have, I'd have gotten up and moved away, but I was stuck in a damned clam-shell and couldn't get up off the low couch under my own power. "Steven, if you are willing to accept my baggage, then I am willing to accept yours. Remember, I'll have Natalie back with us soon."

I'd almost forgotten about Natalie. "Nick, why is she still with her grandmother, anyway?"

"You remember that week I went to Pennsylvania?" Nick asked. When I nodded, he continued. "Grace—Maureen's mother—she is challenging me for custody."

"Nick!"

"I have spoken to my lawyer. We are going to challenge, and I will bring Natalie home. But... that is something you must decide. She is my daughter. Are you willing to become an instant stepfather?"

"Nick, I..." I started, then turned and somehow found my hand on his thigh. He covered my hand with his, then slowly slid his hand up my arm.

"I don't think Maureen would have wanted either of us to be alone," he said softly. "She loved you very much."

I nodded. I knew that, had known it for a long time. "I loved her, too. She was... special."

"She had that way about her," Nick agreed. "Now, we have a long day tomorrow, and you need to rest. In which bedroom would you like to sleep tonight?"

I wanted to. God, how I wanted to! But something made me stop. I think that I was afraid, which was ridiculous. What on earth was I afraid of? I had just spent the past couple of months with Nick, with him helping me every step of the way, seeing me in just about every state there was, including some in which I didn't think most married couples ever saw each other. We'd grown close, and I liked him. I liked him a lot. Given a chance, I could probably fall head-over-heels for him. And he was offering me that chance. He *wanted* me. Even now, even as damaged as I was. But if I went to him now, confused and scared, it wouldn't be... right.

"I don't think I'm ready yet, Nick," I answered. "I think I need a little more time." His hand on my arm tightened. "If you change your mind, I will be waiting. And I will always take no for an answer," he said. He stood up and helped me to stand. For a moment, we just stood there. Then he took my face in his hands and kissed me. It was soft, tender. More a promise than anything else.

And that was the moment when I fell head-over-heels in love.

Chapter Three
Magic Happens

We fell into a comfortable routine, Nick and I. He would drop me off at physical therapy in the mornings, going off to client meetings or to work at home. I would spend hours working with the physical therapist, the massage therapist, the chiropractor, and the pain specialist, until Nick picked me up and took me home for lunch. After lunch would come lessons in Braille, or more therapy, or just time spent around the house, getting used to living in the dark. And Nick waited patiently for me to tell him what I wanted. There were a few mornings where he spent far longer in the shower than he usually did, and I had a good idea what he was doing. But, then again, I was doing the same thing most mornings. He never once pressed his advantage, never again even mentioned sleeping in the same bed. He had promised, and he was a man of his word. He was going to wait for me to make the first move.

And then he went ahead and made it for me.

It was mid-November, and I had been living with Nick for nearly a month. Just that afternoon, I had finally been told that I no longer needed the back-brace. At home, I was standing in the great room, slowly testing my range of motion, getting used to being able to move freely again. Some part of my brain was afraid that if I moved too quickly, I would break something and end up back in the brace.

"How does it feel?" Nick asked. I wasn't sure how long he'd been there, and assumed he'd just come into the room.

"Strange," I answered. "I feel lighter. More... fluid, I think. It's weird." I started to move towards the couch, stopping when I heard a soft sound from Nick. "What?"

"You stopped," he said, sounding disappointed. "I was enjoying watching you."

"You were watching me?" I asked, suddenly feeling more self-conscious than I had in years.

"You are very beautiful when you dance," he murmured softly, his accent more pronounced than I'd ever heard it before.

"I... I wasn't really dancing..." I protested. In answer, I heard something click, and then Nick's footsteps as he came towards me. He took my hands in his and pulled me close, sliding one hand over my waist to the small of my back.

"You were dancing," he repeated. "Dance with me."

As he said that, I heard familiar music, a guitar and mandolin riff that repeated itself. I normally didn't care for John Cougar, but for some reason I always did like that one song. How the heck had Nick known that? He pulled me more tightly to him and whispered, "Dance with me." He slid his hand into my back pocket, just like the song said, and I could no more have said no than I could have sprouted wings and flown away.

We weren't really dancing. It was more like swaying to the music, with Nick holding me with one hand while the other gently roamed up and down my back. I slid one arm around his neck and pressed closer, very aware of his body against mine, and of my cock, which had gone from limp to rock-hard and aching in a heartbeat.

"You're so very beautiful, *mily moy*," he whispered in my ear.

"What does that mean?" I asked.

"My darling," he answered, his lips touching my ear. The tip of his tongue traced my earlobe, and I moaned softly at the touch, pressing harder against him. He laughed softly and took a step back, sliding his hand down my arm and lacing his fingers into mine. "Come with me, *mily moy*. This will be better in bed."

I let him lead me, through the great room and down the hall towards the bedrooms. At the end of the hall, instead of making the right turn towards the room that I was using, we turned left. I hadn't been in Nick's bedroom yet, and when he let my hand go just inside the door, I stopped. There was carpet under my feet, thick plush that muffled sound and made it hard for me to tell where Nick was.

"Steven?"

"I don't know where I am," I said weakly. A heartbeat later, his hand was in mine again, and he was leading me forward.

"The bed is here," he said, and I felt my knee brush against it. I reached out and felt thick blankets and a cold metal bedpost. "Sit down. I won't be a moment." I sat down, hearing him moving around the room, hearing drawers opening and closing. Then he came back and drew me back to my feet. I stood there for a moment, and shivered when his hands ran down my chest. They slowly ran back up my sides, and I realized that Nick was slowly pulling my shirt up. When I started to help him, he stopped. "No, *Styopa*. Let me do this."

So I stood there and let him slowly strip my clothes off, pulling my shirt over my head, teasing open my jeans and sliding them and my underwear down over my hips, his warm hands brushing over my skin. He steadied me as he helped me step out of my pants, then drew his hands slowly back up my legs, over my hips, coming to rest at my waist. His body pressed against mine, and I could feel that he was still dressed. I had never before felt so naked, so unsure of myself, and I shivered under his touch.

"Cold?" he asked softly.

"No." I almost didn't recognize my own voice.

"Ah. Nerves," Nick chuckled softly and his lips brushed mine in a feather-light kiss. "I think I like having you nervous. Do you have any idea how damn sexy you are, *mily*?"

I didn't answer. There was no way I could answer that question without sounding like an idiot. Instead I waited, and Nick stepped away from me. I could hear him moving, hear the sound of fabric sliding over skin, and when he came back and pulled me into his arms, he was as naked as I was. I slid my hands over his waist and up his back, feeling odd ridges under my fingers when I reached his shoulders. Scars? Why would Nick have scars? Then his mouth closed over mine and I stopped thinking about scars. I stopped thinking at all, letting him guide me down so that I was lying on my side on the bed, and feeling the bed dip as he lay down with me. We lay facing each other, our legs intertwined, touching each other, exploring each other's bodies, exchanging gentle kisses. Every time I breathed, I could feel his cock brushing against mine, until I just couldn't take it anymore and let my fingers trail down his length. He shuddered as I touched him, then kissed me again, harder than he had before, his hand sliding up to cup the back of my head. For a brief, crazy moment, I wished my hair was longer, the way it had been before the accident, just so that Nick could pull it. Then I shoved that thought away. No more of that, Stevie. That kind of thinking got you in trouble.

I pulled back against his hand and broke the kiss, whispering against his mouth, "Now?"

"Not yet. I don't want to hurt you," he answered, rolling onto his back and pulling me with him. I felt him shift, felt the bed shake as he did something. Then he rolled towards me and pushed me onto my back. "Spread your legs, mily."

I did, and felt Nick shifting. Then something cold and wet touched my ass—I gasped in surprise and heard Nick laugh. "Relax, Styopa. Relax. It's been some time for the both of us. I want to make sure that you're ready for me. And I need to remember everything I've read."

"Huh?"

"Researching safe positions for sex with someone who has had a major back injury."

I propped myself up on my elbows. "You... you've been doing *research?*"

He laughed. "*Mily moy,* I've been thinking of very little else for the past few weeks. Yes, I did research. The last thing I want to do is hurt you. Now, relax."

I took a deep breath and let myself fall back, fall limp, feeling Nick sliding his finger in and out. One finger was quickly followed by a second, and I whimpered as his fingers curled to hit the sweet spot, then retreated. He kept on teasing me, until I was biting my lip and trying not to scream, my hands clenched in the sheets so hard that my fingers cramped. I moaned when he pulled his fingers away, then gasped in surprise as he stretched out on top of me and kissed me deeply.

When he pulled back, he was laughing, his breath tickling my lips. "Now, *mily*. Just stay where you are." I heard quiet, wet sounds from someplace nearby and ignored them as I tried to force myself to track what he was doing. With firm pressure and gentle instruction, he guided me so that I was lying across the bed, on my back, and with my hips raised on a firm cushion. He rested his hands on my knees and pushed them up towards my chest.

"What are you doing?" I asked.

"This is supposed to be easier on your back," he said as he stopped, his hands sliding down my legs to rest on my ankles. "Hold your knees, keep your legs up. Have you never tried this position before?"

"No. This is new." I wrapped my hands around my knees, feeling very open, very vulnerable. And, because my life is one big song cue, I had to add, "Everything up to now has pretty much been *Bend Over, Greek Sailor*."

Nick burst out laughing. "Later, you will tell me how you know that song. For now, I want all of your attention." He ran his hands back up my legs, down over my inner thighs, running his nails lightly over my skin. I caught my breath and realized that if I wanted him to fuck me, I couldn't move. I was bound in place as strictly as if he'd put me here with rope. I think the only thing that kept me from calling it off was the fact that the only thing that really held me there was my own will, and his instruction. I felt the bed shift, and the heat from his body as he moved to cover me, his hands brushing my shoulders as he braced himself over me.

I closed my eyes and pictured him there. I had never seen him naked, never really saw him at all except for the night that I'd met him, but I had a very good imagination. So I pictured him, pale skin just starting to shine with sweat, the dark hair on his chest, his long hair loose and wild over his shoulders. I wondered what his cock looked like, then decided I didn't care. Especially as he started to press against me, and I moaned at the feeling of pressure against my ass, the slow burn as I was filled for the first time in months. I heard Nick moaning, could feel him trembling and knew that by taking it slow, he must have been driving himself insane. By the time I had taken him completely, Nick was whispering brokenly in Russian: "... *Styopa... spasibo...*"

I knew *spasibo* meant "please." I could guess at what he wanted to know, and I whimpered softly, whispering, "Please, Nick. Please, fuck me."

He leaned down and kissed me, then started to move against me, pumping slowly at first, gaining speed in answer to my moans. It was amazing, incredible, and I was reveling in the feeling of being filled, of being loved by someone who actually cared. The position had a lot going for it, too; Nick kept on leaning down, kissing me, nibbling my neck and my ears, whispering into my ear in Russian. I had no idea what he meant, but it sounded wonderfully filthy.

Nick shifted, his back arching, the movement driving him into me harder. He moved his hand away from my shoulder and rested it on my left knee. I heard him laugh, then he moved my leg, slinging it over his shoulder. "*Eto horosho?*" he murmured. Then he laughed again and said, "Is this good?"

The only answer I could make was a moan. His cock was hitting in just the right place, and I wanted more. I wanted him to drive me right off the bed. I nodded, and he rested his other hand on my right knee. With my hands freed, I reached out and touched him, running my fingers up his arms. I could just barely reach his chest, and I wasn't sure if he'd like it if I touched him. Joey had hated it if I played with his nipples... and those thoughts had no place here and now. I pushed the thoughts of Joey away. Not quickly enough, apparently.

"*Styopa?*" Nick sounded worried.

"Not you," I answered quickly. "Thinking."

"Ah. We cannot have that," he breathed, his voice deep and dark, and feeling as if it was resonating in my bones and in my boner. He leaned over me, pushing my left knee into my chest and almost folding me in half. Something landed on my chest; I touched it and discovered a tube. "Touch yourself, *mily*. I want to see you bring yourself off."

I fumbled with the tube, squirting lube into my palm, then slid my hand down between our bodies, biting my lip as my fingers closed over my cock. I closed my eyes as I started to jerk off, and as I did, Nick let my leg go, bracing himself once more with one hand on the bed over of my shoulders. He started moving again, thrusting against me hard enough that I could feel myself moving, feel my shoulders pressing against Nick's wrists as my head tipped over the edge of the bed. The feeling that I was going to fall off the bed some-how added to the intensity, and I was gasping and moaning, my hand on my cock pumping as hard and as fast as Nick was pounding my ass. I could hear him growling, his breath fast and hot against my skin. I wanted him to push my legs back again, I wanted him to pin me down, but I couldn't find the words. All I could manage were wordless sounds that I think he understood as meaning: *more, harder, faster,* and *oh-sweet-fuckety-fucking-Jesus!*

Nick's breathing grew ragged, and I could tell he was getting close. I was close, too. Really close, and I wanted this come so badly I could scream. I picked my legs up, intending to hook them over Nick's hips, trying to get closer to what he'd done to me before. I wasn't expecting him to stop between thrusts and push himself up, catching me behind the knees with his arms and pressing back down, pinning me to the bed and trapping my hands between our bodies.

"What you wanted?" he mumbled. He didn't wait for an answer, going right back to the same punishingly amazing pace. This time I couldn't move, and the only thing keeping me on the bed was his weight. It was perfect, and I came, howling and struggling underneath him like a mad thing until all my tanks ran dry. As I went limp, I heard him gasping, rapid staccato breaths that ended with him shuddering and falling still, slumping a little over me and making it hard for me to breathe. He took a long breath, then squashed me a little more as he leaned down and kissed me. The movement was almost too much for me, and I whimpered a little against his lips; he pulled back immediately and lifted himself off me, letting my legs fall to the bed. He moved out from between my legs, and I gasped, just a little, as he slid out of my ass and left me feeling... empty. Then he took my hand and tugged it, pulling me back onto the bed to lie next to him.

"I'm sorry. Forgot myself," he said as he ran his hands down my chest. "Are you all right? I didn't hurt you?"

I smiled, feeling sleepy and sex-stupid. "I'm perfect. You're amazing." I ran one hand up his thigh, feeling tension there. Huh? "But I did not hurt you?"

He was getting more tense, and I blinked my eyes and shook my head to clear it. "What? No! No, Nick. I'm fine. I might be sitting a little more slowly the next couple of days, but I'm fine."

He relaxed, letting go a deep breath that ruffled my hair as he pulled me into his arms. "I was worried. I forgot myself, and... I should have been more careful."

I could hear something—regret, maybe—in his voice, something that shouldn't be there. I did the only thing I could, fisting my hand in his hair and kissing him as hard as I could. He held onto me tightly, returning the kiss with interest. When he finally let my mouth go and let me breathe, he didn't loosen his arms.

"You are sure I didn't hurt you?" he asked, his voice low.

"I'm fine," I repeated, smiling. "Tired, but fine. Let's get some sleep."

He laughed. "It is only eight o'clock!"

"So?"

His answer was to pull the covers up over the both of us and snuggle down with me. It was odd, that he wanted to hold me. No one had ever done that before, and I never would have expected it from Nick. But it was nice, too, and I fell asleep resting on his chest, hearing his heartbeat, steady and slow under my ear.

✿

I woke up in the circle of Nick's arms, my back against his chest. I lay there, briefly wondering what time it was, then deciding it wasn't important. I yawned, enjoying his warmth, the smell of his skin and the feel of his body next to mine. I thought he was still asleep, and was surprised when he kissed my shoulder.

"Hi," he said, his voice rough.

"Hi," I answered. My mind went blank, and I wondered what I should say to him. Did you enjoy yourself? Was it good for you? Do you still respect me?

"Thank you," Nick said, relieving me of the responsibility of saying anything.

"I should be thanking you," I said, turning so that I was facing him. "Nick..."

"I wanted to talk to you," he interrupted, catching me off guard. Those aren't really words that you wanted to hear the morning after the night before. If it was morning. I had no idea what time it was.

"Sure," I said slowly. "What is it?"

"You know that I know what Joey did to you," he said slowly.

"I know that," I answered.

"We have never called the police, or spoken to a lawyer. I thought..."

I stopped him, resting my hand against his chest, "Nick, it's been months. There's no proof any more. Right now, it would be my word against his, and I really don't want to go through that. I'm done with him, and that's all."

"Are you sure?" Nick asked. I nodded.

"I'm sure," I said, closing my eyes and trying to relax. "Why?"

"I... was curious," Nick said, and I heard the hesitation in his voice. Why would he hesitate? What was he really asking? I thought about it for a moment, and then remembered Maureen's little TMI moment that last night. She had been a Mistress...

"You're a top, aren't you?" I blurted out. "You... you're a dom?"

"Steven, you didn't know?" he asked, sounding shocked.

"No!" I said, pulling away from him and scrambling out of the bed. I was sweating all over, shaking. It would start again, and this time, I wouldn't be able to run...

"Steven, please. Listen to me." Nick said quietly. He was nowhere near me, which was good. "Steven, have I given you any reason not to trust me?"

"You didn't tell me," I answered. "You knew about Joey, and you didn't tell me that you..."

"Do not insult me by comparing me to that..." Nick snapped. His voice trailed off before he finished the sentence, and I heard the bed creak. Soft footsteps padded towards me, then stopped. "Honestly, Steven, I thought you knew. I thought Maureen had told you why she wanted to introduce you to me. She knew you were a sub, and she wanted to see you in a relationship where you would be safe. I give you my word, Steven. I will never hurt you. I... I will not even touch you again, if that is your wish." The footsteps moved away, and I heard the bathroom door close. I didn't wait for him to come back out, fumbling around until I found my jeans, grabbing them and pulling them on. I managed to find the wall, then the door, and fled for the guest room, locking the door and curling up on the bed. I slept for a while, and then lay there, listening to the wind outside the window and trying to think.

"Okay, brain. Stop reacting and start thinking. Why did we panic?"

My brain answered, *"Well, because of Joey..."*

"This isn't Joey," I told myself firmly. "This is Nick. *We've been living with him for almost a month now. If he wanted to rape us, he could have done it the first night! It's not like he hasn't had the chance. And it's not like we could have fought back."*

"Exactly. How are we going to fight back?"

"Who says we're going to have to? He promised that he wouldn't hurt us. And we trust him."

"Do we?"

"Yes," I told myself firmly. "*We trust him. And... I think we're in love with him.*"

"*Yeah, but is he in love with us?*"

Only one way to find out. I got up and unlocked the door, walking out into the hallway. My back was stiff and aching from the cold, and I shuffled down the hall like I was eighty until I had loosened up enough to walk properly. The house had that it's-really-late stillness to it, and I wondered how long I'd slept, how long I'd been lying there, arguing with myself. Nervous, shivering a little at the chill, I thought about going back into my room, stretching out my back, and grabbing a shirt, then decided not to. It would be too tempting to just stay in the room and avoid this conversation. Better to just go and talk and have done with it. I ran my fingers over the wall as I walked down the hall towards the great room. The room tasted empty, and I kept on going, walking into the kitchen.

"It's half past three, Steven. You should be asleep," Nick said softly.

"I... I wanted to talk to you," I answered. "I'm sorry I freaked out."

"It's understandable, after what you went through. I didn't realize that you didn't know, or I'd have told you before I ever asked you to sleep with me." I heard the scraping of a chair on the floor, then Nick's warm hand on my arm. "You're like ice. Sit. There is tea made."

"Is there anything to eat?" I asked as I sat down.

"I'll make something. And we will talk." Without warning, something warm and soft was draped over my shoulders. "Put that on," Nick said. I fumbled with it, discovered that it was his bathrobe, and shrugged into the warm, soft terrycloth. It smelled like Nick, and I rubbed my cheek against the collar, feeling oddly comforted. I sat and listened as Nick moved around, opening and closing the refrigerator and the cabinets as he prepared to cook, making the comforting, homey sounds that I never used to pay attention to when I could see. I heard the hissing of a spray can, then the clicking from the igniter on the stove.

"Joey was your first, wasn't he? You'd never bottomed to anyone else before?" Nick asked over the sounds of rattling pans and cooking noises.

"I've always been a bottom. But if you mean gone all out, with the ropes and gags and all that, then yeah. He was the only one who ever did that to me. It was fun, in the beginning. Then..."

"Then it became more about his need for power and less about your need to serve and the balance between them," Nick finished for me. "That happens. Too often, in my opinion. You were lucky to get out when you did. Not everyone is that strong." I heard the soft thump of something being put on the table. "Tea in front of you. Be careful, it is hot."

I nodded my thanks and wrapped my hands around the mug, letting the heat soak into my cold fingers. "How is it supposed to be?" I asked.

There was a click and clatter on the table in front of me, and I caught the scent of melting butter. "Three in the morning food. Otherwise known as scrambled eggs and toast," he said, moving away. The chair scraped again, and Nick continued speaking as I started to eat. "In a good relationship, there is balance. My need to be served is balanced by your need to serve. There is respect. Your respect for me as your dom, my respect for you as a submissive. There must always be trust. In the best relationships, there is love."

I stopped eating and laid my fork down, "Nick..."

"Yes," he said quietly. "I do."

I stood up and walked around the table, going to my knees next to Nick's chair. "I do, too," I said. From above my head, I heard his soft laugh as he took my arm and tugged.

"Get up. You shouldn't be on your knees to me, *Styopa*. At least, not yet."

I tipped my head back and asked, "Will you show me how this is supposed to be?"

There was a moment of silence before he asked, "Are you sure?"

I nodded, "I love you. I trust you. I want to be with you. And

I want to know if this," I gestured, taking in myself on my knees, "is really what I want."

"Fair enough. Go and sit down. Finish your eggs. I'll be right back." He pushed back from the table and I heard him walking away, so I got up stiffly and returned to my own chair, easing gingerly down to avoid jarring my back. I was just finishing off my last bit of toast when Nick came back. I heard something metal settling onto the table, and then Nick took a deep breath.

"I am going to start you at the beginning, the way I would start anyone who came to me and said 'I'm interested in learning about BDSM,'" he said. "That way, I can make certain that there will be no holes in your grounding."

"That makes sense," I agreed. "Where do we start?"

"We start with asking what do you like? Do you like being hurt? Do you like restraint? Do you want to be forced or humiliated? Made to dress in costumes, or in female clothing? How do you feel about slavery? I want you to tell me everything."

My jaw dropped, "Really? This is how you start?"

He paused for a long moment, then cleared his throat. "I was taught this way," he said slowly. "If you were a complete stranger, I would hand you a checklist and ask you to write an essay telling me about your sexual history and your fantasies. If I thought it necessary, I would ask one of my colleagues to interview you as well. But I think I know you well enough that we don't need that. Although I might have you do it later, if I see the need."

"You did this. And you didn't run screaming." I ran my fingers through my hair and leaned back in the chair. "I don't like being hurt, although a little bit... can be fun. Spanking, that kind of thing. I don't think being humiliated would be a turn-on at all. I don't know about being made to cross-dress. Being in the theater... costumes just *are*, you know? I don't think that's my kink. I think you know how I feel about being forced. Back in the beginning, back when it was fun, I really liked being tied up so I couldn't escape. Ropes, chains, that kind of thing. And... Nick, are you taking notes?" I'd been hearing a scratching sound as I spoke, and had just finally realized that what I was hearing was the sound of a ballpoint pen on paper.

"I am. That way, I can refer to them later, if I need to." He wrote something else down, then asked, "You like being bound, you said. Inescapable bondage."

"The tighter, the better." I felt my temperature rising, and not from the tea and the thick terry bathrobe.

"Interesting. Anything else you can think of? Any other special turn-ons? Hair-pulling? Gags? Knives?"

"Knives?" I repeated, suddenly scalding hot all over. I knew I had to be blushing, and couldn't help it. How had he known? "I... wow."

"Thought you were the only one?" Nick asked, sounding amused. I felt my face getting impossibly warmer, and nodded. He chuckled and touched my hand. "Mily, I don't think there is anything you can tell me that would shock me. But some of the things you find yourself liking may shock you. How about water sports?"

"What, like swimming?" I asked. What did this have to do with sex?

Nick laughed again, "I didn't realize you were quite that innocent. I meant piss play."

"Oh, ugh!" I shivered with disgust. "Tell me you're not into that?"

"I'm not. And now I know that you aren't either." He kept up that line of questioning for some time, and I found myself telling him about games that I played as a child, where I somehow always ended up being the bad guy who was captured and tied up by the heroes at the end of the game. I told him about my first lover, Mary's older brother Kyle, who had delighted in having what he called a pliable lover, and who had taught me the right way to suck him off. After Kyle was Frank, my college roommate, who, for two years, had loved to find new and interesting, not to mention public, places where he could fuck me.

"You know, that was probably my introduction to all this," I said, running my finger around the rim of my now-empty mug. "He never tied me up, but he would order me not to make a sound, or he'd stop what he was doing and leave me there with my pants around my ankles. Then he wouldn't touch me again for the rest of the night."

"You're probably right," Nick said. "Did you ever get caught?"

"No. Then, after Frank came one or two little things that didn't last very long. Mo used to say I attracted creeps. And then there was Joey..."

"Ah," Nick said, and that seemed to say it all. He was quiet for a few minutes, and the only sound in the kitchen was the scratching of his pen. Then he cleared his throat, "I think I have a good idea as to how to proceed. So now, we'll discuss safety measures. Tell me the one food you hate most of all."

"Food?" I asked, confused by the change in topic. "That would be oatmeal. Makes me gag."

"Good. That is your safe-word."

I laughed. "*Oatmeal?* Oatmeal is my safe-word?"

"Are you likely to forget it? Or say it in the heat of passion?" Nick asked. He sounded very amused.

"Well, no," I admitted. "To both."

"That is why your safe-word is oatmeal," Nick said. "Do you trust me, *Styopa?*"

I didn't even hesitate. "Completely."

"Then give me your hand." I held my hand out, and felt something cold being coiled into my palm. When I touched it, it was a round, metal chain.

"What's this?"

"If you accept it, it will be your collar," Nick answered. "It will symbolize the agreement that we've made and the relationship between us. You will wear it at all times, unless I ask you to remove it." He paused, then cleared his throat and said, "I have never offered a collar to anyone before, *Styopa*. You are the first. If you accept it."

I ran one finger over the chain on my palm, feeling the slight texture of metal, understanding what this meant. And wanting it more than I'd wanted anything, ever. I heard the hope in Nick's voice, and slowly got to my feet. Walking around the table, I stopped and went back onto my knees next to him, holding the chain out. "I think you should be the one putting this on me?"

I felt the chain being removed from my hand, then the chilly metal slipped around my throat, coming to rest just at the base of my neck, warming against my skin. Nick's fingers trailed over the skin at my collarbone, then ran up my neck.

"You look very good on your knees, *Styopa*," he said, his voice husky. "Shall I show you the beginning?" I swallowed and nodded, not trusting my voice. Nick took my hand and stood up, drawing me to my feet. Hand in hand, we left the kitchen and he led me back to his bedroom. There, he drew his bathrobe from my shoulders and ran his hands up and down my arms. "I will try to make this something you enjoy, *mily moy*," he said. "If you do not like it, use your safe-word and I will stop. If anything hurts you, use your safe-word. Do you understand?" I nodded, and he moved away, leaving me standing alone. I heard drawers opening, the soft jingle of chain, the sound of something thumping down onto the bed, and then a ripping noise. Nick came back and took my hand in his, kissing my palm. "Hold your hand out."

I did, and felt something heavy wrapping around my wrist. "What is it?" I asked.

"A cuff. Easier on your wrists and ankles than rope," he answered. The cuff tightened, and I heard a click, then the ripping sound again just before Nick put another cuff on my other wrist. Now the sound made sense.

"Velcro?"

"Yes, actually. Velcro for adjustments, and locking straps to secure them." Another click, and Nick drew his hands away. "Go ahead."

I ran my fingers over the cuff on my left wrist, feeling the lock dangling, the heavy ring, and the strap that wrapped around the wrist. Experimentally, I tugged on the ring. Lightly at first, then harder. The cuff didn't budge.

"These will hold a much larger man than you, mily," Nick said, taking my hand. "Come and sit and I will do your ankles. Then I will position you the way I want you."

I sat down on the bed and felt cuffs snugging down over my ankles. Then Nick made me stand and get onto the bed. He directed me firmly, telling me exactly what to do and where to move, so that I ended up lying face down over what I thought might have been the same cushion as before, with my arms and legs chained to the corners of the bed frame. And still wearing my jeans.

"Nick?" I called out, turning my head to try and hear him. I'd lost track of where he was, and wasn't sure if he was even still in the room. "I think we forgot something."

He laughed, the sound coming from my left, and ran one hand up my leg to rest on my ass. "I've forgotten nothing. Hold still."

I was still puzzling over the instructions when I felt the left leg of my jeans pulling hard against the outside of my calf. For a moment, I couldn't figure out what he was doing. Then I felt cool air on the inside of my calf, and a brush of cold metal against the inside of my knee, and I knew what he was doing.

"... Oh my God..." I moaned, shuddering as the knife started moving up my thigh.

The knife paused, and I heard Nick's voice, "Do not move. The knife is very sharp."

I closed my eyes and fought to stay still as Nick continued cutting, the sharp blade passing through the denim as if it were paper. He slowly sliced open the left leg, then the right, then slipped the blade into the waistband at the small of my back. By the time he was done, I was shivering uncontrollably, whimpering softly, and I was harder than I'd ever been in my life. It was almost enough to drown out the pain in my back.

"Very nice," Nick murmured. He moved away, then came back and knelt between my spread legs; I could feel his knees pressing against my inner thighs. I wasn't sure what he was going to do, until a pair of warm and soft somethings swept down my back.

"...What..." I croaked out.

"Fur gloves. Relax, mily. Let me play."

His idea of playing equaled turning me inside out with need. He used the fur gloves to give me the most erotic massage I'd ever had, running them up and down my back, over my arms and then down my ribs, over hips and ass and down my inner thighs to my ankles. He avoided the tops of my thighs completely, and by the time he was done, I was near frantic and begging.

"...Nick, please..." I moaned, struggling to move, squirming against the cushion under my hips. The cushion cover was ribbed, softer than the remains of my jeans. The contrast felt good as I rubbed against the surfaces.

"Soon, Styopa. Soon," Nick crooned from somewhere over me. The bed shifted, and I heard his footsteps moving away. I moaned and pulled on the chains again, stopping only when his hand came to rest on the back of my head.

"If you fight too much, you will hurt yourself. We've had enough of that," Nick said sternly. "Be still."

I tried. God, how I tried. But I couldn't seem to stop shivering, no matter how much I wanted to obey. The bed moved again, and Nick's hands trailed up the backs of my thighs. Without a word, he started the massage again, this time with bare hands. This time, he didn't stop at the tops of my thighs, sliding his fingers up to play with my balls, circle my anus, massage my ass hard enough that I was torn between pleasure and pain. I shifted, pushing back into his hands, the rough-and-soft underneath me doing incredible things to my cock as I pumped against it. So close...

"Not yet, Styopa. Not yet. If you come now, it will hurt when I fuck you." Nick ran his nails over my ass, hard enough that I knew I'd find welts in the morning. Then he slapped me. Hard. Hard enough that I jerked and yelped, more in surprise than in pain. Nick didn't say anything, and the slap was followed up by soft, gentle strokes, almost as if he was starting the massage again. I relaxed slowly, until he slapped me again, this time on the other side. What followed was the strangest spanking that I'd ever experienced, one that interspersed erotic massage with blows hard enough to rattle my teeth and make my ass feel like it was on fire. When his hands finally moved away, I held still for a moment, expecting another slap, another touch. Something.

There was nothing for what felt like a long time, enough that I wasn't even sure where Nick was. I hadn't heard the door open, so I was sure he was still in the room, but I couldn't even imagine what he was doing. I wasn't even sure if he was still on the bed. I shifted, hearing chains jingling and nothing else.

"Nick," I whispered, my voice shaking. "Nick?"

"I'm here, mily." Nick's hands trailed up the backs of my legs, and I gasped, squirming under his touch. He leaned over me, his body pressing mine down into the mattress, and his lips burned like a hot coal against my spine as he kissed his way down my back from the nape of my neck to my tailbone, then back up. When he reached my neck again, he stopped, leaning against me, his body warm against mine, his cock hard against my ass.

"Nick, please..." I whispered, my voice catching. "I want you..." Pinned underneath his weight, I struggled, tugging hard on the chains. I wanted him so much, was desperate enough to have him that I somehow thought I could maneuver myself onto his cock. That thought was completely destroyed when I felt something pop in my back; for a moment, there was nothing, then a wave of pain spread outwards, enough that I yelped and jerked hard against the restraints. Nick must have heard something, something that told him that my new vocalizations weren't happy noises—he jumped off me, and I felt his hands on my back, resting just over where the pop had been centered.

"Steven! What is it? What happened?" he demanded.

The only word I could get out between clenched teeth was "back." I tried to move and couldn't, held in place by the chains and the pain; I couldn't even roll onto my side to try and take some of the pressure off. I felt Nick's fingers moving over my back, heard him mutter something in Russian. Then he did something strange: he rested his open hand on my lower back and started chanting in Russian. I couldn't for the life of me figure out what he was doing, even if I had been able to think. I noticed, though, that my back under his palm was growing colder. Icy cold, enough that it almost felt like heat. And it spread, moving out and down and through the area that hurt, numbing the pain enough that I gasped in relief. Then Nick stopped chanting, and his hand grew warmer, a gentle, soothing kind of warmth that spread throughout my body, relaxing me, completely. For some reason, I tasted butterscotch, the really good stuff my grandmother used to make.

"Sleep, *Styopa*. Sleep, and it will feel better when you wake," I heard Nick say softly. It seemed like a fantastic idea, so I did just that.

I woke in the circle of Nick's arms, just the way I'd been before. Briefly, I wondered if it all had been a dream. That discussion, my taking Nick's collar, the scene... all of it. Had I been dreaming? I blinked and shook my head, and two things immediately hammered it home that I hadn't been dreaming: the weight of the chain around my throat, and the weight of the cuffs still locked around my wrists and ankles. I shifted and was surprised to find that the wrist cuffs were fastened together, as were the ankle cuffs. Then an arm tightened around me, and Nick murmured into my ear, "How's your back?"

I looked over my shoulder, and grinned when my nose bumped into his; he kissed me and rolled me onto my back before repeating the question. I let my bound wrists fall onto my chest and stretched, rolling my back gingerly. And felt nothing.

"Doesn't hurt," I answered, surprised. "Doesn't hurt at all. I thought I'd done something really bad there."

"You pulled a muscle," Nick answered, lightly running his fingers up and down my stomach. "You'll be tender for a while. I'll do well to remember that."

"I pulled... then why doesn't it hurt?"

He laughed softly and leaned down to kiss me. "Magic."

I started to laugh, then realized that the usual, snarky, smartassery that I was used to hearing when someone said that a miraculous fix was due to magic was missing from Nick's voice. He wasn't joking. "You're serious?" I asked slowly. "You... magic?"

"I was going to tell you over breakfast. There can be no secrets between us. I was just... worried how you would react. You are Christian, no?"

"Not really. Not since my dad used it as an excuse to kick me out on my ass. Not really religious anymore," I admitted. "And... well, Mary is Wiccan. I've never had a problem with that. I just didn't know..." Something finally connected, a question that had been in the back of my brain for years. Why was a legal assistant/part-time musician such good friends with a theater director? They don't usually run in the same circles... unless they run in the same Circle. "Mary... and Mo? Mo was Wiccan, too?"

"Oh, you are quick!" Nick sounded delighted, and leaned down to kiss me with a bit more heat. "Yes. Maureen was our High Priestess. But there's a bit more than just Wicca going on in our coven. There are a few of us who have something... more. Real magic. Real mages, as opposed to witches. Maureen was a Master Mage. As am I."

Master Mage? What was he talking about? "I... don't think I quite follow," I said slowly. "Can you explain more later?"

"Of course, *mily*. Over breakfast. Once we have coffee, I can explain anything."

I grinned. "You probably could. So, you fixed my back, using real magic?"

"I did," Nick paused a moment before continuing. "It is about the extent of my ability to heal. There was nothing I could do to..." He stopped, but I knew what he was going to say—he couldn't save Maureen. He sighed and rested his hand on my chest, just under my linked wrists. "I will introduce you to the coven, and to the other mages. We will be having our Yule ritual here."

"What's that going to be like?" I asked. I shifted, then grinned as I raised my hands. "And what's this all about?" His answer was to take hold of the cuffs and pull them up over my head, towards the head of the bed. I heard something click, and when he let go, I couldn't move. I tugged for a moment, then laughed and said, "Oh."

"Oh," he echoed, running his hand down my chest. "I will explain the ritual later. I have just one more question before we get back to where we were. Was it you who taught Maureen to play that hand drum?"

Not the question I was expecting. I nodded. "The tonbek? Yeah. She was pretty good. I was going to teach her bodhran, too, but we never got around to it."

I heard him grunt, and he slid one leg over both of mine, pinning me to the bed. "Would you consider drumming for us at the Yule ritual? It wouldn't be too complicated—we need someone to keep the beat during a guided meditation."

"Oh, sure. I can do that... oh..." I hesitated, reminded of Joey's callousness. "Nick, I don't have drums anymore."

"Blin. I'd forgotten. I'm sorry, Steven." Nick sighed, and it was almost as if I could feel the weight of his thoughts, growing heavier and heavier until he grunted once more. I assumed he'd decided something, because he leaned down and kissed me, and his hand started roaming again, trailing down over my stomach. When he grabbed my cock, I almost levitated off the bed, held down only by the chains at my wrists and his leg over mine.

"We will talk more about this later," he growled into my ear as he started to jerk me off. "For now, I don't want you to speak at all. Unless it is to beg."

Before long, that was just what I was doing; Nick seemed to know just how to play with me, how much I could stand and how hard, just when to pull back and let me catch my breath and squirm helplessly, waiting for his next touch. And he knew when I was reaching my limit, because that was when he straddled my thighs and wrapped his hand around both of our cocks. The feel of his cock rubbing against mine, and the pressure of his hand jerking the both of us off at once, was enough to send me into orbit; I shot hard enough to hit myself in the chin. Or maybe that was Nick, who shouted as he came, then flopped onto the bed next to me, breathing hard into my armpit. I went to lower my arms and groaned as I was stopped short—I was going nowhere until Nick let me up.

"Want to move?" Nick mumbled. He reached up and unhooked something, bringing my arms down to my chest. "I'll get the keys in a minute."

"Leave them. I'm comfortable," I told him. I rolled onto my side and raised my arms, only to hook them around his neck. He took the hint and kissed me, and it would have been perfect if it hadn't been broken by my yawn. Nick chuckled and started to nudge me into position so that we were spooned together, his soft cock resting against my ass. He wrapped his arms around me again and murmured into my hair, "Sure you don't want to be untied?"

"Not if that means you have to move."

He ran one heavy hand down my side. "I don't want to move. I want to sleep. The both of us need sleep. We're going out in the morning."

"We are?" I asked, settling comfortably on the pillow. "Where?"

He yawned again, and I realized that he'd been awake far longer than I had. He must have been up all night after my freak out. "First, we will be going into Catonsville. And if we cannot find what we want there, Takoma Park."

I turned over my shoulder and asked, "Why?"

He kissed my shoulder, and when he answered, his voice was thick with sleep, "To pick out drums, *Styopa*. My first gift to you."

For a moment, I was speechless. He was going to buy drums? For me? "Oh. Nick... you... you don't have to...."

"I want to. Merry Christmas, if that is what it will take," he said, laughing tiredly. "Go to sleep, *lubov moy.*"

It wasn't hard for me to guess what he meant. "I love you, too," I whispered. "Thank you, Nick."

My only answer was a soft snore. I smiled and snuggled in next to him. Safe in his arms, bound by more than chains, I slept.

Chapter Four
This Longest Night

I flopped onto the futon and tipped my head back, breathing deep through my nose and enjoying how the scent of the live tree that Nick had surprised me with yesterday mingled with the wonderful cooking smells coming from the kitchen. Somehow, both scents had come out of the same trip—we had been doing some frantic pre-party shopping, and had walked past the trees for sale outside the supermarket. I remembered mentioning that I hadn't had a real tree since I was a kid in Boston. When I came home from PT the next morning, there was one in our living room, already decorated and everything. Poof, magic!

I snorted, running my fingers through my hair. Magic. That was an appropriate thought. Tonight was the night of the Yule ritual. Everyone would be here before sunset, Nick had told me. He was downstairs, in the basement I didn't even know we had until today, doing... something. He'd promised to explain it later, but he'd been distracted by something, and was now running late, with everything needing to be done before the first people got here. There wasn't anything I could do to help him, so I just stayed out of the way.

The futon shifted, and I heard a soft snuffling next to me. I grinned and held my hand out, feeling a cold nose, followed by a wet tongue. "Not supposed to be on the couch, baby-girl," I chided gently, hooking my fingers into my guide-dog's collar and tugging. "Down, Mirage."

She whined and got off the couch, resting her chin on my knee so that I could scratch her soft ears. The past month had been a whirlwind, mostly centered around the half-grown Golden Retriever currently drooling on my knee. The insanity had started the day of our drum shopping trip, when we'd come home to find a message on the answering machine from the guide dog school, telling us that the dog that they hoped would be mine was ready. I knew within five minutes of meeting her that Mirage was mine and that we would work beautifully together. The school, however, had needed me to spend the next four weeks proving that to the instructors, and we'd only just gotten home three days ago. It was good to be home. Good to sleep in our own bed. And not sleep in our own bed, I thought with a grin. I turned as I heard Nick's footsteps coming up the stairs.

"Time check?" he called out. I ran my finger over the face of my watch.

"Five after three," I called back, once I'd puzzled out the Braille. I was getting quicker, but it still took me a minute.

"Oh, good. We have time before people will be getting here," he said as he flopped down on the couch next to me. He slid one arm around my shoulders and pulled me against his side. "Now, let me think. The ritual space is ready. The turkey is in the oven..."

"And smelling wonderful." I interrupted as I tipped my head back against Nick's shoulder, studying his mood. He was relaxed, more so than he'd been all day. I knew that something was bothering him, and I also knew that if I asked what it was, he'd clam up. He'd tell me when he was ready. But this was the most at ease he'd been since yesterday afternoon.

"Thank you. That still has an hour and a half. The drinks are on ice on the porch, the fire is laid, the candle is also on the porch," Nick paused, then sighed and pulled me closer. "I think everything is ready."

"Can you explain it now?" I asked. I felt his body move as he nodded.

"Tonight is the solstice, the longest night. According to legend, it was believed that if the need-fire wasn't kept burning all night on the longest night, that the sun wouldn't rise again in the morning. So that is what we're doing. We'll light the need-fire from the rays of the setting sun, and we'll keep it burning all night. There will be music, and presents, and far too much food."

"So, an all-night party," I said. "Sounds like fun."

Nick nodded again, his cheek rubbing against my hair. Without warning, I felt the chain around my neck tighten, and he pulled gently until I was lying on my back across his legs, held in place by firm pressure across my throat. He laughed softly as he ran his free hand down my chest. "Look what I caught," he murmured.

I fought the urge to squirm and closed my eyes as he slowly unfastened the buttons on my jeans and tugged my shirt up. His hand slid underneath my undershirt, nails dragging hard along my skin and making me whimper.

"Nick..." I murmured. "Nick... time?"

"No one will be here for over an hour. Plenty of time. I missed you, *mily*." He tugged on my chain gently, enough to make me catch my breath as the metal pressed against my throat. "This is lovely, having you spread out for me. But there isn't much I can do to you like this. Come up here, *mily moy*." The pressure on my throat eased, and Nick helped me to sit up, then pulled and tugged me until I was kneeling astride his legs. He laughed, sliding his hands up my chest and down my arms, dragging my shirt along with them.

"I missed you," he repeated.

"You were there," I said with a smile. "But I know what you mean. I missed you, too."

"A month without you in my bed was too long, Steven. I thought I would be all right with just seeing you every day. I had no idea how much I would miss you. I don't think I slept at all the first few nights. And I need you. Today, I need you." As he spoke, Nick slowly stripped me of my shirt and pushed my undershirt up, then eased my jeans and shorts down over my hips, leaving me bare from hip to chest. He pulled me closer with one hand at the small of my back, trapping my erection between our bodies as he hooked his finger under my chain. "Hands behind your back."

I did as I was told, crossing my wrists behind me and grinning as he placed his hand over them. I liked this, liked being half-dressed and at his mercy. I wished for a moment that he'd taken the time to get something to tie me, but this was still nice. I slowly started pumping my hips, rutting against his body as he leaned forward and started licking my nipples, tipping my head back and just reveling in having him, in being with him. In what he was doing, and what he was going to do. I moaned... and heard the front door creaking as it opened. Nick's arm around me tightened, and I knew he'd heard it, too. Mirage barked once and I heard the clatter of her nails on the wood floor as she ran towards the door.

"Hi, guys... oh, who is this darling? Nick? Stevie? Oh...oh, dear." I felt my face light up at the sound of Mary's voice. She sounded both shocked and deeply amused, and I knew what she was thinking. Her next words confirmed it, "Stevie, we have *got* to stop meeting like this!"

Nick burst out laughing as he let me go and tugged my undershirt back into place. "He makes a habit of this?"

"I do not!" I answered before Mary could spill all of my secrets. I'm not quite sure if I managed to sound indignant, since I was laughing, too. "It was just that once... and you're early!"

"I promised to come and help cook," Mary answered. "Looks like the cooking started early."

"*Bozhe moi*," Nick groaned. "I forgot, Mary. I'm sorry."

"Not me you should be apologizing to, Nick. Now, I know where the kitchen is, so I'll go get started. Why don't you two go... cook?"

"Mary!" I gasped.

"What? It's a kitchen. I know how it works. And neither of you is going to be good for anything unless you get this out of your system. So git. Come on, Max. Show's over," she said, giggling, and I heard her footsteps and another, heavier set moving away. I sat down on Nick's lap, buried my face in his shoulder and started to laugh.

"Did this before, hm?" he asked, his voice in my ear sounding very amused.

"Not on purpose!" I protested. "Anyone around?"

"No. Mary and Max are in the kitchen. Let me help you up." Nick steadied me while I got to my feet and pulled my pants back up, tucking my cock in gingerly and trying to ignore just how turned on I was. As soon as I was put back together, Nick took my hand and led me out of the living room, past the kitchen where I could hear Mary fussing over Mirage, and on down the hall into our bedroom.

As the door closed, Nick cleared his throat, and I heard my cue.

"I was seventeen," I said. "It was the summer between high school and college. Mary's brother... did I tell you about Kyle?"

"He was your first, wasn't he?"

"Yeah. Him. He was home from college, and we hooked up," I stopped talking as I tugged my shirt up over my head. A cold shower, as much as I hated them, was just what I needed right now. "His parents were out for the day, and we thought we had the house to ourselves. Mary got out of her summer job early, though, and she came home and caught us." I smiled at the memory. "She knew what my dad thought about fags, so it was her idea for us to pretend we were dating. Protective coloration, she called it."

"And in the meantime?"

"In the meantime, I was making time with Kyle. But yeah, the first time, Kyle bent me over the pool table in his parent's basement. That's how Mary caught us." I heard Nick opening and closing drawers as I talked, and figured he was getting changed for the party. And it was time for me to do the same; I turned and shucked my jeans, picking them up and putting them onto the bed, and following them with my shorts. I took my watch off and put it aside, then, naked except for my collar, I turned towards the bathroom.

"Where are you going?" Nick asked, his voice coming closer.

"Shower. A cold one," I said, and grimaced. "Otherwise, I'm not going to get through the night. You want one?"

"I might join you," Nick said softly. "But not cold. I hate cold showers." I felt the heat radiating from his body as he moved in behind me, from his fingers as they ran down my arms until his hands closed around my wrists. As I realized he was up to something, he pounced, pulling both of my wrists behind me and turning me, using firm pressure to force me to bend over the bed. I don't know if this was something he was planning, or if it was just a spur of the moment thing, but there was a strap ready and waiting; before I could pull myself free, my wrists were bound tightly together. Nick helped me to stand, then pushed me back so that I was perched on the edge of the bed.

"Stay here," he said, sounding pleased with himself. "I'll go start the shower." He kissed me and walked away, and I heard the water running in the bathroom. I took advantage of the noise to test my bonds, tugging hard, and grunting when the strap proved to have no give at all. I was not getting loose anytime soon.

"You know, one of these days, I'm going to tie you up and just let you wiggle. I'll enjoy watching you."

I grinned as I turned towards Nick's voice. "That sounds like a challenge. Can I get free before your willpower gives out? Nick, we have company coming..."

"Not before you do. We have time. Mary knows what to do, and we'll be done before anyone else gets here. But just in case..." I heard him coming closer, then he tapped my chin. "Open."

Panic flared, and I quickly tried to push the wave back. This was Nick. Not Joey. But Nick must have seen something in my face, because he stroked my cheek gently, then reached behind me and tucked something into my hand. "That is your safe-word. Drop it, and I'll hear. Now, open?"

I rolled what he'd given me between my fingers, hearing the soft, familiar chime. A jingle bell. I giggled and sang "*Oh, what fun it is to ride?*"

Nick snorted. "No riding today, mily. Not enough time. Open?"

This time, I opened my mouth and let him gag me, using a big ball gag that he strapped tightly around my head. Then, secure and silent, I let him lead me into the bathroom.

We have one of *those* showers—big enough for a Wonderland caucus race, with jets everywhere, a fancy shower head that does everything but make coffee, and a wide bench for just lounging. Nick had set the shower-head to a fine mist setting, filling the bathroom with steam. He put me on the bench and kissed my forehead.

"I have a new toy for you," he murmured, and his hands traced down my damp skin as he knelt in front of me. Something wrapped tightly around each of my ankles, then Nick pulled my legs apart. I heard two loud, sucking sounds—first on my left, then on my right—and when it was done, my feet were off the floor, and I couldn't close my legs. I squeaked a little behind the gag as Nick ran his nails up and down my inner thighs.

"Waterproof cuffs. With suction cups," he answered the question I couldn't ask. "Very good for playing in the shower. Or in a hot tub." He pressed his lips to my left thigh, nipped me gently, then moved away. A moment later, the fine mist changed to the hard, pummeling massage spray I usually used on my back. He centered the spray right on my crotch; I yelped, unable to move out of the way of the punishing waterfall, and not entirely sure I wanted to. It felt amazing—pleasure and pain all at once, and I tugged hard on the ankle cuffs so that I could pump my hips into the water, moaning and biting down hard on the gag.

"Oh, you like that, do you?" Nick asked. From the position of his voice, he was back on his knees, and I couldn't think why until the wet heat of the shower was replaced with the hot wetness of Nick's mouth closing over my cock. He slid his arms underneath my legs to hold me in place as he slowly swallowed me whole, taking me deeper than anyone ever had before.

I admit freely that I'm a cockslut. I love going down on my partners, and I love it when they return the favor. Having someone suck my cock hadn't happened in a long while, because Joey had thought it beneath his dignity as a dom. I was the bottom, so it was my place to be on my knees with his cock in my mouth, not the other way around. Nick, apparently, had missed that day at dom school. He was good. He was really good, and before too long, I was screaming into the gag, thrashing against his arms and the cuffs, completely out of my mind as I came and came. To my shock, Nick swallowed the load, and proceeded to lick me clean before sliding up my body and unfastening the gag; the ball came out of my mouth with a loud pop, and was immediately replaced by Nick's tongue. I could feel his erection poking me in the stomach as he pressed against me, and I groaned.

"You all right?" Nick whispered against my lips.

"Yeah. Yeah, I'm fine. Do I get to return the favor?" I asked, leaning against him. "I want to suck your cock, Nick."

He kissed me again, long and slow, running his fingers through my wet hair. His answer shocked me even more than his swallowing. "No, thank you."

"No?"

"It's... no, thank you. I do appreciate that you want to, Steven," he said, his voice quiet. "Perhaps... perhaps another time."

"Oh," I said, unable to think of anything else. "Well... what can I do for you? I want to."

"Oh, you'll do for me. Don't you worry."

Which is how I ended up re-gagged, and on my knees on the shower floor, my chest on the bench and my ankles released from one position only to be refastened to either side of the shower, spreading my legs wide and leaving my ass open. Nick knew just what I liked, and he toyed with me until I was whimpering through the gag, and I was turned on enough that my cock was somehow starting to rise again. That, I was pretty sure, was him doing some kind of mystic mumbo-jumbo, because never in my life had I come twice in one session. By that point, I was convinced that Nick had planned this out—we don't usually keep the silicone lube in the shower. Or the condoms.

I heard a knock on the door, and Mary's muffled voice. "Nick, time check."

I moaned softly, the sound swallowed up by the water. Nick twisted the three fingers he had in my ass and called back, "Thanks, Mary. We'll be out soon." He pulled his fingers free, and moved his cock into position. I was so open, so well-greased and ready for him that he didn't hesitate at all, ramming home and pounding my ass hard, holding tight to my shoulders for leverage. It was quite probably the fastest, dirtiest, most amazing fuck of my life, and I howled my second orgasm into the gag, then howled again as Nick leaned over my back and bit my arm to keep from screaming as he came. He stayed slumped over me for a long moment, the water pounding on both of us, until I grunted and shifted underneath him. "Ah... I'm sorry, *Styopa*. That was... amazing." He pushed himself up and kissed me between my shoulder-blades, then slipped out of me and stood up, freeing my ankles and removing the cuffs. He helped me to stand, then changed the shower head to a gentle rain setting and started rubbing his hands over my chest. I smelled soap, and realized he was washing me! He laughed at my strangled protest. "Let me, *lubov moy*. Let me have you to myself before I have to share you with the rest of the coven. I need to have you to myself, for just a little while."

It was hard to argue with that, even if I could, and I had no idea what had happened to the bell. Down the drain, I guessed. So I nodded and let him rub me all over with soap, whining a little when he reached my cock and balls. Nick seemed to realize that coming twice had made me super-sensitive, and that even the lightest of touches was almost too much, and he carefully soaped me up and washed me off, then turned me around and washed my back and my ass. Once he was done, he settled me back onto the bench and washed my hair for me, using the hand-sprayer to rinse the soap out. He left me sitting there, while I assume he scrubbed himself. When he finally came back and started to undo the gag, it was after he turned the water off.

"We're going to have the biggest water bill on the block," I said once the gag was out of my mouth. Nick laughed.

"But we will be very, very clean. Let me see your arm... ah, good. I didn't break the skin. You will bruise there, though. I'm sorry for that. Shall I dry you as well, or should I untie you?"

I tipped my head back against the tile and took a long, satisfied breath, feeling very well-fucked and very much loved. "Don't be sorry. I liked it. And it's up to you. Nick, you didn't do anything, did you?"

"What do you mean?" he asked, taking me by the shoulders and standing me up.

Obediently, I turned around, and over my shoulder said, "Magic. I mean, I've never, ever come twice before. I was wondering if you... I don't know... zapped me or something?" Nick went very quiet and very still. He took his hands off my arms, and the next thing I knew, I was being hit was a blast of cold air as the shower door opened. Then the bathroom door opened and Nick was gone, leaving me soaking wet and shivering in the shower, with my hands still tied behind my back.

"Nick!" I called his name as I gingerly made my way out of the shower and through the bathroom. If I slipped like this, if I fell... the idea scared the crap out of me. Once I was on the bedroom carpet, I stopped. I'd screwed up. I knew I screwed up. I just didn't know how! "Nick? Nick, are you still in here?" There was no answer.

I forced myself to think. He had to still be in the room; there hadn't been time for him to get dried off, let alone dressed, and he wasn't going to leave the room wet and naked. I swallowed hard and closed my eyes, trying to listen and not able to hear anything over the rushing in my ears. I couldn't tell which way he was, where he was, and I was starting to get scared. I'd messed up. How do I fix it? What do I *do*? With nothing else to fall back on, I automatically turned to what I'd learned from Joey.

Slowly, carefully, I got down onto my knees. Down was good. It wasn't as far to fall from down, especially when someone hit you. I tucked my head, feeling my collar bumping against my chin as I leaned forward. "Master?" I whispered. "I... I'm sorry."

"Steven!" Nick's voice was sharp. I heard him coming closer, and I couldn't help it. I flinched. But the slap I was expecting never came; instead I was pulled to my feet, and pulled into Nick's wet arms. He held me tightly, murmured apologies into my hair as he reached around me and loosened the strap binding my wrists. "I'm sorry, Steven. I'm sorry. I shouldn't have left you alone. Wait... where is the bell? What happened to your safe-word?"

"I don't know," I said, not resisting as Nick slowly massaged each of my wrists in turn. "I lost it, I think. Master, may I dry off now?"

"Stop that!" Nick snapped. "You do not call me master. I'm sorry, Steven. I lost my temper." He let me go and walked away, coming back and wrapping a towel around my shoulders. He started rubbing me dry with another one, and sighed before saying, "That was a very insulting question, Steven."

By that point, I'd forgotten what I'd asked him, and said so. Nick snorted, the sound muffled since he was working on my legs that that point. "When you asked if I'd put a spell on you. I wouldn't do that to you, Steven. That... I wouldn't try to control you like that. It's completely against everything I believe."

I shivered, and I wasn't sure if it was just from the cold. "I didn't know that. I'm sorry, Nick. I was stupid."

"No," Nick corrected, his voice coming from near my hip. "Not stupid. Just ignorant. Ignorance can be fixed. And I should have realized that, and not lost my temper and gone off to sulk. Are you all right?"

"I'm fine. Just cold," I answered. It didn't seem as if Nick was going to stand up, so I sat down next to him on the floor. "Nick, I really am very sorry. I had no idea..."

He snorted, "I know. I tend to forget sometimes, just how much you don't know." He patted my leg and stood up. "Come on. We need to get you dressed before you freeze. I'm going to need to think about how to have you safe-word if you are gagged. Something that can be dropped won't work."

I clambered to my feet and went back into the bathroom to finish drying off and comb my hair. Still cold, I was pulling a heavy sweater on over my head when Nick started talking again.

".... need your permission."

"What?" I said, pulling the heavy knit into place. "Sorry, the sweater ate most of that. What did you say?"

"That there is something I would like to do," Nick said, sounding tentative. "Something magic. But I would need your permission."

"Oh. Okay, sure." I ran my fingers through my damp hair and frowned, trying to remember where I'd put my watch.

"That's it?" Nick gasped. "You don't even know what I want to do!"

"S'okay. I trust you. If you want to tell me, you will. You promised not to hurt me, and most of the time, I remember that. Even if you had done something to me in the shower, all it did was make me come twice. How can I complain about that? I was just curious, is all. Wanted to know if you could do it again. Do you see my watch?"

Nick burst out laughing, then he pulled me into his arms and kissed me. "I don't deserve you, you know. No, what I want to do is enhance your energy levels. I'll be doing it to myself, as well. Or we will both fall asleep in our dinners."

I grinned. "Yeah, that was really kind of intense."

"And it built up quite a bit of energy. Energy that I can harness and use to keep us going. If you don't object?"

"No objections here. Fire away." I don't know what I was expecting. Fireworks, maybe. What I got was surprisingly sedate— Nick took my head in his hands and whispered something, his voice too faint for me to make out just what he was saying. His hands felt as if they were vibrating, and they got warm far too quickly. The warmth spread down through my body, but instead of relaxing me, I felt invigorated, ready to take on anything, and again, I tasted butterscotch. Weird.

"Wow," I murmured. "You're welcome to do that anytime. That feels good."

"What?" Nick sounded surprised. He touched my forehead, his fingers lingering there for a moment. "Huh," he said. "I was not expecting that. I wonder if that is what Maureen saw."

"Expecting what?" I asked. "Saw what?"

"You should not have felt what I did," Nick said, his hands falling away. "When we have more time, I want to test you. Not now, though." Almost on cue, I heard the doorbell ring. I turned towards the door, stopping when Nick took my arm and tucked my watch into my hand. "Now, it's time for you to meet the coven, Steven."

❖

The first person to arrive was someone I already knew: Cheryl, she of the fantastic brownies. She hugged me warmly, asked me how I was feeling, and promised to sit down with me and talk. That made me wonder just what Mo had told her. There was no time to ask her, though, because the coven started to arrive at that point, and some of them were other people I knew: John, the stage-hand from the theater; Maggie, who had been Natalie's regular babysitter; Anton, who ran the costume shop; and his partner Jesse, who I vaguely remembered from some party or other. They were all happy to see me, telling me how good I looked, and how glad they were that I'd landed on my feet. All of them asked Nick about Natalie, and I could feel him growing more and more tense. He didn't say anything, but I could feel it growing in him, and I knew that he needed a break, and fast.

"Nick?" I murmured.

"Hm?"

"Is there anyone in the kitchen?"

A moment of quiet, then he answered, "Not at the moment."

"Good. Kitchen, please?" I linked my arm into his and hopefully made it look as if he was leading me. In reality, I dragged him along with me into the quiet, fragrant kitchen.

"What, Steven?" he asked, sounding snappish. He let my arm go and I heard him moving away, and the creak of the oven door.

"You needed a minute," I answered. I found a chair and pulled it out, gesturing for him to sit down. "Something is bothering you. I wasn't going to ask, but... now I'm asking. You're upset, and I want to help."

He blustered, just like I was expecting. "I'm fine!"

"Nick..." I crossed my arms over my chest. "Not to put too fine a point on this, but... bullshit. Now, you haven't told me much about what you're doing tonight, but I have read enough fantasy that I don't think you are in any shape to do magic. Not now. So talk!"

The chair scraped across the floor, and I heard Nick grunt. When he spoke again, I could tell that he had sat down. "I... you're right. I should have told you already. When the mail came in yesterday, did you hear the doorbell?"

"I did, but you didn't tell me what it was."

"It was a registered letter," Nick said slowly. "Grace has taken her challenge to another level. She is contesting Maureen's will, and she is claiming that Natalie is not really my daughter."

"What?" I was shocked. "Nick, that's crazy!"

"She wants to keep Natalie. She says I cannot give her a proper home, that we..." he stopped, huffed, and fell silent. But he'd already said enough.

"It's because of me, hm?" I leaned back against the wall, my arms across my chest. "Or rather, because of us. Because Nat would have two daddies. Christ, she's as bad as my father."

"Perhaps. It will be a long, ugly fight, and I wonder... perhaps it might be better? If Natalie lived with her grandmother..."

"'Scuse me, Nick?" I interrupted.

"Hm?"

"Have you lost your fucking mind?"

I don't know if it was the question, or the angry disbelief in my voice, but I heard the chair clatter to the floor, and Nick was in front of me, his hand fisted in my sweater. "I do not take that from anyone, Steven. Least of all from you..."

"You're taking it from her," I snapped back. "Natalie is your daughter. Maureen said so, and I know she wouldn't lie about that. So why the hell are you giving up?"

Stunned silence, and Nick slowly let go of my sweater. He took along breath, then sighed. "Is that what I'm doing? I... I want what is best for her. Perhaps being with Grace... is better?"

"Really? Do you really believe that?"

Another shaky breath. "No. But it will be ugly. I don't want her to have to go through this."

"She's little, Nick. Will she even remember?" I cocked my head to the side. "Will she remember you, if you let her go?"

Silence, for long enough that if I couldn't still hear him

breathing, I'd have thought Nick left the room. Finally, he answered, "I do not think so. She will know... only what Grace tells her. About her mother, and about me."

"Do you think Maureen would have wanted that?" I asked him quietly.

For a few minutes, there was only the sound of Nick moving around, doing something. I assumed it had to do with dinner, since I heard the oven door creaking. When he came back, he stopped in front of me, close enough that I could feel his chest brushing against mine.

"Steven? Am I doing the right thing?" he asked, sounding so tentative, so lost, that I put my arms around him and held on tight. He buried his face in my shoulder, and I could feel him shaking. "I don't want to lose her," he said against my neck. "I don't want to lose... to lose Maureen all over again. And you... what about you?"

"I know. I know, *Kolya*," I whispered, rubbing his back. "I think you're doing the right thing. I think Maureen would want you to bring Natalie home. And no, it isn't unfair to me, or unfaithful. You loved Mo first. I know that. I loved her, too. She would want you to be happy. You and Natalie..."

"Guys?" Mary's voice was soft, gentle. "Nick, you're resonating all over the place. What's wrong?"

Nick straightened, keeping one arm around me as he turned towards Mary. "A... crisis of faith. I'll be fine. Steven... he helped me clear my head."

"He's good at that," Mary said. "He was always the one people went to when they had troubles. In high school, they called him the Counselor."

"You're never going to let me forget that," I groused. "I wasn't that good, Mare."

"Stevie, you talked someone down! You'd have been a great crisis counselor."

"Talked someone down?" Nick repeated. "This means... what?"

"Talked someone out of killing himself," Mary answered. "One of the other kids in the theater program. He blew his Julliard admissions testing, and he was going to jump off the school roof."

"He'd pinned everything on getting into Julliard. When he didn't make it..." I let out a long breath. "I'd forgotten about Chaz, honestly."

"He hasn't," Mary told me. "He called me, the other day. Right out of the blue. Asked about you. His wife just had a little boy. They named him Steven." I heard Nick laughing, no doubt at the look on my face. "So, what is it and how can I help?"

Nick stopped laughing, and his arm around me tightened. "I... am going to be calling my lawyer tomorrow. Maureen's mother is trying to take Natalie away from me, trying to say I am not her father. I am going to get my daughter back."

Mary made a very self-satisfied sound. "Good. You need her back here. You know that the coven will help however we can. Now, can we borrow Stevie? I've been telling Maxie about the wonder drummer, and he doesn't believe me."

I perked up, but Nick wouldn't let me go. "It's early to start, Mary. Wait until after the ritual and dinner. I want to hear you play, too. But not yet."

"All right. Nick, do you need someone else to take the ritual? Give yourself time to settle? It's just about sunset."

"No, no. I will be fine. And I'm coming. Thank you for offering."

I heard Mary walk away, and turned to face Nick. "You're sure you'll be okay?"

Nick took my face between his hands and kissed me, then said, "I have you. Why should I not be?"

The ritual, which Nick had told me in advance would be a little like going to church, was actually nothing of the sort. We all trooped out onto the porch, and Mary took over Nick's usual job of explaining what was happening around me. So I knew that Nick lit a specially-made candle from the light of the setting sun, and that when we had all gone back inside, he'd used that candle to light the fire in the fireplace. Once the fire was lit, Mary left me sitting in the corner, listening to a lot of fussing over directions and watchtowers and incense and salt and water, after which Nick had already warned me the house would be sealed. How, I wasn't quite sure, but Nick had been firm about that; until dawn came and the sun rose, no one would be entering or leaving this house. I missed the end of the chanting, which annoyed me, because they had some really nice harmonies building. But for some reason, my ears kept popping; by the time they cleared, it was time for me to get my drum.

Nick had set up with me that morning what he'd wanted for the ritual, walking me through the meditation that I was to accompany, explaining as much as he could to someone without a proper frame of reference. I understood enough of what he told me to know that he wanted something like a heartbeat. For that, I chose the djembe, the biggest drum I had, and with the deepest voice. I put the drum between my knees and started, closing my eyes as I started and hearing Nick's soothing voice as a counterpoint. I almost immediately lost what he was saying, so focused on the drumbeat that I didn't really care; I just let the rhythm take me.

I'd heard about trance drumming, knew some people who did it as a regular thing. I had never experienced it before, and I certainly wasn't expecting to get pulled into trance, but that was just what happened. I fell into a deep, relaxed state, concentrating completely on my hands and the drum and that deep, dark heartbeat that felt as if it was coming up from the soul of the earth. I could feel the darkness pressing against my skin, drawing me deeper into itself, deeper into the rhythm. From somewhere, I could hear a slight echo, another rhythm calling me, as seductive as anything I'd ever heard. I had no idea what it was, but I knew I had to find it. It was something I had to have, something I needed, the way I needed food, or air, or Nick. I followed the sound, wondering what the heck kind of drum that was, until it seemed I was standing on top of whatever it was. The new rhythm surrounded me, warm and soft and just so *right*, and as I let it settle into me and become part of my own heartbeat, I heard Nick's voice, clear as a bell, calling me back.

For a minute, I felt as if I had just been put back into my skin, and it didn't quite fit right. I shook my head to clear it, and took a long breath, only then noticing that my hands were numb. I grimaced and started massaging my right palm. All around me, I could hear people moving, talking in low voices. Then I heard Mary, her voice ringing like a bell.

"Stevie, that was tight!"

"Yeah. Best path-working we've ever done. I really felt that one," someone else said.

"You're going to keep playing for us, aren't you?" Cheryl asked, her voice plaintive. "We'll make sure it's worth it for you!"

"She's going to bribe him with brownies," someone muttered, loud enough for everyone to hear, and everyone laughed. Over the giggles, I could hear Cheryl calling out that yes, she would bribe me with brownies, if that was what it took to keep me.

More laughter, and I laughed with them as I moved the drum off to one side so that I could stand up. I really needed something to drink, and sitting for however long it had been had made my back stiffen. I stood up... and then next thing I remember was someone holding something under my nose and saying "Drink this!"

I drank, and tasted orange-flavored piss. "What the hell is that?" I sputtered.

"He'll be fine," Nick said from behind me. His hand was warm on the back of my neck, and there was heavy, furry warmth over my legs that I identified as Mirage. I wondered just what Nick was doing on the floor, then realized that I was on the floor, too. What was I doing on the floor?

"Sports drink." Whoever-it-was told me. "Drink some more, Steven. It will help."

"Do I have to?" I asked, wincing at the whine in my voice. I ran my fingers through Mirage's fur, and she whuffed softly and licked my hand. "I'm fine."

"Steven..." Nick's voice had a definite warning tone to it. So I drank the damn piss, and, annoyingly, felt better.

"What happened?" I asked once I handed the cup back.

"Scientific explanation or magical?" Mister Sports-Drink asked.

"Either. Both. Who are you?"

"Sorry. It's Jesse. Scientifically speaking, you overexerted yourself, causing hyponatremia, a drop in blood pressure, and loss of consciousness. In layman's terms, you blew your electrolyte balance to kingdom come, made your blood pressure bottom out, and fainted when you stood up. Hence, the sports drink."

"I... what?" I blinked. "I fainted? Is that why I'm on the floor?"

"And," Jesse continued, as if I hadn't said anything, "In magical terms, you've got a nasty case of circle sickness. Drink some more." He put another cup into my hand.

"Circle sickness?" I repeated, taking another sip. This time, it tasted marginally better.

"It means you were not ready for the path-working. Which I never thought to prepare you for, because I did not think you would get pulled into the trance," Nick said. He moved his hand, and I noticed then that it had been warmer than it should have.

"You were doing something?" I asked.

"Grounding you," he answered.

"What, like an electrical line?" I asked, licking my lips. The orange stuff was tasting better. Sweeter. More... buttery. Nice.

"Very much so," he agreed. "Evening out your energies, so that you would recover faster. It is very basic, and it appears that it is something I am going to have to teach you. I understand now, I think, why Maureen wanted to bring you into the coven."

I coughed on my drink. "She what?"

"Yes. She didn't explain why." Nick paused, then snorted, sounding amused. "She rarely explained why. But she said she wanted to bring you into the coven, if you were willing."

I shook my head and put my now-empty cup down on the floor. "Okay. Help me up. This conversation cannot happen with me on the floor. It just can't." I had to wait until Mirage moved, then I got to my feet, feeling Nick's hand on my back, where it remained until he was sure I wasn't going to fall down again. As I got back up, I heard conversations starting up around me, and realized that we hadn't been alone. I turned towards Nick. "This isn't going to be a private conversation, is it?"

"This effects the whole coven, Steven," he answered. "We discuss this as a group."

I nodded, sitting back down in my chair, this time with Mirage between my knees. It took me a minute to arrange my thoughts, and everyone fell quiet when I cleared my throat and started talking, "All right. I can understand not private. I'm... well, thanks for the offer. Really. I'm flattered. But... I'm not real big on religion anymore." I knew I'd mentioned my reasons to Nick, and Mary knew because she'd been there. But the rest of the coven wouldn't know why I was saying no. I could feel the tension growing in the room, and I needed them to know, to understand, so that they'd know it was all me and my issues. So I raised my voice. "My father... he's a really religious man. Old school Irish Catholic, you know? And... he kicked me out of the family the day I came out of the closet. He told me that there'd never been a faggot in the Ahearn family, and by God, there was not going to be one now."

Someone hissed, and it was as if that hissing was the tension leaking out of the room. A man's voice whispered, "Harsh, man."

"Yeah. He told me I was damned, damned in the eyes of the Church, and damned in his." I stopped, dragging my fingers through my hair, then raking them through Mirage's fur. "After the accident, Mary called them, told them. Even though... even though I could have died... they never came..."

"You don't have to go on, Steven," Cheryl interrupted, her voice firm. "We understand. Will you at least play for us?"

I smiled and nodded. "Sure. I liked that. Just... someone is going to have to show me how not to do whatever it was that I did."

Laughter, and Nick rubbed my back gently. "I will show you. Now, shall we eat?"

I went to stand up to walk to the kitchen, and almost tripped on Mirage, who absolutely refused to move.

"I agree with the dog, Steven," Jesse said. "Stay in the chair. We'll feed you."

So I stayed in the chair for the next hour or so, being waited on hand and foot and stubborn dog—someone brought Mirage's food bowl and water over when she decided to do her best impression of a doorstop. My cup was never empty, nor was my plate, not until I waved off a third offer of dessert.

"Not unless you want to roll me out of here," I protested.

"We're trying to fatten you up for the winter. You're too thin," Mary teased me.

"You have a point," Nick said. He'd pulled a chair up next to me to eat his own dinner. "If I want to stay warm this winter..."

"You can sleep with the dog!" I finished, laughing. Nick leaned over and kissed me.

"If you're done, Stevie, why don't you show us the new drums?" Mary asked.

"All right. Mirage, let me up." I reached down and scratched her ears, and was rewarded by her getting up, shaking herself, then turning and licking my hand. "You stay out here, baby-girl. You don't like the drum." She whined as if she understood me, and moved away; I heard her collar jingling as she settled herself somewhere else.

"She's gone to her bed. Go play, *Styopa*," Nick said. He kissed me again, and I stood up, hesitating a minute to get my bearings.

"That's a very smart dog," Mary said. She took my arm and hugged me, then followed me as I made my way out of the room. She didn't try to lead, which I appreciated. In my own house, I knew how to get from here to there.

"She is," I agreed. "It's a little creepy just how much she understands. Even the instructors at the school said so—that she's one of the smartest dogs they've had." I ran my fingers over the wall, stopping outside the door to what had once been my room. It was still my room, technically. But no one slept here anymore. I opened the door and heard Mary gasp.

"Stevie, what did you *do*?"

"Blame Nick. He went a little nutty." I knew what she was seeing—the three other djembes in their cases, lined up with a pair of conga drums in their rack. The shelves where several different types and sizes of tonbeks were sitting, the bodhrans that lay flat atop those same shelves and the flat box of wood tippers that went with the bodhrans. And in the center of the room was my new pride and joy—the high-end professional drum kit, the best of the best. I still couldn't believe I owned them. "Not that I'm complaining. You have got to hear these."

"I can't wait. Let me get Maxie, and we'll get our gear." She nudged me, giggling. "Just like old times?"

"Just without the bigots?" I asked. Old times had been when I'd played in my father's band.

"Ouch. Sorry for bringing it up."

"Sorry. Bit of a sore spot tonight. Come on, let's play." I heard her hurrying away down the hall, calling Max's name. I walked around the perimeter of the room, picking up a pair of drumsticks from another flat box. I was just taking my place behind the drums when I heard the low rumble of people coming towards me.

"So, it's a concert?" I called out, and heard laughter out in the hall.

"If you don't mind," Mary answered. "Everyone is curious."

"No problem for me," I said, twirling one of the sticks between my fingers. "I know your axe, Mare, but what does Max play?"

"Bass. Keys, sometimes. What's your pleasure tonight?" Max asked.

"Mare? You're calling the shots here. Pick something."

She grumbled something about being put on the spot, and started tuning her guitar. "*Mari Mac*?" she suggested. "The rocked up version. Max knows it."

I burst out laughing, "Woman, are you trying to kill me?"

"We could just play, if you're not feeling up to it," Mary answered. "You probably don't even remember all the lyrics."

I snickered. Mary knew I'd never forgotten a lyric in my life. Oh, I'd missed this kind of teasing. The theatre had been rife with it, and it had been wonderful. "Woman, the day I'm not up to singing is the day they plant me. You finished torturing that thing yet?"

"Just count us in, drummer-boy."

A rapid four-count, and we were off, with Mary picking out the tune lightning-fast. *Mari Mac* was a patter song, full of tongue-twister lyrics that drove most singers crazy when it was sung at regular speed. The rocked-up version was half again as fast, grueling for a drummer and torturous for a singer. Being the perverse bastard that I was, I loved it. From *Mari Mac* we swung into *Whiskey in the Jar*, and the next half an hour turned into a concert of rocked-up Childe Ballads, selections from a fantastic metal a capella-and-drum group from Germany, and classic Celtic rock. There was something different about the music, about the drums, something I couldn't put my finger on. The music felt more... alive, more vital, than anything I'd ever felt before. If this was what professional drums did, they were worth every single penny!

"All right, all right. You've proved your point," Mary called out after the last song. "You haven't lost your touch."

"He's as good as you told me, Mare," Max added. Then, cryptically, he asked, "You going to ask him?"

"Ask me what?" I asked as I stood up and stretched. "Ugh. I need another shower after that."

"Really?"

I grinned at the undisguised eagerness in Nick's voice. "Down, Nick," I called back, drawing giggles from Mary.

"What we were going to ask you is if you wanted a gig," Mary asked when she stopped laughing. "You know about Grail, right?"

"Grail? Ah... wait. The band you were starting? Yeah, you told me something about that. What about it?"

"Our drummer quit," Max said. "Mare said you might be interested, but I wanted to hear you before we offered."

My jaw dropped. "This was an audition?"

"Yeah, sort of." Max sounded a little sheepish at the admission.

"So, interested?" Mary asked.

I didn't answer right off, going over and putting my sticks away. I hadn't played in a band in years, not since before I left Boston. It was a huge commitment, and my evenings and weekends would be shot. No guarantee of getting anywhere, either.

Sounded a lot like being back in the theater company.

"Nick?" I asked.

"It's up to you, *mily*," he answered. "You're very good. If you want my opinion, I think this would be good for you."

"We can't offer much yet, Stevie," Mary said, all in a rush. "But we've got a gig in for Valentine's Day, out in Fells Point. You already know most of our set. It's pretty much the same as what we played in Gypsy Dance."

"Oh, Lord," I murmured. "You're playing the same set we played in high school? Honey, you need to bring it into this century."

"You have ideas?" Mary sounded so eager, so hopeful, that I had to grin.

"Yeah. Lots of them. When and where do we rehearse?"

Mary squealed and threw her arms around me, hugging me tightly as people around us applauded. Max shook my hand, and asked if he could hear me on some of the other drums. I picked up one of the bodhrans and turned to ask, "Mary, do you remember *Coal Quay Market?*"

"Oh, of course. That's a fun one."

The rest of the evening was filled with laughter and music, with the energy level waxing and waning as the night passed into early morning. At some point past two in the morning, I headed for the kitchen for a nibble and some tea.

"You're in good voice," Mary said, her voice thick with sleep.

"So are you," I answered, turning and leaning against the counter. "This is going to be fun, isn't it?"

"I think so," Mary said. She was quiet for a moment, coming over to stand next to me, close enough that her arm was pressed against mine. "You know, I don't think I've ever seen you this happy."

I smiled, sipping my tea. "I don't think I've ever been this happy, Mare. I feel a little silly for asking, but is this what being is love is like? Really being in love?"

"Looks like it. And it shows," she said. "Especially in your music. Stevie, you've never played better. And you said you were out of practice?"

"I haven't played in months. I haven't sung in months, except in the shower." I shrugged. "Mare, when I played tonight, it was... as if the music was alive. It was incredible. I'd had some good performances before, on stage, but nothing that held a candle to... to the sheer energy that we had going tonight." I drank more of my tea and smiled. "When I woke up in the hospital, I thought I'd lost everything. Now... now I've got everything I ever dreamed of. Happy? Mare, I wake up in the morning and have to pinch myself to remind myself that I'm not dreaming. And it's only going to get better from here. I'm sure of that."

Interstitial
Signs and Portents

He didn't look up, didn't turn from his work, but the servant knew that his master had noticed his presence. Noticed, and was very displeased.

"I said I was not to be disturbed." The deep, accented voice rumbled through the dimly lit room like distant thunder, and the servant flinched and cowered lower, his forehead almost touching the floor.

"Mercy, my lord, mercy," he whispered. "You left orders... he has been found..."

Silence, and the man standing turned slightly, enough that the servant could have, had he dared, looked at his master in profile, seen the breathtaking beauty of his features. But raising his eyes to look on his master would have meant seeing also the writhing, whimpering... thing lying on the worktable. That thing, the servant knew, had once been a mortal servant. Like he was. So the servant kept his eyes down and waited.

"You've found the Heart's Master?"

There was no denying the malice in his master's voice, or the eagerness. The servant nodded and dared to rise up a little. "Yes, my lord. The Heart's Master walks the mortal realms again."

"That is... inconvenient. How will this impact my plans? Have the seers spoken?"

"Yes, my lord," the servant hesitated, knowing that his life was now balanced on the edge of a blade. If his master didn't like the seers' rede, he would take his displeasure out on the closest target; the servant bowed low and spoke to the floor, "The seers all agree. If the Heart's Master lives, your plans will fail, and you... you will fall."

His master was silent for a moment, and the servant could hear him moving, pacing. Suddenly polished boots appeared underneath the servant's nose.

"How long has the Heart's Master been aware?" His master's voice rumbled from over his head.

"Not long, my lord. In mortal time, one cycle of the moon, perhaps two."

His master sniffed derisively and the boots moved away. "A child. If I allow him to live, by the time he comes into his full power, my rule will be absolute."

"My lord, forgive me," the servant blurted out, amazed at his own daring. "The Heart's Master is a man grown..."

"What?" The servant mewled in pain as one of those polished boots lashed out and caught him in the chin, sending him tumbling across the polished floor. "How could this happen? A man grown? With a man's strength? No. No, I cannot allow this. I will not be challenged. Find him! Find him and eliminate him!"

The servant slowly got back to his knees, his head bowed and blood forming a small puddle as it dripped from his mouth. "My... my lord, do you wish us to act directly? That... that might attract attention..."

His master stalked back towards the worktable, his boot-heels ringing on the floor. "No. No, do not act directly. If the Heart's Master is a man, he must have made some enemies. There must be someone who can be used as a vessel. Find that vessel, and eliminate the Heart's Master."

Chapter Five
The Hand You're Dealt

The house shook as the front door was shoved closed, and I heard Nick's footsteps overhead, moving towards the stairs. The circle had gone well, and with the last of the coven gone, I knew that Nick was going to be in a mood. Circle high, he called it. I called it frisky, when I was being polite. When I wasn't, I told him that he was a slut.

Not that I minded much. I could be a slut, too, and Nick's moods suited me just fine. But before playtime came work; I had told Nick that I'd clean up my toys. I picked up the drum I'd used to accompany the ritual and made my way over to the wall and the cabinet that Nick had set up for storage of odd-sized ritual items. It smelled of cedar and incense as I opened it, finding the shelf by touch and sliding the bodhran into its place. Behind me, I heard footsteps on the stairs, and then Nick was behind me, sliding his arms around my waist and pressing a kiss onto my shoulder.

"Everyone gone?" I asked, and felt him nod, the stubble of his late-evening beard scratching on the side of my neck.

"All gone. Just you and me now," he nuzzled my neck. "Want to play, Styopa?"

I grinned. He knew what my answer would be, and he knew I loved the Russian diminutive of my name. After all, it was a hell of a lot more sophisticated than Stevie. "I'll always play with you, Kolya. What are you up to?"

"Something... random," he laughed, backing away. "Get yourself ready, Steven. I'll take care of the dog and get a few things, and meet you in the playroom."

The playroom. Oh, that kind of play. My heart sped up, and I nodded without saying a word, hearing him going back up the stairs. Nicolai was the love of my life, my sanity, the single best thing that had happened to me after the accident. He was also one hell of a dom, and if he wanted me on my knees, I'd be there immediately.

But he didn't want immediate. He wanted me ready, and I knew what that meant. I also knew that it meant I'd better hurry. It didn't take that long to feed the dog and lock up, and if I wasn't in position when Nick got to the playroom, he'd keep right on going and head to bed.

Only one thing worried me, and that was his choice of words. Random? What was he talking about? Random and BDSM usually didn't go together, and especially not where Nick was concerned. Every planned scene we'd ever done had been precise, structured, and intense. Even the impromptu ones had their own rules. Random wasn't a word I'd ever heard Nick use.

But I wasn't going to find out what he meant just standing here. And if I didn't move it, I wouldn't find out what he meant at all.

The playroom door squeaked slightly, something that Nick was always meaning to fix and never getting around to. So I knew when he came in, and I knew what he'd see. Me, kneeling in the middle of the room, facing the door (I hoped—he still teased me about the time I'd knelt off center and had been facing the closet when he came in). I was naked, and I'd assumed the position he'd taught me—knees apart, back straight, with my hands resting easy on my thighs. I'd been hard before I'd even gotten my pants off, and the chilly breeze caused by the opening of the door washed over my skin, raising goosebumps and making me shiver. Outside this house, it was February, and cold. Inside my skin, it was scalding.

"Very nice," Nick murmured, and I could hear the barest hint of the accent that he never could manage to lose in his voice, stronger now than it usually was. He really was in a mood. I heard his soft footfalls, almost-but-not-quite muffled by the thick carpet as he walked around me, trailing his fingers over my shoulders and brushing my hair out of the way.

"Very nice," he repeated. He linked one finger through the

heavy silver chain I always wore and tugged on it. I closed my eyes
and took a sharp breath; he laughed and let me go.

"All right. Hold your hands out." I did, and he dropped a pile
of something slippery into my waiting palms. I grabbed them before I dropped them, feeling slick, narrow cards.

"What's this?" I asked.

"That's a tarot deck. I want you to think about what you want
tonight while you shuffle the cards," Nick said as he moved around.
I heard cabinets opening, and knew that he was getting the toys
ready. "Once you shuffle the cards, I'll lay them out. Whatever the
cards say is what I will be doing to you tonight."

I almost dropped the cards, "Nick, I don't know about this..."

"Do you trust me?" he asked.

I nodded. "You know I do."

"What's your safe-word?"

"Nick, you don't think I'm going to need..."

"Safe-word?" he repeated, his voice a little harsher, a little more
stern, the accent even more pronounced, the tone edging towards
strict formality. His dom voice. I ducked my head in response.

"Oatmeal," I said quietly. I heard Nick move, and then he was
kneeling in front of me, tugging on my chain again, pulling me
towards him and claiming my mouth in a hard, possessive kiss that
left me gasping and wanting more.

"I made a promise, *Styopa*," he whispered into my ear, sliding
his hands up my arms. "I promised you that I would never hurt
you. If you do not like what the cards say, we will stop. We will play
another way. Or not play at all. Do you understand?" I nodded, not
sure I could speak at the moment, still trying to find my breath. He
kissed me again, more gently, than stood up, "Good. Shuffle the
cards."

So I shuffled, trying to focus on all of the wonderful, horrible
things that Nick did to me in this room. The sounds of the room
became a soothing drone as I concentrated—Nick's breathing, the
hum of the fan blowing, the hiss of the rain outside, all of them
harmonizing around the bass line that was my own rapid heartbeat.
Finally, I held the cards up. "I'm done."

Nick came over and took the cards from me, "Good. I'll lay out the pattern, and then we'll get started."

I nodded, returning to my resting position. "May I speak?"

"Go ahead."

"Which deck is that? That's not the usual one, is it?" I was sure it wasn't; as I'd handled the cards, I'd noticed that it had felt different from the deck I knew Nick used when he did readings. Not as heavy... no, that wasn't it. The cards felt like they were the same paper-weight as Nick's usual deck, but for some reason, they felt like they had less of something. They were... different.

When Nick answered me, I could tell my question pleased him, "One of the art ones. The one that you gave me for Yule, as a matter of fact. How did you know?"

"It feels different," I answered, letting my confusion show.

He laughed, "Of course it does, *mily*. My working deck is consecrated. This one isn't. You really are more sensitive to magic than you give yourself credit for, Steven."

I restrained the urge to snort; just because I was sleeping with a mage didn't mean I believed him when he told me I had magic of my own. Which he'd mentioned at least once a week ever since Yule. I didn't give any religion any real credence any more. The extent of my participation in the coven was to play drums for them, and that was how I liked it. But I couldn't get over how different those cards felt.

I heard the snap of the cards. "What are you doing?"

"Laying them out. Face down, so it will be a surprise for both of us. I did keep one card out. The Knight of Cauldrons. Tell me why."

Oh, this was going to be a lesson, too? I knew the answer to this one, "That's my card. For my age and coloring, and because I'm a musician."

"Very good. All right, next card," another card snapped, and Nick snorted. "Well, that makes sense."

"What?"

"The Devil. In this deck, it's called Temptation. But... the meaning behind it is perfect." Nick moved over to walk around me again, lacing his fingers into my hair and pulling my head back, making me whimper with delight and need. "Depravity. Submission. Perversion. Lust. I think that's a very good description of what's going to happen to you tonight, don't you?"

I swallowed, trying not to shake from wanting him so much. "Yes, sir."

He kissed me again. "Next card." He moved away; I shivered and tried not to break position. I missed the snap of the card, but not Nick's delighted laugh.

"The Emperor," he announced.

That caught me by surprise. "That's your card!"

"Yes. Yes, it is," he said, still laughing. "Well, I suppose that's a relief. I wouldn't want to think that you were going to submit to someone else tonight. Although... do you know what the meaning of this card is?"

I was caught in spite of myself, fascinated by the game he had orchestrated for us, "I don't have a clue."

"This card signifies the masculine force of the universe. Dominance and discipline, and at the same time, paternal. The Emperor is the universal father figure."

I cocked my head to the side. "Did you choose the card because he was a dom or because he was a dad?"

Nick laughed, "Both. Neither. The card chose me. Now, let's see what the next card you chose is." Another card snapped, followed quickly by two more. Nick grunted, and then all I heard was movement. Nick walked away, and then came back towards me, standing behind me. I stayed still, and was rewarded by the slithering of a silky rope over my shoulder.

"Nine of Swords, the Six of Swords, reversed, and the Chariot, also reversed," Nick murmured. "Hands behind your back."

I nodded and crossed my wrists behind me; he lashed them together firmly and then drew them up, running the ropes over my shoulders and down, crossing and re-crossing my chest until my arms were immobile. I could feel the ends of the rope trailing down my belly in a long tail, and I shifted slightly so that the rope swayed and slid over my cock. That felt good, but the movement earned me a sharp slap on the thigh and I fell still.

"You look very good in rope and nothing else," Nick tugged on the ropes, checking their placement. "There's no point in blind-folding you, *mily*. Except for aesthetics, that is."

"And while we're at it, we can take owls to Athens," I muttered.

Nick snorted his amusement, and there was a steady tug at the center of my chest; he had gathered up the tail and was using it as a leash. "Come on."

"Are you going to tell me what the cards mean?"

"In a minute," he answered, pulling me along for a few steps before stopping me pushing me up against the edge of the massage table that stood off to one side of the room. I'd been surprised by this table when I'd learned about it—both by the fact that we owned one, and by the fact that Nick knew what to do around one. He was damned good at massage, something I appreciated when the cold got into my back. He said it had been part of his training as a healer.

Nick bent me over the edge of the table and pressed one hand on the back of my neck, forcing me down until my cheek was pressed against the surface and all I could smell was leather. Then he pushed me forward; when he was done, my head and shoulders hung off of one edge of the table, and my rock-hard cock was pressed against the other. "Don't move," he ordered me, and then moved away again. When he came back, it was with heavy cuffs that he locked around my ankles, and a spreader bar that he used to force my legs apart. "How long can you hold this position?" he asked.

I thought about it for a moment, shifting gently in the ropes and judging how it made my back feel. "I don't think this will be a problem. I've got pretty good support from the table. If I start to cramp, I'll call red."

"Good boy. Oh, and the two cards? The meaning of the nine of swords really doesn't apply to anything we're doing here tonight, but the artwork shows a lovely young man tied up with rope." He patted my ass and moved away, and I felt a tug on the rope leash as he pulled it towards my chin and then down over the edge of the table. Nick moved around the table again, and there was a tug at my feet as pressure was put on the spreader bar.

Nick patted my ass again when he was done, and then ran one hand slowly down over my hip. "Can you move?" I tried and failed, finding myself unable to stand up straight. He must have tied the rope tails off to the spreader bar, trapping me over the table. I could move a little from side to side, but not much, and I told him so. He ran his nails down my spine. "Good. That's the next two cards. Six of swords, and the Chariot, both reversed."

"What, they mean bondage?" I asked, shifting a little, testing my limits.

"Not in so many words," he slapped my ass and then slid his hand down, between my legs, stopping just before he reached my balls. I whimpered and thrust back, and he laughed and pulled his hand away. "Reversed, the Six of swords means hindrance, and the Chariot means lack of control."

"Which means bondage," I said again, pushing my ass back towards him. "Well, I'm hindered, and I've got no control. Is there a card in there that says I get fucked?"

"If that's something that you were focusing on when you shuf-fled, than perhaps. There are five cards left, and they're all face down. So... let's see what the next card says. Maybe it'll say you need to be gagged; you're awfully chatty tonight." The next card snap was so close to me that I jumped when it sounded. Nick made an odd sound, and then another card snapped. "Interesting."

I wanted to ask what was so interesting, but I really didn't want to be gagged, and I can take a hint. So I waited. Patience is a virtue, and virtue gets rewarded. Or at least, that's what I've been told.

It seemed to work in this case. I heard another snap, different from the sound of the cards. This one I recognized it as the top of the lube bottle being opened. It was followed by a cold dribble down the crack of my ass. A fourth snap, and I almost cheered; latex has a very distinctive sound, and condoms don't snap—Nick had put on a glove. He ran his gloved nails up the back of my leg, making me twitch, then slowly started to spread the lube, making long sweeping strokes that ran from my balls to my anus and didn't come nearly close enough to either. I groaned and tried to push back more, earning myself another slap.

"Stay still," he ordered. He circled my anus with one finger and then slid it in slowly. The next stroke was two fingers, and then three, and I moaned in response, closing my eyes. He growled, leaning forward over me and reaching forward with his free hand, shoving his fingers in my mouth. "Is this enough for you, *Styopa?*"

I whined around his fingers and set to work, sucking as hard as I could and running my tongue over his knuckles the way I knew that he liked. He growled again as he started to finger-fuck me into a frenzy, then whispered into my ear, "You are such a hungry little slut, aren't you, my *Styopa?* You want nothing more than my cock up your ass, down your throat, however you can get it. Don't you?" I whined again. He was right, of course. I did want him, however I could get him, as often as I could get him, and as hard as I could get him. He laughed, pumping harder and shoving his fingers further down my throat; I had just enough slack in the ropes to pump against the edge of the table, and the sweat pooling under me made it easier, so I was building to a wonderful come.

And the phone rang. My eyes flew open as Nick laughed and pulled his fingers out of my mouth.

"So that's what those cards meant!" he said. I heard the snapping of latex as he stripped off the glove, then the padding of his feet as he walked away.

"Nick!" I squirmed, pulling against the ropes. "You can't answer that!"

"I have to. It's George," he said, and I groaned. George was his lawyer, and was handling the messy custody case over Nick's daughter. If he was calling at this hour on a Saturday night, Nick had to take the call. I heard the beep of the phone as Nick picked up the receiver, and knew that the only thing I could do was relax and wait. I sighed softly, not really paying attention to what was being said. So when Nick tapped me on the top of the head, I was surprised. And even more surprised when he tapped my lower lip, a silent signal for me to open my mouth. When I did, he shoved his cock in so roughly that I choked on it, needing a moment to catch my breath before I started sucking. It was wonderful, the velvet-soft skin tasting slightly salty and sweet, accented with the scent of soap and musk and the sandalwood incense that they used in the ritual. I loved going down on Nick, now that he'd finally relented and allowed me the privilege, and he'd told me over and over again that I was good it at. So how he was managing to keep up a conversation with me using his cock as a Popsicle, I will never know.

"What? Oh, no, it's all right. Steven just had something caught in his throat," Nick sounded amused, and startlingly normal for a man who was pounding his dick down my throat. "He's fine. He says hi... no, he can't come to the phone. He's... a little tied up right now. I'll tell him. What did you need?"

I couldn't hear the other end of the conversation, so I gave myself over to doing my damnedest to disrupt it. Or at least shorten it. When I started humming, I heard Nick's breath catch, and shortly thereafter he was promising to call George first thing in the morning. A click, a thump, and he rested one hand on my head. "You are terrible, *mily*. But I suppose I deserved that. Even if it was your own fault."

My fault? His cock muffled my indignant protest, and he laughed, "Yes, your fault. You shuffled the damn deck. Do you want to know what the cards were, or don't you?"

Curiosity won; I opened my mouth. Nick stepped back, then leaned down and kissed me, still laughing.

"What's so funny?" I demanded, feeling the slight soreness in my throat. Not enough soreness. Damn it, I *wanted* his cock!

"The last two cards. Ace of Rods and Wheel of Fortune. Both reversed," he answered, reaching down and cupping my chin. "Are you still hungry, *mily*?"

Oh, I knew that cue. I closed my eyes and started to beg, "Yes, please. Please, *Kolya?* I want you. Please?" I would have added a little begging in Russian, but my accent was horrible, and it only made Nick laugh when I tried. Laughter was *not* what I wanted from him right now.

"You ask very nicely. Open wide."

Obediently, eagerly, I opened my mouth, going back to work on his cock, and pumping my hips against the table as best I could. I was so hard I ached, and it didn't look like I was getting any relief any time soon. Nick groaned over me and locked his fingers into my hair, dragging the nails of his other hand over my shoulder, hard enough that I was sure it was going to leave welts.

After only a few minutes, he was moaning hard. "Stop," he gasped out, pulling on my hair. "Steven, stop, or this is going to end too soon." He pulled back, and I let my head hang, working my jaw silently and listening to him walk around. When he touched my back, I whined, pumping my hips again.

"Nick, please..." I moaned, ready to beg again, ready to crawl, ready to do anything to have him again. It didn't even matter how. He ran his hand down my back, then leaned over and kissed my spine.

"The last two cards—the Ace of Rods reversed means sexual deprivation," he said, leaning over my back. "And the Wheel of Fortune reversed means situations interrupted. I couldn't figure out why you were going to end up frustrated, but I was ready for anything. Well, almost anything. If I'd fallen over dead, you'd have been in a very bad situation. And the cleaning lady would have a very interesting surprise on Monday."

"Don't say that!" I blurted out, pulling up hard on the ropes, and gasping as they dug into my back. Immediately, Nick pushed me back down, his hands gentle on my skin.

"*Styopa*, I'm sorry. I was teasing, and it wasn't funny. I am not going anywhere. Are you all right?"

I nodded, "Yes. I'm fine. Are we going to finish?"

"Do you still want to? We have three cards left."

"Do it." I grinned. "I want to see what the 'time to fuck Steven' card is."

He laughed, and I heard the cards being turned over, one at a time. Then there was a long silence. Finally, Nick cleared his throat.

"Steven, you really do have a knack for this," he murmured. "You need to start studying magic with me. Soon."

"Why?" I turned my head, hearing him gathering the cards. Then he was back, and his hands were warm on my hips. He moved in close, resting against my ass; I could feel his cock pressed against me. I strained back towards him. "Nick? What did the cards say?"

Nick laughed softly, "Time to fuck Steven."

"You're joking!"

"Explanations later," he started to move against me, his dick sliding up and down the crack of my ass. "Now is the time for fucking."

I moaned; I don't think I could have been more ready. I felt more lube, like ice on my skin, and then Nick was leaning over me. He pressed forward, little by little, teasing and almost tortuously slow, until finally he was balls deep in my ass. He braced himself with one hand on the edge of the table next to my shoulder, his other hand reaching forward to stroke my cheek.

"So beautiful," he murmured, his accent as thick as I'd ever heard it. "Tell me what you want, *Styopa*."

What did I want? I wanted him to pound me until I screamed, shove his fingers down my throat until I couldn't breathe, and make me come until I passed out. But I didn't have the words to tell him that. Instead I twisted my wrists in the ropes, turning until I could splay the fingers of one hand over his chest, finding his nipples with my fingertips and gently stroking them until he growled and whined over me, setting his teeth into my shoulder like a wolf or a big cat. I howled, and he growled again, reaching forward and grabbing my hair, pulling my head up and back.

"Tell me!" he whispered.

It was like the floodgates burst at his command. The words just came pouring out, "...fuck me please God I want you pound it in don't stop don't stop yes yes yes...." It stopped only when Nick shoved three fingers into my mouth, and even then I kept on moaning and whining as he slammed into me, holding me down with the weight of his body, his free hand burning like a brand into my shoulder. It was almost perfect, except that with his weight on me, I couldn't move against the table any more. No doubt if I couldn't come by the time he was done, he'd go down on me, or order me to jerk off for him. But that wasn't what I wanted. I wanted his hands on my cock. No way to do it, the way I was tied.

Nick grunted again, and picked up the pace, pounding into me hard, the way I liked it. And the part of my brain that just doesn't want to sit down and shut up identified the rhythm of the pounding and pulled up the appropriate song lyric, an off-color sea shanty I'd learned from a friend: *Put your shoulder next to mine and pump away, pump away. Put your shoulder next to mine and pump away.* I closed my eyes, amused at the lyric, and started humming it around Nick's fingers. And nearly jumped out of my skin when a hand closed around my cock. For a split second, I wondered how Nick had managed it. Then I wondered when he'd grown a third hand, because I could still feel his one hand next to my shoulder, and the other hand was still checking out my lack of tonsils. When the hand started pumping, hard and fast and matching Nick's rhythm perfectly, I gave up thinking. Now it was perfect.

Perfection never lasts long enough. I did get my wish, though; I came screaming around his fingers and blacked out. When I woke up, Nick was still leaning over me, his forehead resting between my shoulder-blades and his fingers out of my mouth. I turned my head, feeling all the little aches that marked a really good scene.

"You good?" I managed to croak out.

Nick laughed, kissing me between the shoulder blades. "I am good. You are magnificent. And I must move before you end up with something kinky in back."

I snickered, amused; he must have come really hard if he'd lost all command of idiom. "It's a kink in my back, Kolya. Right now, I do have something kinky in back."

Nick laughed again, delighted. "Let me let you up." He kissed me again and shifted slowly off of me; I shivered as the air hit my sweat-damp skin. "Just a minute, *Styopa*." I felt him behind me, kneeling down, and the spreader bar was unhooked from my ankles. Then the cuffs were removed, and Nick stood back up, resting one hand on the small of my back, just under my bound wrists. "Stand up slowly."

I did, and he steadied me when my balance failed, walking me over to a chair and helping me sit. He covered me up with a blanket, and I frowned. "Aren't you going to untie me?"

"In a minute. I will clean up first, and then I will take you to bed. And then, perhaps, untie you," Nick answered, then kissed me on the lips, gently.

He moved away, and I closed my eyes, tired, listening as he moved around, hearing cabinets open and close as I slipped into a half-doze. When Nick came back over to me, I was leaning against the side of the chair, almost asleep.

"*Styopa, lubov moy,* if you want to sleep, let's go to bed," he said, his voice low. He moved the blanket and helped me to stand up, sliding one arm around my waist and gathering up the rope tails so that I wouldn't trip on them.

"Nick, where'd the third hand come from?" I asked, suddenly curious.

"What?"

"Third hand. You had one hand on the table, one hand in my mouth. How'd you grab my cock?"

He stopped. "Steven, I didn't."

"Sure you did," I insisted. "I felt it. It felt great, just the way I like it."

"Steven, I promise you, I didn't. I couldn't. I couldn't reach. That's why I put my fingers in your mouth," Nick sounded confused, and I blinked slowly, realizing that I was not quite awake enough for this conversation.

"Maybe I imagined it, then." I said at length. "But it sure felt real."

"You have a very good imagination, Steven, but I don't think it's that good," Nick said slowly, "Perhaps it's time I insist. You will start learning from me. Immediately."

"Learning?"

"Magic. I think you should be dedicated at the next full moon, Styopa. You've got the gift, and it's starting to show."

I was definitely too tired for this conversation. "Gift? Nick, I don't know what you're talking about. I don't have magic!"

"I know. But... that hand came from somewhere. There was no one else in the room, and I swear to you, I did not do it."

I paused, thinking that over, "So, you're saying that I used... magic... to *masturbate?*"

"I don't know. We will have to talk about this, Steven, and this is not the time to do it. We are both too tired. Bedtime."

I nodded, more concerned about sleep than magic. Then I thought of another question, "Are you going to tell me what the fuck-me cards were?"

"Of course. Let's get you untied, and I will tell you." Nick led me out of the playroom and down the hall to our bedroom, where he had me sit on the edge of the bed. As he started to untie and unwind the ropes, he cleared his throat. "The next two cards were the important ones. The Ten of Swords and the Ace of Pentacles."

I nodded. "Isn't the Ten of Swords the one where the guy is stabbed?"

"You remember that? Good. Yes, the Ten of Swords is the only card of the suit that has that... feature. And in this deck, the young man who is... impaled is the same one from the Nine of Swords."

I frowned, then blinked as I remembered. "The one who was tied up?"

"Exactly," Nick said as he unwrapped my wrists and let them fall. He picked one up and gently turned it over. "You will have marks, I think. I'm sorry."

"Don't be. I had fun. What was the Ace?"

"The Ace of Pentacles. Or Coins, if you're using another deck,"

Nick paused a moment, bringing my hand to his lips and kissing it. "It means attainment, with an emphasis on ecstasy."

I snickered, "You mean there's a card that means orgasm?"

"In this context, yes. Come to bed, *lubov moy*. I'm tired."

We climbed into bed and curled up around each other. I listened to Nick's breathing, the rain on the roof, and knew that I was a very lucky man. Then I realized that Nick had only told me two cards. There had been three left.

"Nick?"

"Hm?"

"What was the last card?"

He laughed, a sleepy chuckle. "You can't guess?"

I shook my head. "No. I've no idea. What was it?"

He laughed again, pulling me closer. "The Lovers. I love you, my *Styopa*."

I smiled, closing my eyes and resting my head on his shoulder. "I love you, too, *Kolya*."

I woke up when the bed shifted, and rolled over to find the other side of the bed still warm, but empty. "Nick?"

"Sorry. I wasn't going to wake you yet," he said quietly.

"S'okay. You going for a run?" I rubbed my hand over my face. "Want company?"

Nick, I had found out shortly after the new year, had been an avid runner before the accident. He intended, at some point in the future, to train for a marathon, but for now, he just did it for fun. To clear his head, he said. Occasionally, Mirage and I went with him, and I was slowly learning the intricacies of running on a track that you couldn't see.

"I was going to trail run this morning," Nick answered. "The college track is being resurfaced."

"Ah." Trail running was not something I was up to. Not yet, anyway.

"Go back to sleep," Nick said, and the bed shifted again. He pressed me down into the mattress with his body, kissed me deeply, then rose and pulled the blankets up to my chin. "I'll wake you when I get back, and we'll shower together. Then I'll take you out to breakfast."

I smiled. Showering together had taken on an entire other meaning since Yule. "All right. Have fun," I said.

Nick kissed me again, and I rolled over and let the sounds of his getting ready lull me back to sleep. The last thing I remembered was the sound of the door closing as he left.

I woke all at once, the way I never do, completely alert and alarmed, sweating and shaking. Nightmare. It had to have been a nightmare, although I couldn't remember what it was that I'd been dreaming. Whatever it was, it must have been a doozy—even awake, I couldn't shake the feeling that something bad was coming for me. I got up, went into the bathroom and washed my face, then pulled on the t-shirt and sweats that I wore in lieu of pajamas. There was no way I was getting back to sleep after that. I'd go get some juice, listen to the TV for a while, and calm myself down. Maybe play with Mirage... I opened the bedroom door and heard, very faintly, the sound of Mirage barking. That was strange. I whistled and called her name, and her barking grew even more frantic.

"Mirage?" I called again, following the sound. Where was she? I walked out into the living room, stopping there and listening. I'd never heard Mirage bark like this—there was a definite menace in her voice that I had no idea she could even manage. Was she outside? Maybe that was it. She was out on the deck, and getting all worked up over... over a squirrel or something. Sure. Nick had probably let her out before he'd left, and...

That line of thought stopped there. There was no way Nick would put the dog out and forget to bring her back into the house.

But maybe she'd followed him into the garage, and gotten stuck out there when he'd left. It would not be the first time that had happened.

I turned and headed towards the kitchen, and sure enough, the barking got louder. "All right, Mirage. I hear you. I'm coming," I called.

The garage door was in the laundry room, which was more like a laundry hallway, and I had to go through the kitchen to get there. I stopped just inside the kitchen door to get my bearings, and almost gagged as my mouth was suddenly flooded with a vile, almost coppery taste. I had no idea what caused it, but it was almost as if I had put a penny under my tongue, or suddenly had a mouthful of blood. In the garage, the barking took on an even more frantic tone. Then I heard it—a single, heavy footstep. I turned... and my head exploded in pain. I hit the floor hard, and the last thing I remembered was hearing more heavy footsteps...

I woke up on an icy-cold floor, unable to move and wanting desperately to puke. It would have been a very bad idea, because my mouth was sealed shut with tape. My arms were pulled back behind me, and I could feel something holding them there tight enough that my elbows were nearly touching. Something similar bound my legs from knee to ankle. I forced myself not to struggle. It would only hurt if I fought it—my back was already screaming at me, a painful counterpoint to the throbbing in my head. I smelled blood, and was pretty sure it was my own. And far away, I could hear Mirage barking. I was still in the house. I tried to relax, tried and think. What had happened?

Someone had hit me with a brick, that's what happened. Or maybe not a brick. Maybe the fridge. My head felt about right for that. Someone... someone had broken into the house. Either Mirage had already been in the garage, or he'd lured her out there, then jumped me in the kitchen. I took a deep breath through my nose to try and quell my nausea, and smelled incense. Incense. Basement. I was in the basement.

Heavy footsteps, coming down the stairs. I closed my eyes and tried to play unconscious, and earned a boot in the ribs that brought tears to my eyes. Then I heard laughter, and I knew I was in very deep shit indeed.

"Well, looks like my boy has done pretty well for himself, hasn't he?" Joey taunted, laughing. "I took a look around while I was waiting for you to wake up. Got some nice toys up there, hm? Shit you used to complain about me using on you. Slut." He kicked me again, and I screamed behind the gag. I hurt, everything hurt, and it was getting harder to breath. Nick... when would Nick be home? I held on to that thought while Joey ranted on above me about how much of a whore I was, and how I'd bend over for anything with a cock and a credit card. Then his voice went darker, and I whimpered in pain and fear as he pushed me onto my back.

"So easy to find you. So easy. And so disappointing. You're no threat to anyone, are you? No matter. Soon, you'll be dead." Cold metal brushed over my throat; I held myself very still as Joey ran the knife over my skin. "I'm going to let you live a little while, though. Just long enough." He moved away, and I heard him thumping around the room. "I'm going to let you live long enough to hear that bastard who took you from me scream."

I went cold, then hot. He was going to kill Nick. No! I started to struggle, growling into the gag. I heard Joey laughing, and then... I heard nothing. Everything went still and quiet, but only for a moment before the silence was replaced with a deafening roar as something washed over and through me, leaving me limp and dizzy on the floor.

That was when the laughter turned to screams. But only for a few minutes. There was a solid thump, then... silence. I heard the heat kick on, heard the whirring of the fans, and Mirage, very faintly, still barking. I couldn't hear Joey at all. I had no idea what had happened. Maybe, when I woke up from my nap, I'd be able to figure it out then.

"Mr. Ahearn? Can you hear me?"

I grimaced as the pleasant female voice penetrated my foggy consciousness. I hate it when people call me Mr. Ahearn. Mr. Ahearn is my father, not me.

"He's waking up. Mr. Ahearn?"

I blinked slowly, took a long breath, and realized that there was one of those funny oxygen things in my nose. Enough of the surrounding air got in for me to identify "hospital," and I blinked again and croaked out, "'M awake."

"Mr. Ahearn, I am Dr. Garrity. Can you tell me what year it is?" she asked.

"Steven. Name is Steven. And... 2009. No wait, 2010." Something itched on my cheek, and I moved slowly, raising my hand to my face and feeling bandages. My arms and back ached. "Can't ever get it right until March."

She laughed. "Oh, I'm the same way. I used to have to predate my checks or I'd write the wrong year for months. Now, if I'm going to call you Steven, you can call me Celia. I'm going to examine you. Then there are some police officers outside who would like to speak with you."

"Right. All right. Wait. Nick. Where's Nick?" I felt a surge of panic. Did he know where I was?

"Nick is outside. He's very worried about you, Steven. Let's get this taken care of so that he can come in and see you for himself. I need to ask an uncomfortable question, first. Your attacker..."

"He didn't rape me," I answered quietly. "At least, I don't think he touched me like that. Not this time."

"I... see. You be sure to tell the police that." She did the usual doctor things—lifting my eyelids to check out my eyes, checking my reflexes. "Any pain?"

"My head feels like one of my drums. And my back hurts, and my ribs. I have a concussion, don't I? Broken ribs?"

"Stop trying to do my job, Steven," she teased gently. "Yes, you have a concussion. Only bruising on the ribs, though. I'll want to run a few more tests, but I don't think there will be any nerve damage or circulatory problems to your hands or arms; given how you were restrained, I think you were very lucky on that count. But it's a good thing that the police got to you when they did. Ready to talk to them?"

"I think so. Can Nick come in?"

"Not until they're done. They just want to ask you some questions. Once you're done with them, then Nick can come in. We'll be keeping you overnight for observation and a few more tests, but from what I've seen so far, I think you'll be going home tomorrow." She patted my arm, helped me to raise the head of the bed, then I heard her soft footsteps moving away. A door opened, and Dr. Garrity said, "He's awake and ready to answer questions. No, Nicolai, not yet!"

I chuckled and called, "Tell him to sit down and behave himself." From outside, I heard Nick's voice clearly, saying something in Russian that I was glad I didn't understand. Then his voice was drowned out by a pair of footsteps.

"Mr. Ahearn?"

I turned slightly towards them. "You can call me Steven. Hi. Can you tell me what happened?"

"We were hoping you could tell us." The chair creaked, and the same voice continued. "I'm Detective Morrison."

"Wish I could say it was a pleasure," I said. "Ah... Nick went out for a run. I went back to sleep..." I retraced my steps, telling them about waking, about hearing Mirage barking. About being jumped in the kitchen. "After that, I don't know. Joey..."

"Your attacker? That would be Joseph Delaney?"

"Yeah. He was my ex," I told them. "Broke up... August of last year."

"And have you seen him since then?" the detective asked.

"Ah... the last time I talked to him was... September or October. I was still in the hospital after the car accident. Did you know about that? The accident?'

"Mr. Rozhenko told us."

"Okay. While I was in the hospital, Joey came to see me, to try and get me to come back to him. I don't know the date, though. Time was a little fuzzy then. Nick would know. He was there. Anyhow, I told him to get bent, and I haven't seen... I haven't heard from him since."

"Dr. Garrity says that you told her Mr. Delaney assaulted you in the past," the other policeman said. "Did you ever report that?"

I shook my head and winced. "No. It happened the morning of the car accident. By the time I was in any shape to report anything, it was over six weeks later. If there'd been any evidence on me, it was long gone."

"True. Did he say anything or do anything that might have told you why he was attacking you after all this time?" That was Detective Morrison again.

"He said..." The words got stuck in my throat, and I had to swallow before I could continue, "He threatened me. Said he was going to kill me. He didn't say why. I don't know why. He just said that he was going to keep me alive long enough to hear Nick die. He was going to kill both of us. Then... I don't know what happened. He started screaming. That's really the last thing I remember."

"Do you know if Mr. Delaney ever used any illegal drugs?"

I shrugged slightly. "I don't know. I remember that I started suspecting that he might have started using. The night we broke up, I could smell something on him. But I don't know for sure, and I never had a chance to report that, either. Was he high?"

"We won't know until the toxicology reports come back," Detective Morrison answered. "Mr. Delaney is in no shape right now to answer any questions. He's been unresponsive since he was brought in. When he comes around, he's facing... well, a long list of charges. Breaking and entering, assault with a deadly weapon, and false imprisonment to start out with, and from what you've

told us and the injuries you sustained, I'm fairly certain that the
DA will be adding attempted murder to the list. I'm assuming that
you intend to press charges this time?"

"That kind of goes without saying," I said sourly. Both cops
snickered.

"Thank you, Mr. Ahearn. We'll be in touch." Both cops walked
away, and I heard them talking in low voices outside the door. I assumed with Nick, since he didn't come right in. I closed my eyes
and leaned back against the pillow, and tried not to lose my grip.
Of all the things I'd ever come to expect from Joey, having him try
to kill me was not one of them.

"Steven?"

I jumped when I heard Nick's voice, quiet and tentative, and
far too far away. I sat up, and almost immediately found myself in
his arms.

"I'm sorry," he murmured into my hair. "I'm so sorry. I should
have been there. I should..." he lapsed into Russian, and I just held
on and shook in his arms, terrified by the possibilities. If Nick had
been home...

"He was going to kill you," I said into Nick's shoulder. "He was
going to wait until you got home and kill you in front of me."

"I... this is my fault. I forgot to set the alarm when I left. I was
terrified, Steven. I got home, and there were police everywhere and
an ambulance..."

That startled me enough that I pulled back to face Nick. If he
hadn't set the alarm, how had the police gotten there before he
had? I opened my mouth to ask, and felt Nick's finger press on my
lips. He kept on talking, his voice shaky, "They'd broken down the
door, and they wouldn't let me in to find you. I didn't see you until
they took you out on a stretcher." He stroked my cheek gently. "You
were so pale. They questioned me..."

"What? But you weren't even there!"

"They had to be sure, I suppose. That this was not something I
was involved with. That I didn't invite that bastard into our home.
As if the broken window wasn't enough of a clue."

I shuddered and took Nick's hand. "And... Mirage? Where's she?"

"By now, home from the vet," Nick answered, and silenced me again with his fingers. "She is fine. She attempted to go through the garage door to get to you. The vet visit was just to be on the safe side. Mary took her, and Max is supervising the replacement of the window and the front door. I will bring her with me tomorrow morning."

"She tried to warn me. I've never heard her bark like that, Nick. If she hadn't been locked in the garage, I think she'd have ripped his throat out," I said. Something he'd said made me pause, and I frowned. "Nick... isn't the garage door metal?"

Nick snorted and squeezed my hand. "You have an exceptional dog, *Styopa*."

I found out later that I'd been unconscious for two hours or so, and that while I was out, they'd done just about every test they could think of. Which all needed to be rerun once I was awake. So the rest of the day was one test after another, leaving me cranky and tired, and aching in all sorts of places. The nurses were really sweet, and let Nick stay well past official visiting hours. When he finally left, it was past ten; he promised to be back first thing in the morning, with Mirage and a change of clothes for me. Then he was gone, and I was left alone. I tried to get comfortable and get some sleep, but I hurt too much, and every time I closed my eyes, I heard Joey's voice. I tossed and turned, restless and far too wired to sleep.

"Mr. Ahearn?" I recognized Celia Garrity's voice.

"You're here late," I said as her footsteps came closer. "And it's Steven."

"I was on my way out, and I thought I'd look in on you. Steven, you should try to sleep."

I sighed and turned towards her. "Trying. Can't. I keep... I keep hearing him. And everything hurts. Dr... Celia, I know I have a concussion, but is there anything I can take? For the pain, and so I can sleep?"

She sighed softly. "The strongest thing I can safely prescribe is acetaminophen. I can't give you anything to help you sleep because we still need to monitor your coherence. Want the acetaminophen?"

"Yes, please," I answered. I heard her leave, and a few minutes later, she was back. "Sit up."

I did as I was told, and swallowed the pills she gave to me. Then I leaned back and shook my head. "I still don't know if I can sleep," I said.

"You're safe here, Steven. No one is going to get to you. Not here."

"That's what I thought about home," I retorted.

"I guess that means that no one told you about the guard outside your door?" She sounded amused. "Or the industrial-strength wards on this room?"

I blinked, sure I'd misheard her. Or that I was hallucinating. "Wards? Wait... you?"

She patted my leg and lowered her voice, "Nick is an old friend of mine. We trained together, and I used to be part of the coven. And the overnight on-call doctor is another mage. You're safe here. We look after our own."

I couldn't think of anything else to say, so I nodded. Then I did think of something, and asked, "Celia, can you magic me to sleep?"

She laughed. "Yes, Steven. I was just waiting for you to ask. Goodnight." She touched me between the eyes, and warmth crept over me, different from what I knew as the feel of Nick's magic. I was trying to figure out the difference as I started to fade around the edges, but what she'd said came back to me, distracting me. We look after our own. Was she talking about me? Or about Nick?

❖

I slept all night, and woke up the next morning when they brought in my breakfast. Nick arrived before I'd finished, bringing Mirage with him. She jumped up on the bed and washed my face for me, then settled over my legs and refused to be moved. She stayed right where she was throughout the rest of the morning, regardless of what tests they came in to run. When Celia arrived, she was already laughing.

"I hear that you've acquired a personal bodyguard," she said as she came in. "The floor nurses are all very amused."

I ruffled Mirage's ears. "She takes her job seriously," I said.

"And well she should," Celia agreed. She cooed nonsense to Mirage for a moment, then laughed again. "You've got quite the familiar here, Steven," she murmured in a low voice.

My jaw dropped, and I sputtered, "I'm sorry, what?"

Celia hesitated, then asked, "She isn't? Nick, I thought..."

"He's new, Celia. Just broke through."

She whistled, low, and I blinked and demanded, "What are you two talking about?"

"I'm sorry, *Styopa*," Nick said. He sat down on the edge of the bed and rested his hand on my leg. "Do you remember the other night, I said you needed to start learning from me?"

"Yes..." I said slowly.

"Now it is imperative," he hesitated, then cleared his throat. "Steven, tell me what you think happened to Joey."

I frowned, unsure of where this was going. "He... I don't know. He started screaming, and then... I think I heard him fall before I passed out."

"And before that? What happened before that?"

"He... he threatened you. He said he was going to kill you." I thought back, and remembered the rush of energy that had left me limp. And I realized what they weren't saying. "Oh, my God... I did that? What did I do?"

"Saved both our lives," Nick murmured.

"When you came in, you were suffering from profound magic shock," Celia said. "The kind of thing we only ever see with unrestrained magic use, or uncontrollable magic use. What we call wild magic."

"There's a reason I insisted that we come here, Styopa..." Nick started to add.

"And where is here?" I interrupted. "We're not at St. Ann's?"

"No. This is Howard Central," Celia answered. "Or Hex Central, if you're in on the fact that there are six mages on staff here."

"When I saw you, I knew what had happened. Your magic broke completely free. I just didn't know why," Nick told me, his hand warm on my leg. "I insisted that they bring you here, and I called Celia on the way so that she would be ready for you..."

"Can we turn it off?" I blurted.

"I'm sorry?" Nick asked.

"Turn the magic off. Put it back. I don't want it. I don't want to be a mage. So... can you take it away?" I turned my head, listening for one of them to tell me they could make me normal again. "My God... I... I almost killed someone."

"He attacked you," Nick said firmly. "He would have killed the both of us if you hadn't stopped him. Steven, it isn't your fault... Celia, what? What's wrong?"

Celia took a long breath, then let it out. "You'd be told one way or the other. Ah... Joseph Delaney died early this morning."

I went cold, numb, hearing her continue as if she were a mile away, telling us that Joey had had some kind of seizure, that the coroner thought it was possible that he'd had a stroke because of whatever drugs were in his system, but of course they wouldn't know anything until the autopsy reports came back, and the entire time I was thinking: *My God, I killed him. I killed him... with magic.*

"Styopa?" Nick called my name, and I got the impression that he'd done it more than once. "Styopa, do you understand now why you must start learning how to control your magic?"

"No." My voice was sharp, harsh to my own ears. "Nick... I killed someone..."

"Steven, listen to me. You have power. That kind of raw power must be trained, or it will run wild. And it cannot be shut away, not now that it is free. To do that... I don't even want to consider the possibilities. If you do not wish for this to happen again, you have to be trained."

Happen again? I could kill someone else? The unwanted image of Nick lying lifeless on the floor filled my mind. Could I do that, if we ever had a real fight?

Probably.

"All right," I whispered. "Where... where do we start?"

"Once you are out of the hospital, and healthy. Then we start," Nick said firmly. "For now, you will rest, and you will heal."

I nodded, then murmured, "Nick... I don't think I'm going to want to play again for a while."

Celia's voice startled me—I'd forgotten she was there. "And that is my cue to leave. I'll check in with you again before you're discharged, Steven." She walked away, and when I could no longer hear her footsteps, Nick cleared his throat and took my hand.

"I understand. You will tell me when you are ready. Do you... are you going to take off your chain?"

I reached up and touched the silver chain, and shook my head. "No. That stays. Nick, I have a question."

"I was expecting that you would. The alarms?"

I nodded again. "If you didn't set the alarm when you left, how did the police get there first?"

"There is more than one kind of alarm on our house. And I see I forgot to tell you about the magical ones. You didn't know about the house wards, did you?" he asked. When I shook my head, he continued. "I felt Joey break the wards when he broke into the house. I knew that it had to be an intruder, because the wards know you. So, I triggered the physical alarms remotely, and ran a full mile back to the car to get back to you." He laughed suddenly, a short, sharp sound. "And I tell you, I remember none of that mile!"

I grinned, then leaned back and sighed. "Nick..."

"The house is being cleansed right now. There will be no sign of him ever having been there. No trace of him physically or magically. And I will rebuild the wards when we get home."

I nodded. No trace at all... except for my memories.

Chapter Six
First of May

"Try it again," Nick said firmly. Frustrated, I restrained myself from either yelling at him or tearing my hair out. Instead, I closed my eyes and once again turned my mind to the magical exercise that I'd been struggling with for weeks. I fumbled for the warmth that I now recognized as magical energy and tried to form the twisting, unruly thing into something resembling a wall. It was very much like trying to put a cat into a bag, and after several minutes of wrestling with it, I let the energies go and slumped back into my chair.

"It isn't working!" I snapped. I dragged my fingers through my hair, wincing as the tangles caught and pulled. "Maybe... maybe I can't. Maybe I've got that wild magic Celia was talking about..."

"No. That you do not have. You have managed some of the exercises. You can draw power to you, and release it." Nick sighed, and I realized that this was as frustrating for him as it was for me. "I do not understand why this is so difficult. These are basic exercises for any prentice-mage!"

"I don't think it's the way you're teaching me. I'm just an idiot," I said, tipping my head back against the couch. I smiled ruefully and added, "Is there such a thing as magical special-ed? How about vo-tech?"

"You are not an idiot," Nick said as he joined me on the couch. "It is my teaching, I think. I've never taken a prentice before. Perhaps I am going about it wrong. Perhaps you would respond better to another teacher. I will talk to Celia, perhaps? She has a prentice."

"Maybe," I murmured. I didn't want another teacher. I liked Celia, but letting my guard down around anyone besides Nick was something I was finding very hard to do since the attack. I'd been struggling with these lessons since the end of February; here it was the end of April, and even though I was a recognized and acknowledged prentice-mage, I still wasn't advanced enough to be properly sworn into the coven. I participated, played the drums for them, but until I could shield properly, I wasn't allowed into the actual magic working.

"We will talk about it later," Nick said, patting my leg. "We have ritual tonight. How is your head?"

"Oh, I'm fine," I answered and, because I was still a little fuzzy on rituals, asked, "Which one is this?"

"Beltane."

I woke up to a searing kiss. Nick pushed me onto my back and pinned me there with his hand curled around my throat. When I reached for him, he pulled away, laughing. The Beltane ritual with the coven had run late, turning into a raucous party sometime around the point when the ritual usually calls for cakes and ale. Since the ritual was essentially over, Nick let the others play, finally taking control of the group and closing the Circle sometime around two in the morning. Everyone had left soon after, and we'd finally fallen into bed somewhere between three and four. I fully intended to sleep in this morning, maybe get out of bed in time for lunch. Nick, however, had other ideas.

"Good. You're awake."

I scrubbed one hand over my face, "I'm not so sure of that. What time is it?" I felt like I'd only just gotten to sleep.

"A little after seven. Breakfast is ready." I heard him moving away from the bed, "Come and eat, then you can shower and get ready. I've already fed Mirage."

I blinked. "Nick, what the hell are you talking about? Why are we getting up? We only just got to bed!" I didn't usually get snappish at Nick, but too little sleep did that to me. And the frustration alarm clock was not helping my mood at all.

"We have an appointment. Get up and get moving." The door clicked shut and I frowned. Was I forgetting something? Probably. I groaned and untangled myself from the sheets. No point in heading for the bathroom right now, so I felt around the foot of the bed until I found my robe. All the while, I was thinking: what appointment? It was Sunday, so I didn't have physical therapy or an appointment with either the doctor or the chiropractor. Nick didn't work on Sunday, so he wasn't meeting with a client, and in any case, there would be no need for me to go with him if he was working. The lawyer handling the custody case over Nick's daughter was out of town until next week. I frowned as I fumbled into my robe and opened the door, trailing my fingers over the wall as I headed for the other side of the house and the great room that was our kitchen, dining room, and main living space. Who the hell did we have an appointment with today?

Just outside the great room, I was met by the four-legged welcoming committee. Mirage was off-duty, out of harness, armed with her tow-rope, and making happy, little "play with me!" barks. I indulged her a little, getting down on the floor and playing tug-of-war with her until Nick came looking for me.

"How old are you again?" he asked, a fond note in his voice. He helped me up off the floor and took my elbow as we headed into the dining room. I settled in my chair and ran my fingers through my hair to get it off my face, yawning. I smelled coffee close by. That, at least, was something positive.

"Kolya, I'm forgetting whatever it is that we have today. What appointment?" I asked, finding my coffee cup and taking a long drink.

"Your breakfast is getting cold. Eat." I heard Nick's chair scrape against the floor. "There are eggs at six, toast at eleven and sausage at three."

I nodded, picking up my fork. "Thanks. What kind of sausage?" I asked.

"That chicken and apple one that you like. And you are not forgetting. This is a surprise."

I stopped with a forkful of eggs halfway to my mouth, "A surprise? Nikolai, you woke me up after no sleep for a surprise? Isn't this something we can do later?"

"No. It needs to be done early, and it must be done today. Trust me, you will enjoy it. Now eat."

He refused to answer any other questions; I gave up and ate my breakfast, drinking two cups of coffee in rapid succession, then lingering over a third while Nick cleaned up. I was feeling almost human when Nick took my cup from me and then escorted me back upstairs. His attentiveness should have been my first warning that he was up to something; usually, he pushed me to do things by myself. Today, he was at my elbow for everything, overseeing my morning routine and insisting on laying out my clothes while I showered.

As I got out of the shower, I heard the bedroom door close, and Nick's footsteps moving down the hall. I toweled off and found the clothes that Nick had put out for me on our bed. And stood there, confused. He'd laid out a shirt that I used to wear back when I went clubbing—it fit like a second skin and was made from thin mesh, so it left nothing to the imagination. With it were the tiniest pair of shorts I owned, a pair that I knew I'd told Nick were getting too tight to be comfortable. Oh, and socks. I ran my hand over the surface of the bed, trying to find anything I'd missed.

The door opened. "You're not dressed yet. Good. I forgot something."

"You forgot a couple of things, Kolya. Underwear? Some real clothes, maybe?" I started to turn towards him, and was surprised when he stopped me, taking my arms in his hands and pushing me towards the bed.

"You won't need anything else," he whispered into my ear. "I have many surprises for you today, but you must trust me."

From the sound of his voice, he was deep in dom space, had probably been there all morning, waiting patiently to spring this on me. I wondered what else he had planned for me. "I trust you, Kolya," I said.

"Good." He ran his hands up and down my arms. "I am taking you on a hike."

"A hike? Where?"

He laughed when I named a series of streets in the city that were notorious for male whores, then answered, "No. A nature hike. It is Beltane, after all."

"A nature hike," I repeated. "In *these* clothes?"

"Trust me. Now, let me get you ready."

I found myself ordered to stand still as he slathered every inch of me in sunblock. He sent me back into the bathroom with orders to take an antihistamine and a decongestant, and he was waiting for me when I got back.

"Now, bend over." He pushed me gently into position, my upper body resting on the bed, my legs spread. I heard him moving around behind me, and then something hard, cold and wet was pressing against my asshole. I jumped, and Nick put his hand on my back. "Relax, *Styopa*."

I nodded, my cheek scraping against the blanket, forcing myself to relax and accept the butt plug. When it was seated, Nick ordered me to get dressed. The tight shorts pushed the plug in deeper, and I bit my lip to hold back a moan as the erection I still hadn't quite lost started to regain its former glory. Nick just laughed and helped me to put on my socks.

"Now, before we go, give me your chain."

That surprised me. I'd only just given Nick the green light about a week ago, and he'd simply agreed that I was ready, and hadn't done anything one way or the other. Apparently, he was waiting for this. I hesitated, then reached up and unclasped the chain, holding it out. Nick took it, and then moved behind me and replaced the chain with a soft leather collar; I heard the click of a lock and felt my cock growing harder. Nick started to laugh, and I knew that he could see my reaction clearly through the tight shorts.

"You're more than ready, aren't you?" Nick murmured. He took my arm and we left the bedroom.

It was a gorgeous day for early May, hot and sunny, feeling more like late June than early spring. And it was an interesting drive, with me fidgeting and trying to find a comfortable position that wasn't going to drive that plug in any further. When we turned off onto what had to have been the worst-paved road in Maryland, I called Nick every foul name I could think of, stopping only when it was obvious that he was going to either hyperventilate or drive into a tree because he was laughing so hard.

We stopped for a moment, and I heard a woman's voice, asking for money. A parking fee, which told me that we were probably at one of the state parks near our house. Nick drove a little further, then parked the car and turned off the engine. We sat there for a moment in silence.

"*Styopa*, before we leave this car, we need to discuss this," he said at length. "Because once we leave this car, there will be no time for negotiations. I am going to ask you to trust me completely, and to give me complete control. No safe-words, no stopping. Once we go, we're committed."

I was stunned. He'd never asked anything like this before. "Nick, what are you up to?"

"Nothing you won't enjoy. But it's a little... illegal." He sounded almost embarrassed. "I will make sure that we do not get caught. But I can't do it if you're not completely in agreement. So, do we get out, or go home?" He rested his hand on my leg. "I will make sure you enjoy it, either way."

Part of me was saying that this was insane. I still had no idea what he was up to. But at the same time, I was excited. This was insane, and I'd always been one to take risks. And I did trust Nick.

"Let's go," I said, and opened the car door. We'd left Mirage at home, something that hadn't made sense to me at the time. Now I understood, but it still left me at a major disadvantage. All I had to guide me now were my cane and Nick. In the time it took me to shake out my cane, Nick was out of the car and had come around to meet me. He kissed me and tugged the cane out of my hand.

"You won't need that. Just let me get my bag. There's no one else here, but that won't last. We don't have a lot of time to get into position. Once we're there, we should be fine."

I heard the trunk open and close, and then Nick had my arm

and was leading me away from the car. The path was unpaved, uneven and steep in places, which slowed our pace down to a crawl. After a long hike, the path seemed to get very overgrown. There were branches and leaves that brushed against my arms and legs, and I heard more crackling underfoot. It took me a minute to realize what must have happened.

"Nick, did we leave the path?"

"Yes. We're almost there."

As soon as he'd said that, the space around me opened up. Nick stopped. "We're here. Stand still for a moment. I have a couple of things to get set up."

What followed was a bizarre set of sounds. Birdsong and the sound of the wind in the trees interspersed with pounding and the unmistakable jingling of chain. Then Nick came back to me, taking my arm.

"This way." He steered me further into the clearing, then said, "Take your shoes and socks off. You're standing on a blanket."

"I might need some help with the socks," I said, toeing off my sneakers. Nick knelt down in front of me and tugged my socks off, and then shocked me by wrapping heavy cuffs around my ankles. He wanted to scene here? That was what this was all about? My reintroduction to BDSM? I had been expecting something quiet, something sedate. Something private and indoors, in our own bedroom, or in the playroom. I certainly wasn't expecting anything like this!

I'd agreed to all this, though, so I didn't argue when Nick took me by the shoulders and steered me into a specific position off the edge of the blanket; I could feel dirt under the balls of my feet, as well as something metallic and cold that pressed against the arch of my right foot. Nick did something around my feet, then stood up and kissed me before saying, "Open your mouth."

When I did, Nick stuffed a wad of cloth into my mouth, kissed me again, and then pressed a wide piece of tape over my lips. Startled, I pulled back slightly, and found out that what Nick had been doing at my feet was chaining me in place. I nearly fell, but Nick grabbed my arm and pulled me back, steadying me until I had my balance back.

"Stay still."

I nodded and held my position while Nick added more tape to the first piece, layering it until I couldn't have opened my mouth if I'd wanted to and the only sound I could manage was a strangled grunt.

"Give me your arms," Nick ordered. I held both arms out so that he could strap cuffs around my wrists. Once he started, I knew which ones he had brought: our suspension cuffs, unusual ones that Nick had told me that he'd found somewhere in Europe. These were more like wrist braces than cuffs, extending from my knuckles to halfway down my forearms. They were riveted together along the insides, and when I was locked into these, I couldn't bend my wrists or use my hands at all, and could just barely use my fingers. Nick tugged my arms up and I heard him laugh.

"The ring is still here. I thought I was going to have to run a chain," he said as he locked the cuffs to whatever ring he was talking about that hung somewhere over my head. An overhanging branch, I assumed. "Maureen put that ring into this tree branch when she did this to me."

I mmphed my surprise; Maureen had topped Nick? He had never told me that! I had no idea that he was a switch, or that he'd bottomed to Mo. Briefly, I wondered what else he hadn't told me about their relationship. Then Nick stepped away, and that was the point when I stopped thinking about Maureen, realizing that there was one thing that Nick hadn't thought of—the differences in our heights. Nick was a full five inches taller than I was. Thankfully, branches bend, and I could still keep both feet flat on the ground. I didn't have a lot of wiggle room, though.

"That's very nice. Are you comfortable?" Nick asked, running his hand over my stomach. I thought about it for a moment, and then nodded. This wasn't too bad, actually.

"Good. On to the next step." Nick moved behind me and I felt something cold trace down my spine. I tensed, feeling my shirt grow loose as he cut it open. Then he cut the sleeves open and the ruined shirt fell to my feet. My shorts followed, leaving me bound and bare in the middle of a clearing in a Maryland state park. I certainly didn't mind being naked in public. Nick knew that I was something of an exhibitionist, both by temperament and by training. What amused me was that he had said this was only a little illegal. My darling Master of the understatement!

There was a splash of cold water on my back, then Nick's hand on my shoulder, and he was doing something, tracing one finger over my skin. It tickled a little, and I squirmed in protest. Nick just pressed down on my shoulder until I stopped moving, then finished tracing a pentacle between my shoulder blades. He let go of my shoulder and walked around me; there was another splash of cold water, then he traced another pentacle on my chest, from nipple to nipple, down to my sides and up to the hollow of my throat, then back down and ending at my nipple again. I hadn't been studying magic with him for long enough for this to make sense to me, so I was completely lost. What was he *doing*?

Nick ran his hand down my stomach again, stopping just short of heaven. I moaned, thrusting my hips forward, making him laugh. "We're not ready for that yet. But this should keep you busy while I work." I heard a faint click, and the butt plug came to life. I moaned again, barely noticing when Nick walked away. When had he picked up this wonderful little toy?

I could hear Nick moving around, doing something, Not that I was paying any attention to him now; I had other things to keep me occupied. I twisted slightly, enjoying the vibrator and the feel of the sun and wind on my skin. This *was* very nice. The bondage was restrictive but comfortable, just the way I liked it. The vibrator was just intense enough to tease without being frustrating, just enough to make sure that I would be hot and ready. And I knew Nick was always very inventive when it came to a scene. I couldn't wait to find out what else he had in store for me.

Then I heard something in the distance, so softly at first that I thought I was imagining it. But my hearing had gotten very sharp since I'd lost my sight, so I knew in a moment that I wasn't imagining things. There was someone coming closer. A few someones, from the sound of it, people out to enjoy the day and the weather and the park, and who were about to see more than just nature's wonders. We hadn't walked that far from the path, so I didn't think there was any way they could miss seeing me, hanging here like some kind of perverted banner. This way to the freak show, ladies and gentlemen!

Words like "public indecency" and "false imprisonment" ran through my head, as well as the cold knowledge that if we were arrested, Nick would lose any chance of ever getting Natalie back. I could hear him, doing something off to my left. I was sure that if he'd heard the voices, he'd be reacting, coming and getting me down. Then I caught the scent of incense, and heard Nick raise his voice in the now-familiar Quarter call.

He was casting Circle! That was when I remembered what he said, why we were here in the first place. Finally, this made sense! We were here for a private Beltane celebration. And now we were going to get caught in some very extreme *flagrante*!

I tried to get his attention, shouting through the gag, fighting the cuffs, hoping that he'd see or hear me and come to find out what was wrong. It was a slim hope; Nick was notorious for getting so wrapped up in the ritual that he saw nothing else going on around him. And true to form, Nick didn't notice me at all. He finished invoking East and I heard him move, heading to the South. I tried interrupting again, more muffled shouting, more futile struggling. I'm not sure exactly what happened then. Maybe the branch had been caught under something else, or maybe Nick had pulled it down and anchored it at the right height. Whatever it was, I had no warning at all before the branch suddenly shot up like a catapult. With a startled, albeit muffled, yelp, I went up as well; when the branch stopped moving, I was stretched out taut, trapped between earth and sky, with the only thing keeping me near the ground being the chain attached to the ankle cuffs.

There was no way for me to get Nick's attention now, not when he was so focused on setting the Circle. All I could do was listen and wait. Listening to Nick saying the words that created the sacred space, I automatically fell into the rhythms of the ritual, my mind clearing of everything mundane. It was almost a Pavlovian response from me; I hadn't realized how much I'd missed having something spiritual in my life until Nick had started involving me with the coven. Now, even bound and gagged, naked and about to be discovered and almost certainly arrested, I found myself silently repeating the responses as Nick finished invoking Fire in the South, and moved on to the West. In my head, I could hear the drum rhythms that I would normally be playing throughout this part of the ritual.

Somewhere in between the drums beating in my head and drumming of my pulse in my ears, I became aware of... something. A steadily growing sensation, right behind my breastbone, that I almost dismissed at first. Then I recognized the warmth, and realized that my magic was swelling. I tried to drain it back into the earth, the way I'd been taught, but it refused to obey me this time. I could tell that something was different from the last time. The last time, it had been wild, like a raging river, and had damn near killed me. This time, there was no pressure, no weakness; it was more like... anticipation. It felt like when you were a kid, waiting up all night for Christmas morning. Like the moment before your first kiss, or when you realize that you are going to have your first lay. Or that instant just before a really amazing orgasm. It was building, growing, blending seamlessly with the rhythm of the invocation and the rhythms in my head, turning the cold fear of discovery into steaming hot lust. I'd lost my erection when I realized we were going to be found, but now I could feel myself getting harder, getting hotter, pulsing in time to the beat that echoed in my ears. The butt plug, which had gone from tantalizing to an annoyance that I was doing my best to ignore, suddenly felt like the intensity had been turned up as high as it could go, and the vibration was resonating up and down my spine. Mindlessly, unable to stop myself, I started to struggle, trying to pump my hips, almost frantic with need and want.

From behind me, I heard Nick finish the invocation of North.

There was a pause and I heard him take a breath before he began the final part of the invocation. His voice moved, circling me, tracing out the sacred circle and setting in place the power that he'd been calling from each of the four quarters. He made the circuit three times, and with each pass, the rhythm in my head grew faster, the growing sensation in my chest stronger; I threw my head back, eyes squeezed shut tight as the blood roared in my ears. I could barely hear Nick's voice as he finished casting the Circle.

There was a thud of something striking the ground right in front of me, and then it was like my chest exploded. The magic that had been building within me burst outward, leaving me behind, somehow both drained and oddly exhilarated. And very, very horny. All I wanted was Nick. I could hear him moving around, doing something. The rest of the sounds around us, the wind, the birdsong, had all gotten very distant. To my ears, it sounded as though we were listening to them through thick glass. I had no idea what had just happened. Nor did I care. What was *taking* him so long?

Then he came up behind me, pressing himself against my back, and I knew what he had been doing. He was a naked as I was, and I could feel his cock pressing against my ass as he wrapped his arms around me and pinched my nipples hard enough to make me groan.

"Don't get too far ahead of me, *mily moy*," he murmured as he nibbled my shoulder. I tipped my head back, and he moved up to my ear, still playing with my nipples. It was maddening; there was nothing I could do to make him speed up or urge him on.

"They *had* to have come this way!" a woman's voice, far too close for comfort, and coming closer. Nick froze, and I heard him swear in Russian.

"That's what you said about the overlook." Another woman, this one sounding decidedly bitchy.

"You saw them! They came this way. There are only two paths down here. They weren't at the overlook, so they had to have taken this path."

"Tell me why we're doing this again? And why the hell would they have come this way? It's a dead end!"

"We're doing this because they were hot! Come on." Voice number one started to take on a wheedling sing-song, "You can have the tall one..."

"They're getting closer!" Nick reached up, fumbling. "Blin! Steven, what happened here? I can't reach the lock!"

There was a muffled crack, someone stepping on a branch, and then voice two spoke up again, "Dee, wasn't there a clearing around here?"

"Who cares? They're not here, and we can see the end of the path. Let's go back."

We heard the two women walk away. When we couldn't hear them anymore, Nick wrapped his arms around me and rested his head on my shoulder.

"I don't understand. She was looking right at us. How did she not see?" he asked, his voice muffled by his position. "They didn't see the clearing, they didn't see us. How?"

I shook my head, silently asking the same questions myself. Nick moved away, and I heard rustling. It fell quiet, and I wondered where he had gone. Then he was back, taking my face in his hands, "What did you do?"

I blinked, confused. I knew I'd done something, but I had no idea what it could have been. I shook my head, shaking his hands off. He took a long breath, and when he spoke he sounded shaken.

"Styopa, the clearing is gone. You cannot see it from the path. You can see nothing but trees. This is nothing that I did. Nothing I know how to do. So..." he stopped, and swore again. "You heard them? Is that what happened, when I was calling the quarters? You heard them, and you were trying to warn me?"

I nodded emphatically.

"Oh, Styopa. I'm so sorry. I should have come to see what was wrong," he apologized, then snorted. "I thought you were coming." My turn to snort, and he laughed. "Very well. It seems that you've made sure that we will not be discovered. So, I will leave it up to you, mily. Do we continue?"

Without hesitation, I nodded. He laughed again, leaning in and pushing my head back so he could kiss my throat.

"I was hoping you'd say that," he murmured. He nuzzled my neck for a moment, then stepped away. There was some rustling, and then he was back. "So, do you know what you are today?" he asked.

I blinked again, then shook my head. In answer, he moved in close, pressing against my back as he did something over my head. When he was done, he leaned into my ear and whispered, "You are my Maypole."

A Maypole? Visions of church Mayday festivals from my childhood flashed through my head, with all of us kids in our Easter clothes, bringing in the May to celebrate the Virgin Mary. There was nothing even remotely sexual about that pseudo-Victorian claptrap, so I thought he was joking, right up until the moment when he started weaving long, soft ribbons around my forearms.

I'd done mummification bondage once, at a play party with Joey. It was interesting, but I thought it took too long for too little reward. But this... this was somehow very different. Nick twined the ribbons tightly around my arms from the base of the cuffs to my upper arms, then wound them around my arms until he could bring them down and wrap my chest, starting just under my collarbone. That wrapping went to below my navel, over my hips and my ass, leaving my cock and balls exposed while covering everything else. He continued on down my legs, sealing them together before finally finishing at my ankles, leaving me even more helpless than I had been when he'd first chained me up here. He stood up, running his hands over my body until he reached my chest, where he shifted the ribbons slightly. I wasn't sure what he was doing until he set the first nipple clip; I yelped into the gag at the first and then shook my head violently when the second one was in place. I hated the nipple clips, but Nick loved how I reacted to them. And I loved his reactions to me, so I put up with the clips.

"Oh, yes. Perfect. The perfect Maypole," he murmured, tugging the chain between the clips and making me groan. "Do you know what the Maypole is, *Styopa?*"

From the tone of his voice, this was another lesson. That meant that there was something more than the claptrap I'd learned at school and in church. I didn't know what he meant, and shook my head to let Nick know. He laughed, running his hand over my chest and belly, smoothing the ribbons that enveloped my skin.

"The Maypole is a phallic symbol. It symbolizes the World Tree, and to dance the Maypole is to guarantee fertility for the coming year." He ran his hands down my sides and over my hips. I moaned, trying to thrust forward, trying to encourage him to move his hands someplace a little more useful to me. He laughed again and pulled his hands away, leaving me swaying slightly and growling through the gag. When he spoke again, his voice was lower down. Was he kneeling?

"Now, time to polish the Maypole." There was another faint click, and the vibrator roared to life. I jumped, pulling on my bonds, thrusting my hips forward in surprise... and Nick swallowed me whole, grabbing my ass with both hands to hold me in place.

It always felt odd to me to have Nick going down on me. Not that he wasn't good at it; he was amazing, and he seemed to have no gag reflex at all. I loved what he could do to me. It just felt strange to have my dom on his knees, doing to me what I thought I should rightly be doing to him. Now, knowing that he'd bottomed to Maureen, I wondered what it would be like to top him—to tie his hands behind his back and put him on his knees, to sit back in one of the chairs by the fireplace and order him to suck me off, then put him on his face on the hearthrug, bent over one of the overstuffed cushions from the couch, so that I could fuck him until we both fell asleep on the floor. Would he like it? Would he accept that, from me? I wondered how I could approach it... and then he did something indescribable with his tongue, and I stopped having anything approaching a coherent thought.

Between the bondage, the vibrator, and Nick deep-throating me, it didn't take me very long to reach a screaming come, straining against the cuffs and the ribbons as I shot my load. Nick must have known I was about to come because just before I did, he moved, letting me shoot into the air until I was finally drained and hanging, limp in every possible way. When Nick came back and touched me again, he was pressed up against my back, reaching for the lock over my head.

"That was magnificent," Nick whispered into my ear as he strained upwards. This time, he managed to catch the lock; he released the cuffs so that I could lower my arms, one of his arms wrapped around my waist so that I didn't lose my balance. At his whispered instruction, I brought my hands up and he fastened the cuffs to the ring on my collar. He helped me down onto my knees, kneeling down in front of me and wrapping his arms around me. For a moment, I thought it was a hug, then I realized that he was wrapping my arms to my body with more of the ribbon. I made a gargle of protest—the increasingly tight bondage was forcing my arms into my chest, and putting pressure on those evil little clips. Nick chuckled in response as he finished binding my arms, wrapping another length of ribbon around and around over the tape gag and tying it off behind my head. Then he wrapped his arms around me again, guiding me gently down onto the blanket so that I was lying on my back. He stretched out next to me and ran one hand over my belly.

"The next time I do this, I must remember to pick a better color of ribbon," he said idly. "This one is green. Appropriate for the day, but it does make you look like a beached merman." He ran his hand lower, grabbing my cock gently. "What is it they say? I've caught a whopper?" He scraped his nails over my balls and then gently started to nudge me until I was on my side, slightly curled up. Nick shifted, pulling at the ribbons to bare my ass; I could feel him pressing against my back as he started to slowly fuck me with the still-vibrating butt plug. It was a good thing that he started slow; that thing had been in for a while, and although Nick had used a lot of lube when he'd put it in, there wasn't much left. Thankfully, he noticed that, or had planned for it, and I felt more wetness being added as he manipulated the plug. Once there was enough lube, Nick turned the vibrator off and just used the plug to fuck me while I moaned and squirmed like the proverbial beached merman. I tipped over onto my front, yelling as that put even more pressure onto my already aching nipples. It was easy to get past that, though, with what was going on behind me. Nick shifted again, moving to sit astride my legs, all the while still fucking me with the plug. Then he shifted, moving down to sit on my calves, grabbing the ribbons that crossed my back and pulling my upper body into an arch that must have made me look like the figurehead on a sailing ship. It eased the pain in my nipples not at all, as it pressed my arms even tighter into my chest. Surprisingly, I felt myself getting hard again.

I must not have been the only one getting hard, because suddenly Nick stopped what he was doing and lowered me back down onto the ground. Then he was gone, only to return a moment later to kneel next to me and put one hand at the small of my back. "Don't move," he warned, and I felt something cold and metal slide between my legs. It slid down my inner thighs, and the ribbons parted, freeing my legs from thigh to ankle. Nick got rid of the knife, slowly pulled the butt plug out, then shifted to kneel behind me. He grabbed my hips in both hands, pulling my ass up into the air. "My turn," he said in a harsh voice. It was a good thing he'd added more lube to the plug, because he didn't hesitate, going balls-deep on his first stroke and then starting a fast, hard rhythm.

It was *good*. Better than good, even, although I wasn't sure why it was. I had been worried that I was going to be too sensitive, because of the vibrator and how hard Nick had been fucking me with it. I had known what he'd wanted from the point when he'd cut the bindings on my legs, and I'd thought it was going to hurt. It didn't. Far from it, actually; this was *wonderful*. The only failing was the position. I couldn't push back, even though I wanted to. And it wasn't very comfortable; with my arms bound the way they were, there was no way for me to brace myself, or keep my right cheek from grinding into the blanket. I was sure I was going to end up with rug-burn on any bit of skin on the right side of my face that wasn't covered by multiple layers of tape or ribbon.

Behind me, I could hear Nick making little grunting sounds, and the beginnings of the deep keening that he always made when he came. Sometimes, when we played together and it got this intense, I imagined that I could feel what he was feeling, as if I was inside his skull. This was one of those times. I could feel his arousal, how much he loved taking my ass, how turned on he had been by looking at me lying on the blanket, completely helpless and at his mercy, wrapped up like a gift just for him. How flattered he was by the level of trust that I showed when I gave him complete control, and how much of a turn on that was. There were also faint hints of annoyance and regret, and I couldn't, for the life of me, figure out why I was imagining those, but it didn't matter, since all of that was slowly being drowned out by the orgasm that was building like a tidal wave. His thrusts grew more erratic, the keening louder, and I felt the ribbons around my waist tighten as he twisted his hands into them for a better grip. When he came, he went rigid, his hands pulling the ribbons tight enough to pinch, and somehow managing to swallow the keening, which I had been pretty sure was going to be heard clear to the parking lot. Then he relaxed, gasping his pleasure as he folded slowly over me, pushing me down flat onto the blanket and pinning me there simply by lying mostly on top of me. He nuzzled my neck and hugged me tightly, murmuring something indistinct in Russian before sighing contentedly and resting his cheek on my shoulder.

It always struck me as being slightly incongruous that Nick, who was a beautiful, badass dom and a coldly analytical computer guru, was also such a devoted snuggler. It just never seemed to fit any of his personae. But he was, and I thoroughly enjoyed lying curled up with him after sex. I relaxed into the inevitable, enjoying his comforting weight on my back, waiting for him to roll off of me and either untie me or do something about the hard-on that was currently pressed between my body and the ground. I was hoping that he untied me first, since the pain in my nipples was quickly reaching my limits. Instead, he seemed to get heavier, and as his breathing on my neck grew deeper and more regular, I realized that Nick wasn't just snuggling. He was asleep!

Waking him wasn't even an option. I couldn't manage more than a grunt through the gag, and I was still bound down, with even less leverage to move than I'd had before. Until Nick woke up, I wasn't going anywhere. I settled in to wait, and found my eyes growing heavy as my too-short night and truly impressive orgasm caught up with me at the same time. Maybe a nap wasn't a bad idea after all.

As I gave in to sleep, I could have sworn that I could hear someone close by, laughing.

I woke up cold, thirsty, hungry, with a growing need to piss, and absolutely certain that someone was watching us. None of that mattered, though, since Nick had me in an interesting position: one arm wrapped loosely around my throat in a headlock and his fist tight around my cock. I came fully awake with a jolt, grunting in surprise and trying to turn, stopping when Nick tightened his arm and cut off my breath. I could feel his cock between my thighs, poking me in the balls from behind. I knew this game well, it was something that Nick would occasionally do to me if he woke up horny in the middle of the night.

Nick whispered something in Russian that sounded delightfully profane as he tightened his arm around my throat a little more. When I moaned, he bit the back of my neck, hard enough to hurt, then started to nibble my neck and ear, jerking me off with his free hand while he fucked my thighs. He must have gotten more lube before he'd woken me up, and it wasn't long before we were both coming again, together this time, with him muffling his cries in my shoulder while I shook and moaned in his arms. He loosened his hold, rubbing his cheek on my hair before pulling me onto my back. "Blessed Beltane," he murmured, leaning down to kiss the tip of my nose. I tried to glare at him, and either succeeded or failed miserably, because he started to laugh.

"All right. I'll unwrap you." He sat me up, untying the ribbon that covered the gag, unwrapping it and then gently teasing the tape from my skin. I spat the soaked cloth wadding out of my mouth and started coughing. Almost immediately, I felt something held to my lips, and Nick was urging me to drink. The cold water felt good on my throat; being gagged doesn't stop you from screaming your throat raw, it just keeps you from disturbing others while you do it. I must have drained at least half of the water bottle, and, before I could get a word out, Nick covered my mouth with his. The kiss went on for a while, until we were both moaning and whimpering again. He pulled away slowly, saying something about two being enough.

"Intense," I mumbled, shaking my head a little. "Unwrap me, please?"

"Oh, I was thinking of leaving you like this," Nick sat down behind me, pulling me back to lean against his chest. "Carry you up the path, pop you in the trunk, take you home, and put you to bed. Maybe let you loose in the morning."

I sniffed. "*Kolya*, even if I thought you could get me back to the car without getting us both thrown in jail, I'd still want to be let go now. My tits hurt and I have to piss. And..." I stopped, frowning slightly. The sensation that we were being watched was gone. Had I dreamed it?

Nick must have assumed I was done talking, because he kissed me again and laughed. "You're so romantic," he teased.

I felt a tug on the ribbons over my right side, then things started to come loose; the ribbon fell in pieces around my waist until all that was left was a few twists around my arms, and the only things that bound me were the cuffs around my wrists and ankles. I hissed in pain as the chain that connected the nipple clips shifted and the movement tugged on the clips.

Nick sighed. "This... will be interesting," he said. "I hadn't thought you would be this sensitive. I should probably gag you again, or else they'll hear you all the way down to the dam."

The chain shifted again, and I closed my eyes tightly and shook my head. "I don't want another gag."

"It's going to hurt like hell, *Styopa*. You're going to scream."

"I know," I nodded and tipped my head back to rest on his shoulder. "Kiss me?"

Nick was quiet for a moment, then he tipped me backwards until I was lying across his legs, my back supported by his arm. "Since you ask so nicely..." he murmured, leaning down to cover my mouth again. I felt his arm shift slightly, and his fingers brushed mine as he took hold of the ring on my collar.

This kiss was even better than the last one, and I forgot damn near everything except how good it was, how much I loved kissing this man. Then Nick released the first clip. He was right—it *did* hurt like hell, and I *did* scream. But he kept his mouth on mine, and his free hand caressed my chest and stomach, gently skimming over my aching nipple with his nails. Very quickly, the screams turned into muffled moans, and I was once again writhing in pleasure under his touch. At least, right up until Nick released the second clip.

The orgasm hit me like a lightning bolt. There was no warning, no build up, just an immediate and intense force that took me all at once. This time, I not only screamed, I thrashed wildly, losing complete control as the waves of pleasure rushed over and through me. I couldn't do more than flail ineffectually in Nick's arms, though. My ankles were still chained to the ground, Nick still had a firm hold on my collar, and he wrapped his other arm around me, embracing me tightly and never letting go of my mouth, thrusting his tongue deep to better swallow my screams. When my shaking finally stopped, he pulled back and let me lie in his arms, gasping for breath.

"If this is your reaction to the clips, I should use them more often," he said as he let go of my collar and slid his fingers over my shoulder. I whimpered in response, shaking my head weakly.

"...gonna hide..." I mumbled.

He laughed. "If you hide these, that leaves me with the Japanese ones."

I frowned, not liking the sound of that. "Tighter?"

"Yes, the ones that get tighter." Nick squeezed my shoulders and started to shift around, moving out from under me and laying me down on the blanket. "But not tonight. We've both had enough, I think. We need to finish the ritual and close the Circle." He moved away and I heard him rummaging around with something.

I nodded. The sooner we finished, the sooner we could go home. Which raised another question, "*Kolya*? Did you bring something for me to wear?"

"Of course I did," Nick said as he sat back down and helped me sit up. He tapped my lower lip with something, "Open up."

I accepted a bite of what turned out to be a piece of crusty bread, chewed it slowly. "You know, if you untied me, I could feed myself."

Nick chuckled, pulling me back to lean against his chest again, and then pulling the blanket up to wrap around the both of us. "I like taking care of you. Now, apples, cheese, or bread next?"

We shared the light picnic that Nick had brought, with him feeding tidbits to me and holding a bottle of water for me to sip. I had a thought as I finished a bite of apple. "You're going to have to untie me and let me get dressed before you close the Circle," I said. "Whatever it is that I did that's keeping us hidden, it's tied into the wards."

In response, Nick reached under my chin and unlocked the cuffs from the ring on my collar. He made quick work of releasing my wrists and then turned to my ankles before getting up and walking away. Once I was free, I stretched, shaking my arms out, feeling the stiffness that came from being in the same position for so long. Then a bundle was dropped in my lap, and I unfolded it to find a pair of jeans, a sweater and socks. And again, no underwear.

"Nick!"

I could almost hear him smirking at me when he answered, "You look better without. Get dressed. I want to close the Circle."

I dressed quickly, keeping my place on the blanket while listening to Nick release the Quarters and close the Circle. As he dismissed the final Ward, I felt a rush of tingling warmth, and the sensation that something was being pulled away from my skin. Once, with Joey, I'd tried liquid latex, letting myself get completely painted in the stuff, before having the latex cut from my body with the edge of a blade; the feeling of the magic leaving me reminded me of the feel of the latex as the strips were peeled from my skin. I shook my head to clear it, hearing Nick as he worked around me, cleaning up and packing things away.

"I really do like this place," he said. "We should have the coven here. It's a good location, and with that ring..."

For a moment, I thought he meant the ring that he'd suspended me from. But that didn't make any sense. "Nick, what ring?"

"Oh, I didn't mention it?" he asked as he came over and helped me to my feet. "There's a ring around this clearing. It's a perfect circle. Maureen told me that sometimes you find mushroom rings like this, but that she'd never seen one this large before."

I went cold, with all the stories that my grandmother had told me suddenly ringing shrill in my ears. I turned, aware that whatever it was that had been watching us was back, watching and waiting. "Nick... we need to get out of here. Now!"

Nick must have seen how alarmed I was, because he didn't stop to ask me why; he grabbed my arm and dragged me along with him. But as we crossed the clearing, the presence grew stronger. And I felt...

"Nick, do you feel that?" I asked, pulling to a stop.

He stopped next to me, and his hand on my arm tightened slightly, "I... yes. What is that?"

"Elf call," I murmured. "Gran said..." I shook my head to clear it, then frowned. This wasn't the seductive call that my grandmother had told me to beware of. This... "Nick, are they calling for *help*?"

"I think so. You know what this is?"

I nodded. "We're in a faery ring. And... they want our help." I raised my voice, "We hear you! What do you want?"

It was a man's voice that answered, one that sounded distant and pained. "You hear us?"

"Yes!" I called back. "What can we do?"

"The ring..." the voice faded away, and all that was left was a faint sense of hope.

"What did he mean, the ring?" Nick asked. "The mushroom ring?"

"That can't be it. The mushrooms are the border between their world and ours." I turned towards him. "A faery ring is... a bridge. Between our world and the world of the *Aos Sí*. There are stories about people passing a single night in a faery ring and finding that a thousand years have passed in the mortal world. But something is wrong here." Then I blinked, "Nick, the ring in the tree! What is it made out of?"

He hummed for a moment, a habit he'd picked up to let me know when he was thinking. "It's... a steel ring, I think."

"That's it!" I pulled away from Nick's hand and took two steps back, listening. And felt a surge of excitement when I crossed one spot. I tipped my head back. "Here?"

"What are you doing? How did you know?" Nick asked, and I heard him coming closer.

"We need to take it out. The *Aos Sí* can't bear the touch of iron in any form. That ring... it must be poisoning them."

"*Bozhe moi*," Nick murmured. "I didn't know... all right. Steven, I will need to lift you up. The branch bounced up too high for me to reach..."

I felt Nick's arms encircle my legs from behind, and then he was lifting me into the air; I fumbled for a moment, then found the branch and the ring. I tried to turn it, and couldn't get it to move.

"I don't have enough leverage," I called down to Nick. "I need..."

"Can you hold onto the branch?" Nick interrupted. "Pull it down so I can reach?"

"Yes, I think so."

"Good. Hold on."

I wrapped my arms around the branch and thought heavy thoughts as Nick let me go. The branch bent slightly, but I was still left dangling in mid-air. I could hear Nick moving around, moving away. Then he was back, and I heard him grunt as the branch bent further.

"Hang on, *Styopa*. This will take me a moment," he said. I heard something cracking, and the branch shook as Nick did whatever he was doing. I just concentrated on holding on until finally, the branch shook once more, Nick grunted again and then said, "Got it! All right, *Styopa*. It's out."

"Get it out of the clearing," I said through gritted teeth. I heard Nick move away, and decided to jump down. It wasn't that far to the ground, after all, and my arms were tired. I let go of the branch and dropped, and felt a sickening crack in my left ankle as I landed. I yelped at the sudden pain and kept on going, ending up on the ground, grabbing for my ankle. Not this one, not again!

Nick was back beside me before I'd stopped moving, "What happened?"

"My ankle," I gasped. "The left..."

"Oh, no." He sounded as horrified as I was. Breaking this ankle had been the least of the injuries I'd sustained in the car accident that had killed Maureen. They'd told me when the cast came off that I was lucky. I should still be able to walk. If I'd broken the ankle again...

"May I help?" It was the same voice I'd heard before, only closer. Much closer.

.

Chapter Seven
The Singer and the Song

I froze, unable to get up and run. "*Blin!*" Nick cursed, startled, and put himself between me and the voice. "Who are you? Where did you come from?"

I touched Nick's arm, "He's *Aos Sí*. He's the one who called us, Nick. Quick, describe him for me."

"He's taller than I am. Red coat..."

I caught my breath and silently thanked my grandmother, "He's a *fear dearg*. Ah... *na dean maggadh fum.*"

There was a moment of silence, and then an amused laugh, "Well now. You're one who sees further into the millstone than most. You do know that your accent is terrible?"

I nodded carefully. "I haven't had much call to practice. Do I need to say it in English?"

"No, I understand you, and you are safe from our tricks. You needn't even have said it; we owe you a great boon. But... you have the gift, you know the words, and you're still not smart enough to stay out of a faery ring?"

Despite the pain, I grinned. "I didn't know it was there."

"Well, you're the wiser for it now. May I help?"

I nodded. "Nick, let him."

Nick moved to kneel next to me, and I heard footsteps approaching, then my pants leg was rolled up and I felt cool fingers on my skin. "Ah, lad. You've done yourself a world of hurt to help us. I can't have that." All of a sudden my ankle was flooded with warmth; I tasted something pure and cool, like spring water, and when the *fear dearg* took his hand away, the pain was gone.

"What did you do?" I gasped.

"Put that right." was the very self-satisfied answer. "The bones are still mending, so you'll be sore for a few days. Make certain he walks gently."

"I'll take care of it," Nick said. "Thank you." He hugged my shoulders tightly. "Air cast, the minute we get home."

I nodded. "Thank you. Ah... how did you get here, if you don't mind my asking? And... do you have a name?"

"You can call me Fergus. And we came with the men who laid the rails, back when this part of the world was young." I felt a hand on my leg, "Now, a question for you. How is it that you can hear us? And that you know? The one who set the death metal ring in the tree, she couldn't hear. Neither did this one, the last time he was here. You hear, and you can grant him the hearing. How?"

I blinked, "I... my grandmother taught me about the Good Neighbors when I was small. She told me that I could hear them, if I tried. Honestly, I just thought she was telling me stories!"

"Your grandmother was uncanny, then?" Fergus sounded like this all made perfect sense to him. Nice that someone understood! He touched my hand, then my cheek, making me jump. He ignored it and made a soft sound in his throat. "Ah. I see now. Very interesting. I didn't know there were any left in this area. What else did she teach you?" he asked.

I shrugged. "Nothing, really. She died when I was eight."

"I'm teaching him now," Nick volunteered.

"Trying to, anyway. I'm a slow study," I said ruefully.

"That is because you are trying to learn the mortal way of magic. That will never work for you. You bear the old blood in your veins. Our blood. It marks you clearly to those who can see."

I coughed. "I what?"

"Somewhere in your line, you've an ancestor who was full-blooded *Aos Sí*. Not too far back, if the strength of your power is any indication. Possibly that grandmother of yours, or her mother." I heard Fergus stand. "Stay with me, cousin. Let me teach you our ways."

Nick's hand on my arm spasmed "What?"

"You... want me to stay?" I asked, stunned.

"For a time. You can both stay, if you wish. I would not separate true lovers." Fergus laughed. "And I'll admit that I've not been this entertained in many years. You put on quite the show."

I ignored the commentary on our sex life. "Fergus, how long? In our time, how long would we be here?"

Fergus was quiet for a moment, then answered, "Your time is... unfamiliar to me. You would be with us for a year of our time, perhaps two at the very most. In your years? Ten? Twenty? I'm sorry, I cannot be more exact."

Next to me, I hear Nick whisper something under his breath. I wasn't sure, but I thought it was his daughter's name. That decided it for me.

"We can't. Thank you for the offer, Fergus. But we have responsibilities in our world. We can't leave."

"I see. You have a child?" Fergus asked.

"A daughter," Nick answered. "She was taken from me. I have to get her back."

"Ah. Of course. I understand that. My own children are long since grown, but I am a father, too. Go with my blessing, then, and with the knowledge that we owe you a boon." I felt something, almost like a current in the air, then something hard was slipped into my hand. I rubbed it with my thumb, and discovered that I held a smooth stone, one that had been pierced through. There was a cord threaded through the hole, and I understood that I was supposed to wear it. Silently, I slipped the cord over my head and tucked the stone into my shirt.

"That marks you as being under my protection, cousin," Fergus said. "Should you need assistance, a drop of your blood on that stone will summon any of our blood who are near."

Thank you didn't seem to be enough, but it was all I could think of to say. "Thank you," I murmured, touching the stone through my sweater. It was already warm on my skin, and it felt like it was tingling.

Nick helped me to my feet, and put his arm around me to

support my left side. I heard footsteps moving away, and called out, "Fergus?"

"Yes, cousin?"

I smiled. "My name is Steven. Would it be all right if we came back to visit with you?"

There was a long pause. "Of course. If you wish to learn from me, I could even teach you here," Fergus offered.

"I wasn't joking about being a slow study. I... don't have a lot of talent... I can't... I can't do it right..."

"That is not the truth. You have talent, but you are afraid," Fergus said. "Why are you afraid, cousin?"

I hesitated, then ducked my head. "I... I killed someone," I answered in a low voice. I felt the comforting warmth of Nick's hand on my back. Fergus grunted once, coming closer. His fingers brushed my forehead, leaving a breath of warmth behind, and grunted again. Then he was gone; I heard Nick yelp, and there was a cold spot on my back where Nick's hand had been. I gasped and turned, reaching and finding only empty space. "Nick?"

"I've claimed him," Fergus' voice came from somewhere across the clearing. "I wonder how long it will take me to break him?"

"No!" I shouted. "No, you promised!"

"I lied."

I felt the rage building in me, and with it, the magic. At that moment, everything that Nick had been trying to teach me, everything that I'd been struggling to learn for months, all of it was startlingly crystal-clear. Shields snapped in place around me, and I reached out my hand, feeling under my fingers the ghostly weave of Nick's sweater. I grabbed, pulled, and caught him as he fell against me, gasping in shock. My shields closed around him, and I stepped in front of him, ready to strike out at the bastard who dared to try and take him from me.

"Steven, no!" Nick grabbed my arm. He gabbled something in Russian, then cursed and said in English. "It was a test! He was testing you! He never had me! He was twenty feet away from me."

It took a moment for his words to sink in, and when they did, the power that surrounded us blew away like dandelion fluff. A test? There hadn't been any threat at all. I slumped, and Nick caught me before I hit the ground.

"That was impressive, cousin," Fergus said, still at some distance away. "May I come closer, or will you rip my throat out with your teeth?"

I whimpered softly, pressing against Nick for comfort. "I... I could have killed you... and you're laughing about it?"

"You don't have enough control of your power yet to kill me, cousin. I'm still a better mage than you. For a while, at least. You've a great deal of power at your disposal, but you act only on instinct, which is very dangerous. Nicolai, are you all right?"

"I'm fine. A little dizzy, but that will pass. Will you explain why you did that to him? To us?"

I heard Fergus' footsteps coming closer, crunching on the grass. Then he grunted, and when he spoke again, his voice was at the same level as we were. "When I touched Steven's forehead, I saw a memory. You were attacked?"

I swallowed hard and told him about Joey, about how I'd killed him. Before I'd finished, Fergus interrupted, "Answer me this, cousin. If you'd been free, and armed with a sword, or a dagger, or one of your mortal weapons that spit fire and cold iron, would you have struck him down to save your Nicolai?"

I didn't even have to think about it. "In a heartbeat," I said softly. Nick hugged me close and kissed my temple, whispering "I love you, too" in my ear. I smiled slightly and turned towards Fergus. "You'll still teach me? I'm still... well, I'm not very good..."

"I think that your fear is only part of your problem, cousin. The other is that mortal magics are—excuse me, Nicolai—mortal magics are far more primitive than what you are capable of wielding. It would be akin to putting a flint knife in the hands of a master carver—the end results would be functional, but not what they should be." He patted my knee, and he and Nick helped me to my feet. "Shall we start now?"

"Oh," I gasped, surprised and uncertain. "Ummm... sure?"

"Go ahead. I'm curious," Nick said. He moved back, and I felt a moment of fear. Then I took a deep breath and stepped forward, taking care of my weak ankle.

"Where do we start?" I asked.

"You had some very basic shields. Raise them again," Fergus told me. I nodded and closed my eyes, struggling to mentally re-build the wall the way Nick had showed me. And stopping when Fergus sniffed.

"I'm doing it wrong?" I asked.

"As I said, primitive. When you think about it, you build shields like a bricklayer builds a wall. But when you act on instinct, you cloak yourself in power as fitting your bloodline. Take my hand, Steven. This is important that you know, so I will show you, the same way that I taught my children." I grimaced a little at the idea of being taught like a child, but I held my hand out anyway. Fergus's hand was warm and callused, and he took my hand firmly before saying, "This may be a bit disconcerting at first."

Disconcerting was a very apt description. All at once I could feel his presence in my mind, feeling as if my childhood imaginary friend had grown up and gotten bossy. He poked and prodded me into doing what he wanted, then ran me through some kind of mental exercise several times in succession, until he was certain that I could do it at speed. Then, all at once, he was gone. I blinked and let his hand drop, running my tongue over my lips to catch the lingering taste of pure spring water. Where had that come from?

"That was it?" I asked.

"That was all. Now, shield!"

I heard the urgency, and threw the shields up just the way he'd showed me, and just in time to feel the impact of something splat-tering all over them. "You... what did you throw at me?"

"The magical equivalent of a rotten egg," Fergus answered, laughing. "You pass. Now, go home before you fall over, cousin. Come back in a week's time for your next lesson."

Over the next several weeks, the Parks Department made a bundle off of Nick and me. Every Sunday, without fail, we packed up a picnic and headed out to the park, always arriving as soon as the gates opened. The guards came to know our car, and were always willing to chat with us and admire Mirage. One of them confessed to be a little surprised that a blind man enjoyed hiking as much as I did.

They had no idea.

We'd head down the path to the dam, and make our way to what we'd started calling Fergus's Tree. The first week, we arrived to find absolutely nothing and no one, and had stood there, confused, until Fergus' voice on the breeze told us that he wasn't coming out until I put shields on the whole clearing.

"Oh, come on," I called back, laughing. "I'm still in kindergarten!"

"No shields, no lessons," Fergus answered, and I could hear him laughing at me.

"What are you going to do?" Nick asked.

I frowned, thinking, running through the steps that Fergus had shown me the week before. I'd practiced like crazy all week. Now I needed to improvise. "Can you help me find the middle of the clearing? And then take Mirage?"

"All right. What do you need me to do?"

"Umm..." I considered it. Considered what might happen if I screwed this up. "Wait outside the clearing? Just in case."

"*Styopa...*"

I turned, grabbed him by the front of his shirt, pulled him in and kissed him. "Humor me, *Kolya?*"

He kissed me back, his hand closing over the back of my neck, then took Mirage's harness from my hand. I heard him moving away, and waited until he told me he was clear. Then I closed my eyes and brought up my shields, feeling them enveloping me in their warmth. Now, how to expand them? I considered the exercise that Fergus had showed me, then twisted it a little in one place, and told it what I wanted it to do. Like an eager puppy, the energy scrambled to obey, and I laughed out loud as I felt the shields spread out and settle in a perfect circle around me, at what I assumed was the mushroom ring.

"Nicely done," Fergus said from behind my shoulder. "Now, what about personal shields? I could attack you now, and you would not be able to stop me." I hadn't considered that, and hurried to put shields on myself. And only succeeded in collapsing the shields I'd put on the clearing.

"Oh, damn it!" I swore as Fergus laughed.

"Come in, Nicolai. Who is the lady?"

"This is Mirage," I said as she pressed herself against my leg. "My eyes. And, according to some, my familiar."

"I can see that. But you need to grow into her," Fergus said. "We'll work on that. Now, shall I show you what you did wrong?"

"Please?"

And that set the pattern. Every week, we would start once I had set shields on the clearing, and then Fergus would set me to doing something that built on whatever it was that he'd shown to me the week before. Sometimes I figured out how to do it myself, sometimes I didn't. Fergus was a patient teacher, explaining things over and over, and only once, after the first time, did he have to resort to getting into my head and showing me.

It was the hottest day of July, and all three of us were panting by the time we reached the clearing. Once we were inside shields, Nick groaned, and I heard the dry grass crackle under his feet. "It is too hot," he complained. "As many years as I have lived here, I have never gotten used to this heat."

"There's cold water in the cooler," I reminded him. "When you're in there, pour some out for Mirage?"

"For you also?"

"Yes, please." I turned around, frowning. The shields were up. Where was Fergus?

"Is he coming?" Nick asked, coming up next to me and putting a cold bottle into my hand. "Perhaps he does not like the heat, either, hm?"

I grinned. "Maybe. Or maybe it's another test. Let me drink this, and I'll call him." I drained half the bottle in one gulp, then handed it back to Nick and raised my hands, holding them cupped over my heart, preparing to send out an elf call of my own. I hadn't done this yet by myself, but Fergus had assured me that I was perfectly capable, for all that I had, as he called it, a diminished bloodline.

To my ears, the elf call was loud, and sounded very much like a military signal drum, and not at all like Fergus' more lyrical call. Startled, I took a step back, losing the concentration that the call needed; the drums faded away into wind and bird-call.

"Must you shout?" Fergus asked. "You're early today."

"It's blasted hot today," Nick answered, and I could hear the repressed temper in his voice. "We came early to try and beat the heat."

"I see. But why so loud, cousin?" Fergus asked me. "Show me what you did."

I repeated the call, and it came out just as loud. I shrugged as I let the magic fade. "I don't know what I did to shout like that, Fergus. I thought I did what you told me."

"You did, cousin. You did," he sounded intrigued, and I was pretty sure I knew what was coming. He did exactly what I was expecting: he touched my forehead with his fingers. Instead of the usual, feather-brush touch, his fingers lingered for a moment, and I heard him laugh out loud. "Well, of course!" he said. "I missed it earlier, cousin! Or did you know you were a bard as well, and just chose not to tell me?"

"A bard?" Nick repeated, sounding curious.

"I have music magic, Nick," I said matter-of-factly. At this point, I was well and truly past the point of being shocked by anything that Fergus told me.

"I know. In Russia, we would call you a *kaliki perekhozhie*." Nick sounded both amused and impressed. "Wandering singers and tellers of tales. Now that I think of it, they were usually described as being blind men."

"Really?" This was fascinating! "Will you tell me about them?"

"Later, cousin," Fergus interrupted. "Now, tell me. Have you noticed any difference in your magic when you around music?"

I frowned, thinking back on the times I'd used my magic outside the grove, either consciously or unconsciously. "Ah... not when I took out Joey. But... oh..." I felt my face get warmer.

"You were humming," Nick said softly. "I remember it."

"Yeah," I laughed. "And when you had me here, I was running through the ritual drum in my head, right before I set the shields on the clearing. So, yeah. Music makes it... interesting."

Fergus laughed, then took my chin in his hand like I was a kid and teased, "You have been keeping tales from me! I want to hear all of your magic experiments. Especially if they are as interesting as the one I witnessed."

I stepped back, breaking the contact and feeling a little odd. Was Fergus... hitting on me? "I... Fergus, get out from under my bed," I stammered, turning away slightly. "Nick, can I have the rest of that water, please?"

He handed me the bottle, his fingers lingering over mine, then placed his hand on my back; I smiled and turned my head so that I was facing where I'd last heard Fergus' voice. "What are we going to do today, Fergus?"

"I should explore more of this bardic ability of yours, but that will have to wait. There is currently no bard in our court, so I must look further afield for instruction on how best to train your gifts, or perhaps for another teacher," Fergus answered. "We will temper your call, and perhaps work on refining your defenses a bit more. You're still too uncertain with them. And we will finish early, I think. You are both right. It is too hot for lessons."

"Is there a way to change the temperature inside the shields?" Nick asked.

"Hey, that's a neat idea," I said, laughing. "Magical AC. Can I do that, Fergus?"

"Not as yet, no," Fergus said slowly, drawing out each word.

"Oh. Okay. Is that something you can do?" I asked, realizing that I really didn't have any idea just how powerful Fergus really was. He said I couldn't hurt him, but that could just mean that I didn't know enough, yet.

He hesitated, then slowly admitted, "It is not something that I can do."

"Oh. Well, it was a thought. Nick, can I have some more water before we start?"

"Yes. And then I must ask that you let me out. I've had too much water. I'll take Mirage."

"The shields are already keyed to let you back in," I told him. Nick handed me a cold bottle and kissed me on the cheek, then I heard him walking away. We'd come to the agreement after the first week that if we needed to water the grass, or if Mirage did, we did it outside the circle. It only seemed polite.

When I could no longer hear Nick's footsteps, I turned back towards Fergus. "Shall we get started?" I asked.

"In a moment," Fergus answered. I heard him coming closer, and was surprised when he stopped close enough that I could feel his breath on my face. Holy crap, he *had* been hitting on me!

"Fergus, stop," I said softly. "You don't..."

"Steven, I want you to know that I find you attractive. Exotic. And..."

"Fergus, I'm involved with Nick," I cut him off. "I'm in love with Nick. So... thank you. But, no thank you."

"And I would not separate true lovers," he continued as if I hadn't said anything. "But you are *Aos Si*, as I am. You should know what that part of your blood can offer you."

"Fergus, no. No, I..." I wanted him to understand, so I held both hands up to try and ward him off, and ended up with them trapped between us, pressed against Fergus' chest as he pulled me close and kissed me. Shocked stupid, I froze, my mind frantically trying to deny that this was happening to me, was happening again. I went from denial to panic, and from panic to pure anger. That woke my brains up, and I shoved Fergus away, backing up my own strength with a good, hard magic push; Fergus gasped and cursed, and I felt his anger flare.

"How dare you...?"

"How the fuck dare *you*?" I demanded in return. "I told you no! Now keep your hands off me!" I heard him coming towards me, closed my eyes, set myself and swung. I'm not sure who was more surprised that I actually connected—me or Fergus. But I got him, right in the chin, and heard the heavy thump as he went down.

"Steven!" Nick called my name, obviously alarmed. "Steven, what happened?"

I was so angry I was shaking, and when Nick touched my arm, I shook him off and stalked out of his reach. "He made a pass at me. He wouldn't take no for an answer," I snapped, too wired to stay still. "Where's Mirage?"

"Here. Are you all right? *Styopa?*"

"Out. I want out. I want to go home. Now." I pulled my shields back in, feeling them snap back hard; I'd probably have a headache when I finally came down off the anger rush, but I didn't care. "Nick, now!"

"Steven...*Styopa, lubov moy*, I... may I touch you?" Nick asked softly. I paused, then realized why he was asking and nodded; he handed me Mirage's harness, then took my hand and guided me out of the circle. "You knocked him out, Steven," he said as we walked.

"Really? Wouldn't have thought he'd have a glass jaw," I said. "He was asking for it."

"Did you hit him with your fist or with magic?" Nick asked.

"Does it matter? I'm not going to be a victim, Nick. Not again. We're not coming back."

"I heard that," Fergus' voice floated on the wind. "There is something that you did not tell me? Did you not trust me?" I winced and turned.

"I trusted you. Once. Not anymore," I called back. "Now you can hear this. You can keep your magic, and your bloodline and your *Aos Si*. If sex is what you want in return for magic lessons, you can forget it. You're never coming near me again." I fished the elf-stone out from under my shirt, pulled the cord over my head and threw the stone as hard as I could back the way we'd come. Then I turned and reached out, catching Nick's arm. "Come on, Nick. Let's go."

We shifted as we walked, when my hold on Nick's arm proved too awkward. The rest of the way to the car, I felt Nick's hand at the small of my back, just barely touching me. I was grateful for the minimal contact; I felt as if I was going to spontaneously combust from anger and fear, and I knew that if he touched me—really touched me—I was going to rip his head off. I think he knew it, too, and he didn't say a word until we were in the car.

"Steven, tell me what happened?" he asked gently.

"He waited until you were gone. He made a pass at me. Told me he thought I was attractive and... what did he say? Oh, yeah. Exotic. I told him no. I told him I was with you, and I wasn't interested in him. That should have been the end of it. But he pushed, and before I could explain anything, he grabbed me and planted one on me."

Nick let out a long breath. "There is no way to mistake that, is there?"

I turned, my jaw dropping. "You think I made that up?"

"No! No, *Styopa*, I was not calling you a liar. I was wondering if perhaps there was," he hesitated. "Excuse me, I am thinking of the words. If it was a... a cultural difference? I made a great many mistakes like that, my first few years in this country."

"You think it may have been an elf thing?" I asked. I shook my head, feeling the ache I'd been expecting starting at the base of my skull. "I don't know. I really don't think that 'No, I'm not interested in you' is hard to understand, Nick."

"True," he agreed as he started the car. I closed my eyes and tipped my head back against the headrest. The throbbing had started, and I knew that nausea wasn't far behind. My center was blown, and try as hard as I could, I couldn't get it back; I was too frazzled. All I wanted was a shower, and then maybe a nap. "If you had not beaten him, *Styopa*, I would gladly have done it for you," he said after a long while. I turned, and realized that the anger I was still feeling wasn't entirely my own. "He had no right to touch you."

"Thanks," I murmured. "Can we not talk right now? My head aches."

"Of course." He was quiet for the rest of the way home, only breaking the silence when he finally stopped the car. "Steven? Is there anything..."

"I just want a shower, Nick. Then maybe some sleep." I let myself out of the car and winced; the headache had gotten to the point where my back teeth hurt.

"Go on, then. I'll see to Mirage."

I grunted my thanks and headed inside, making a beeline for the bedroom. Once I'd started the water in the shower, I stripped naked and grabbed something for my head while I waited for the hot water to come up. I dry-swallowed the pills, then stepped under the spray and leaned against the wall, letting the heat stream down the back of my neck.

What was it about me? What the hell had I ever done to deserve the cosmic-karmic-kick-me-sign? It was starting to feel as if every single man in my life was there to fuck me over, either literally or figuratively. With the sole exception of Nick, I reminded myself. He'd promised he would never hurt me. He loved me.

And with the most incredible bad timing, he picked that moment to come up behind me in the shower. I had my head under the water, and I was lost in thought, so I didn't hear him at all. Didn't know he was there until he touched me, his hand coming down on my shoulder. There was nothing at all unusual about it— he did it every day. But today...

I reacted before I even had a chance to think, yelping in shock and alarm, spinning and lashing out with my elbow, and almost ending up on the shower floor as I lost my balance. Nick cursed and grabbed me... and that made it worse. I panicked so completely that thinking wasn't even an option anymore; I screamed and fought, and somehow ended up on the floor anyway. Only this time I was wrapped up in Nick's arms, and he whispered into my ear things I don't even remember until I finally stopped fighting him and went limp. I was exhausted, and I felt as if I'd been wrung out, except for the aching in my head that still hadn't gone away. "Steven, it's all right," Nick murmured. "I've got you. It's safe. It's all right."

I closed my eyes and pressed my ear against his chest, listening to his rapid heartbeat. "It isn't all right," I answered. "It's not. I'm not. There's something... something wrong with me."

"No, *mily moy*. There is nothing wrong with you. There is something wrong with them, that they need to take advantage. They need to hurt someone. They need a victim..."

"And I'm the victim," I whispered. "Why? Why me? Why am I always the victim?" I pulled away from him and sat up, brushing wet hair out of my face. "Nick, what's *wrong* with me?"

He sighed, and rested his hand on my ankle. "Steven, there is nothing wrong with you," he repeated. "But I think it is past time that you speak to Cheryl."

It took me a minute to realize what he meant. Cheryl. The rape counselor. Mo had wanted me to talk to her, I remembered now. Cheryl had offered, at the Yule circle. And at every meeting of the coven since. But I'd never gotten around to it. I was fine. Or so I thought.

"Yeah. Yeah, I think so," I mumbled.

"All right. You shower. Take something for your head, unless you want me to work on it?"

"No!" I blurted out. "No... no more magic. I... I think I need a break from magic. I took a pain pill."

"All right. Then finish here and take a nap. I will call Cheryl, and have her come for dinner." He patted my ankle again, and I heard him grunt. Then he tapped my shoulder, and I knew he'd stood up. "Come on. Off the floor."

He helped me back onto my feet, and I leaned back against the wall and closed my eyes. "Nick..."

"It's fine, *Styopa*. Whatever you need, I will help you with. It is fine." I felt his body against my arm, and his lips quickly brushed against mine. Then he was gone. I heard the bathroom door close, and I slumped down onto the seat, resting my elbows on my knees and letting the water pound on my back. Even with the heat of the shower, I felt cold, and I finally gave up and turned the water off, toweling off roughly and pulling on my old sweats. I climbed into bed, pulled the blankets up over my head, and did my damnedest to shut out of the rest of the world.

When I woke up, I could tell that Nick wasn't the only one in the house. I could feel Cheryl's presence. And, oddly enough, I could feel Nick—he was upset. Probably about the attack, I decided. I got up and dressed, then headed out in search of company. I smelled coffee, and at the moment, that sounded like a really good idea.

"... I just do not want him to hurt that way, Cheryl. So you must tell me what I can do. I know you helped Maureen..." I heard Nick saying as I came up to the kitchen. His voice stopped abruptly as Cheryl said, "Hi, Steven."

"*Styopa?*" Nick said softly. "I..."

"I'm all right, Nick. I think. For right now, anyway," I answered. "There's coffee?"

"Decaf. I don't know about you two, but I need to sleep tonight."

"Decaf is fine," I said, finding the empty chair and sitting down. "So... what did Nick tell you?"

"That your magic tutor tried to take advantage of you, and that you laid him on his ass. Well done," Cheryl answered, telling me clearly that Nick hadn't told her *everything*. "And that you're having flashback reactions. We're well and truly past the time when we should have talked about the rape, Steven."

I nodded slowly, clasping my hands on the table-top. "I thought I was fine. I thought... I was over it."

"You don't get over that kind of attack, Steven. It gets better over time. You learn to live with it, you learn to be more comfortable with yourself, but you do not get over it," Cheryl said, her hand resting warm on mine. "And one of the things that will help is talking about it. So now, we talk."

And talk we did. For hours, it felt like we did nothing but talk. Or rather, I talked, and Cheryl asked questions. About Joey, about our relationship, and how it changed. About waking up that morning bound and helpless, just a nameless, faceless hole for Joey to fuck whenever he felt like it. To my surprise, I remembered so much more about that morning than I thought I did. I'd told myself that I really didn't remember any of it, but I found myself recalling little details that normally I would never think about. Like the fact that the phone rang in the middle of it all, and someone had left a message on the machine.

"You know, I never did find out who called," I said, stopping to sip my now-cold coffee. "I never stopped to listen to the machine, and I never went back to the apartment. I..." I stopped, licked my lips, suddenly overwhelmed. I opened my mouth, then shook my head. "I... don't want to talk any more, Cheryl. Is... is that okay?"

"That's fine, Steven. We've covered a lot for today, I think. I'll come over in a couple of days, and we'll talk again. For now, I want you to rest. Be gentle with yourself. And... if I might be so bold, Nick? No power games."

"I knew that," Nick said stiffly.

"Steven doesn't. Right now, he's too... raw. There are too many emotions, too close to the surface. You do not want to damage anything between you by something being misread or misunderstood. So, until he finds his footing, I think you two are stuck on vanilla."

"Stuck on... oh," I said, finally catching up to what she meant. I ran my finger over my chain. "You think that might happen?"

"She is right, Steven," Nick answered. "I startled you in the shower, and you almost broke my nose."

"I came that close?" I asked, amazed.

"You did. So... until you are ready, I think you should perhaps give me back your collar?"

My breath caught in my throat, and all I could hear was my

blood rushing in my ears. I managed to squeak out the words, "My... my collar?" before Nick grabbed my hands.

"Steven, listen to me!"

I nodded. "I am."

"I am not asking this because I do not love you. I am not asking this because I do not want you. Or because anything has changed between us. You are still mine. But until you are healed enough that we can safely play, we should not. Do you understand?" His voice was very firm, his hands on mine solid and warm. I closed my eyes and nodded. I believed him. I trusted him. I loved him.

"When I'm ready...?"

"I will give it back."

"All right," I said. I worked my hands out from under his and reached up and back, undoing the clasp on the chain. My neck felt light, naked as I held the chain out and Nick took it from me.

"Now what?" I asked. In answer, Cheryl took one of my hands, and Nick took the other.

"Now, we put you back together," she answered.

Interstitial
Heart Strike

"You failed me."

The servant cringed and tried to disappear into the polished stone floor. "Mercy, my lord," he whimpered, hearing his master sniff. He dared glance up, to see the gloriously handsome elf-lord sprawled inelegantly over his throne. His eyes glittered like death-metal as he considered the servant groveling before him, and the servant ducked his head and repeated, "Mercy."

"Your vessel was flawed, and the Heart's Master lives. You failed. It is only by some great good fortune that he is not warned of our presence. Or our threat."

The servant nodded, knocking his forehead against the floor with a hollow-sounding thump. "He is... untrained. Untrained and powerful. He is... unpredictable. And he is protected."

"Protected?"

"A mortal mage. A lover, from what we can see. And one of the minor lords of *Aos Si*, but that protection has been refused."

The servant heard the creaking of wood and leather, and looked up to see his master leaning forward. "Which minor lord?"

"Fergus, my lord."

His master scoffed. "The old gatekeeper? Hardly a threat. Tell me more about this mortal mage."

The servant nodded, this time without hitting his head on the floor. "He was born on foreign soil, my lord. The same soil that you once called home, I believe. He has not yet claimed the place where he lives with the Heart's Master as his home territory. His magic is not as strong as he has the potential to be, for that reason. He is powerful, though, for a mortal. The shields that he has placed on their home and on the Heart's Master himself will not be easily defeated. And there is the potential that he will decide that his new place is now his home. It increases the longer he remains with the

Heart's Master. They've a true pair-bond between them, the seers say."

"A pair-bond? Have they started to merge their magics?"

"Not as yet. The seers say that will come, but the cusp has not yet been reached."

"What else? You've studied him?"

"We have watched him, my lord. It has been several cycles of the moon since our... failure, and we have watched. The mage is wounded in spirit. An old wound, but one that can be used against him. And he places much value on the Heart's Master and on their bond. Too much, perhaps. If they can be separated, then perhaps..."

"A sound theory," his master interrupted. "Use the scrying bowl and show me this mage. I am... curious."

The servant rose and went to a plinth that rose along one wall, and which served as a resting place for a large black bowl. The bowl, the servant knew, had been carved from a single piece of jet, consecrated in blood, and was priceless; his hands shook as he filled the bowl with water. He heard footsteps behind him, and felt the looming presence at his shoulder.

"Show me," his master crooned. The servant swallowed his fear and murmured the words that would allow him to show the image of the mage to his master.

The surface of the water rippled, and an image formed, that of a young man, scandalously dressed in a shirt with no sleeves and short trews that showed his long, muscular legs. He was running, from what or to where the servant could not say.

"He does this most days when the weather is fine," he said. "He leaves the house under his strongest shields, and he runs."

"Interesting," his master murmured, and there was enough heat in his voice that the servant knew that it was not his words that his master was reacting to, but the image of the mortal mage. "So, you plan to do what?"

"Separate them. Remove the protections of the mage, and destroy the Heart's Master."

"A simple plan for a simple mind," his master answered, walking away. "And how do you plan on accomplishing that?"

"The seers have found us another vessel, and a time and place in which to use that vessel. If he succeeds, then we will be rid of the Heart's Master, and the mage will be crippled by the loss. If he fails, then both the Heart's Master and the mage will be disoriented by the attack, and open for a direct assault."

"Well thought out, my servant," his master said, real approval in his voice. "If you succeed in this, I may even grant you a name. But I will change one point in your plan."

"My lord?"

"Bring the mortal mage to me."

Chapter Eight
So Shall Ye Reap

"Okay, Steve, you can do this," I whispered to myself for the nth time. N at that moment was some number that I'd lost track but was surely approaching a million. I ran through the steps in my mind—put the frozen chicken breasts on the baking sheet and put the sheet in the oven. Set the broiler and the timer. Rub the potatoes with oil and salt and wrap them in foil, and put them in the oven with the chicken. Pull open the salad bag and put it in the bowl, and make a pot of coffee. Easy. So why was I so terrified?

Probably because this was my first solo flight in the kitchen. Nick was not only not looking over my shoulder, he wasn't even in the house. Today had gotten to him badly, and he'd been snappish all day, stalking around the house, unable to settle, and unwilling to talk. It was worse today than it had been since I'd really started working with Cheryl and we'd stopped playing, because today was a year since the accident. A year since Maureen died, and he'd lost both her and his daughter. I understood, but I doubt I was much help, since I was dealing with my own anniversary today. I kept remembering that day, remembering my last performance, the things I seen and done, the look on Maureen's face when I'd kissed her.

Nick had finally announced he was going for a run. He'd been gone for nearly an hour, and while he was gone, I'd gotten the brilliant idea to make dinner. Maybe that would help, I thought. We had everything we needed in the house. I pitched the idea to Mirage, who had whined at me, then left the kitchen. That should have been my first warning.

I'd never been much of a cook, but I watched a lot of cooking shows back when I still could actually watch them, and I still listened to them. I honestly thought that was enough. I guess not. I don't remember any of those shows ever telling me that I needed to stick a fork into the potatoes before putting them into the oven, so that they wouldn't explode. The idea never even occurred to me, so I was not expecting the twin explosions half an hour into the cooking time. Of course, it happened when I was attempting to pull open the bag of salad, which meant that lettuce flew every-where. Scared silly, I figured out that the sound came from the oven, and as I went to investigate, I heard the timer on the coffeepot chime, which meant that the brewing cycle was starting.

Opening the oven, I was hit in the face with a wave of steam and smoke. Something was burning, and I wasn't sure what. I grabbed the oven mitts and pulled trays out of the oven, dumping them onto the stove-top as I kicked the oven door closed. Okay, what was wrong with the dinner? I had no idea, and as I stood there and tried to figure it out, I heard hissing, and a new stench mingled with the smell of burning whatever-it-was. This one, I knew—burning coffee. I must not have seated the pot correctly, and everything was overflowing in the brew basket. I went for the coffeepot, slipped on spilled lettuce, and ended up on my ass in the middle of the kitchen.

And that, of course, was the minute that Nick chose to walk in on me. "Steven, what are you doing?" I jumped when I heard his incredulous voice.

"I... I was trying to make dinner..." I gestured with both hands, then let them fall helplessly to my sides. "... help?"

Technically, I wasn't supposed to be doing this. Nick had told me more than once that he wasn't comfortable with me trying to cook without supervision. So I was expecting him to completely blow his top, to start yelling and cursing in Russian. I wasn't expecting him to start giggling, and I sat there in shock as the giggles turned to uproarious laughter. I heard a soft thump, and the laughter continued, occasionally punctuated by a gasp-and-wheeze as Nick tried to take a full breath. I felt pressure in my chest, and knew that I wasn't going to be able to keep it in; I started to laugh, imagining just how ridiculous I looked. My laughter set Nick off harder, and we sat there for I don't know how long, laughing like idiots. When Nick finally managed to stop, he coughed a few times, then sighed and snorted, "Just... what were you trying to do?"

"Make dinner?" I answered. "I thought... it might help?"

"Well, I haven't laughed that hard in a long, long time, so I suppose that it did. Can you stand up?"

"I don't know." I heard movement, coming closer; to my surprise, Nick was on the floor, too, on his knees in front of me. "What are you doing on the floor?" I asked.

"I couldn't keep standing. I was laughing too hard. Tell me what you were doing?" he asked as he helped me up.

"I... I put chicken under the broiler, and put potatoes in. Something went boom, and the salad went flying. I don't know what happened, but it was in the oven...."

Nick laughed again and pushed me into a chair. "Steven, *Styopa*, make a promise to me?" he asked, his hands on the back of the chair, leaning over me so that his face was close enough that I could feel his breath on my face.

"Okay? What?"

"Promise me that you will never touch anything in my kitchen, ever again?" He sounded as if he was going to break into laughter again, and I nodded once without saying a word. "Good. Now, let me see what it is that you did here." He moved away, and I heard him gasp. "*Bozhe moi*, what did you do to the coffeepot? I think that is a lost cause, *Styopa*."

"Sorry," I offered.

"Don't be. It was a sweet thought, and I do appreciate it. How did you manage to burn the chicken? And... Steven, this is still raw on the inside. How... how did you *do* that?" He sighed, then started laughing again. "What a mess! I will get the broom. Then... what do you want from the take-away?"

An hour later, we sat facing each other on the couch, eating Chinese take-out directly from the cartons and passing a bottle of vodka back and forth between us. I was feeling pleasantly relaxed, but not quite drunk. Or maybe, just drunk enough.

I took the bottle, took a long sip, then put the bottle down on the floor. I set my carton of lo mein down on the couch and made up my mind. "*Kolya*, may I have my collar back?"

He coughed, sputtered, and for a minute, nothing else was said. How was I supposed to know he'd just taken a mouthful of rice? Once he could talk again, he asked me, "Are you sure?"

"Yes. I love you. I know what Cheryl said, and I understand that things are going to be weird for a while. Maybe a long while. But..." I took a deep breath and continued, talking fast, "I love you. I want you. I don't belong with anyone else, I know that. I know you won't hurt me. I know you can't hurt me. And I trust you. So... I'd like things to go back to the way they were. As much as they can. Regardless, I want to be yours again, completely. Because without the collar, I don't feel like I am. So can I have it back now, please?"

I waited, and a few minutes later, Nick asked, "Are you going to finish that?"

My lo mein, I guessed. "Ah... no. Not hungry anymore."

"I'll clean up, then," he said. The couch shifted, and I heard him picking things up and moving away. Suddenly, I was very tired. I'd said just about everything there was for me to say, and every ball I had was now squarely in Nick's court. It was all up to him.

"I'll be in my room," I called. No answer, so I headed down the hall and let myself into my room. I turned the light on for Nick, grabbed a pair of sticks, and sat down behind my drum kit.

Nick had, for my birthday present, taken a bunch of my CDs and run them through some program in his computer. I'm not sure exactly how he did it, but he'd managed to isolate the drum tracks and remove them entirely, then he'd loaded the resulting tracks onto a dedicated music server that fed into a sound system that he installed in my room. I didn't understand half of what he explained to me, but I did get that this meant that I could play rhythm for some of my favorite bands. My current favorite was in the player already, so I picked up the remote, started the music, and let the tight harmonies on Lost Forever wash over me. Five words in, the drums started, and I was off.

I was not, by any stretch of the imagination, a heavy metal drummer, which was why I liked this song in particular. It was a fast rhythm, and tricky in spots. I really had to focus on what I was doing, which left me no brain-space to fret over what Nick was doing or why he hadn't answered me when I asked him for my collar. Or to worry that he would say no.

I was well into the fourth track and working hard when I felt Nick coming into the room. There wasn't any urgency to him, so I didn't stop, but I did grin at him and send a soft "nudge" of energy to kiss his cheek, just to let him know I knew he was there. There was a phantom touch on my cheek in return, along with a waft of the butterscotch that for some reason my brain associated with Nick; some small part of my brain that wasn't engaged in banging drums marveled at the way I'd become so accustomed to using magic. Nick moved around and behind me, and waited there until I was done; I picked up the remote and turned off the music, then grabbed a towel and wiped sweat from my face as I turned around.

"Hi," I said quietly. "Is... is everything cleaned up?" He didn't answer, stepping forward to stand between my knees. I felt cold metal on the back of my neck and shuddered as Nick clasped my collar around my throat. When he let it fall, I touched the chain and let out the breath I didn't know I'd been holding. "Thank you," I murmured.

"Come to bed?" Nick asked. I nodded and stood up, setting my sticks on top of the shelf as I passed on my way to the door. Nick followed me, his hand coming to rest on my back. "I do not think that we will do more than cuddle tonight, *mily*. I think I have drunk enough that nothing else should happen," he said, and I could hear the apology in his voice.

"I'm fine with cuddling, Nick," I told him. "But I'm a mess right now. Keep me company in the shower?"

"I will just watch, I think."

I stopped and turned, stunned. This was the first time since... well, the first time that he'd ever refused an invitation to play in the shower. "You..."

"Not yet, *mily*. Not until my head is clear."

"All right," I turned back towards our bedroom and let myself in, stripping my shirt off over my head as I walked, and stopping outside the bathroom so that I could strip off the rest, dropping everything into the clothes hamper there. Inside the bathroom, and once the water was on, I couldn't hear Nick at all, but I could feel him behind me. All right, he was just going to watch? I would give him something to watch.

I stepped under the shower-head and reached up to set the spray to the steady, pounding massage that I liked so much, then picked up the soap. I lathered up, then leaned against the wall and started to stroke my cock.

"Steven!"

"You wanted to watch," I said. "So enjoy yourself." I tipped my head back and started to tug on my cock, imagining that it was Nick doing it. I thought for a moment about using my other hand in my ass, but decided against it. I needed a hand free if I lost my balance, and besides, soap would sting. I pumped a little harder, a little faster, and blinked in surprise as something cold dribbled over my fingers.

"You will hurt yourself using just soap," Nick said. His hand covered mine, and he pressed me against the wall of the shower and kissed me. When his body pressed against mine, I realized that he hadn't bothered to strip; he was standing in the shower, fully-clothed, helping me jerk off. I moaned into his mouth and damn near came on the spot.

It didn't last long; I'd had quite a bit to drink, too. Nick pushed me down onto the seat, took my cock in one hand and my collar in the other, and that was all she wrote—three-stroke Charlie and I was done. I sat there, panting, and felt Nick sit down next to me. I turned, resting my face on his soggy shoulder, and started giggling. "You're all wet."

He snorted. "And you aren't?"

"I'm at least dressed for it," I protested. And we sat there, giggling like idiots, until the hot water ran out. Only then did Nick strip, and we helped each other dry off and fell into bed; I fell asleep in his arms. All in all, not a bad way to spend a sucky anniversary. Even if we were going to have to clean petrified potatoes out of the oven in the morning.

The next morning, after breakfast, I was lingering over my coffee when I heard Nick shuffling papers. "What have you got?" I asked.

"Yesterday's mail. I didn't get a chance to read it. Ah... this is interesting."

"What?"

"Do you know the big BDSM group in DC? They have an annual conference?" he asked.

"Yeah, I know them. I went to a munch last year with Joey. Why?"

"Did you?" Nick sounded surprised.

"It was before he turned into an asshole, yeah. What about it?" I asked as I finished my coffee. "It's coming up soon, isn't it? Is that what this is about? You want to go?"

"Perhaps. If you are interested. This year, an old friend is the conference coordinator. He sent a note. He wants to know if we are interested in attending. He thinks that it will be good for people to see... well, you."

"Me?" I asked. "Oh, because I'm blind?"

"Exactly. His thoughts are that it may help show that kink and disability are not mutually exclusive. So, is this something that you might be interested in doing? Or should I tell him no?"

I considered the idea, then nodded. "No, I think I'll be okay. The policies at these things are usually hands-off unless you get permission, right?"

"That's right."

I picked up my coffee cup, took a sip, then nodded again. "So long as you don't mind me being stuck to you like green on grass, then yeah. Sure. Let's go party with the kinky people."

Which is how I ended up sitting on the bed in a hotel room, feeling the slick, synthetic hotel bedspread under my thighs, and listening to Nick finish up in the bathroom. I rubbed my hands together, then rubbed them over the waistband of the very short, very tight leather shorts that were the only thing I was wearing.

Nick and I had spent the day cruising the convention, shopping and sitting in on panels. But now, the panels were over, the vendors shut down, and the lower floors of the hotel given back to the people who worked here. Now, it was time to play.

"Are you ready, mily?" Nick asked as he came out of the bathroom.

"I think so," I answered, standing up. In truth, I felt naked. It wasn't the shorts that did it. It was the lack of my chain. The only thing I was wearing other than the shorts was my medical emergency bracelet. Nervous, I rubbed the bare nape of my neck.

"It's all right, mily. If you decide that this is too much, we can stay here and play in private." Nick came closer, running his hands up and down my arms with a soft touch that raised goosebumps in its wake. I shivered and moved closer, feeling the smooth leather of his vest against my bare skin.

"No. I want you to be able to show off. I want to make you proud of me," I whispered. "Let's go."

He laughed and kissed me gently. "We will. But you're not quite ready yet." Quickly, he buckled cuffs onto my wrists and around my ankles, and slipped my leather collar around my neck. It was the first time I'd worn it since Beltane in the clearing, and I smiled as Nick locked it in place.

"Remembering the last time?" he asked.

"How could I forget?" I murmured, shocked that he'd brought it up. And even more shocked that it didn't trigger any kind of reaction in me.

Nick laughed and kissed the back of my neck, just above the collar. "Now you are ready. Mirage has food and water for the evening, so she's set. I'll get the leash."

This was going to be the hardest part. As much as I wanted to, I couldn't bring Mirage with me into the play-party. As well trained as she was, I was pretty sure that she'd never understand what she'd see in the party, and I didn't want her to freak out. So tonight, Nick was going to be my eyes, and he was going to guide me with twenty inches of narrow leather clipped to my collar. I swallowed as I heard the metal clip snap, licking my lips with a tongue that was suddenly as dry as a desert.

"Ready?" Nick asked again.

"Lead on."

I wasn't expecting the guards at the elevators. As the signal chimed and the doors opened, a rough voice challenged us: "Invitation only!"

"I have an invitation," Nick answered. I heard the rustle of paper, and then the guard's voice. "Very good, sir. Enjoy yourselves."

"Thank you." Nick led me along, the carpet deep and plush under my bare feet. We hadn't gone very far when I heard a man's voice call Nick's name.

"Nicolai? Darling, how are you?"

"Hello, Harry. Good to see you again," Nick answered, real pleasure in his voice. The old friend, I assumed, as I heard the sound of kisses, an assumption confirmed by Nick's next words, "Thank you for inviting us. We've enjoyed the day. Now, what rooms do you have?"

"Oh, the usual. Medical play, the Nursery, the St. Andrews Cross. There's a suspension rig in that room over there, too. And a few private rooms. Your new boy is lovely. May I touch?"

"Warn him first, Harry. You know he can't see you."

"I know. I'm sorry we never got the chance to meet earlier. I've been so busy. I saw you all around today, but I never could catch up with you. Hello, gorgeous. I'm Harry."

I knew he was talking to me, and I bowed my head towards his voice, "Sir. A pleasure, sir. Thank you for letting me know."

My answer prompted a lilting laugh and a warm hand down my arm. "Oh, Nicolai, he's a nice one. And so polite. You've done well for yourself."

"Yes," Nick answered. "I have."

"So have I," I added softly. I heard them both laugh, and I smiled, the tight knot of nerves loosening. This might not be so bad after all.

"Of course I have an invitation, you idiot!" A sharp male voice from behind me, one that sounded somehow both angry and petulant. At the sound, Nick gasped, and I felt a sharp tug on the leash.

"Harry, what the hell is he doing here?" Nick hissed.

"He's back in town, Nicolai. Has been for a month or so. This is his first outing, from what I hear. You didn't know?"

"If I'd known, I wouldn't have come," Nick growled, and I wondered who he was talking about. "Why didn't you warn me, Harry?"

"Good lord, that surely can't be Nicolai!" It was the same voice, but now the anger was replaced with an oily smarm that made my skin crawl. I swallowed against a foul, coppery taste in my mouth, shivering slightly and trying to remember why the taste was so alarming. "It is! Nicolai, how lovely to see you again."

I could feel Nick's anger radiating off him like waves of summer heat off of asphalt. The leash tightened slightly, and when Nick spoke, he was standing directly in front of me. "Trevor. How interesting to see you here. When did they start letting you back into the public play-areas?"

Trevor laughed. "Starting trouble already? Really, Nicolai? And who is this?"

I knew he meant me, and I shuddered, trying to hide behind Nick. Nick growled, "You don't go near him. No one touches him."

"Of course, Nicolai. But it is telling, is it not, that the only boy you could get to take your collar was one who was already... damaged?" Laughter, and the voices moved away. I moved closer to Nick and rested my hand on his waist.

"We can go. I don't mind," I whispered.

Nick growled softly and turned, his cheek brushing against my nose. "No. I won't have him thinking he's chased me off. Not again."

"No one would think that, Nicolai. We all know..." Harry started to say, but his voice trailed off. I wasn't sure why, and I wasn't sure I wanted to find out. But I had to ask.

"Who is he?" I asked.

Nick growled softly, "He is no one I want you near. You stay with me, you let no one touch you without my express permission. You tell them you do not have permission to play out. Is that clear?"

"Crystal." The last thing I wanted was for that one to touch me in any way. I licked my lips to try and clear the taste from my mouth, and was about to mention it to Nick when there was slight tug on the collar pulling me forward. I filed it for later, and we headed into the party.

This wasn't my first play-party. I'd been to a couple before, with Joey, so I wasn't surprised when people recognized me. Some of them had the balls to ask about what happened with Joey, and Nick basically told those people to get bent. Most of the people who knew me from before made a point of telling me that I was well rid of Joey, and that they thought I'd traded up.

Well, to be honest, so did I.

Harry seemed to have appointed himself our guide, and he took us on a tour of the rooms, describing the themes with an attention to detail that I greatly appreciated. All around me, I could hear the sounds of men and women moaning in pain or pleasure, the heavy sounds of paddles or straps, the lighter sounds of floggers, the sharp snap of canes and the crack of single-tails. We lingered in several places so that Nick and Harry could watch the action, which they took turns describing for me in terms that left me hungry for my turn. Every time we stopped, I knelt between Nick's knees and just listened to them talk, enjoying Nick's vivid descriptions of what was being done to the lucky or unlucky subs in the room.

"I notice you don't have an instrument, Nicolai," Harry said over my head as we sat in one of the rooms. "I'd be happy to loan you one of mine. You prefer a heavy flogger, no?"

I stiffened, and felt Nick smooth his hand soothingly down my spine. "I can't use it on this one, Harry. Steven's had back surgery. Turn and show him your scars, *mily*."

I shifted, leaning forward and resting my forehead on my folded hands, the better to display the line of my back. Warm fingers trailed down my skin, tracing the surgical scars. Harry made soft tut-tut sounds over my head, and I moved back to my place between Nick's knees. "Well, I can see that heavy play is right out," Harry said. "So what do you do together?"

"Strict bondage. Nipple play. Knives," Nick answered, then laughed as I shivered. "He likes knives."

"I can see that. Come here, Steven," Harry said. I hesitated, waiting for direction, and felt the leash fall loose over my shoulder. Permission granted; and Nick telling me without words that Harry was to be trusted at least this far. I crawled out from between Nick's knees and made my way around to kneel in front of Harry. I felt the leash move, grow taut, and Harry pulled me so that I was kneeling up in front of him. I shivered all over, and Harry laughed.

"Oh, he is delightful. Very responsive," Harry said. I gasped as he gently prodded my crotch with his foot, rubbing his toes against my half-hard cock. "You know, if he likes strict bondage, there's a room you'll want to see."

"And that would be?" Nick asked.

"The Parlor."

The transition from one room to another was marked, for me, by the change in the carpet and the sudden, absolute silence that was broken by Nick's laughter.

"I see what you mean, Harry. This is... impressive. Where did the idea come from?"

"It's called forniphilia. I saw something like this online and thought it might be fun. And some of the tops seem to think this is a good place to park the pets for a while so that they can go have a drink or play in another room. We've got monitors in here the entire night, so it's perfectly safe. People are allowed to touch, but not to remove the pets. Shall we?"

"Oh, you want to..." Nick sounded thoughtful, then eager. "Yes, I think so."

"I'll get the straps."

The leash fell slack, and I felt tugging at my wrist. "Have you ever been a piece of furniture, Steven?" Nick asked as he removed the cuffs from my wrists.

"Furniture?" I repeated, sure I hadn't heard him right. "No."

"You're about to be," Nick told me as he stooped to take the ankle cuffs off of me. "What are we making him, Harry?"

"A table, I think," Harry called back. "It will be easier on his back. Strip him and bring him over here."

Nick tugged on my shorts, pulling them down over my hips slowly and steadying me while I stepped out of them; I had to bit my lip and keep myself from moving, when what I really wanted was to press myself against Nick, rub up against him until he was as hot and ready as I was. He had to have known, because he trailed his fingers up my thigh and over my hip until I moaned. Then he stood up and tugged hard on the leash, and I knew that this was something that he really found arousing, too. And that it was something I was probably going to find myself doing at home now. The two of them moved me into position, and heavy leather straps were wrapped tightly around my ankles, knees, and around my upper thighs.

"Arms behind your back, pretty boy," Harry cooed. I did as I was told, feeling my wrists firmly bound with another leather strap.

"Elbows, too?" Harry wanted to know.

"Not with his back. Just strap him down."

"Of course," Harry said, and more straps were wrapped around me, binding my arms to my body.

"Cock strap?" Harry asked.

"I have one. I'll do it."

I gasped as Nick grabbed my cock and wrapped the leather tightly around me then slowly started to toy with my erection, softly at first, then harder, until he was almost slapping my cock and I was moaning and pumping my hips at him, desperate for more. Harry had come around behind me when Nick started, and he held me still, steadying me and keeping me on my feet while Nick tormented me. Then the two of them guided me to my knees and into an odd frame. There was a soft mesh sling that cradled my belly, and that was held up by two arches, one wide enough for my hips, the other just the right size for my neck. There was a third arch that was slightly padded and that adjusted to make a place for me to rest my forehead. The arches, I soon found out, were equipped with straps to secure me in place, as well as more straps that went around my thighs, and something that wrapped around my ankles and pulled them up towards my ass. By the time they were done, I was more strictly bound than I think I ever had been in my life. I literally couldn't move a muscle, or even turn my head. It was incredible. I tried to shift and moaned softly at the feel of the straps all over me.

"What have you got there?" I heard Nick ask.

"Breather gag. Good for long term wear. This one is new. You're welcome to it."

"Thank you," Nick said, and I knew what he was going to ask me. Before he was even in position, my mouth was open for the gag. He laughed and buckled it in place, then ruffled my hair.

"Just a minute, Harry," he said. A moment later, something hard was tucked into my hand. "Test, Steven." I understood that command completely, and opened my hand, hearing distantly a faint, tinny squeal.

"What on earth is that?" Harry asked.

"Something I'm working on. It is an electronic safe-word," Nick told him. "That controller is on a dead-man switch, and it is linked to my headset. If Steven lets it go, then the alarm sounds and I know he needs me."

"Clever! Have you thought about marketing that?"

"Not yet. This is the prototype. I'm still refining the technology. Shall we finish this?"

I wasn't sure what he meant by finish, until I felt something cold and hard settling down onto my bound arms, shifting slightly as they moved it into position. Oh, of course! The table top!

I could hear them moving around me, and then Nick's voice, coming from my level. He had to be sitting on the floor. "This is very nice, Harry. I think he likes it." I moaned through the gag, agreeing with Nick, who laughed. I felt fingers run over my side, then I heard Nick grunt, and knew that he'd stood up. There was a click from over my head, and I realized that I was in use. Someone had put something on the table.

"Nicolai, there's a heavy demonstration going on three rooms down. Are you interested? It's Marco."

"Really? I thought he'd stopped showing." Nick paused, and I knew he was thinking about me. I could almost hear him thinking *Can I leave him? Should I, after the last time?* Oddly enough, I was fine with the idea. After all, this was safe space. It was all hands-off here.

"The monitor will keep an eye on him, darling," I heard Harry say. "No one will bother him. They may pet him a bit, but nothing more. And he has that cunning little safe-word. We won't be very far..."

There was silence for a long moment, then I heard movement next to me. "Steven, I will be back in a few minutes. If this starts being painful, or you start getting uncomfortable, call me immediately."

I grunted to tell him I understood, and he patted my hip. I heard them moving away, and then the room fell silent. Just me, and the other bound pieces of furniture.

I don't think I'd ever been so turned on before, and there was nothing I could do about it at all. I could hear people around me, coming in and going out, quiet conversations and the click of glasses on the table-top above me. I heard one brief, intense interchange that sounded as if someone had been turned over their master's lap for a spanking. And there were many, many people who circled me, commenting on my bondage, on my looks, on the impression that they'd had of me from the day. A few people reached under the table and touched me, pinching and poking. I assumed that they were trying to make me make some noise. Only one succeeded, a woman with sharp nails who pinched my nipple hard enough that I yelped. She laughed and moved away, and for a long time there was no one else who came near.

Things were just starting to get a little uncomfortable, and I was starting to wonder where Nick was, when the table-top shifted off of my back and I felt straps falling loose. My legs were freed, and two pairs of hands steadied me as they helped me to stand. The straps around my arms fell away, although my wrists remained bound behind me and they didn't unbuckle the gag. I wasn't worried at all until whoever was behind me grabbed my arms hard and held me still so that the person in front of me could jam a hood over my head, pulling it down hard and fast. I pulled back, suddenly alarmed. Nick didn't use hoods, for some reason didn't like them. I didn't think we even owned one. I stepped back, my back coming to rest hard against the chest of the man holding my arms. I tasted copper again as I felt silk against my skin, and I panicked, knowing full-well that Nick had been bare-chested. This wasn't Nick. Where was Nick? Terrified, I opened my hand, sounding the alarm as I tried to pull away. I couldn't break his grip, though, and I felt someone doing something under my chin. A slight tugging... a leash. Someone had clipped a leash to my collar.

"What have you got here?" I heard a man say. The transmitter was taken from my hand; when I made a mumbled protest and started to struggle, whoever held the leash tugged on it hard, pulling me down to my knees.

"Get him up and take him to the private room." I recognized

that smarmy voice. Trevor. I pulled back against the lead, fighting
as they dragged me forward, trying to delay them, give Nick a
chance to find me. But it didn't do any good—someone started
pushing me from behind, and before I could try anything else, I
was pushed to the side and heard a door closing behind me.

"Good. Get him on the cross." Trevor again, and he wasn't one
of the ones manhandling me. At least three, then. Too many to
fight, and they'd be able to force me to do whatever they wanted.
Not that I cared about odds—I fought like crazy, especially when
they released my wrists. It didn't do any good, though. Three of
them, one of me—it was over before it had really started. As they
finished fastening my wrists and ankles to the cross, someone ran
their hand down my back.

"Trev, these look like surgical scars." I grunted and nodded
hard, and the hand moved away. "Trevor, I don't think he's up for
heavy."

"He'll be fine," Trevor snapped. "Please, he's a toy."

"Not yours, though. Trevor, you told us he was good to go.
That you could use him," someone else said.

"He's my boy's pet. He's mine to do with whatever I please."

"Your former boy," the first voice scoffed. "The one who got
you charged with assault and thrown out of the DC leather com-
munity. Trev, this is a bad plan. I'm letting him down."

There was the sound of a resounding slap, and someone
grunted in pain. Trevor's voice was cold, "You'll do what I say,
Lee. If you don't want a turn, then get over in the corner and
watch."

I knew what they were going to do to me now. Heavy... they
were going to use a whip, or a strap. Something with some weight
behind it. Something that would do damage. I shook my head and
grunted again, panic growing stronger. No safe-word. I had no
safe-word. They were going to beat me up and then...

My mind rebelled on the "and then." I started fighting the
bonds, straining and struggling, trying to call for help. When it
was clear that none of them were going to help me, I reached in-

side for my magic. It had worked against Joey, and against Fergus, it had to work now!

Nothing. Emptiness. I was too far gone in my panic to find the threads, let alone use them. I heard someone grunt behind me, felt the rush of air, then the strap connected with the backs of my legs. I screamed, my knees buckling with the pain.

"Oh, he's a lightweight." I could barely hear Trevor through the sound of the blood rushing in my ears. "This will never do. Straighten him up and make sure he can't move."

Rough hands, pulling me back into position and wrapping rope around my waist, tying me into place. I moaned and shook my head, trying to get them to stop. It didn't work, and the next blow took me right across the ass. I screamed again... and the magic hit me harder than the strap had. I was suddenly surrounded with warmth and light, and I could feel Nick's anger and fear. He was looking for me, had found the transmitter. The monitor who had been in the Parlor had vanished, and no one knew where. No one had seen me...

Nick! Kolya, help me! I screamed in my mind. And to my surprise, he answered.

Styopa? Where are you?

A room. A room near the Parlor. Don't know how many paces, but we turned left. It had a whipping cross. Kolya, it's Trevor. He's got a strap. I can't stop him...

White-hot rage rolled through my mind like thunder. *He hit you?*

Before I could answer, I was distracted by the incoming rush of air, and tensed just as the strap came down across my shoulders. I screamed again, and I knew without knowing how that Nick had felt the blow as well. *Kolya!*

Behind me, I heard someone pounding at the door, heard Nick's raised voice, ordering Trevor to open the door. Heard Harry calling for the keys. Trevor laughed. "Pathetic. Come on, pretty boy. Let's see how red I can make your back turn before I give you back to your poor excuse for a master."

I felt Nick's magic flare, and heard the door come crashing open just as the strap connected with my lower back. I heard Nick roaring in anger as crimson pain swallowed the room whole...

I woke up in pain, face down on what smelled like a hotel bed. At least it wasn't a hospital, although I wasn't sure why it wasn't. I groaned when I tried to move, and jumped when Mirage stuck her wet nose into my armpit. Then I heard Harry's voice, "He's awake!"

There was a scrambling, and I felt a hand in mine. Nick's hand, I was sure of it. "*Styopa?*" he whispered. "Steven, talk to me?"

I blinked. "'m hurt. How bad?"

"You're all right, I think. Just bruised. We'll call Celia, get you in tomorrow and make sure."

"... not ER?" I asked, confused.

"Do you think you're hurt that badly?" Harry asked, sounding nervous. It took me a minute to realize why, and the reason pissed me enough to clear my head. He didn't care about me, he was worried about his convention.

"Maybe. Dunno," I shook my head and winced. "Why didn't they call an ambulance?"

"Because Harry is an EMT," Nick answered, his voice clipped, his accent thick with anger. I'd never heard him that angry before, not even when dealing with Maureen's mother. "If you want a real doctor, we can go now that you're awake."

"Okay. Trevor. What happened to him?" I asked.

"He's gone. We kicked him and his friends out of the conference," Harry answered.

"What?" I gasped, turning towards his voice. "That's it? Didn't anyone call the cops?"

"No," Nick answered. "I was going to..." His voice trailed off, and I wondered why he hadn't.

I grimaced and pushed myself up, feeling the bone-deep aches in my shoulders and legs. "Nick, help me up. I want to walk."

"Steven, are you sure?" Harry asked.

"If you thought it was bad enough that I shouldn't walk, then you should have fucking called an ambulance and the cops!" I snapped. Nick sniffed once—in amusement, I thought—and helped me to my feet. The pain was intense, but I was used to the pains in my back enough to know that it was all surface pain. I'd still want Celia to take a look, but I didn't think there had been any real damage done. I tottered across the room and then back to the bed, realizing as I lay down that I was still naked.

"Nick, can I have a blanket?" I asked.

"Cold, mily?" he asked as he tucked me into bed.

"No, just... tired of being meat." I sighed and closed my eyes, feeling myself starting to shake. "Harry? Get out."

"What? Steven, I should..."

"You should get out. We'll call you if we need anything," Nick said firmly. I heard the door open, and a few whispered words before the door closed again. Then Nick came back and sat down on the edge of the bed.

"Talk to me, Steven?" he repeated, his hand heavy on my arm.

I opened my mouth... and burst into tears. Nick drew me into his arms and held me, murmuring in Russian soft words that I couldn't have translated even on a good day, and rubbing my back until I somehow managed to calm down and breathe again. That was when I realized that somewhere in there, he'd started speaking in English.

"... after my father died. I was alone, for the first time in my life, and I was still fairly new in this country. I had just started grad school. I was still dealing with being open about my sexuality. I kept it hidden from everyone. I didn't date, I didn't do much besides study and work with my father. I knew he would never approve. I wasn't as brave as you were, mily.

"I was living then near Dupont Circle, and I met him in a bar. I must have looked to him like a sacrificial lamb. Before I knew it,

I was his boy. I was living in his house, wearing his collar. I had no idea what BDSM was then, and yet I was living the life that people write lurid stories about—24/7, with no contracts, no agreements, no safe-words. I didn't know anyone in the scene then, didn't know that what he was doing to me wasn't the way it was supposed to be. He made me think I was in love with him. I don't know. Maybe I was."

It didn't take a brain surgeon to figure out that he was talking about Trevor. Trevor had been his introduction to the scene, the way Joey had been mine. I wondered if his time with Trevor was the source of the scars he refused to talk about.

"How did you get out?" I asked, barely recognizing my own voice.

"He took me out to show me off. I was his perfect slave, and he never could resist showing off. He brought me to a conference like this one." Nick paused for a moment, and the bed shifted. I heard him swallow, then clear his throat. "That was where I had my eyes opened. I realized that I had choices. That I could say no to him. So I did."

"And?" I prompted when the silence grew too deep.

"He laid my back open with a single tail whip. After that, he broke my jaw, my left wrist and three of my ribs."

"Jesus, Nick!" I blurted out. Nick sighed and pulled me to him, my head resting against his chest.

"We were still at the conference when it happened, so he couldn't hide it the way he'd hidden everything else he'd done to me. The conference coordinator didn't try to ignore things, didn't try to bury them the way Harry is trying to bury this. She went with me to the hospital, stayed with me while I made a statement to the police, made sure I pressed charges." With my ear pressed to his skin, Nick's sudden laugh sounded strangely hollow. "Can you guess who that was?"

I frowned at the question, and then the penny dropped. I sat up facing him and blurted out, "Maureen?"

"Maureen," he confirmed. "She took me in when I had no place else to go, went with me and the police when we went to

Trevor's to get my things—what little I had. I'd given up my apartment, dropped out of grad school, sold my car. I didn't even have a bank account at that point. Trevor had made me sign everything over to him."

"What happened after?"

He sighed, "After... Maureen helped me put my life back together. Pushed me back into grad school. Cosigned the loan for my car. I lived with her for a year. And..."

"You fell in love with her," I said.

"I did," Nick sighed. "It took some time. I was somewhat... wary..."

His hesitation made me grin in spite of everything. "Oh, I wouldn't know anything about that."

He chuckled. "Of course not. It was when I graduated with my Masters. She asked me what I wanted for a graduation present, and I told her I wanted her collar. I loved her, I trusted her, and I respected her. The questioning that I did with you that first time? That was nothing to the interview that I had with Maureen, and when she was done, she had me interview with a dom friend of hers. She wanted to be very sure that I knew what I wanted, and she wanted to be sure that I was comfortable with my body and my choices."

"That's what you did with me," I murmured. "I didn't realize it was because you... you knew. You understood. And... now I understand what you were talking about. With Cheryl. That night... I heard a little. That's why you didn't put up a fuss when she told me to give up the collar. You knew... because you'd been there."

"Yes. I knew you'd been through something very similar to what I had experienced. I didn't want you to make a mistake. I didn't want to be the one who led you into something you would regret..."

"I would never regret you, or anything I've done with you!" I interrupted him, shocked that he could suggest such a thing. He hugged me gently and kissed my forehead.

"Ah, *mily*. Steven, my Steven. I should never have suggested this. I should never have left you alone. It was a mistake right from the start... Do you still want to call the police, mily?"

"Why didn't you, Nick?" I asked. "You started to say."

"I... remember what it was like," he said softly. "They questioned my motives, my sexuality, my past. In court, I was called promiscuous. I was told that I was asking for everything happened to me. I was blamed for what Trevor did to me. They presented my entire sexual history in court, and made me look as if I was a whore. By the time it was over, I had no reputation, personal or professional. It is why I work alone. I thought... I can protect you from this, if I can protect you from nothing else. But perhaps that was high-handed of me."

"Maybe," I agreed. "I'll decide tomorrow, after we see Celia. Now, Nick, there was something else. Something weird." I quickly told him about the copper taste that I'd had in my mouth when we'd first run into Trevor. As I told him, I realized where I'd felt that same thing before. "And... it was the same when Joey broke into the house. I had exactly the same reaction, right before he clubbed me. I tasted copper."

"Hrm..." Nick hummed softly. "I've never heard of such a thing before. An early warning system, perhaps?"

"Wonderful. My horse sense is tingling," I snorted. "Nick, let's go home."

Half an hour later, we were in the car, heading back to Baltimore. It was late, and I heard no other cars on the road, even with the window cracked open.

"Nick," I said quietly, breaking the silence that had reigned since we'd left the hotel. "I think I need to go back to the park."

"No," Nick said, his voice flat. "You are not going back to... there is no need. We will find another way to teach you what you need to know."

"How many *Aos Si* do you have on speed dial, Nick?" I asked. "I should have been able to save myself tonight, and I couldn't. I didn't have enough control over my magic, and I was scared, and I lost it. I... I need to learn more. I need to be able to control it."

Nick was silent, and I could feel his anger simmering again. It struck me then that I had been feeling him the whole time—his anger, his fear, his pain. It was all as clear to me as my own emotions. I closed my eyes and realized that there was more to his anger than just what had happened, and what I was proposing.

"Nick, what are you afraid of?" I asked. "If I go back to the park, and start learning from Fergus again? I'm not going to give him an opening to try again, you know. And you'll be there."

"Every moment," he said. "No, that is not what is bothering me. And how do you know this?"

"You... I think you're thinking loud. Either that, or I'm in your head," I answered. "I can feel what you're feeling. It's... a little strange, actually. So, what is really bothering you?"

"I am never going to have another secret from you ever again, am I?" Nick muttered. I heard the turn signal start to chime softly, and the car bumped a couple of times. Then we stopped, and all I could hear was the wind in the trees outside, Mirage snoring in the backseat, and the ticking of the car engine.

"He is powerful, Fergus," Nick said. "He is... ancient, and he knows what you are. What you can be. I... know none of these things. I cannot teach you. I am..." he stopped, and I unclipped my seatbelt, turning gingerly towards him and waiting for him to find the words. "I am... flawed..."

"You and everyone else in this car, *Kolya*," I interrupted. "Are you really saying you're afraid of losing me to Fergus?"

"Yes. Yes, that is what I am saying. Or not saying. He is... powerful. He is very handsome, *Styopa*. He can give you much, much more than I can..."

"And I love you," I said, reaching over and resting my hand on Nick's leg. "I love you. I love only you, and I want only you. He has nothing that I want. You are my everything."

Nick was quiet for a moment, then asked in a low voice, "Do you mean that? You cannot mean that. I am... not a prize, Steven."

"If I wanted a prize, Nick, I'd buy a box of Cracker Jacks. Look, would it help if I made some kind of grand gesture?"

Nick snickered. "Such as what?"

"Do you have a soldering iron?" I asked, grinning. "I swear to you, if I have to have a collar permanently fastened around my neck in order to finally prove to you that I am not leaving you for an elf with crappy fashion sense, then that is what I'll do."

"Steven!" he gasped, then started giggling.

"I'm serious!" I insisted. "I'll even have a little tag put on it that says 'Property of Nicolai.'"

"That," he said around giggles, "that is stupid, Steven."

I laughed. "All right. How about this? Marry me?"

Nick's giggles chopped off abruptly. "What?"

"Marry me," I said again. "We can go to Hawaii. Or Massachusetts. I don't care where. Just... I love you. I want you with me forever. I don't have a ring to offer you, but I can get one if you'll take me shopping. Ummm... you'd have to pick it out. So, will you marry me, Nicolai?"

Absolute silence. Even the wind went quiet, and the silence stretched on for so long that I was afraid I'd break. Then I heard something I wasn't expecting—the car door opened, and Nick got out. I heard crunching footsteps, then my door opened.

"Out of the car," Nick said. I couldn't tell what he was thinking, he must have shielded or something. Or I'd shocked him enough that he wasn't thinking at all. I wasn't sure, so I slowly got out of the car, hearing Mirage whine behind me as I closed the door.

"Nick?"

I was expecting an answer. I wasn't sure what the answer was going to be, but I thought there would be something. I was not expecting Nick to grab me, push me against the side of the car hard enough to make me yelp in pain, and then try to kiss me into next week. Not that I was complaining! I wrapped my arms around him and tried to give as good as I got, but the pain in my back started to get distracting. So, I twisted, taking Nick with me so that he was against the car, and I was the one in charge. I pushed him hard against the car and kissed him, grabbing his hair and tugging his head down to mine. I don't know who was more surprised by his reaction; he froze in shock, then groaned softly. I felt him shift, and when I ran my hands down his arms, I discovered that he'd tucked his hands behind his back.

"Umm..." I couldn't think of anything to say. No, that's not right. I could think of one thing. "Safe-word?"

"Tolstoy," Nick answered immediately.

"You're sure about this?"

"Yes. Please." I could hear the begging in Nick's voice, and every fantasy that I'd had since he'd mentioned that he'd bottomed came to life, right then and there. I stepped back and undid my belt, pulling it out of the loops and holding it up.

"Turn around, Nick," I told him. When I touched him again, he was facing the car, his wrists crossed behind him. He moaned softly as I tied him up with the belt, and when I turned him back around, I could feel his erection clearly through his pants. Grinning, I unfastened his belt and slowly unzipped his fly. His pants slid neatly down his legs, followed by his shorts, and I leaned against him, grinding into his cock with my hip. "Nearly naked... where the hell are we, Nick?"

"Side... side of the highway," he stammered. "No... no traffic."

"So, I've got you nearly naked on the side of the highway. No one to hear you scream when I make you come." I leaned in and bit his neck gently, wrapping my hand around his cock and listening to him whimper and moan as I played with him. I was incredibly turned on by being the one on top for once, and I hoped that the lube was somewhere where I could find it.

It turned out that I was wrong, though. There was someone to hear us. I tasted copper, and I starting to turn, hearing the footsteps coming at us fast. Nick reared back and shouted something in Russian, right before someone grabbed me, pulling me away from Nick, away from the car. I tumbled to the ground, hearing Nick shouting, a mix of angry sounding Russian and English, and Mirage's muffled barking from inside the car. Then someone threw me down, and I felt hands fumbling at my throat.

"Nick!" I shouted, grappling with my attacker. I landed a good punch, and he fell back; I scrambled to my feet and ran towards where I could hear Nick calling me. Calling for help, with terror clear in his voice. I felt my magic boiling up, and heard people shouting around me. Apparently, I was glowing. Good, let them run. But before I could reach Nick, I was hit from behind and knocked down. I twisted in his grip and snarled, "You are not going to hurt him!" Then I reached down, grabbed my attacker's wrist, and shoved my magic into him.

I felt him die. I didn't care. I'd left Nick helpless, bound and hobbled, and I'd left him alone. They were going to hurt him, and I wasn't going to let that happen. I kicked the body off my legs and got to my feet... and realized that everything around me was quiet, except for Mirage's barking, muffled by the closed car doors.

They were gone. And, somehow I knew, they'd taken Nick with them.

Chapter Nine
Down the Rabbit Hole

I found my way to the car by following the sound of Mirage's barking. I scrabbled at the door handle, almost ready to cry in frustration, until I got the door open. Mirage bounded out, pressing up against me and whining.

"Find Nick," I told her. "Come on, baby-girl. Find Nick."

She didn't move, and I could feel her shivering. She couldn't see Nick. Or smell him. What the hell had happened here? I mean, they had to have dragged him into the woods. Why couldn't she follow the trail? I shook my head and tried to fight back the urge to panic, climbing into the car. I had to call the cops. Where the hell was Nick's phone?

Answer: in Nick's pocket. I slumped into the seat and tried not to burst into tears. I was alone, along a highway and God only knew where, and I didn't have a phone. No way to call for help, no way to save Nick...

"Wait a minute, maybe..." I frowned, trying to think. I'd managed to transport Nick, once, when I'd thought he was in danger. Maybe I could do it again? I got out of the car, concentrating hard, trying to remember what I'd done that morning in Fergus' circle. I'd thought he was trying to hurt Nick, so I reached...

Nothing happened, except I immediately got a headache. Bad plan. Apparently, I had a range. Who knew? Okay, back-up plan. Maybe... maybe the guy who hit me had a phone! I found Mirage's harness and said, "Mirage, find the body."

Definitely smarter than the average dog, my Mirage. She led me right to it, and I got down on the ground and started trying to find his pockets. There was something strange about his clothes: his shirt was longer than I expected, and belted, his pants were rough cloth, and didn't seem to have pockets. Then I found the sheathed dagger at his belt. "Oh, no," I murmured. The only person who'd be dressed like this was an escapee from the Renaissance Festival... or an elf. Since we were nowhere near Crownsville, that left me with only one choice; I ran my hand up his body and found a delicately pointed ear.

"*Aos Si*. Why the hell are the *Aos Si* attacking us?" I said out loud. Then I shook my head. "No. I don't think Fergus would go this far. I think..."

I stopped talking, stopped thinking. If I thought about it, I'd never try it. I needed help, and the only help I was going to be able to get to was Fergus. We were far enough from his park that I knew he'd never hear an elf-call, and I didn't want to open myself up to any other crazy elves who might want to pound on me. I was going to have to go to him.

"Same thing I did with Nick," I told Mirage. "Just in reverse." I put one arm around her, grabbed the body by the belt, and closed my eyes. "Please work," I murmured, and wrapped my magic around us. Just a jump to the left...

I didn't remember any of it, which was probably the best thing that had happened to me all night. All I knew was that suddenly the feel of the place, the smell of it, changed, and I was laid out flat on the cold ground, with a rock digging into my back and Mirage licking my face. I hauled myself up to my knees and leaned against Mirage to steady myself as I prepared to send the elf-call. I held my hands up, tried to send the call, and passed out cold.

I woke up with someone shaking me. "Steven! Danu's tits, boy, what happened?"

It was a good thing I recognized Fergus' voice, because I came up swinging, and managed to pull back in time. I gasped and rolled over, setting off a wave of nausea. "... gonna... gonna be sick..."

He held me while I puked, then helped me sit up and pressed something—a flask—into my hand. "Drink this. A small sip. Then tell me what happened that made you take such a damned stupid risk."

I sipped the liquid and coughed; it was like drinking liquid lightning. But I did start to feel better almost immediately. "Nick... Fergus, we were attacked. They took Nick..."

"And they did some damage to you, I see."

I realized then that my shirt was untucked, and had rucked itself up. The welts on my back must have been an eyeful. "Um... no," I said, shaking my head. "No, that was different. Fergus, I killed one of them. He's *Aos Si*..."

"What?" Fergus let me go and moved away. I heard him cursing softly, then he was back at my side. "That... thing is not *Aos Si*, Steven. Well, it is a *Si*, but not *Aos Si*. There are others. That... we call them... well, what we call them is of no concern. What does matter is that if they have come from the Elvenlands to attack you here, then they are hunting you."

"Me? Hunting me?" I squeaked. "Why? Why would anyone be hunting me? And why would they take Nick?"

"Bait," Fergus said softly. "He is bait, to lure you to them. How do you feel, Steven?"

"Better," I answered, running my hands over my face. I had never felt so lost, and I noticed that Fergus hadn't answered my question about why anyone would be hunting me. But now I had another question. "Fergus, there was something weird. This time, and when Joey attacked me at home, and... and when I was attacked at the hotel..."

"Hotel?"

"Long story. Later. Fergus, I... I *tasted* something. Like... blood, or copper. It was really weird."

"And it was the same each time?" Fergus asked, his voice suddenly sharp.

"Yes. Nick said it might be some kind of early warning system..."

"No. No, it is not," Fergus said slowly. "Tell me, Steven. When you are with me, and I use my magic, does the same thing happen?"

"Clean water," I answered. "Like spring water." I frowned, thinking about it. "Is... is that what is it?"

"Perhaps. And Nick? Is there a taste that you associate with him? Not... not that..." Fergus stammered, and I grinned.

"Butterscotch. Really good butterscotch. Why is this important, Fergus?"

"Because I think you are perhaps tasting the magic. It is rare, but not unheard of. The way that I can see a mage's aura and identify it, you can taste that power."

I nodded, swallowing hard, trying to think. And all I could think of was Nick, packaged for their convenience. "Fergus, what do I do?" I demanded. "I can't leave him. I need to go after him. But I... I'm not a fighter..."

"There's a corpse starting to stink that disagrees with you, Steven," Fergus said, sounding amused. "You fight, when it is some-one you love you are trying to defend. And I will help you."

Hope flared wildly. "You will?"

"Yes. Tell me, where did this happen?"

I laughed, "How the hell do I know, Fergus? We were driving home from New Carrollton, and we pulled over to talk and..." I stopped, not wanting to give Fergus any ideas.

"More than talk?" Fergus filled in the blanks, and I felt my face get warm.

"Yeah. And that was when they hit us." I closed my eyes and ran my fingers through my hair. "Nick couldn't get away. Couldn't fight back. And that's my fault."

"Ah, so you finally gave him what he wanted from you?" Fergus asked, and I sputtered.

"What the hell... Fergus! How did you know?"

"You forget, I saw him with his lady when they came here the first time. He loves the chains as much as you do," Fergus answered. "I think, perhaps, we can discuss this more later. We should go."

"Where?" I asked as I got to my feet. Whatever was in that flask had done wonders for my balance. "Back to the car? I don't know if I can do that again."

Fergus snorted. "No. We must go to the Court. This is more than you and I alone can handle. We need help." He took my hand, and I felt his magic swelling. "I am taking you to the Elvenlands, to the

Court of the High King over the Seas, to meet the Steward. It is... time. Possibly past time."

"What?"

"I will explain it all when we are safe, Steven," he said, tugging me forward. I grabbed Mirage's harness, took three steps, and felt the world shimmy. Then... we were somewhere else.

I stopped, feeling my head spinning. Not from the transport, which was a hell of a lot smoother than when I'd done it. It was the sheer amount of magic in the air—it was like being dropped head first into a barrel of whiskey. I swallowed once, then again, and wondered if wine-tasters ever had it this bad.

"Are you all right?" Fergus asked.

"Yeah," I answered, nodding. "Just... wow. Where are we?"

"In the Elvenlands. In the courtyard of the Steward's palace. Come with me," he said, walking away. Without being told, Mirage followed him.

"What did you call this place?" I asked.

"The Court of the High King over the Seas," Fergus answered. "The High King of the *Aos* Si has his primary court in Eire, but the Steward rules here in his name, and keeps the Court here ready, in case the High King should ever cross the seas. It is a shame that you cannot see this, Steven. It is a beautiful place, and part of your heritage."

"You can tell me about it later, Fergus. Once Nick is safe, I'd love to know more," I told him, and I meant every word. Just the sounds were amazing. I could hear music coming from somewhere, and it was like nothing I'd ever heard before. I wanted to know what instruments they were using, and if I could somehow record what they were playing. Then the music stopped, and I started to hear voices, all of which seemed to be talking at once. I didn't understand what they were saying—it sounded like Irish, but more fluid than anything Gran had taught me. More than once, I heard the phrase 'Máistir an Chroí,' always said in a tone of amazement.

"Fergus?" I murmured, suddenly uncomfortable, tightening my grip on Mirage's harness. "Are they talking about me?" He took my arm and stopped me without saying anything, and I nearly jumped out of my skin when he leaned in and blew in my ear. "Fergus!"

He chuckled and said, "Not what you think. Listen."

I frowned, listening, then blinked in surprise. I could understand them! "Universal translator?" I asked.

"It is a translation spell, yes. It needs a focus, which is why I did that. That, and the look on your face."

I scowled at him, "You have pooka blood, don't you?" He laughed outright, and tugged me into motion again. Now that I could understand the voices around me, I could tell that they were talking about me, the dark-haired mortal mage with the familiar. And I kept hearing them say something about the Hearth's Master, and about the High Wizard. I wondered if that was who we were going to talk to about getting help, then kicked myself mentally when the songster in my brain started up with the *Wizard of Oz* lyrics.

"Ready to meet the Steward?" Fergus asked.

"Is he going to give me a brain?" I asked in response, unable to help myself. Unfortunately, or maybe fortunately, Fergus didn't get the reference. I shut up and let him lead me into a place that echoed wildly. It was disorienting, and I hesitated for a moment, trying to get my bearings.

"My lord Steward," Fergus said, his voice booming out. "I bring an ally."

"We see that, Gatekeeper. Welcome to the Court, High Wizard."

For a moment, I thought that he meant Fergus, and I started to turn and ask him why he hadn't told me. Then he nudged me, and I realized just who the Steward meant. "High Wizard?" I repeated. "You... you mean me?" Vocal training kicks in at weird moments, and I think they heard me in every corner of that room. There was bright laughter, from all around us, and I felt my face grow warm. I turned towards Fergus and demanded, "You knew about this? Why the hell didn't you tell me?"

"You were not ready to know the extent of your powers," Fergus answered. "Given your fears, I thought that it would be for the best to bring you gently to your potential. If this had not happened, and if I had not damaged our relationship so badly, then I would have trained you gradually, and found another teacher when you surpassed me. But now... you must know the truth, and all of it, if we are to find and save your Nicolai. I will explain more once we have finished here. Now, speak to the Steward. And do not bow, Steven. The High Wizard bows to no one, Si or mortal."

I nodded, swallowing hard and urging Mirage forward. "I... thank you, my lord Steward. I... I need your help."

"The High Wizard has only recently come into his powers," Fergus said from behind me. "Someone is hunting him, and attacked him and his lover tonight. Whoever it was took the Wizard's lover captive. However, the Wizard killed one of the attackers." I heard a dull thud, and someone screamed. I covered my face with my hand and sighed.

"Fergus, did you drop the body in the middle of the floor?" I asked.

"Yes."

"Subtle. Really subtle," I snapped. "I... apologize, my lord. But he's right. This guy and others attacked me and... and Nick. They took Nick, and I need to find him. So I need your help."

"Fergus, do you know what it is you've brought here?" the Steward asked.

"One of the Uaigneach, yes."

"The what?" I asked. The spell that Fergus had put on me translated the word as "lonely," which didn't make any sense to me.

"They are outcasts among our society," Fergus said. "Why they are outcast is not terribly important. Why they are hunting you..."

"Is probably unimportant as well," the Steward interrupted. "You were probably a convenient target, High Wizard."

"What?" I snapped. "Once, maybe. These guys have tried killing me three times!"

"An attractive target, then," the Steward said, so dismissively that I wanted to scream. We weren't going to be getting any help here, and his next words confirmed it. "If you wish to hunt them, the *Uaigneach* live—if you can call it that—in the forests north of the Palace. You may be able to raise a hunting party amongst the younger nobles."

"A hunting party," I repeated. "These... things have been hunting me for almost a year. They've tried to kill me, they've stolen Nick, and... and you are just blowing me off?"

"They are no threat, High Wizard. They have no society, no rules, no laws. They reject law and order, and there are none among them who can be said to lead. They war with each other, they occasionally prey on mortals, when they can pass through the veils between our world and yours. They are a nuisance, nothing more." He sniffed, as if that would end the discussion. "Your presence honors us, High Wizard," he continued, and I could tell that he was lying. He wasn't honored. He was annoyed. But he was also afraid I'd squash him. "On the morrow, if you so desire, you can take a hunting party into the forests and see if you can find your mortal. I will warn you, though: mortals taken into the forests rarely last long enough to be rescued."

Conversations started up again, all around me, and I could tell I'd been dismissed. Furious, I stepped forward and opened my mouth; I have no idea what I was going to say, because that was the moment when Fergus grabbed me and hissed in my ear, "No! Let it be, Steven. If you anger him, there will be no hope. I will try to convince him. Come with me, and I will explain."

There didn't seem to be many choices, so I let Fergus take the lead, and we headed off... somewhere. There were too many twists and turns for me to keep track of, and when we finally stopped, Fergus let go of my arm.

"They've given us a suite of rooms, Steven. We can talk now."

Talk? Yeah, right. "He blew us off!" I yelled. "You said we'd get help here, and he fucking blew us off!"

"I know what I said. It has been some time since I last saw Barra—that's the Steward's name. He's gone... I don't know. He used to be more open. Now... I will talk to him. Convince him of the threat..."

"He won't believe you," I said over my shoulder. Mirage had pulled me forward, and I discovered a couch. I sat down and groaned as my back came in contact with the cushions.

"I will try, Steven. Do you want me to heal the wounds on your back?"

I thought about it, hesitated, then nodded. If we were going to fight, I needed to be in full form, not distracted by the aching welts. "Please. Then... let's go back. I can find the car, I think. We can search from there..." I fumbled at the buttons as I spoke, stopping when Fergus touched my shoulder.

"No, you do not need to take your shirt off. But you should lie down. Come, there must be a bed in here somewhere." He took me by the hand and tugged me to my feet. "Now, if the Uaigneach have taken Nick, he is here somewhere. He is no longer in your world, Steven, he is in mine. If we go back, we may lose any chance of finding him."

"If you say so," I said. I was suddenly tired, and I realized that, by this time, I'd probably been awake a full twenty-four hours. I needed some sleep. "Lying down will be good right now. Just let me see to Mirage." In response to her name, Mirage came and pressed herself up against my legs; when I leaned over her to unfasten her harness, she licked my face and whined. I rubbed her ears and sighed. "I know, baby. This is usually Nick's job. We'll find him. You and me, if it comes right down to it. We'll find him."

"Am I counted in that?" Fergus asked. "I promised you my help."

"Will it get you in trouble with the court?" I asked, setting the harness on the couch. "Can we get a bowl of water and maybe some meat scraps for Mirage?"

"I'll send for it. And something for you to eat as well. Thintreach leachtacha may cure many ills, but it is no substitute for a meal."

I frowned, the words filtering through my exhaustion and the translation spell. Then I giggled. "It really is called liquid lightning?" I asked.

"It is. It is a restorative. Come now, you will sleep, then you will eat." He took my arm and led me through the suite, settling me down onto a huge bed. I felt the mattress shift as Mirage jumped up and lay down next to me, then again as Fergus sat down and rested his hand on my back.

"Fergus, what's this whole High Wizard thing?" I asked, tasting his magic and knowing that he'd started putting my back to rights. Already, the pain was fading. "Can you talk and work at the same time?"

"Yes, I can," Fergus answered. "The High Wizard... there is only ever one at the time. The last one died of age... I think it would be just over a year ago on the mortal realms. That person is the most powerful mage, and is recognized as the master of all other mages. You rule the magic world, Steven. In both the mortal realms and the Si."

"I didn't wake up this morning expecting to be king, you know," I murmured. "And... what was the other thing they called me? Hearth's Master?"

He chuckled. "Not hearth. Heart. The Chroi is the heart of all magic. It is from the Chroi that magic flows, very much as a river would flow, growing more dilute as they flow. Mages tap into those power flows..."

"The ley lines?" I interrupted, showing that I remembered at least a little of what I'd learned from Nick.

"Yes. The closer to the Chroi, the more potent the magic, and the more powerful a mage must be in order to access the power. There is only one mage who can tap directly into the Chroi."

"And... that would be me?"

"Yes, Steven," Fergus answered. "That is you. I knew from the moment I saw you who and what you were. That is why I offered to teach you. How is your back?"

I shifted, nodding when I found the pain was gone. "Thanks. Fergus, I'm..."

"It is still healing, under the skin. Be gentle with yourself, as much as you can," Fergus said. "Now... do not apologize to me,

Steven. I am the one who is sorry. I overstepped my bounds, and I damaged your trust in me. What was it that you did not tell me? You mentioned it, when you left that last time. That you would not be a victim again?"

I nodded, rolling over onto my back. "Fergus, a little over a year ago, I was raped."

"Oh, Danu... I'd no idea." He let out a long breath, and I felt his hand on my arm. "And when I pushed..."

"You set off an emotional avalanche that I'm still working on getting through."

"Tell me, the one who did it. Did he pay?"

"You could say that. You know who it was, Fergus."

"The one who attacked you? The one you killed?" Fergus asked. I nodded, and he made a small, satisfied noise. "Good. He deserved it."

"Maybe." I ran my fingers through my hair and yawned. "Fergus, I asked Nick to marry me."

"Well! And he agreed?"

I shook my head. "He never had a chance to answer. That was when we were jumped." I swallowed around a lump in my throat. "Fergus..."

Fergus patted my arm. "We will find him, Steven. I promise you that. Now, sleep."

Best idea I'd heard all day.

Interstitial

In the Hall of the Mountain King

Cold. It was cold. His hair was in his face, and the floor was hard. He couldn't imagine Steven putting him on the floor. Not the way Trevor had. So why was he sleeping on the floor? Then he remembered the car. The attack. Falling to the ground, bound by his clothes and Steven's belt, unable to fight or flee. Seeing Steven trying to get to him, only to be taken down by one of the... they weren't Si, not like Fergus was. But they were not human either. Then, they had grabbed him, and the world had fallen apart.

Now... where was he? Nick opened his eyes, and immediately focused on the manacles on his wrists, and the thin chain that stretched between them. He jerked, hearing chain jingling as he moved, and felt a weight around his neck. A collar, and another chain, this one attached to a ring set into the floor. There were manacles and chains on his ankles, too. Nick swallowed and closed his eyes, then opened them again and tried to think. Where was he?

Answer: large room. Ornate room, with a dais and a gaudy chair that could probably be called a throne. So, throne room. Whose throne room? And what was he doing here?

Prisoner. That was the easy answer. But, prisoners aren't usually chained to the throne. Nick blinked again and looked down at himself, finally seeing how he was dressed. Or, not dressed. The only thing that he was wearing was a chain around his hips, from which hung an almost transparent loincloth.

Not a prisoner, then. A slave. Nick revised his assumptions and tried not to burst into hysterical laughter. Tried and failed, and he ended up sitting down with his face in his hands, trying to muffle his near-hysterical giggling. This was easily as bad as any of the horrible fantasy movies Maureen had enjoyed making light of over cheap wine and popcorn. All he needed now was the iron-thewed barbarian and the dark...

"Do I amuse you?" a silky voice came from the shadows. Nick

stopped laughing and turned towards the voice. Dark wizard, right on cue. Nick stared as the man came into view, shocked speechless by the sheer beauty of the man. He smiled down at Nick, arching an eyebrow. "Well?"

Nick stammered and found his voice. "I... have seen this movie. This is where you tell me that I am your helpless slave, yes?"

The man laughed. "So we can dispense with the trivialities. Good. You know your role. You know mine. What else is there to say?"

Nick realized with a jolt that the man was speaking without an accent. "You... you're Ukrainian."

"I am from that part of the world, yes," the man answered, smiling. He climbed the dais and sat down on the throne, reaching down and picking up the chain, tugging on it roughly. "Come here, my pet. Let me look at you."

There was a shuffling sound from the shadows, coming closer. Nick turned, and gasped, backing instinctively away from the approaching group of what appeared to be various kinds of monsters.

"My people," the dark wizard crooned. "My clan. My army. You'll see more of them, once this is over with, my pet. Come closer."

For a moment, Nick thought about resisting. Then he swallowed and bowed his head. If he cooperated, he could win time for... someone to find him. His mind rebelled against the thought that Steven had been left behind in the middle of nowhere alongside the highway, without access to help. That he might already be dead. No, he had to believe that somehow, someone was coming. And he needed to give them time; slowly, he started to get to his feet, then gasped as the chain jerked hard against his neck, pulling him back down to his knees.

"I did not give you leave to rise, pet," the wizard warned. Nick nodded and crawled slowly towards the throne, only to feel a hand in his hair, feeling far too much like Trevor; Nick gasped and pulled away, throwing himself off-balance and tumbling down the dais steps, ending up sprawled and strangling at the bottom, clutching at the collar chain. The wizard held it taut in his hand, slowly picking up the slack as he came down the stairs to stand over Nick. "Don't touch me!" Nick snapped, tugging hard at the chain. The wizard just laughed and held one hand over Nick's body; without warning, Nick found himself unable to move.

"Leave us. I wish not to be disturbed," the wizard called out. Nick heard grumbling and movement, fading away into the distance. Then the room was empty, echoing as the wizard paced a wide circle around Nick. "Foolish little pet," he murmured. "You're mine now. I chose you. I *saved* you, when the others would have slain you along with the Heart's Master."

"Heart's Master?" Nick asked. The wizard turned and looked down at him, surprised amusement on his face.

"You don't even know, do you? You have no idea what he was, your lover. What he could have been, had I let him live. No matter now. Now, you're mine. And you will learn your place." He gestured again, and Nick yelped as it felt as if every pleasure center on his body had all been stimulated, all at once. It went on for several minutes, leaving him shaking, desperate for more and hating himself for it, his erection very visible through the sheer loincloth.

"You do not know what he was," the wizard continued. "Do you know what I am?"

Nick shook his head. "No."

"You should. You're of the blood, you should have been warned. My name is Vikentiy, and I am *Perelesnyk*." He smiled, cocking his head to one side. "Interesting. You do not even know what that is. Your education is sorely lacking, pet. Perhaps you know of my kind by our other name?" He went to one knee next to Nick, running one finger down Nick's chest, leaving him gasping and moaning. "That name is incubus. You will learn to enjoy being my pet." He froze, and his eyes narrowed. "I gave instruction not to be disturbed."

"Mercy, my lord. But the Heart's Master lives. He is in the Elvenlands."

Vikentiy rose in one fluid motion, turning on the servant crouching just out of reach. "What?" he roared.

"He was seen, my lord, by your men at the Court. He and the gatekeeper have gone to the Steward."

Vikentiy scowled, then shook his head. "It is time, then. Contact my puppets in the Court and have them rise up. Bring the Court down, and destroy the mortal mage with it. Make ready the troops, and we will march."

"Yes, my lord." The servant scuttled away, and Vikentiy turned back to Nick, a cruel smile on his face.

"So. Your mortal lover lives. I am impressed. He'll be formidable, assuming he lives so long. But he will not. My men will destroy him..."

"That's what you said last time," Nick snapped. Vikentiy laughed.

"Oh the bravado is quite charming, little mortal. No, he will die. If my men at the palace fail, then he will come here for you." He knelt again, reaching out to toy with Nick's hair. "And I'm of a mind to give you to him. For a little while, at least." He tugged hard on Nick's hair, making him whimper. "Yes, that is very promising. You'll do nicely, my pet, as the bait in my trap. Very nicely indeed."

Chapter Ten
At the Mirk and Midnight Hout

"Steven!"

I sat bolt upright in bed, feeling the bed shake as Mirage jumped off, barking furiously. What the hell? Why was Fergus screaming?

Then I heard it, the sound of metal crashing on metal. I'd spent too many years doing stage combat, followed by a stint as a performer and stunt fighter at a renaissance faire: there was no way for me not to know that noise. Sword-fighting. We were under attack. I heard Mirage barking and snarling, and scrambled off the bed and towards the sound without another moment's thought. I damn near ran into the half-open door, then stopped. It was all a blur of sound. A coppery tasting blur of sound. I had no idea how many there were, even though I had a pretty good idea who was doing the attacking. The *Uaigneach*. Looking for me, I figured.

"Fergus!" I shouted, "How many?"

I heard another clash of metal, then Fergus shouted back, "Too many! Get back inside! Bar the door!"

"Like hell!" I snapped. I stepped back, but only to give myself a bit of cover and some room. Then I closed my eyes and flooded the other room with magic. What I was thinking, and what, to my amazement, actually happened, was that by filling the room with my own magic, I'd surround everything else, and get an accurate picture of how many people were out there. It wasn't as accurate as I'd have wished, but I knew where every single one of the *Uaigneach* were in that room. And that Fergus was already wounded. And failing fast. I growled, grabbed as many threads of coppery magic as I could, and *pulled*.

And half of the *Uaigneach* vanished completely. There were still some out there, but not as many. Seven. Maybe eight. It was hard to tell, since they were moving. I stepped forward, out of the bedroom, prepared to find the rest of them and do to them what I'd done to their friends.

That was the point where I heard Fergus cry out in pain, and the point where I tripped on something and ended up sprawled out on the floor. The something turned out to be a sword, probably dropped when I made the other fighters go *poof*. I picked it up as I got to my feet, and that turned out to be exactly the wrong thing to do. Now that I was physically armed, I was a target; I felt one of the *Uaigneach* break off from the others and rush towards me. I backed away and found myself with my back against the wall. Nowhere to go, and I had no idea how he was attacking... until I realized that I did know! The magic surrounding him showed me his movements, and if I concentrated on him alone, I could see. Sort of. It was like watching a moving silhouette. I couldn't "see" his sword, but I could track his sword arm; his arm started to come down, and my stage training took over. I parried the blow, feeling the impact rattling my teeth. Thank God for sadistic sword-masters who insisted on full-speed, full-impact drills—I didn't drop the sword, and I was able to get a good swing off in return. I felt the sword bite, heard him yell, then tugged back hard and heard a solid thump as my opponent hit the floor. No time to think, no time to react. Who's next?

Turns out, there was no one else next. The outer doors crashed open, and I heard shouting and more fighting. I thought for a moment that it was another attack force, but when I focused on my magic that was still filling the room, I could taste all the different threads, and none of them were copper. The cavalry had arrived. I stayed on guard until the last coppery tang blinked out, then cursed myself for not thinking to have them keep at least one for questioning. Then I lowered the sword, suddenly feeling as if my arm were made of lead. Mirage whined at me and pressed up against my leg, and I went down to my knees and hugged her.

"You all right, baby?" I murmured, running my hands over her fur. I could smell blood, and I wasn't sure if any of it was hers. "Let's not report this to your trainer, okay? I don't want to lose you." She licked my face, and I grinned and ruffled her ears, then stood up. "Fergus?" I called. "Fergus, are you all right?"

"High Wizard?" I didn't know the voice, but the magic tasted right. I turned, keeping my sword ready. "High Wizard, are you unhurt?"

"I think so. Where's Fergus?" The hesitation told me all I needed to know. I closed my eyes and felt the chill run down my back, realizing that the taste of pure water was gone from the room. "He's dead, isn't he?"

"I'm sorry, High Wizard."

I nodded, took a long breath, then stood up straighter. "Where's the Steward?"

"High Wizard..."

I didn't let him finish, pulling all of my magic in fast enough that I swore I heard a snap, then wrapping him in a hand made of pure power, picking him up off the floor. "Where is the fucking Steward?" I repeated. I'd never been this angry before.

"Put him down!" I recognized Barra's voice, and I let the other man go.

"This is your fault!" I snarled. "If you hadn't blown us off, if you'd taken the threat seriously, none of this would have happened!"

"I know," he answered, and I could hear the sadness in his voice. "I know, High Wizard. And I regret it. Fergus was a friend. I have many other friends who will go to the fires tonight. The entire Palace was overrun. There are few who were not injured. For centuries, we have regarded the *Uaigneach* as an annoyance, an amusing distraction. No one ever believed that they could be anything more. I should have seen the attack on you, in your world, as a sign that something had changed. Something has been changing, and for far longer than any of us would have believed. They had agents inside the Court, men whom I have known for years, and who I would never had suspected of being traitors. You are correct, High Wizard. This was my fault."

"This was an inside job?" I asked, then shook my head. "All right. Now you believe me. Now what do we do?"

"I need to find if there are other traitors amongst my Court..."

"I can do that. If you bring them all into that big hall where you met me and..." I stopped and bit my lip. Damn it. Losing Fergus hurt far more than I thought it would. "Where we met before. They all have a tell-tale magic thread, some kind of influence from whoever is behind this. I'll find them. What else?"

"Healing, High Wizard. There are few who escaped unscathed."

"Right. And then?"

"Then... we must assemble our forces. I will find someone to work with you in planning the assault. Now, I must see the healers myself."

His final words pushed me past the mind-blowing idea of me planning an assault on anything. "You're hurt?"

"Not badly, High Wizard," he said, and I could tell he wasn't telling the whole truth. "Not as badly as some. I will send someone to see to Fergus, and to set your rooms to right. And I will send someone who will work with you. By your leave."

"Yeah, sure. Go get patched up. Don't... don't worry about me." Something was nagging at me. Something I'd said, or he'd said. Something important. I managed to find my way to the couch, and I sat there, my sword next to me and my knees pulled to my chest, thinking. I was like that for quite some time, and my stomach was growling furiously when I finally stretched out and ran my fingers through my hair.

"I'm missing something, baby-girl," I muttered. "I'm missing something important. I just can't tell what it is!"

"Perhaps it is something that another person could help with?" a strange voice asked. I jumped, pulling up shields and grabbing the sword. He gasped, then laughed. "High Wizard, I apologize. I didn't mean to startle you. I am Liam. The Steward sent me."

"Oh. Oh, okay. Sorry. I... I was thinking. And I didn't hear you come in."

"Considering that you no longer have a door, I'm not surprised," he said, sounding amused. "How is it you didn't see me come in? You were staring right at the door."

I blinked, surprised. "You didn't know I was blind?"

"You are? And yet... you fought. I heard from my men that you acquitted yourself well for a mage. Most who wield a great deal of power do not favor weapons. They prefer to use magic."

"Well, I was. Sort of," I said, and explained to him what I'd done, and where I'd learned to fight. By the time I was done, he was sitting next to me on the couch, and I could feel the disbelief rolling off of him.

"You learned to fight... as a player? A... a minstrel of sorts?" he asked. "Oh, I can see that I will have to work with you. We can refine that spell, I think. And I will make sure that you won't kill yourself of any of your men should you be called on to take up a blade again."

"I didn't do that badly," I protested.

"Against one, no. But would you have been able to fight two, or three? And cast spells while you did?" he asked. I shook my head, and he snorted. "When I am done with you, High Wizard, you will be able to do that and more."

"If you say so," I said. "You said your name was Liam?"

"Yes. Sir Liam mac Fhergusa, *Ridire airgid an Rí Ard-thar na Farraige*. I am the Knight-Commander of the Steward's Guard."

"Silver Knight of the High King over the sea," I repeated. "That's... impressive." Then I really heard his name, and my jaw dropped. "Mac Fhergusa? Oh..."

"Fergus was my father," Liam said quietly.

I was completely floored. "Oh. Oh, God, Liam. I'm... I'm so sorry." I got up and turned to face him. "And the Steward wants you to work with me? Damn. If... if you want to bow out, Liam, I'll understand."

"Bow out? You mean, turn my back on my responsibilities?" he sounded insulted, and I shook my head.

"No! No, I mean... I got your father killed. If I was in your place, I'd hate my guts right now."

"My father died defending the Court and defending the High Wizard. There is no shame in that. And you did what you could to try and save his life, as ill-trained and inexperienced as you are. Again, there is no shame to be found. I asked for this duty, High Wizard..."

I grimaced, stung at his description of me. Ill-trained and inexperienced? True, but did he have to say it? "Steven. My name is Steven," I told him.

"Steven," he repeated. "Steven, I asked to be able to serve you, to assist you in finding whoever is behind this..."

My jaw dropped. That was it! That was what I was missing!

"Steven, what is it?" Liam asked, sounding concerned.

"You nailed it. Liam, you nailed it! That was what was bothering me! Every single one of the attackers had the same taste. The same *magic!*"

"You taste magic?"

"Don't distract me, Liam," I muttered. "They can't all have had the same magic signature, not unless they were all under some one, some single person's control. So, if they had the same magic signature, then... there's one person behind this whole mess. One person ordering the *Uaigneach* around. The Steward said that they don't have any leaders. I think he's wrong. I think someone's managed to figure out how to herd the cats."

Liam was silent for a moment, then grunted. "Your logic is sound. There must be a leader. Which means that, in all likelihood, there is an army out there in the forest. I must speak to the Steward. This will change many things, I think. I'll be back, Steven, and we will begin your training when I return. You should eat something."

Since my stomach took that moment to remind me that I hadn't eaten in what felt like days, I wasn't going to argue. "All right. Should I get anything for you?"

"No, thank you. But you can explain one thing when I get back."

I nodded. "Sure. What?"

"What do cats have to do with this?"

I was still giggling when he gave up waiting for an answer and left.

It took me twenty minutes to find the bell-pull, so I was still eating when Liam came back. I heard him coming this time, and grinned as he came closer.

"Come and sit," I said. "They brought enough to feed the army, and I'm never going to finish this...whatever it is."

I heard the chair scrape across the floor, and Liam sighed as he sat down. "There are scouts heading into the forest now. We will, I hope, have news by sunset. Or by dawn tomorrow at the latest. Tell me, are you a bard?"

I blinked, surprised by the change in subject. "Yeah. Fergus said I was. He said he was going to have to find someone to train me. Why?"

"Because I was remembering something that he told me," Liam answered. "About a young half-blood bard, and how he'd made a grave error..."

I waved him silent and said, "We buried that hatchet, Liam. I mean, I forgave him. He knew that."

"Will you tell me what happened?" Liam asked. "He did not, although he did get very, very drunk over it."

That surprised me. "He did? Really? Wow. He... ah... he made a pass at me. An aggressive pass. Wouldn't take no for an answer."

I could hear Liam trying to make sense of what I'd said. Then I heard him hiss, and he asked, "He tried to force himself on you?"

"He kissed me. That's as far as it went. I... kinda knocked him out."

Liam let out a long breath. "That damned old fool. Always with his half-bloods. I swear, the man seemed to have a sense for them..."

I burst out giggling. "You mean I was a fetish?"

"Fetish?" he repeated. "That... I don't think you mean what I think of when I hear the word. A religious item?"

"No. Ah..." I thought about it, trying to define the word. "Something that shouldn't have a sexual meaning, but does."

"Oh. I see. You mean like old Mad Muirenn and her horses..."

"More information than I needed!" I interrupted, laughing. He laughed with me, and for a moment, it felt good. Like none of this had happened, like I wasn't sitting at a table in a palace in the Elvenlands, with the Si who was going to help me save Nick. Then it all came crashing back. I was sitting at a table, in the Elvenlands, with the son of the man who had died to protect me, and who was going to be helping me plan an assault on something I'd never seen.

"You realize I have no idea what I'm doing?" I asked.

"You mean with the assault?"

"With the assault, with magic, with... pretty much all of it," I said, pushing my plate away. "Liam, I'm an actor. I was a dancer. I can handle a sword, somewhat. And... that's about it. I don't know what I'm doing!"

"And yet, so far you do well," Liam said gently.

I shook my head. "You don't get it. You said it before. I've got no training. I've got no experience. I'm a Prentice-Mage, and not even a very good one. They won't even swear me into the coven, I'm that backwards!" I dragged my fingers through my hair and tugged hard enough on it to make my scalp ache. "I don't know what I'm doing. I'll get someone else killed —"

"Who has had the training of you, Steven?" Liam interrupted.

"I... Nick. My lover. And then Fergus. And then... no one," I answered. "I'm... I'm a magical idiot."

"Is that so? And how did you track the man fighting you? How did you lift my man off the floor? You had some impressive battle shields when I startled you. How did you do that?" My mouth opened and closed a couple of times, but nothing came out, and he continued without even acknowledging me. "It seems to me that both your teachers have neglected to teach you the most basic magical fundamental." He stopped, and I could tell he was waiting for me to ask.

So, I asked, "All right, Liam. I'll bite. What did I miss?"

He chuckled softly. "Steven, there is one thing that controls magic, that makes it do whatever you wish it to do. And that is your will. If your will is strong enough, you can make the magic do anything at all. It is what you have been doing. You don't need lessons, Steven, you need confidence."

"I... really?" I clenched my hands in front of me on the table. "Fergus told me once that I needed to not use mortal techniques. That when I did, it was like I was laying bricks. He said I needed to use my instincts."

Liam sighed. "Trust the old fool not to come out and actually say what needs to be said. You must learn to trust yourself and your magic, Steven. You are the one in control. You did quite well during that attack. Do you remember that I said I want to refine the spell you used?"

"Yeah. I thought you meant I didn't do it right?"

"Hardly!" he said with a snort. "Steven, you did something I'd never seen done before. I want to help you refine it, in part so I can learn what you did and how to do it. And how to block it, if I can. Perhaps refining is not the best word. Perhaps honing is a better choice. Honing the way one might hone a fine blade."

I rubbed my hands together and flexed my fingers. "I'm a blade, hmm?" I asked. "And... all it takes is will? Well, everyone always said I had a hard head." Saying that reminded me of just who I was talking to, and I cocked my head to one side and said, "You know, I still don't understand why you don't hate my guts."

"Why, because of Fergus?" Liam asked. When I nodded, he was silent for a moment, then asked, "Steven, how old are you?"

"Me? Twenty-eight. Why?"

He chuckled. "I understand now. You're so young! I hadn't realized. Among us, you'd barely be out of the nursery."

I laughed. "Really? How old are you?"

"Oh, in your years? Ah..." he was quiet, and I let him think. Eventually, he answered, "When I was born, the Shining Queen still reigned. I came over the seas with Father, back when they laid the rails in your part of the world. I was a man grown, then. But young, looking for adventure. No more than a pair of centuries behind me."

"The Shining Queen? In my world? You mean Queen Elizabeth?" I asked, incredulous. "That makes you... four hundred years old?"

"Perhaps," Liam answered. "I'm not as fluent in your time periods as Father was."

"And how old was he?"

Liam laughed softly. "He used to tell me tales of when he was a child, before Cothraige was a slave in Eire, and the Si and the mortals walked amongst each other. It must have been grand. Then... it changed."

"Cothraige?" I frowned, thinking. The translation spell didn't work on the name, and I tried to figure out why a slave in Ireland would be so important... and then I remembered why a slave in Ireland was so important. "Patrick? You mean Saint Patrick?"

"Is that what you call him? Yes. The one who brought the belief in the carpenter to Eire, and closed people's minds to us."

I nodded. "So Fergus was almost two thousand years old. Wow. That's amazing. If you guys live so long, why don't you rule the world?"

"Because we don't breed the way you mortals do," Liam answered. "Children among the Si are rare and precious. It is why we once stole them from your people. But, do you understand now why I am not angry?"

"Not really, no."

Liam laughed again, "Because we have so much time. Attend. Among the Si, when we are young, we leave our parents' house when we are old enough, and we fly or fall on our own merit. Once we have made ourselves what we will be, then perhaps we return to our families, if they will have us. I do love my father, but I have been grown and my own man for so long that he has long since become my friend. The pain of losing him, it is not as... immediate, as it would be amongst those who live and die in an eye blink. Does your own father yet live?"

I wasn't expecting him to ask me that. "Ah... yeah. Last I heard."

"You are not close?"

"No. Can we leave it at that?" I got up and found my way to the couch, picking up and rattling Mirage's harness. She came over, and I started to strap her into it.

"If you wish," Liam answered. "Do you need help with that?"

"No, thanks," I said. "And just for the record, I'm jealous."

"What?"

"Your relationship with your father. You could be friends. Mine..." I shrugged.

"I thought you wanted to leave it."

"Sometimes my tongue has other ideas," I said. "My dad kicked me out because I loved a man. He couldn't approve of who or what I was, and he decided that meant he didn't have a son any more. I haven't spoken to him in seven years."

Liam was quiet, sitting down next to me on the couch. "And will you let him close you out of his life forever?"

I shrugged. "Doesn't seem like I have much say in it."

"You're a man grown among your people, Steven. So you always have a say. You always have a choice. A man does not allow his parents to make his choices for him," Liam said, his voice firm. He patted my leg and rose. "Now, we should begin our training. Bring your sword and come with me."

"Where are we going?" I asked, fumbling around under the couch until I found the sword I'd stashed there. It had seemed like the safest place for it.

"The armory. Then the training ring."

In the armory, Liam had me run through a series of exercises with the sword, then replaced the one I'd picked up during the fight with another one, this one lighter and more comfortable in my hand.

"This one feels good," I said.

"I thought it might," he answered. "The one you had was serviceable, but too heavy for your hand and your frame. We'll need to get you a sword-belt. And proper clothes. For now, what you have will do. Come with me."

I told Mirage to follow him, and he led us outside. I heard something click and squeak, followed by Liam saying, "Leave your familiar here. Will she attack, if you're threatened?"

"I don't know," I answered. "She's gone nuts the couple of times I really was in danger."

"Then perhaps she shouldn't be here?" Liam said slowly. I could understand why. Mirage had an awful lot of sharp teeth. I reached down and rubbed her ears.

"I'd like her to stay," I said slowly. "Can we try and see if there's a problem? I think she might understand the difference. She's pretty bright."

Liam hesitated, then grunted. "If you will. If she tears my throat out, you have to plan the assault on your own. Come here and show me what it was that you did."

"First, I need to know where we are," I told him.

"You are in the training ring."

I grinned. "That doesn't tell me anything, Liam. I know there's a fence of some kind. I heard you open the gate."

"Ah. I understand now," he said, taking my arm. He led me to the fence, a rough-timber thing that was about chest-high; I ran one hand over it as I walked slowly around the perimeter of the ring. "I apologize, Steven. I've never taught a blind man to fight before."

"That's all right. I've never learned to fight as a blind man before. I've never fought blind before this morning," I answered. "I learned all this before I lost my sight."

"Is that so? You did very well."

"Thanks. So, the ring is a perfect circle? What's the ground like? It feels like sand."

"It is sand. Are you ready?"

I nodded and let him lead me. "I think so."

"Good. Show me what you did when you fought this morning."

I took a deep breath and let my magic flow, wrapping around Liam and then around the people I'd hadn't even realized were there, watching us from outside the fence.

"Interesting," Liam said. "Now what?" He started pacing, moving around to my left, and I turned with him. He stopped abruptly, probably when he noticed I was tracking his movements.

"Now? I can... well, sort of see the disturbances in the magic when you move."

"Can you see my sword?"

I shook my head. "No. I have to... intuit that it's there."

"So if it were a mace, or a war hammer, you wouldn't know," Liam said. "That isn't good. The movements are similar if I were to attack with either of those, but the defense is different. There must be a way... how did my father teach you?"

"If he couldn't explain it, he went into my head and showed me. Why?" I asked.

"Because I must do something similar, I think. If you will allow me?"

"Anything if it will help me save Nick," I told him. He came around behind me and rested his hands on my shoulders. "Now, bring your magic back, and do it again. Let me see what you do."

I nodded and did as he told me, and as I let my magic flow out into the training circle, I tasted Liam's magic, sharp and tannic, like really strong tea. He nudged at my magic gently, showing me how he wanted me to mold it, what he wanted me to do. Then, without warning, there was a man in front of me; I stepped back, right into Liam.

"What is he carrying?" he asked me.

"I..." I stuttered for a moment, then frowned and shook my head. "I can't tell." Another surge of tannic tea, and the silhouette in front of me sharpened and shifted. But there was still no weapon "visible" to me, and I told Liam so. "I don't think magic can show me dead metal, Liam. I think what I'm seeing is my magic bouncing off their auras."

Liam stepped back, and the tea taste vanished. "I think perhaps you may be correct. I will have to think on this. Perhaps talk to other mages. You are... an anomaly, Steven."

"You said that already," I said with a sigh. "I'm weird because I can do magic and fight." I turned towards him and realized something. "But so can you! You're a mage."

"A very minor one, by any standards," he admitted. "I've never had the strength of gift to go further. Your magic is an inferno, mine is barely an ember. So I fight with physical weapons. But perhaps I can find someone among the elders, or something in the records. You're not the first High Wizard who was sightless, you know."

"I'm not?" I said, surprised. "No one said anything about another."

"I'm not surprised. It was quite a time ago. They still sing of him, though, and I've a friend who is a bard's son. He told me about the other. Mogh Roith, his name was. He was a great warrior, and a very powerful druid. There may be some in the court who knew him. I'll find out. Now, shall we see what you can do with that sword besides look decorative?"

We spent the rest of the afternoon sparring, honing what skills I had. Liam seemed less than impressed once he actually saw me going against another fighter. I think the kindest thing he said about my sword-master was that he was a flaming idiot. When I pointed out that stage-combat was more about looking good than actually winning a fight, I swear he called me, my teachers, and my sword everything but children of God.

He did show me some neat tricks, though. Like how to shield around my ankle to strengthen it, so that I didn't have to worry about the weak bones. And, of course, telling me that gave me the idea of shielding the rest of me against physical attack. My first attempt didn't work very well, leaving me in a magical, full-body cast, and leaving Liam unable to speak from laughter. Second attempt? Better but clunky, this one left me feeling the way I'd always thought that the Thing, the superhero in the comics, felt. When that didn't work, I asked Liam if I could have some real armor to play with, so that I could feel how it went together. He left me, coming back a little while later with something he called dragon scales. I knew what scale armor was, but this was different. I could feel hundreds of little scales under my fingers, overlapping to form a nice, tight barrier.

"How well does this hold up?" I asked.

"These suits are imbued with protective spells, so they'll stop almost anything," Liam answered. "We could simply have one made for you, Steven."

"That will take too long," I answered. "But I'd like that. I think I really need to know how to fight. So let me see if I can copy this."

That attempt worked, and I ended up wearing a full-body suit of flexible and damn near impenetrable armor shielding. Liam and I ran through another sparring run, and this time, I let him hit me; his blade scraped over my skin without leaving a mark, although the impact made me wince.

"That's the problem with armor," he said. "It will stop a cut, but not a blow. I could hit you with a war hammer and crush your ribs without piercing your shields."

I nodded, touching the sore spot on my arm. "So I noticed. Still, it's a start."

"It is, and I'll want you to show me how you did this. You should show the armorer, as well, so he can teach others." Liam clapped me on the shoulder. "Come, High Wizard. Let's get you cleaned up and properly dressed so you can be seen in polite company at dinner."

I had no idea what he was talking about. No idea what I was in for. First, I was met in my room by servants who were prepared to bathe me, something I refused to allow. They did, however, have to help me dress, and when I was finally pronounced ready, I felt like a refugee from an Elizabethan drama, minus the dinner-plate collar. Silk shirt and leggings. Boots to my knees, and a doublet that felt like real velvet. The only thing I ended up wearing that was actually mine was my chain, and only because I refused to remove it.

"Well, you clean up nicely," Liam said appreciatively when he came back for me. "Are you ready?"

"Ready for what?" I asked, taking Mirage's harness in one hand and letting Liam take my free arm. He led me through the halls, and I heard a lot of voices, both around us and off in the distance. "Where are we going?"

"Dinner," Liam answered.

"Liam, I thought we had an assault to plan? I figured we'd have a quiet dinner and work." Then we entered a room that echoed and reechoed with chattering voices and half-drowned out music. I stopped in my tracks. "Liam..." I murmured under my breath. "What the hell?"

"The Steward is attempting to make amends. Smile, Steven. I'll be at your elbow, if you need help." He stopped me, and I wondered why. Then, there was a hush, and I heard someone with a fantastic *basso profundo* voice announcing "The Heart's Master, High Wizard Steven Ahearn, his familiar Mirage, and Knight-Commander Sir Liam mac Fhergusa, *Ridire airgid an Rí Ard-thar na Farraige.*"

"How did he know my last name?" I whispered as we started walking again.

"I took a liberty, I'm afraid," Liam admitted. "The Steward asked me to find out, so while you were bathing, I looked in your case with all the cards with your name on them."

"You looked in my wallet? You could have just asked." I sat where Liam told me to sit, and felt Mirage lie down over my feet.

"The servants told me you'd objected to their presence, and I did not wish to make you uncomfortable," Liam answered from my right. "Why do you have all those little cards, anyway?"

I snickered. "It's complicated. The mortal world has a lot of different rules."

"It must. I think I prefer it here. It is far more simple," Liam said, sounding very convinced. "There's wine by your left hand."

"So says the man who lives in a place where the clothes have so many ruffles and flourishes that it takes three people to get you dressed," I muttered, picking up the goblet and taking a sip. Liam coughed, apparently smothering his laughter. I grinned and touched the edge of my plate. "All right. Tell me what I have and where it is on the plate."

"Right now, nothing," Liam answered, still sounding as if he were swallowing laughter. "The servers haven't come around yet."

"Okay, so you'll have to tell me." I leaned back in my chair. "Now, tell me about this party. I assume I'm front and center?"

"We're at high table, yes. You are at the Steward's left, in the place of honor. I am with you as a courtesy, because I told the Steward that you would probably not accept another guide at the table. Normally, if I were to attend a feast such as this, I would not be at high table. But I would normally not attend. Even as Knight-Commander, I don't have the rank to warrant an invitation."

"So who is here?" I asked. What followed was a litany of names and ranks that made absolutely no sense to me, but most of whom Liam seemed to know well. He had interesting gossip about each of them, some it really racy, and I wondered how he'd found out all of these things. Then I realized that all of the raciest things were about women. I leaned over towards him and whispered, "Old lovers?"

He coughed. "Am I that obvious?"

"You're a catty bitch, is what you are," I told him, making him laugh again.

"I'm not, really. It's just... a lot of the worst of those stories? Those are the ones who think they are so very daring for sleeping their way through the lower nobility and the servants. They promise the moon, and leave you in the midden."

"Slumming," I said, nodding. "Yeah, I know the type. Why do you bother?"

He hesitated, then sighed. "Because, according to Father, I'm a hopeless romantic. I was married once," he paused, and I could feel the pain in him.

"You don't have to tell me," I said quietly.

"It's been many years. Mairead died in a hunting accident. We had only been wed... oh, a half century or so. Still newlyweds, almost. Since then, I've had pairings, but no real lover. And those bitches... I believed them when they told me that they loved me."

"Ouch. Sorry," I murmured. Then I turned slightly towards him. "Want to make them jealous?"

"What are you thinking?"

"You strictly straight, Liam? Or do you play both sides of the street?" I leaned towards him as I spoke, a gesture that might have simply been so that he could hear me better in the noisy room. But combined with my running my fingers over the back of his hand, it wasn't likely to be taken that way. I felt Liam startle, then he laughed, and I felt him lean closer to me.

"I'm the catty bitch?" he murmured.

I smiled at him and answered, "I never said I wasn't."

"I don't prefer men. That's fairly well known, I'm afraid."

I nodded and leaned back, still smiling at him. "Ah, well. It was a thought."

"One that appears to have worked. I've turned down the favors of a most powerful mage... I've turned down the Heart's Master! You should see... oh."

I laughed. "Don't worry, Liam. What can I not see?"

"Lady Arania," he answered. "She's sitting directly across from us. She was watching the both of us the way a hawk watches a rabbit. I think she was going to proposition you. Then you turned to me, as if you were trying to seduce me. She looks as if she swallowed a lemon."

At that point, the servers started coming around, and Liam was occupied with telling me what we were eating and where it was on my plate. Or in my bowl. Or in my other bowl. After about fifteen minutes, I stopped him and whispered, "How much food is there?"

"We have another three or four courses."

"Oh, dear God," I groaned. "I'm gonna burst. How can you eat like this?"

He sounded confused when he answered. "Mages eat a lot.

They need it, to rebuild their energy reserves. Surely you've noticed that?"

I thought about it for a moment. "I hadn't, no. But now that you mention it, I have been eating more. Nick..." I stopped, suddenly horrified and damn near sick to my stomach. Here I was, dressed to the nines, sitting at a banquet in my honor, and I had no idea where Nick was. If he was even still alive. I felt Liam's hand on mine.

"We'll find him, Steven," he said softly. "We'll..."

There was a commotion in the hall, and Liam stopped talking, his hand on mine tensing. "Sir Liam!" I heard someone shouting. "One of the scouts has returned!"

I got to my feet, heard the chair clatter to the floor, and a similar sound next to me as Liam jumped up. "Where is he?" Liam shouted.

The answer was shouted back, and chilled me to the bone, "With the healers! Hurry! He's dying!"

We ran.

Chapter Eleven
Aspect and Attribute

I had no idea where we were going, so I held on tight to Mirage's harness and told her to follow Liam, pelting along after them and trying to avoid running into anything that would cause me damage.

"Where is he?" I heard Liam ask as Mirage slowed to a walk.

"Here, Liam. He's doing poorly. I don't expect him to wake," a woman answered, and I wondered at the quiver I heard in her voice.

"He has to wake," Liam snapped. "We have to know what he saw, what did this to him. Where the other scouts are. He has to report."

"Liam, there isn't anything I can do!" she protested. I urged Mirage forward, towards their voices.

"Is there something I can do?" I asked. Both of them went silent, as if they'd forgotten I was there, and I'd startled them.

"Are you a healer as well, High Wizard?" the woman asked.

"I don't know," I admitted. "But... can you show me what to do?"

"It might work, Siana," Liam said.

"Or it might kill him!" Siana snapped back.

"He's dying anyway! You said so!"

I held up my hand, which silenced the both of them. Nice trick. "Do we have a choice?" I asked.

Siana sighed and said, "No. Please, High Wizard. Come with me." She took my hand and led me into a room that smelled uncomfortable, like pain and sickness. I shivered slightly, and she stopped. "High Wizard?"

"I'm fine. Just... too much time in hospitals. Where is he?"

"Sit down," she told me, and guided me into a chair. There was a low bed at my knees, and I knew that the scout was lying there. I could feel his energy, his magic, slowly ebbing.

"What's his name?" I asked.

"Donal," Siana answered. "Now... touch him, and then do nothing. Let me do the work."

"All right," I said. I rested my hand on Donal, noticing how cold his skin was, how still he was lying there. Siana rested her hands on my shoulders; her magic tasted like warmed milk, soft and soothing, and she gathered what she needed from me with a gentle touch of someone who had done this before.

"Not a drop of healing," she murmured. "Not that you need it, High Wizard. I should be able to buy Donal a bit more time. And wake him. He'll be in great pain, though."

"Can we block that?" I asked.

"I can try," she said. I felt her magic flow through mine, pulling some of the energy along with it as it flowed out of me and into Donal. I felt his energy grow, and his pain, right before he groaned.

"Donal. Donal-lad," Liam whispered urgently. "Donal, what happened out there?"

The boy—and why I was suddenly thinking of a Si who was probably older than anyone I'd ever met as a boy was beyond me—groaned again, and I heard him muttering softly. "...army... army... in the forest... hundreds... more...

"Hundreds? Or more than hundreds?" Liam asked.

"... more... keep... center... center of forest...Vikentiy...."

"Donal, where are the others?" Liam wanted to know.

"...dead... all... all dead...Vikentiy... at... at the keep..." Donal's voice trailed off, and I felt his energy slowly fading away.

I'm not sure what made me do it, but it felt right. I reached with my left hand and rested it on his forehead, and I started to sing to him. The song was *John O'Dreams*, a song my mother used to sing to me, when I was sick or sad, or just too wound up to sleep. I remembered her singing it to me when I was five, and miserable with chicken-pox, and how much better it had made me feel. All that was in my mind was that I wanted this poor kid to live, to feel better. I wanted to make it better, the way Mom had done for me.

So I sang to him, and I felt my magic latch on to Siana's. She squeaked, more startled than alarmed, I think. "High Wizard!"

I couldn't stop to explain, and I heard Liam telling Siana to work with me, to do whatever she could. I felt her steady herself, and once she had control, I let her drive, focusing on the song. Under my hands, I could feel Donal's energy growing stronger as Siana did... whatever it was she was doing. Fixing things. Making it better.

"High Wizard, stop. Please. You've done it," she said in my ear as I finished the last verse. I heard her voice break as she caught her breath and repeated, "You've done it. He'll live."

I lifted my hand from Donal's forehead, feeling an almost audible snap as I severed the link between us and slumped back in my seat. I wasn't expecting Siana to hug me from behind, whispering, "Thank you," into my hair.

"Let him be, Siana," Liam said gently. "I think he needs to lie down."

"That would be good," I said. "Is there a place?"

"Of course. This way, High Wizard." She took my arm and helped me to stand, leading me over to what turned out to be another low bed. I lay down, and was only dimly aware of Siana kissing me on the cheek as I fell asleep.

I woke up to hear Liam, talking to someone whose voice I didn't recognize.

"A keep? How could there possibly be a keep in the forest? That close to the Court, and no one knew?" Liam was saying.

"They attacked inside the Court," the other person answered, and I realized that it must have been Donal talking. "Find out who was in league with whoever the leader is out there, and I'd wager you'd also find whoever was in charge of the patrols in that area."

I sat up slowly and rolled my neck, working out the stiffness.

"Liam? Who is Vikentiy?"

"Vikentiy is a who? I thought it a what, myself," Liam answered. "I don't know the word."

"It was the rallying cry of the forces that attacked us," Donal added. "I've never heard it before, but I was certain it was important."

"It's a name," I told them. "A Ukrainian name. Now, every name I've heard since I came here has been Celtic of some kind or other. Why Ukrainian?"

"High Wizard, are you certain that this Vikentiy is a person?" Liam asked. I nodded.

"Vikentiy was Nick's father's name. I'm sure."

"There is no connection, perhaps?" Donal asked. "His father is not a mage?"

"His father died years ago," I answered. "I don't know what connection there is. If there is. But I do know that Nick must be in that keep you both mentioned."

"It is minimally guarded," Donal said. "I thought perhaps we could infiltrate the walls, find more information. But we decided against fool-hardiness, and turned for home."

"And were caught?" Liam asked. "I taught you better."

"You did, Liam. We made mistakes. But with the forces gathering on the other side of the forest, how were we to know that there would be a patrol there?"

I heard a sharp slap, and Donal grunting. Liam snarled at him, "Idiot. Always assume there will be a patrol. That's how you live long enough to teach other young fools how not to get killed."

"Yes, sir," Donal answered, his voice small. "I'll remember."

"It's thanks to the High Wizard that you'll be alive to remember," Liam snapped. "To think that a son of mine..."

"He's your son?" I interrupted.

"Yes. I didn't say?"

"No," I said. "You didn't. No wonder I kept getting the feeling he's a kid."

With all the wounded dignity and righteous indignation of young people everywhere, who think they're so grown up even when they aren't, Donal blurted, "I am not a child!" Dear God, I needed that laugh.

✿

Liam and I walked back to my room, shoulder to shoulder, silent except for the sounds of Mirage's nails on the floor. I finally broke the silence, "So, what's the plan?"

"Plan?" he snorted. "We have a plan? Steven, there is an army amassing in the forest. Ready to march on the Court, from what Donal tells me. There is a keep where none should be, and an unknown enemy of undetermined strength, holding as hostage the lover of his strongest enemy," he answered. "At this point, I should be asking someone to pinch me. I'm having a nightmare."

I snorted. "Right. Shared nightmares. What do we do, Liam?"

He was silent, which I took to mean he was thinking. So I shut up and let him think, walking back into the my room, finding my way to the couch and shucking off my sword-belt and my doublet before I flopped bonelessly down and threw one arm over my eyes. I heard a thump that I interpreted as Liam sitting down hard on a chair or another couch. After several minutes, he cleared his throat and said, "My father gave you an elf-stone."

Surprised, I nodded, sitting up. "Yeah. I threw it back at him after..."

"I know. I have it. Do you want it back?" I heard him get up and come towards me, and felt the familiar stone as he tucked it into my hand. I closed my hand around it, feeling a pang as I thought of Fergus. Maybe I'd get a chance to avenge his death.

"Thank you," I said as I put the cord around my neck.

"It will help protect you," he said. "I'll be with you, during the assault, but if anything... that will help."

"I didn't know that," I said, thinking back to when Fergus had given it to me. "He didn't say anything about that."

"It doesn't hold the same power in your world as it does in ours. I don't think he expected to bring you to the Elvenlands so soon."

"Maybe. He offered. Liam, we're not planning," I pointed out.

"I am," he said. "I am thinking that if we put an attack force against that army, then perhaps a smaller force could raid that keep. I just wonder... High Wizard, is there anything you could do to protect my men?"

I leaned back against the couch cushions, toying with the stone around my neck and thinking. Protect the troops. I wonder if they even make magical Kevlar? "What would I be protecting them from?" I asked. "Remember, this is not my field of expertise. I don't know what the enemy can throw at us."

"True. I want them protected from magical attack. From physical attack..."

"Such as?" I interrupted. I had no idea what level of technology the Si had. Was I dealing with just the slings and arrows of some *really* outrageous fortunes? Or something more?

"Arrows, swords, spears... is this so different from the weaponry in your world?"

I nodded, "Yeah. We've got other things. Nasty ones, compared to what you have. And if there's a Si with an AK-47 out there, then I am well and truly frightened. Anything else?"

"Why don't we just say that I want them protected from anything else you can think of."

I nodded, thinking, and turning my stone over between my fingers. How do I do that? If I wasn't going to be with them, how could I...

"Liam?" I asked, sitting up. "Where can I get more stones like this?"

"How many stones do you need?" Liam asked.

"How many men do you have that I need to protect?"

An hour later, I was standing next to a table that was completely covered with small stones, very similar in feel to the one I wore around my neck. I skimmed my hand over them, just barely touching them, feeling an odd negativity to them. Nothing bad. More like an absence of anything.

"Are they supposed to feel like this?" I asked.

"Until you purpose them, yes," Liam answered. "The spell-stones draw your intent, your will, and amplify it. Any spell that you set into them is set for eternity. Not even the death of the caster will shatter the spell."

"That's comforting to know," I murmured. "All right, let me talk this out so I'm clear on what I'm doing. I'm going to set these things as protective spells. Protection against magical attacks, primarily. I don't want to make these into a crutch, and have your men come to rely on them, so protection against physical attacks will be minimal. Mostly camouflage. I'm going for a 'you can't see me, I'm not here' kind of thing. Until they actually engage."

"If someone is wearing a stone, will they be able to see anyone else with a stone?" Liam asked.

"Oh, good idea!" I grinned. "Yeah, it would be a bad thing if your men were all tripping over each other because they couldn't see who was in front of them. All right. Go over there and let me work." I flexed my fingers over the stones, trying not to fret over what I was about to do. A lot of lives were counting on me, and I was not going to fuck it up!

I growled and shook my head, trying to ignore the thoughts that raced around in the back of my brain, telling me that I could not do this. I could do it, and I would do it. So I rested my hands on the edge of the table, and I did it, pushing my magic through the stones, telling each and every one of them what they were going to do. That they were going to repel any kind of magic attack on their bearer. That when in battle, they were going to keep anyone who did not wear a brother stone from seeing their bearer until the bearer attacked. And I added that they would be bound to their bearer, useless in anyone else's hands, and would remain so for the bearer's lifetime. The stones drank in all that I had to give, keying themselves with my instructions, and then lay there, waiting to be paired with one of Liam's men.

I stepped away from the table and rubbed my hands together. "It's done," I said softly. "We can give them out now."

"Was that all?" Liam asked. "That barely took any time. Are you sure it worked?"

"Only one way to find out," I answered. "Let's hand them out."

I wasn't really all that familiar with military discipline, so the speed at which Liam's men assembled was a little surprising to me. We'd only just brought the box of stones to the training ring when I heard the sound of a lot of footsteps coming towards us. I turned, and heard Donal's voice. "Sir, Raven squadron reporting, Sir!"

"Donal? You can't be well enough to fight again!" I said.

"Siana has said I'm perfectly hale, High Wizard," he said, and I heard in his voice the challenge. He wanted a fight, and he didn't care who he fought. I didn't want it to be me, so I backed down.

"If Siana says you're well, then I can't argue," I answered. "Do you know what we're doing?"

"No, High Wizard," he said.

"Then get your men out of the way so that the others can get in place. We'll explain it to all of you at once," I told him, and turned away, urging Mirage over towards where I could hear Liam, giving a similar speech to someone else. In the end, there turned out to be ten squadrons, each one made up of fifty men and women. Each of them came to me, introduced themselves, and accepted a stone. And as each one took a stone, I felt something— almost an itch, if the inside of your brain can be said to itch. It was as if I'd been touched with a pin, very lightly. I didn't think much of it at the time, deciding that it was simply my magic passing into their hands. When finally all the stones had been passed out, Liam joined me, raising his voice so that everyone could hear him, "Does everyone have one? Good! Now, the High Wizard will tell you what to do with them."

I would? Oh, boy. Good thing I was decent at improv. I cleared my throat and drew myself up, feeling Mirage pressing up against my leg, a warm, soothing constant that helped keep me grounded. "The stones are keyed to each of you. You can't give them away, you can't trade them away. They won't work for anyone else but you. They will protect you from magical attack, and if the person you're fighting isn't wearing one, they won't be able to see you until you hit them. Wear them close to the skin, under your armor. Under your shirts, if you can. And if anyone has any questions, just talk to me later."

I was completely unprepared for the roar of approval from the squadrons. It washed over me, reminding me painfully of the standing ovation that last night at the theatre. I swallowed, then bowed my head slightly, more than a bit overwhelmed. Would any of them still be here to talk to me later? How many of these people were going out there to die?

None of them, if I had anything to say about it. I straightened and nodded, raising my voice slightly and projecting the way I'd been taught, "Good luck. To all of you. Come back safely."

"That sounds like an order, High Wizard," Liam said, his voice only slightly mocking. I turned slightly and decided I was going to take the bait.

"Consider it one," I answered. Then, I grinned and channeled a childhood hero, "Make it so."

They may not have gotten the joke, but they definitely appreciated the attitude. There was another roar of approval, and Liam clapped me on the shoulder. He had to lean in to my shoulder so that I could hear him over the cheers, "I'll get them sorted and ready to march. The Steward wishes to speak to you."

I nodded and waved in the direction of the loudest cheering, which only made it worse. Then Liam led me off, and I heard another voice, "High Wizard, I'm to take you to the Steward. My name is Oscar."

Oh, I had to bite my tongue. I managed to not tell him he sounded awfully friendly for a Grouch, but I'm not sure how. I let him take my free arm and lead me and Mirage back into the palace and through the halls.

"Where are we going?" I asked.

"The Great Hall. The Steward says that you offered to do something for him? The entire court is assembled there."

Now I remembered, and I nodded as we walked. "Oh, yes. Everyone is there?"

"Everyone except for the squadrons you just left," Oscar answered. I nodded again. There had been no coppery taint on any of the men or women who now wore the elf-stones. If there were any traitors left, they were all in the hall.

The Steward met us, and told Oscar to go into the hall. Once my escort was gone, Barra cleared his throat and hemmed and hawed for a moment, his discomfort filling the space between us.

"High Wizard, I—"

"It wasn't your fault, Barra," I said at the same moment. We both shut up, and I grinned and held my hand out. "Let's clean up your court, Steward."

"Thank you, High Wizard," he said softly. He took my hand, squeezed it, then led me into the hall. I heard a million little conversations, all of them at odds with the others, and all of them petering out as Barra and I walked the length of the hall. "Three steps," he murmured. I nodded and walked up onto a dais, letting Barra's hand fall as I turned to face the court.

I realized at that moment that to the assembled Si, I probably looked like something the cat had dragged in—rumpled, half-dressed, wearing only my slept-in shirt and leggings. I probably didn't look a damn thing like they expected the High Wizard to look. I'd have to show them otherwise. Years ago, I'd read a science fiction novel, a classic, about men who were somehow also Hindu Gods. I'd long since lost the details, but I did remember what they called it when they became their divine personas—they took on their Aspects. It was time for me to take on mine.

And if there was one thing that I'd learned in the theatre that I was learning was also true in magic, and that was that showmanship counts for a lot. I raised one hand, and heard every door in the room slam closed. The sound was followed by a rumble of disbelief and alarm; a woman screamed, the sound quickly muffled. I lowered my hand and raised my voice, "I mean no harm to most of you. By now, you all know of the attack on the court, of the attack on me. There are traitors in our midst, ladies and gentlemen, and I mean to flush them out."

Someone—someone braver than the rest of them—raised his voice, "The traitors are all dead! We destroyed them all!"

"If you're right," I called back, "Then I will apologize for the dramatics. If you are wrong..." I let my voice trail off. Anything they could possibly dream up would probably be much more impressive than anything I actually said, or that I'd have the stones and the stomach to do once I found any traitors in this hall. I spoke without turning towards the Steward, "Barra, is this everyone?"

"There are nine men unaccounted for, High Wizard," he answered, sounding unsure of himself. "We'd assumed they'd fled to... to the forests."

"Nine?" I repeated, thinking back to the attack in my rooms. Nine... that seemed about right. "You won't find them, Barra. They didn't run. They were part of the group that attacked me, and I dealt with them. I should have mentioned it."

"I... see," Barra murmured. I could tell he didn't, that he had no idea what I was talking about, and just didn't want to ask in front of everyone. I made a mental note to explain it to him later. If there was time.

"Ladies and gentlemen, please stay where you are," I said. When I didn't hear any objections or questions, I closed my eyes and let my magic flow out into the room. At first, having that many magical auras clashing against mine was more than a bit overwhelming. Something like trying to taste the entire box of jelly beans, all at once—you can't really taste anything at all. Then I caught the copper tang, and I figured out how to pick that one signature out of all the other. One by one, I located the people who had that taint, located them and tagged them until, at last, I had found myself with a full football team of traitors—nine men and two women. Satisfied that I hadn't missed anyone, I gathered the threads of my magic that surrounded the traitors and pulled, bringing each of them forward until they stood before the dais.

"Barra, these are your traitors. All of them have the taint of... what was his name?" I cocked my head to the side and smiled. "Oh, yes. Vikentiy." One of the men whimpered, and I nodded. "I know about him. And I'll be dealing with him next. Barra, these people are your problem. Unless you want me to deal with them?"

"No," Barra answered, very abruptly. Apparently, he had a fertile imagination. "No, thank you, High Wizard," he added, a little more calmly. "We will deal with them. If you will unseal the room?"

"Sure," I said, waving one hand. There was a near stampede as the court fled the hall, leaving me behind. I sighed and turned towards Barra. "I think I scared them."

"I know you did. You frightened me, High Wizard," Barra said. "Will you tell me what you did with the others? What you would do with these?"

I shrugged, tired and suddenly very, very lonely. I didn't want people to be afraid of me. I wanted Nick. It was time to go get him. "You don't have to worry about them anymore, Barra. I sent them to Never-Never Land. Now, if you'll excuse me, I have an appointment with this Vikentiy bastard. He's got someone that belongs to me." I took Mirage's harness and went down the stairs, letting her lead me towards the door. Somehow, I knew she'd lead me back out to the training ring, to where Liam would be waiting for me. From there...

"High Wizard, do you know where you're going?" Barra asked. Now he sounded concerned, worried about me. I stopped and turned around.

"Thank you, Barra," I said quietly. "I know where I'm going. Into that forest. I'm going to take that fortress apart until I find Nick. I need to get him back." I turned back and headed towards the door, hearing Barra's voice behind me.

"Good luck, High Wizard. And good hunting."

Silently, I thanked him again. I was pretty sure I was going to need that luck.

❖

I wasn't surprised when Liam found me before I found him. I figured that he might.

"Steven!" he called as he came towards me. "What are you doing here alone?"

"Not alone. I have Mirage," I answered. "She knows where we're going."

He snorted. "And that would be where, exactly?"

"To find you," I answered. "Are your men ready?"

"They're preparing now. What did you find, in the hall?" he asked, taking my off arm.

"Eleven people under Vikentiy's thumb," I told him. "Barra is going to deal with them. Where are we going?"

"My men are getting ready. Now it's time to get you ready. I've spoken to the armorer, and he says he has something that might fit you. But first we need to speak to Aodh."

"Who's Aodh?" I asked as we walked through the halls.

"The herald. You heard him at the feast."

I nodded. "Oh, him. The fantastic voice. Yeah. Why are we talking to him?"

"His mother was a bard, and he knows the lore," Liam answered. "He might have some help for us before we go into battle. I spoke to him, and he's eager to meet you."

"That sounds like a plan. I'm really playing this whole thing by ear. I don't have the foggiest idea what I'm doing," I said.

"That is not what I hear," I heard in that magnificent voice. "The word among the court is that the High Wizard is one who is not to be crossed. Anger him, and he will make you vanish as if you'd never existed. Cross him, and he will make you wish that you had vanished as if you had never existed. And his voice has the power to bring the dying back from the very brink. Good day, Liam."

"Hello, Aodh. Don't take too long—we're riding out soon and I still need to see him outfitted properly. When you're done with him, bring him to the armory, will you?" Liam squeezed my arm.

"Steven, I need to go back to my men and make sure they remember which end of their swords they're supposed to hold."

"Tell them the pointy end goes in the other guy," I quipped. Liam chuckled, patted my arm, and I heard his footsteps receding down the hall. Then I turned back to Aodh. "That's none of it true, you know."

"Oh, of course I know," he said with a laugh. "Come, I've got wine, and you look as if you need it." He took my arm and led me into a room, pushing me into a chair and putting a goblet into my hand. "Liam says you need information on what a bard can do?"

"Yeah. I don't know what I can do, other than..." I gestured vaguely. "Well, what I've been doing. Liam said your mother was a bard. Did she ever go into battle?"

"Once only, that I know of. We do not go to war often here," he answered, sounding a little embarrassed to admit it.

"Wish I could say the same about the other side of the curtain," I said. "What does a bard even do in battle?"

"From what she told me, she took her harp to the highest point, overlooking the battle, and she sang the heart into the army. What is your instrument, High Wizard? With what will you sing the heart into Liam's men?"

"I'm not singing the heart into anyone. I'm going in with them," I said. "My lover is in there, and I'm going to go and bring him out."

"You're going to fight, High Wizard?" Aodh sounded as if I'd just told him I was planning on sprouting a second head.

"Steven. Please, call me Steven. And, yeah. I know I'm an odd duck."

"A different sort of mage, I would say. And perhaps, the one that is needed. You haven't answered me. What is your instrument?" Aodh insisted. "A bard needs an instrument to take into battle, regardless of how they do battle."

I stopped as I was about to say I was a singer. He seemed to be taking that for granted. My instrument? "Drums. But I don't have one here."

"Is that all?" Aodh said. "What kind of voice?"

For a moment, I thought he meant mine. Then I realized he was talking about a drum's voice. "Deep. Like yours," I told him, and listened to him laugh.

"Of course. Just a moment, High... Steven," he told me, and left the room. I reached down and petted Mirage, told her she was a good girl, and came to another realization. I couldn't take her with me. Not into a fight. I'd get her killed.

"Try this one," Aodh said as he came back. I held my hand out, and took a surprisingly large bodhran from him. Tapping the skin with my fingertips let out a sound like a distant roll of thunder, and I smiled.

"This is nice. Do you have a tipper?" I asked. He tapped the back of my hand with one, and I took it from him and started to play. It was one of the best drums I'd ever held, and I was grinning like a loon when I finished. "Oh, she's sweet, Aodh."

"She's yours," he told me. "Take care of her."

"What?"

"You're a bard. You need an instrument to take into battle, Steven," he said, his voice firm. "I wish that we had more time to talk. Use her well, Steven. When you return, we can talk more, and I will see if I can find a proper teacher for you. For now, I should get you off to the armory."

"One thing before I go," I said, tucking the tipper into my belt. "Aodh, do you like dogs?"

He sounded surprised when he answered, "Yes. Your lady here is quite lovely."

"She's my eyes. My familiar. And I can't take her with me into battle. Would you... Aodh, would you look after her for me? Until I come back?" I left unspoken my request for him to take care of her if I didn't come back. I didn't have to say it—he knew.

"I would be honored, Steven," he said solemnly. Then he took my arm and led me out of his rooms and through the halls, outside into the courtyard, and from there towards the sound of metal ringing on metal. Not swords, though. Different.

"There you are!" Liam called out. "Steven, what have you found there?"

"Aodh says that as a bard, I need an instrument to go into battle. My instrument of choice is a drum, so..."

"So he provided you with one. Good thinking, Aodh."

"Thank you. I'll leave you to your planning," Aodh told us. I stopped him with a raised hand.

"Wait a minute, Aodh," I told him, and went to my knees next to Mirage. Carefully, I unbuckled her harness, then I ruffled her ears and hugged her tightly; she licked my cheek and whined softly. "You go with him, baby-girl," I murmured. "I'll be back. And I'll have Nick with me." She licked me again and I stood up and handed her leash to Aodh.

"I will treat her as if she were my own child," he swore to me before he left. I thanked him again and tried not to cry as he took Mirage away. My last link to the real world... until I ran my fingers under my collar and touched my chain. I'm coming, Nick.

Liam's hand was warm on my shoulder, even through my doublet and shirt. "Let's get you ready. We've got a ride ahead of us."

Chapter Twelve
Into the Darkling Forest

The next hour passed in a blur of activity—in short order, a brusque armorer who never introduced himself had me dressed in a padded jacket, with light gauntlets, while Liam sent someone running to my room to get my sword. When he heard that I was taking the drum with me, the armorer rigged a harness for it, so that I could carry it on my back, with the tipper in my pouch. When I was finally dressed and armed, Liam took my arm and led me out.

"I'm hoping you know how to ride?" he asked, sounding doubtful.

"I assume you mean a horse?" I asked.

"Of course I mean a horse. What were you expecting?"

"Liam, this is the Elvenlands. For all I know, you were asking if I could ride a dragon! Yes, I can ride. It's been a while. And... you'll need to lead me."

"I knew that," Liam said. "I'll have you on a leading rein. I was just worried I'd have to strap you to your saddle or have you ride pillion. And no. We don't ride dragons here. They don't appreciate it."

"They don't... there really *are* dragons?" I sputtered. "I was joking!"

"I wasn't. There are..." he paused for a moment, leading me into a building that smelled strongly of horses. "Four, I think, in this area? They're solitary creatures. We don't see them often. Father was friends with one. Ragnar, I think his name is. They traded books. He'll probably want to meet you. How well do you ride?"

I stopped in my tracks, shaking my head and trying to ward off near-hysterical giggles. I heard Liam come closer, and his hands came to rest on my shoulders. "All you all right?" he asked. That just set me off more, and it took a couple of minutes before I could catch my breath and answer.

I nodded and wiped my eyes. "Yeah. Yeah, I'm fine. Just... it's all catching up with me. Where I am, what's happened. I mean... we're talking about dragons, for God's sake! Me, meeting a dragon! When this is all over, I'm going to have a nice, quiet, breakdown."

Liam chuckled, then hugged me hard. "You're doing amazingly well, High Wizard. Once this is over, you and your lover are welcome to stay on here, to rest and heal."

"Thanks, Liam," I mumbled into his shoulder. Then I pushed him away gently and took a deep breath. "Let's go."

It turned out that I was the last one who needed to get ready—everyone else was mounted and ready to go. Liam had already given them their orders, so as we rode up I heard the sounds of cheers, then the thunder of hooves, all of them moving away.

"How many are here? How many went?" I asked.

"Half a squadron are with us," Liam told me. "The rest have gone to engage the forces in the forest. They'll attack at sunset."

"I thought attacks were usually at dawn?" I asked. Everything I'd ever read said that armies attacked at dawn, so I'd assumed that was what we were going to do.

"Where did you get that idea?" Liam asked, sounding amused. "If we waited for dawn, we'd be up to our ears in *Uaigneach*."

"So, it's not an honor thing?"

"Honor?" Liam repeated. "Steven, honor is a luxury that we do not have, especially not when we are fighting a dishonorable opponent. Attend. When the Sí go to war, which is very rare, there are forms and conventions that must be followed. A battlefield is chosen, agreements are made. There is... a structure, to every part of the battle."

"So it's more like a tournament than a war?"

"Exactly so. Honor is very important in war. This, what we are doing, this is not what we consider war. This is..." he paused for a moment, and I thought I heard him sigh. "This is extermination.

The *Uaigneach* are rogues, feral beasts that must be removed before they can threaten the innocent. And now, it is too late to protect the innocent, we both know that."

"Yeah, I know," I murmured. It bothered me, to hear him condemning the whole group of *Uaigneach* for this. But what did I know? Maybe Barra was wrong, and they had all banded together. Maybe they really were all at fault. I wouldn't know until I faced down Vikentiy. And maybe I wouldn't even know then.

"We must stop them before they harm anyone else." Liam finished. Our horses stopped, and I heard him telling someone else that we would wait here, under concealment, until we were certain that the others had engaged the forces in the forest. That made me think of Donal, wonder how he was faring. What was happening with the others?

It was as if thinking about him conjured Donal up; suddenly, it was as if I was riding on his shoulder, hearing his thoughts. I gasped in shock, heard Liam, and realized that my head was somehow in two places at once.

"Steven, what is it?"

"Donal," I answered, frowning, trying to make sense of what I was feeling. "I... okay, this is weird. I'm in his head... damn, Liam! He's bloodthirsty!"

"His first real battle," Liam said, sounding as if he were talking about his son's first two-wheeler. "He'll learn better. How is this possible?"

I considered it, thankful that Donal seemed to be unaware of my presence. "I think... maybe... two possibilities. Either my healing him linked us somehow, or it's the stone, and he's the only one who has one that I'm close enough with to feel like this."

"Either is possible," Liam said. "Where are they?"

"About to engage, I think? They're waiting... no, wait. They're moving... I... oh. Oh, boy." I felt my face growing warm; Donal's thoughts had taken a sharp turn from the bloodthirsty to the erotic—apparently, Siana had given him a hero's send-off. And from what he was thinking, it hadn't been their first time.

"What?" Liam asked, sounding alarmed.

"No. Nothing wrong," I answered quickly. "Just... nothing you have any business knowing about. Nothing I have any business knowing, and he'll probably strangle me if he ever finds out I do know. Liam, how old is Donal?"

"His age would mean little to you. From your perspective, he is old enough to be your father's father. He left my care... oh, your time escapes me. Not long. Months, I believe."

"Jeez, he is a kid," I breathed. "By my perspective, he may be old enough to be my grandfather, but he's got the maturity of an overgrown teenager."

"We let them go when they are convinced that they know everything and can conquer the world," Liam said. "We welcome them back when they learn better."

I snickered. "Sounds like self-preservation, right there. They're definitely on the move. I... whoa. They're charging. How the hell can you charge like that in a forest? Someone is going to run into a tree!"

"You can *see* what they're doing?"

I shook my head. "Of course not. It's magic, not miracles. Donal can see. I'm just telling you what I'm getting from him." I shook my head, blinking my eyes, finally closing them and finding the thread that connected me to Donal so that I could dampen it. When I opened my eyes, I was just in my head. "They've engaged. Now what?"

"Now we move on the keep," Liam said. Before he finished speaking, my horse was moving.

"You know where we're going?" I asked.

"Of course I do. Now be quiet. We're going to be entering the forest in a moment, and if there are any scouts hidden in the trees, they might hear you."

I shut up, listening as hard as I could, and hearing only the sounds of our horses' hooves. It was far too quiet. That kind of quiet had to mean there was someone out there, scaring the animals. Or so I thought; I spread out my awareness, sending tentative threads of magic out in all directions, and found no scouts. No one at all.

"Liam, there's no one out there," I called.

"Are you sure?" he asked.

"I think so. Unless... do you think they can hide from me?" I asked. He grunted.

"That makes no sense," he said. "No guards, no scouts. What are they playing at?"

"Maybe they didn't realize Donal got away?" one of the other men suggested. "No one is supposed to know this place is here. Maybe they've all gone off with that army?"

"I doubt they're idiots, Gaynor. More likely, they've laid a trap," Liam answered. "Everyone stay on your guard. Steven, keep a sharp eye..." He stopped, and I grinned.

"I'll keep my feelers out for anyone not wearing a stone," I assured him.

I knew exactly when we rode into the forest; I felt a darkness pass over me, as if I'd been touched by a shadow. I shivered, and shielded, and felt the men around me do the same. No one said a word. No one had to, and I wondered who it was in the Court who had been keeping this hidden, keeping patrols from finding out about the keep and the growing army. Was it one of the eleven I turned up? Or one of the ones I made softly and silently vanish away? Did it even matter?

In the end, I decided it really didn't matter, and checked my threads once more. Still, no one around us. There weren't even any animals in the forest. Nothing but trees. It was eerie. I checked my connection with Donal, and found him in the middle of battle, and having the time of his life. Kids, I said to myself, then bit down on a laugh.

Then, we stopped, and I heard leather creaking and a soft jingle. Someone tapped my leg, and I understood, dismounting and letting whoever it was take my arm. It turned out to be Liam.

"We're here," he whispered into my ear. "I'm sending most of the squadron on to secure the keep. We've a party of six, counting you and me. Once it's clear, we'll go in and search."

I nodded and folded my arms over my chest, shivering slightly and trying to ignore it. I wasn't cold. I was scared out of my mind. I stayed as close to Liam as I could, drumming on my biceps with my fingers, occasionally touching my chain through my shirt, and just generally trying not to fidget too much. I didn't want the others to know just how bad off I was.

"High Wizard?" Gaynor said, his voice barely audible. "This is your first, isn't it?"

I nodded. No shame in admitting it. "Unless you count the fight in the palace, yeah," I said.

"Have you been blooded?" Gaynor asked.

"Blooded? What?" I asked. "Liam, what is he talking about?"

"Commander, he hasn't been blooded yet?" Now Gaynor sounded shocked. "He can't go into battle without being blooded!"

"There hasn't been a chance to do it properly, Gaynor. And Danu willing, there won't be a battle. But yes, he should be blooded," Liam said with a sigh. "Steven, to be blooded is to be sealed to a squadron. They become your brothers and sisters. As close as family. In some cases, closer than family. It is customary for a new knight to be blooded before his first battle."

"I'm not a knight, Liam," I said weakly.

"Commander—"

"I know, Gaynor. It is hardly fitting that the High Wizard not be a Silver Knight," Liam cut him off. "Steven, would you kneel?"

"Kneel?" I repeated, shocked. He was going to do what? "Umm... Liam?"

"Humor me, Steven. And kneel."

All right, I'd humor him. I slowly knelt down, feeling soft moss under my knees, smelling the rich, loamy earth below. I heard the scraping of a drawn sword, then there was a firm tap on each of my shoulders. Liam cleared his throat and solemnly said, "Rise, Sir Steven Ahearn, *Ridire airgid an Rí Ard-thar na Farraige*."

I slowly got back to my feet, feeling unreal, a little voice in the back of my head yammering away, telling me that I was surely still in a coma in a hospital in Baltimore, that the past year hadn't happened. That I was not the most powerful mage in existence, getting knighted on a battlefield before I stormed a castle to rescue my lover. This just could not be happening.

And then Liam hit me, hard enough that I thought I was going to lose a few teeth. That brought me back to myself—there was no way that I'd imagine someone hitting me that hard!

"Let that be the last blow you ever accept unchallenged," Liam said, his voice firm. "And now we blood you," he added, taking my hand. I felt a stabbing pain in my palm, and warmth as the blood flowed, filling my hand. I heard Liam hiss, then his hand closed over mine, and I tasted his magic as he did... something. I wasn't sure what exactly it was, but when his hand fell away, the blood was gone, and cut on my palm was healed. When it was done, Liam pulled me close and hugged me. "Be welcome, my brother."

"Thanks. I think. Ow," I told him as he let me go. I rubbed my jaw, and they all laughed. I laughed with them, and it was a good feeling, reminding me strongly of some of the coven meetings. "So what squadron am I part of now?"

"Technically? All of them," Gaynor told me. "You've been blooded by the Commander. He's not part of a single squadron, he's blooded to all of us, since he leads us all. So, you really belong to all of us now."

"Really?" That was an interesting idea. Not one that I had a chance to dwell on too much, because just then one of the others spoke up.

"Commander, they're signaling."

"That was quick," Liam murmured, his voice unreadable. I couldn't tell what he was thinking.

"Is that good?" I finally asked.

"Could be," Liam answered, which told me exactly nothing. "Everyone be ready. I think we'll be going in soon."

Soon turned into immediately—the man who came out to report told us that the keep was secured. There had been passive

shields on the walls, but that was the only thing they had encoun-
tered. There were no guards inside, there had been no other defense
at all.

"All right," Liam said. "We're going inside. Keep the High
Wizard surrounded at all times. We're looking for one man. We're
going in, finding him, and getting out. That is our only purpose.
Understood?"

"Yes, Commander," the men around me chorused.

From the moment we passed through the shields and entered the
keep's walls, I was on edge. The place tasted wrong, tasted like
something rotten. There was so much pain in this place, so much
blood spilled, and I damn near gagged as we broke through the
shields and crossed the threshold into the keep.

"Steven?" Liam whispered.

"I'm all right," I answered. "Just... this place is foul. Let's find
Nick and get the hell out."

"Form up," Liam said, his voice low. At once, I heard the men
who had come with us falling in around me, putting me at the
heart of the group. The entire way, I could feel Liam and his men
around me, acting as living armor for me as they guided me
through the halls. A few minutes into the walk, I cursed myself
silently and extended my shields around them all. Gaynor murmured his thanks, and I nodded, slightly distracted. There was a
small bright thread, running through the carrion feel of the place.
A diamond, hidden in shit. I was pretty sure I knew what it was,
and took me a few minutes to tease it free and find that I had, indeed, found Nick.

"Got him," I murmured. "Liam, turn left at the next chance
you get." We went on like that, me whispering directions, and Liam
making sure we didn't run into any walls. Then, the sound of our
footsteps changed, and the space around me opened up. A room. A
large room. And Nick was very close.

"There's no one here," Liam said. "Looks to be a throne room. No guards, no one. We're quite alone."

"Liam, Nick is in here. I can feel him. Do you see him anywhere?" I whispered. I turned, wanting to call Nick's name, afraid of what would happen if I did.

"I don't.... wait," Liam answered. His footsteps moved away, and I heard him gasp. "Steven, he's here..." I didn't give him a chance to finish, pushing past the guards and running towards Liam's voice. I tripped on stairs, falling to my knees and letting Liam help me up. "He's here. He's half covered by a robe, and I thought... I wasn't sure until I came close. He's breathing, so he's asleep—"

"Or unconscious," I interrupted. I knelt down and reached out, feeling fur under my fingers, and a familiar firmness under the furs. I skimmed my hand over the furs, trying to find the edge. "Liam, tell me what he looks like."

"He's been beaten, Steven," Liam answered. "Badly. No blood that I can see, though. He is bound, chained by the neck to the throne. There are chains on his wrists and ankles, as well."

I nodded. "I'll deal with those later. *Kolya?* Baby, wake up. It's me. It's Steven. I'm here." As I called his name, I found the edge of the fur, and my fingers trailed over Nick's chest, feeling the warmth of his skin, the heat that spoke of bruising. For a moment, all I wanted to do was pull him into my arms and cry.

Then the room was flooded with coppery magic, and the screams started. I wheeled around as Liam and his men howled in pain, trying to find the source of the magic. If I found it, I could stop it. But it seemed to be coming from... behind me.

"No," I gasped, turning and holding one hand over Nick's chest as I did what I should have done first—tested him for magic. And found that my Nick was wrapped in a cocoon of copper-tainted threads. Bait, Fergus had said. Nick had been taken as bait.

"Oh, Fergus. You were right," I breathed. "I should have re-membered."

"Oh, that was entirely too easy," I heard the deep, silky voice, with an accent much the same as Nick's, coming from behind me, and I knew I'd found Vikentiy. I rose and turned towards him, my drum bumping against my back, my hand on my sword.

"I'd say it was a pleasure, Vikentiy, but it isn't," I said quietly. "You have something of mine. I want him back."

"And you are in my way, High Wizard," he said. I could hear a note of confusion in his voice, and I wondered what the trap spell that had caught Liam and his men was supposed to have done to me. They were still alive, I knew. I could feel them. But I could also hear them groaning in pain.

"In your way?" I repeated. "Want to explain that? Because up until a few nights ago, I didn't even know you were here. How am I in your way?"

"The seers have spoken. I will rule the Elvenlands, but only once you are gone."

"So that's what this is all about? Get rid of me so that you can march over the Court?" I snorted. "You know, I think you overlooked something, Vikentiy. Your first attack on me, that was back before I knew I was Heart's Master. It was before I knew I had Si blood, too. So, until you started messing around in my life, I didn't even know you lot existed." I cocked my head to the side. "And even after I did know about the Si, I still didn't give a damn about your power games, or the Elvenlands. That didn't happen until you attacked me and stole Nick. So I wonder, did your seers put you on to me because they wanted you to win... or because they wanted me to stop you?"

"Curious," he murmured, ignoring my implication that he'd been set up by his own people. "My spells didn't affect you. It affected the others, but not you. Why?"

I couldn't hear him coming any closer, and I didn't sense any magic, so I played along. I shrugged and answered, "No idea. What was it supposed to do?"

When he spoke again, his voice came from closer, and to the other side. I jumped, and heard him gasp in amusement. "You're blind? The High Wizard is blind?" He started to laugh, and I wondered how it could sound so merry and so cruel at the same time. I felt his magic surge, and knocked his thrown spell away as easily as I'd once hit a baseball, chasing it back with a magical slap of my own. I felt it impact against his shields, felt it rock him, and felt his surprise.

"I can still kick your ass, you know," I snapped. "None of your seers told you that, did they?"

"No. No, they did not," he answered. "And I believe it was one of them who suggested the flare spell that has left you without guards. So I will reward them suitably, once I deal with you."

"A flare? Oh, I get it. Bright lights. Yeah, just a little useless against the blind guy. So, just who is going to be dealing with whom?" I asked mildly. "Seems like your own people set you up, Vikentiy. And I'm pretty pissed off right now. I think that gives me an edge."

"Hardly. I challenge you, High Wizard. I challenge you to a spell-circle."

Chapter Thirteen
Circle Dance

I blinked, trying not to show how confused I was. I had no idea what he was talking about. Apparently, I wasn't too successful in keeping a poker-face—he started to laugh again.

"You really cannot be that ignorant of the magical world, can you?" he asked. "You don't understand a thing of what is happening here. All right. I'll be generous. Go on, go talk to your little helpers. Let them explain it to you. I'll wait."

Stung by his all-too-accurate assessment, I started down the steps, turning and feeling for Liam's magic, and finding him at the bottom of the stairs, not too far away. I crouched down next to him and murmured, "Liam? You okay?"

"There was a light... I cannot see," he answered, and I heard panic in his voice. I winced, remembering the feeling. I reached out and touched his shoulder.

"It's okay," I told him. "Mister Happy over there said it was a flare spell. Should be temporary. I'll get us all out of here, and Siana will put it right."

I felt Liam's hand on my knee. "I cannot help you, Steven."

"You can tell me what a spell-circle is," I said. "You did hear him challenge me to one, right?"

"A spell-circle?" Liam sounded shocked.

"Yeah. Is that bad?"

"It means that he thinks he can defeat you," Liam answered. "It is a one-on-one challenge, a duel. Once the spell-circle is cast, only the death of one of the participants will release the spell and open the circle. Steven, you cannot do this. You do not have enough experience—"

I cut him off, "I don't have a choice, Liam. Not if I want to get all of us out of here. So... I have to kill him? No other way?"

"You do. And if you are within the circle and you refuse to

fight, then the circle itself will turn on you and slay you," Liam said. "Once you make this choice, Steven, there is no turning back."

I let out a long whistle and murmured, "Do you think I can win?"

Liam answered without hesitation, "Yes. So long as you remember what I told you. Your will controls your magic. He is not more powerful than you, so you can defeat him, if you do not waver."

I took a long breath, let it out slowly, and stood up. "I'm going to do this. I'm not going to let you and the Court down. Not going to let Nick down."

"Good man," Liam told me. "Help me up." I groped for his hand and helped him to his feet, and was startled when Liam hugged me. "Bring me to your Nick, my brother," he whispered into my ear. "I'll protect him. If I can."

"I showed you how to see if someone is coming at you," I reminded him.

"You did. I'll protect him."

"Thanks," I hugged him again and helped him up the stairs to where Nick lay. Then I turned back to Vikentiy. "All right. I'm ready. I accept your challenge."

"I thought you would," he answered. "Come down here, boy. Do you understand the rules of the spell-circle?"

"I know I'm going to kill you," I told him as I walked down the stairs. "And I know you're going to try to kill me. Is there anything else?"

He laughed again. "I do like you, boy. You've a sense of humor. You have no idea how rare that is among this lot." I heard his boot-heels clicking on the floor, moving off towards my left. "You know, I don't have to kill you. We don't have to duel. Not all the High Wizards walked on the side of the light. And you... you have a certain... ruthlessness that I admire. The way you dispatched the first vessel, that was quite nice, especially for one with no training. And I'm told that you did away with more than half of my puppets in the Court. That is marvelous. You could be one I would serve, and gladly. You could join me in my quest. We could overthrow the High King. You could rule your world, and I could hold the Elven-lands in your name. The only thing I would regret would be giving you your pet back. I've grown fond of him." He chuckled again. "He's delightful. Very responsive. Have you had him long?"

I fought down a wave of nauseous anger as he described Nick. Please, let him be lying! "He is not my pet," I growled. "And join you? Like hell!"

"A pity," he said. "You have such potential. It will be a shame to waste. And who knows what the next High Wizard will be? But I'll deal with that one when they come. Perhaps they'll be more open to my offer. Come here, little mortal man. Come and dance in my circle."

I walked towards his voice, hearing my boots ringing and echo-ing through the hall, almost muffling the faint breathing and scuf-fling that had to be the Si guards that I brought into this mess. I hadn't done that great a job of protecting them, but if I had anything to say about it, we were all going to walk out of here. I stopped and cocked my head to one side. "Here?"

"That will do," Vikentiy said. I heard him chanting something, then felt walls snapping up around me, arching over my head, seal-ing me inside the circle. As they rose, I snapped my dragon scale shields up around myself, and added the extra shielding to my ankle. Then I waited, my hands at my sides, gently testing the edges of the circle, getting my bearings. And getting an idea.

"So," I said, taking my drum from my back, setting it down at the base of one of the walls, and putting a light shield over it so that it wouldn't get stepped on. "You challenged. Do I get to choose the weapon? Is that how things are done here?"

"Is that how things are done in your world?" Vikentiy asked.

"Used to be," I told him. "We don't do much in the way of duels anymore."

"Interesting," Vikentiy said, and was quiet just long enough to make me nervous. If he said no, this wouldn't work. "Very well, I can be generous. You may choose the first weapon."

I grinned and put my hand on my sword. "Steel," I said, and had the immense satisfaction of hearing Vikentiy sputter.

"You jest!"

I smiled and drew both my sword and a long dagger, waiting. "No joke. Steel. Or forfeit." Before he could answer, I let my magic flow, filling the circle. I could "see" him now, standing about as far away from me as he could. He moved, his arm sweeping, and I knew that he was armed. All right.

"How is it that a blind man knows how to fight?" he asked, coming towards me.

"I wasn't always blind," I answered. Then there was no more talking. He charged me, and I parried his overhand swing easily before advancing on him. It didn't take me long to realize that my hunch had been right. He was a mage, and therefore not a fighter. I was better than he was. I could end this, right now. So I ran a complicated sword-and-knife pattern that I'd learned when I played Mercutio in *Romeo and Juliet*. It looked impressive as hell, but it really wasn't threatening at all—something a novice swordsman like Vikentiy wouldn't be able to tell. He stood his ground and tried to block me... and failed, his sword going skittering across the floor as I disarmed him. The next blow would end it...

"Mercy!" Vikentiy whimpered, falling to his knees.

I drew myself up, readying myself to deliver the death blow... and hesitated. Mercy? Could I? No. I had no choice, and I'd known that coming in. If I didn't kill him, either he or the circle would kill me. And he'd hurt Nick. I shook my head, tightened my grip on my sword, and too late felt the surge of copper-tinged magic. I'd waited too long, holding the blow just long enough to give him the opening; Vikentiy's blast of magic hit me right in the chest, knocking me backwards and off my feet. It didn't break through my shields, but I landed badly, jarring my still-healing back, losing both my sword and my dagger as abused muscles spasmed. I gasped in pain, unable to move as I heard his boot-heels coming closer.

"Pathetic," Vikentiy sneered. "Soft-hearted, weak-willed mortal wretch. Trust me, I will not hesitate thus when I kill you." I groaned and tried to rise, and he laughed. "Oh, come now. Surely that little tap didn't damage you! It barely grazed your shields!"

I blinked and forced myself through the pain, slowly getting to my knees, and stopping to deflect another magic bolt, knocking it away to splatter harmlessly on the walls of the circle.

"Oh, do stay on your knees, little mortal!" Vikentiy told me, and I could hear him laughing at me. "It will be where you spent the rest of your very short life. It will amuse me to have you for a slave... for a little while. Although I doubt you'd make a very good slave.

For a moment, he sounded eerily like Joey, and that mimicry rattled me so much that when another blast hit me, it hit harder than the first two, throwing me back down and slicing through my shields, my clothes, and my skin like a razor; I howled in pain, feeling the blood spilling, cursing myself for letting things slip. How much time did I have? How long could I go on, bleeding like this? I tried to roll onto my side, one arm pressed to my chest, trying to do something to stop the bleeding, hearing Vikentiy coming closer, feeling him standing over me. He pushed me down, onto my back, and straddled me, almost sitting on my stomach, and that was the moment that I realized that my shields were gone. He knew, too, and I felt cold metal digging into my throat.

"Your head, I think," he said, sounding as if he'd decided something important. "I'll keep your head. You're decorative enough. I'll preserve it, and put it on a spike over my bed. That way, every time I take your little pet, I'll be able to see our reflection in your lifeless eyes."

I swallowed hard, feeling the blade at my throat, knowing that I couldn't fail now. If I died, Nick would spend the rest of his life as this bastard's plaything. Liam would die. Donal and Aodh, and Siana. All of them would die.

"... not... not gonna happen...." I growled. He started to laugh, and stopped abruptly when I threw him off of me with a blast of power and drew my magic back around me. I sealed a shield tight around my chest, hoping it would work like a compression bandage, gritted my teeth, and got back up onto my knees. That was as far as I could go—my head started to spin as I moved, so I crouched there, filling the circle with magic again and seeing Vikentiy across from me, against the far side of the circle. From what little I could tell, he was recovering, trying to get back to his feet. I tested his shields, and discovered them fractured; I'd hurt him. Now... I needed to finish him. But I was in no shape to fight. I couldn't even stand.

"No!" I heard Vikentiy shout. "I will not be defeated by an ignorant, crippled mortal! I will be victorious! The prophecy will not be fulfilled!"

I caught my breath, my lyric brain taking over. Song cue... the prophecy will not be fulfilled... prophecy fulfilled... prophecy fulfilled today. *Magic Taborea.* And just like that, I knew what I had to do. The lyrics... dear God, I'd been listening to Van Canto the morning we'd left for the conference! And for some reason that I couldn't name, I'd been driven to listen to just that one song, putting it on repeat until Nick finally demanded that I either change songs or turn it off. Now I understood. This was why. The lyrics were right, the tone was right. But... could I do it on a bodhran?

Only one way to find out. I pulled the tipper from my pouch and held out my hand, reaching out and grabbing my drum with magic, sailing it through the air to where I could catch it and pull it into position, wrapping myself and the drum in shields that I anchored to the ground. There was something deeply, intensely wrong about using a song from an online role-playing game to fight a magical battle in the Elvenlands. If I'd had a chance to think about it, I'd probably have laughed myself silly. But I didn't have that chance. I had one shot. So I took a deep breath, and breathed out in the deep, chest-resonating hum that started the song.

I heard Vikentiy scoff, heard him coming towards me as I started to sing, heard him laugh outright at the line about being weak and torn apart. But the next line was where the drums started, and I felt my magic rising in response to the call of the music. I didn't try to shape it, to make it do anything specific. I couldn't have figured out what to do with it and sing, not right then. I just poured everything I had into it, into my need to be, as the song said, back where I belonged. And the single, desperate need for this bastard to pay for what he'd done—for killing Fergus, for hurting Nick. For hurting me.

Whatever it was that I was doing, it was working. By the second verse, I felt something building, outside my shields, and I heard Vikentiy swearing a blue-streak in Ukrainian. When I hit the bridge, I stopped singing and concentrated on the drum, feeling a lot of magic start flying around the circle, glancing off my shields, hitting whatever it was that I knew was advancing onto Vikentiy, who was now shouting obscenities in a panic-filled voice. As I started singing the last verse, I heard Vikentiy start to scream, mingled fear and pain. Screaming that stopped abruptly as I reached the final chorus and brought the song to a close. I let my shields go, feeling the walls of the circle coming down all around me. Vikentiy was dead. I'd won. And all I wanted to do was be sick. I sat down hard, shaking my head, trying to clear it. Everything felt like it was spinning, a feeling I remembered from Yule. I had pushed myself too far. Or maybe it was from the blood loss. I couldn't tell.

"Steven?" Liam called. "Steven?"

"Yeah?" I mumbled, my throat as sore as if I'd done a three-hour concert instead of a three-minute song. "You okay, Liam? Can you see?"

"Steven, what is that thing?" Liam's voice was very shrill, which I suppose answered my question about him seeing. I just had no idea what he was talking about.

"What thing? Liam?" I shouted.

"It's... it's your magic!" Liam answered. "Great Dagda, Steven, make it stop!"

My magic? I heard someone scream, and grabbed, finding a handful of my own magic and pulling it back into myself. For some reason, it fought back, and the effort left me panting and dizzy.

"Liam?" I called.

"Steven, it's trying to kill us!"

Oh, dear God. Whatever it was that I'd created to kill Vikentiy was still out there, still loose in the room. Would kill my friends, would kill Nick, if I didn't stop it somehow. I closed my eyes, reached, and pulled as hard as I could, feeling the construct screaming its defiance as I slowly reeled it back in. What the hell had I done? I wrestled with it, pulling it in, refusing to let this wild thing go free, feeling all of the anger I'd filled it with, all of the fear and hate and pain. No wonder it wouldn't just go away, and was seeking another target. There was too much there to burn out with just one death. It needed more. I just wasn't expecting my own magic to turn its rage on me.

I felt the magic thing stop fighting, thought that it had given up, and I let my grip on the threads relax, only to fall back as the construct surged forward, barreling into me and engulfing me with hate and pain and the need for death. For any death. I howled and wrapped my arms around myself, around the thing, trying to fight it down, to force it back, to bring it back under control before it killed me the way it had killed Vikentiy. I could hear Liam, shouting my name, screaming at me to release it. But I couldn't. If I let it go, it would kill everyone in this room, and only God knew how many others before it was finally stopped. I held on, screaming, feeling as if the damn thing was going to rip me apart, feeling it growing weaker, until at last it faded, sinking underneath my skin until it was gone. Gone where, I had no idea. Nor did I care.

"Li... Liam?" I stuttered. Then passed out cold.

Chapter Fourteen
Keeper of my Soul

"Steven?"

Woman's voice. Nice. Really pretty brogue. I knew that voice. Why did I know that voice?

"Steven? High Wizard?"

High Wizard? That was familiar, too. Wait, don't tell me. I'll have it in a minute.

"Liam, I'm not sure he hears me."

Hey, I know a guy named Liam. Nice guy. For a... oh!

With a groan, I opened my eyes. I knew who the voice belonged to now. "Siana?"

It wasn't Siana who answered. A warm hand clasped my shoulder, and Liam said softly. "Welcome back, High Wizard. You had us all worried."

I licked my lips and blinked, feeling really out of it. Much more out of it than I should have if I'd only been out for a while. "How long have I been asleep?" I asked.

"More like half dead, and a full day and night. When we carried you and your Nick—"

"Nick?" I blurted out. "Where's Nick?" I tried to sit up, feeling silk sliding over my skin, which made me realize that I was raw under the covers. Liam pushed me back down onto the bed, and I flopped back down, weak as a kitten.

"Not until your healer gives you leave, Steven," he said firmly. "Nick is in the next room. When Siana comes back from checking on him, I will take you to him myself."

"Take me to him? Why can't he come to me?" I demanded. "Liam, what's wrong with Nick?"

Liam hesitated for a moment, then hummed softly. "You will not try to get up?" he asked.

"Liam!"

"Siana will have my head on a platter if you relapse because I've upset you," Liam protested.

"Not telling me is going to upset me a hell of a lot more," I grumbled.

"All right. Your Nick is asleep. He has not awakened at all since we found him. Whatever spells that Vikentiy laid on him did not dissipate when Vikentiy died, and none of us can unravel them. We've let him sleep, and Siana has tended to him. His wounds are all healed, and she has made him drink tea and broth. There is nothing more that she can do, nothing more than any of us can do. We had to wait for you to wake."

I swallowed and slowly sat up, rubbing my face and feeling the scratchiness and thinking that I had way too much stubble for just two or three days. How long had we really been here? "Do I have clothes, Liam?"

"You'll want to bathe first, my brother. Are you feeling better?" I nodded. "Yeah, I think so."

"Good," he said. Then he slapped me. Not too hard, but in the state I was in, it enough to almost knock me over.

"What the hell—" I sputtered.

"Are you always such a blasted idiot, or did you have to study for it?" Liam cut my rant off at the knees. "Why did you not release the fetch?"

"The *what?*"

"The death fetch," Liam answered. "The thing you created to kill Vikentiy. Why in the name of sacred Danu did you create such a thing? And why did you not release it?" He took a breath, then breathed out. "Oh. Oh, Danu... you had no idea what you were doing, did you?"

"Not a clue. So start at the beginning. What did I do, and how did I screw it up?"

"The death fetch—it is a creation of rage, of pain and of hatred. It takes on a life of its own, and very often will turn on and kill its creator. It is something that no sane mage will ever create."

I nodded, "All right. Never claimed to be sane. And I didn't create it on purpose... no, that's not right. I did create it on purpose. I just didn't know there was a name to what I was doing. And I couldn't let it go, Liam. It would have gone after you and the others."

There was a long silence, broken by a horrified gasp. "Steven!" Liam breathed. "Did no one ever tell you what it meant to release a spell? My father didn't teach you that?"

I shook my head slowly, so it wouldn't fall off. "No. Liam, I told you. I'm a Prentice, and not a very good one. I've done more spells here in the past few days than I have in the year that I've known magic even existed!"

Liam sighed and touched my hand. "Steven, I apologize. I should have remembered that you've not the learning you should have had. I should have been clear. Now..." he stopped, and that was just enough to scare the crap out of me.

"Now? Now what?" I demanded. "Liam, what the hell did I do?"

"You did not release the spell. It should have killed you, Steven. It did not, because you absorbed it. However, that does not mean that the fetch is gone."

I frowned. "I don't follow," I said. "It's gone, but it isn't gone? Where is it?"

My answer was a light tapping on my forehead. "It has become part of you. Part of your magic. While we waited to see if you would wake, I read anything I could find on the death fetch, to see if this has happened before. It has."

"Okay. What do I do?"

"For now, it sleeps. Before it awakens, you must find a way to conquer it," Liam answered, his voice deadly serious. "And you must do it before the creature awakens. If that happens, it will feed on your magic, and it will destroy you. It will consume you from inside out."

I closed my eyes and winced, rubbing my face. "How do I beat it, Liam? Did your reading tell you that?"

"No, Steven," Liam said softly. "I don't think anyone ever has.

There is no record of it that I could find. I will continue to search."
I nodded, running my fingers over the smooth, silk sheets.
"Thanks. All right, so I'm on borrowed time, and I have to make
sure I don't wake the sleeping giant. Any suggestions how I do
that?"
"I wish I could tell you, Steven," Liam answered. "I am sorry."
"Not your fault," I answered automatically. I heard a door
open, and voices in another room, followed by a very familiar
barking. "Mirage? Is that Mirage?"
Scrabbling sounds, more barking, then the bed shook as she
jumped up and damn near bowled me over with her enthusiastic
I'm-still-a-puppy-even-if-I-do-eat-more-than-you-do greeting. I let her wash
my face and sniff me, so that she would be sure I was all right.
When she was done, she sneezed on me, then lay down across my
legs. I tangled my fingers into her fur and smiled. "Aodh took good
care of you, baby-girl?"
"I did, indeed," Aodh answered. "She's a lovely lady, Steven.
And I am very glad to see you awake."
"Thanks, Aodh. Hey. Liam, where's my drum?" I asked.
"In the other room," Liam answered. "I was not likely to leave
something invested with that much power behind for anyone to
find. What you did... Steven, I have never seen the like."
"And hopefully, you will never see it again," I said firmly.
"Now, when can I go see to Nick?"
"After you eat," I heard Siana say, and as she came closer, I
smelled something wonderfully savory. My stomach picked that
moment to let me know I'd been neglecting it, and I decided that
fainting from hunger was not going to get Nick freed from those
spells any sooner. I ate everything Siana put in front of me, without
knowing what it was, and not caring. It tasted good, and that was
the important thing.
When I was done, Siana chased everyone, including Mirage,
out of the room, and helped me out of the bed. I balked for a moment, knowing I wasn't wearing anything under the covers, but
that reaction stopped when Siana pointed out that she'd been the

one to cut my clothes off of me when Liam had dragged me back. Given that fact, I gave up on being modest and let her help me bathe and dress, then lead me out of the bedroom to where Liam and Aodh were waiting.

"Steven," Liam said. "I... you look different."

"You didn't recognize me with my clothes on?" I asked with a grin. Aodh snorted his amusement, and Liam laughed before he answered.

"No, that isn't it," he said slowly. "You look... I'm not sure I can explain it. You no longer look like the bedraggled boy I took you for when you arrived in the Elvenlands. Now... now you are a warrior."

"Yes," Aodh agreed. "It is the way he holds himself, the look in his eyes. He is not one that I would cross. But he is one I would want at my back."

"Really?" I cocked my head to the side and considered what they'd said. Had I changed? I didn't feel any different.

"Are you ready to go to him?" Siana asked.

"Yes. Where..." I frowned, closing my eyes and turning slightly. "Never mind." I could feel Nick, and I turned and started walking, only to have Siana grab my arm. "He's this way," I said.

"And you are about to walk into a door," she answered me with a giggle. "You were following the bond?"

"Bond?" I stopped and turned towards her. "What bond?"

"There is a deep bond between you and your Nick. I saw it when I was healing you, and confirmed it when I was healing him. With time, and training, you will be able to converse mind-to-mind, and you will always know where he is and his emotional state."

I blinked, "We started doing that already. The day—well, the night—this all started."

"Did you? You've more deeply entwined than I thought. Come on, then. Let's go wake him." She held on to my arm as we walked, and led me into a room that I didn't even know was there. And inside... a nauseating mix of copper and butterscotch.

"Why is Nick's magic active?" I asked.

"He is a healer. His magic responded to what I was doing to him, and it continues to work to heal the deep injuries."

I didn't want the answer, didn't want to know. But I had to ask. "Siana, was he... assaulted?"

"Assaulted? You mean, sexually?" Siana asked, sounding shocked. "No, Steven. I found no evidence of that."

I sighed, and felt a tightness in my chest relax. "Thank God. That bastard told me... he lied. Made me think..."

"He lied, Steven." Siana guided me to a chair and made me sit. "He's here. You're next to the bed."

I reached out and groped around until I found Nick's hand, holding on to it tightly as I shifted from the chair to the bed. With my other hand, I gently explored Nick's chest, his throat, his face. If I hadn't known better, I'd have thought him just asleep.

"Hey. Hey, *Kolya*," I murmured. "Hey, Sleeping Beauty. Wake up." The thought jumped into my head that this never happened. Nick was an early riser, so I never got to be the one to wake him up. I fought down a wave of giggles and ran my hand over his chest again, this time to test the magic that kept him imprisoned in sleep.

It was pretty much the way I remembered—strands of slimy, foul-tasting magic that clung to each other with stubborn tenacity. There was one major difference this time, though. When I'd last examined these spells, they had been smooth and unyielding, like latex strips, or the ribbons that Nick had used on me in the park at Beltane. Now, the strands were sticky, and clung to my fingers like cobwebs.

"Siana, could you link with me?" I asked. "I wouldn't put it past that bastard to have left a surprise in this for me. Something triggered by his death. Catch me if I start to go under?"

"Of course, Steven," she answered, and rested her hands on my shoulders. The taste of warm milk as her magic merged with mine was almost enough to clear my mouth of copper. Almost. Time to clean house and take back what was mine. I reached out

and rested my hand on Nick's forehead, closing my eyes and concentrating on stripping away the spells.

I was right about the traps; Siana had to pull me out of spell-
induced sleep four times before I started to be able to recognize
the feel of the traps and defuse them before they got me. It was
painfully slow, and frustrating as hell, and Siana made me stop
twice to eat and rest, ignoring me when I snapped at her, quietly
insisting until she got her way.

Finally, I took my seat and rolled my neck. "I think this will be
it. The last push."

"I think you may be right, Steven," Siana agreed. "We should
have another mage here for this."

"Why?" I asked.

"In case there is anything else hidden in the spells," she answered. "If I were doing this, I would lay something at the end
that would strike out and destroy the mage, who would almost
certainly be tired by this point. And I would have it possibly target
the prisoner as well. That way, even if the mage survived, he'd
have the knowledge that he killed the person he was trying to help.
We should have another mage here, to protect you and Nick."

Caught in equal parts fascination and horror, I turned in my
seat so that I was facing Siana. "Do me a favor, Siana. Don't go
rogue on me. I really don't like the way you think when you think
evil thoughts."

She scoffed gently. "I can think the thoughts. I could never act
on them. I am a healer. This kind of thing... it goes against everything I am. I'll go get Aodh. He's a good enough mage for this.
Wait for me."

"Yes, ma'am. And bring Mirage in with you, too?" I'd kept
her out, mostly to keep from being distracted. But I had a feeling
that I was going to need her. For what I wasn't sure, but I was
learning to listen to that little voice.

I heard the door open behind me, and Mirage's nails on the
floor. She came over to me and pressed up against my legs, then
lay down on top of my feet. I reached down and scratched her ears,
then sat back up. "Aodh?"

"I'm here. What do you need from me?"

I ran my fingers through Nick's hair, wishing he'd wake, wanting to hear his voice. Quickly, Siana and I brought him up to date, and I let him know my worries. "This is it. I'll have all the spells down after this, and I don't trust that Vikentiy not to have hidden something in these spells, just in case I really did beat him."

"I thought he was convinced he could not be beaten?" Aodh asked. "Why then place a trap?"

"Because arrogant doesn't always mean stupid," I answered. "It does, however, sometimes mean paranoid."

"So what do you need from me?" Aodh asked again.

"I need someone who can watch my back," I answered. "Siana says you're a mage, so I need for you to link with us and help me, just in case."

Aodh coughed, and when he spoke, he sounded surprised, "Link with you?"

"Yeah," I said, confused. "Is that a problem?"

Aodh sputtered, "Siana, have you not told him? Has no one told him?"

"Aodh, this is a necessity!" Siana snapped. "Propriety can wait until there isn't a crisis."

"Propriety?" I asked. "What are you two talking about?"

Siana sighed. "Linking magic, the way we've been doing? Steven, that kind of sharing is something that is usually done only between a parent and child. If it is done between adults, it is something more intimate. Usually, it is only between lovers..."

"Intimate," I repeated. "You mean... oh, man." I felt my face burning, and ducked my head. "Oh, boy. Siana..."

She touched my cheek and said, "You didn't know. And I did not mind. Healers are far more open about this kind of thing than most."

I covered my face with my hands and let out a shaky breath. "I... thank you? I think? Siana, you should have told me. If I'd known..."

"We would have done the same thing," Siana said gently. "Truly, we had no choices, in any of it."

I nodded my head and lowered my hands. "So, should I be asking if it was good for you?"

She giggled. "It was very good for me. You've a fascinating mind, Steven. Shall we?"

I nodded, and felt Siana's hand on my left shoulder, joined almost immediately by Aodh's heavier hand on my right. I almost lost all composure and started to giggle when Siana's warm milk magic was met by Aodh's, which tasted to me like a rich, dark buckwheat honey. I ran my tongue over my lower lip, then reached out and touched Nick's hand with one hand, resting my other hand on his forehead. I closed my eyes, and dove back into the mass of spelled tendrils.

Every time I'd done this before, it had been like wading through a jungle with a machete. Granted, it was a glowing machete made of pure magic, but, yeah. Jungle. Machete. Hack, slash. Slash, hack. Lather, rinse, repeat. This time, the moment I was fully surrounded by Vikentiy's tangled threads, they turned on me, attacking like some kind of tentacle monster in a bad Japanese porn. I reacted without thinking, blasting the tendrils closest to me, feeling them crisp and die, only to be replaced by new ones.

Siana? Did that hurt Nick at all?

Her answer was immediate, *The power blast? No. He's fine.*

Good. More than one way to deal with a jungle. I went from hack and slash to slash and burn. I'd once seen a gardener use a small flamethrower to clear a large patch of weedy ground, and I kept that image in mind as I worked, pouring massive amounts of power into clearing away the threads.

Which, it turned out, was exactly what Vikentiy had expected me to do. Siana had called his plan perfectly. I had gone in to this last battle already tired, and the breaks that Siana had insisted on hadn't recharged me all that much. The minute my energy levels began to ebb, the threads reappeared, swarming up and over me, overwhelming my attempts to burn them away and dragging me down. I heard Siana scream, and a deep roar from Aodh, and I knew without knowing how that they were both entangled as well. I felt

Liam, pulling hard against the threads, trying to break through to us. There was nothing he could do, no way to get to us.

Styopa!

Nick! That hadn't been my imagination! I'd heard him, calling to me from somewhere nearby. We were inside the prison with him! Which told me that there was only one thing I could do—I concentrated my power, burning through the strands holding me until they fell away and I was free. Before the strands could attack again, I reached out and grabbed the others, pulling Siana, Aodh, and Nick to me and wrapping them in the best shields I could create. No time to warn them, no time to do anything but pull everything I had and let it all out in a continuous blast of power. I heard screaming, screaming in Vikentiy's voice, and I knew that the spells were dying around us. Almost done... and I felt my power gutter like a candle in a breeze; I was almost tapped out. In despair, I reached deeper, trying to find something—anything— that would let me bring everyone out safely. But I had nothing left, and I wanted to scream... until I found something. Something that I knew wasn't coming from me. A tiny pocket of power, pure and potent, and somehow... furry?

Mirage. I laughed and tapped into her offering, channeling it into the failing blast and feeling the spells that held us scream and falter and die, until there was nothing left of them. Slowly, I dropped my shields and let the others go, breaking the links so that I was alone inside my head. When I felt like I could, I opened my eyes and wiped at an annoying tickling on my face. My fingers came away sticky.

"Your nose is bleeding," Siana said, her voice hoarse. "Sit still."

I cleared my throat, tried to speak, and had to clear my throat again before I could. "Not... not going anywhere," I croaked, and felt a cool, wet cloth on my face. It felt wonderful, and I sighed and slumped in my chair. I felt like my brains had been scooped out and the inside of my skull scraped; ridiculously, I wondered if I could be used as a sort of Jack-o-lantern come Halloween. No, that wouldn't work. The candle would just shine out my ears. I giggled at the image. Look, Ma. Jack Pumpkinhead!

"He's drunk," Liam murmured from behind me.

"Am not!" I protested, still giggling. "Haven't had a drop of anything."

"Magic drunk," Siana said. "Come, Steven. Come and lie down."

"Best idea I've heard all day," I told her. "Wait. Nick? I want to stay here. I'll lie down here, with Nick."

"Do you think that wise?" Siana asked softly, and my euphoria vanished. I remembered what I'd asked her, what Vikentiy had claimed. She'd said no, but magic didn't leave marks. I didn't say anything else, letting Siana lead me out of the room and into another. She insisted that I take off my blood-stained doublet, so I let her boss me around, stripping to my shirt and leggings, then got into bed. I lay down, and was drifting in and out of sleep when the bed shook, and a warm and furry body pressed up against my chest. I wrapped my arms around Mirage and kissed her on the head.

"Good girl," I told her. "Very good girl."

Her tail thumped against my legs, and she whuffed in my face. Apparently, she was feeling pretty smug. She deserved it, I thought. I threw one arm over her and closed my eyes.

It felt as if I'd only just closed my eyes before someone was calling my name. I rolled over, feeling like my head was empty, and noticing that Mirage was gone. "Yeah?" I called. "Who's there?"

"Liam," he said. "Your Nick is awake. He's very confused, and he is asking for you. Siana is with him."

I was out of bed the moment Liam said Nick was awake, stumbling out the door and across the suite to the other room. Thankfully, the door was open; I stopped in the doorway, one hand on the frame. "Nick?"

His voice was harsh, and I almost cried when I heard it. "*Styopa?* Steven, where are we?"

"*Kolya*, I'll explain everything. I promise," I said. I closed the distance between the door and the bed, sitting down on the edge. "*Kolya?*" I was afraid to say anything else. Afraid to touch him. "Steven, you came for me," Nick said softly.

"Of course I did! I wasn't going to let that bastard—"

"*Perelesnyk*," Nick said, his voice clipped. "He was a *perelesnyk*." Behind me, I heard Aodh cough, then start cursing softly. Before he could explain, Nick continued, and I felt my heart drop to my shoes when he said flatly, "An incubus."

"No..." I whispered. "Nick..." I heard whispering behind me, then the sound of the door closing. We were alone. I swallowed hard and reached out, touching Nick's leg. "I'm sorry. I should have gotten to you sooner. I... I never should have gotten you involved in this. I—"

"You should shut up," Nick said firmly. I felt the bed shift, then Nick's hand cupping my cheek. "It is not your fault. You did not know who he was or what he was about. And... is he dead?"

"Yes. I..." I wasn't ready to tell him about the duel. About the death fetch trapped inside me, waiting for me to fall. "I killed him."

"Good," Nick said. He let his hand fall. "Now, where are we?"

"We're in the Elvenlands. At the court of the Steward to the High King beyond the Sea," I said, grateful to be able to talk about something else. "Once you're on your feet, I'll introduce you to Barra. He's the Steward. And... well, you met Siana. She's a healer. There's Liam and his son Donal. Liam is Fergus' son. And Aodh, and..."

"You're babbling."

I shut my mouth hard enough to make my teeth click together, then closed my eyes and clenched my fists. "He hurt you," I said softly. "He..."

"He did not. He said he was going to wait to take me to his bed until after he had disposed of you. He used his power on me, but he did not touch me otherwise," Nick said. "What he did to me, it in no way approaches what was done to me by someone whom I thought I loved. And so I can live with this. Steven, tell me, what is this Heart's Master that Vikentiy called you. He seemed surprised that I did not know what it meant."

I grinned. "Well, in a nutshell, you appear to be involved with some crazy combination of Dumbledore and Gandalf the Gray." I gave him a quick and dirty explanation, and finished by saying, "I didn't mean to be a superhero, Nick. Honestly, if I could give it all up, I would. I... the idea of me having this much power, and not knowing what to do with it, scares the crap out of me."

"Then you are the right man to hold it," Nick said. "And we will see you have the training you need. I am sure there are many people here who will fight over the right to teach you. And the coven will want to help, I know. But for now... *Styopa*, when can we go home?"

"I need to recharge a bit," I answered. "I used up everything I had to beat the spells Vikentiy put on you, and to get us all out of the trap he hid at the end. If we want to go back to the car, then I need to be the one to cast the spell. If we want to go straight home... I don't know. I suppose someone else could do it."

"What about Fergus?" Nick asked. "Is he here? Did you see him?"

I knew that question was coming, but it still hit me hard. I sighed and swallowed, knowing that now, I had time for the grief. "Fergus... he's dead," I said slowly. "He helped me. Brought me here. Defended me when Vikentiy's men attacked the court. And... he died defending me from them."

"*Bozhe moi*," Nick breathed. "Steven, I... I am awake? This is not all some wild dream? We will not wake up at home?"

"Not in the hotel?" I asked.

"No. I wish to have dreamed that, as well," Nick said firmly. "I... you have turned into someone I am not certain I know. But someone I like very much."

I blinked, suddenly alarmed. "I haven't changed!"

"You have," Nick insisted. "You have matured, I think. It will be interesting to see who you become as you come into your power."

"Liam says that now I'm a warrior," I said, remembering.

"Yes, that is what I see as well," Nick said, his hand covering mine. "Steven, I think that Maureen would be very proud of who you have become. Who you are becoming. I know that I am. And I love you very much."

"Even knowing... I don't scare you?"

"Scare me?" Nick laughed. "No! Steven, you killed someone, twice, to save me. You do not scare me. If there is anything that frightens me, it is the worry that I may not deserve you!"

I felt my face grow warm, and ducked my head. "Nick, when we get back... if you want the bed to yourself, I'll understand. I'm fine, if you want to take a break. For however long you want. Whatever you need."

It took him a moment to answer, and when he did, it was the last thing I expected. "What I want is for you to finish what you started," Nick said, his voice low and hesitant.

"Really?" I gasped. "You still... you really... Nick, I don't want to... to push."

"You are not pushing if I ask," he said. "I am asking. Please. I... I liked what I saw. I liked what you were doing. I trust you, Steven. More than I think I have trusted anyone save Maureen. And I love you. You would not hurt me."

I heard in his words the echo of my own, what I'd told him so many months before over the kitchen table the night he'd given me his collar. And I knew that I could do this. I could give him what he needed. So I reached inside, and found a small trickle of magic. It was enough to do what I wanted. I put my hands together, rolling my palms, and spun magic into gold. The effort left me panting, but it also left me with a handful of chain.

"Steven!"

I waved him silent, and held the chain between my hands. "I don't know if I'll be able to be everything you need me to be," I said quietly. "But I'm willing to learn. And... you don't have to answer the question I asked you in the car. Just know that the offer still stands." I held the chain up and asked, "Nick, will you wear this? Will you be mine?"

He answered in a surprisingly clear voice, "I already was. Yes, I will wear your collar."

My hands were shaking enough that Nick had to help me loop the chain around his neck, and I heard him catch his breath as I made the chain shrink to fit him properly, resting flat against the base of his neck. I ran my fingers down his throat, smiling as his pulse jumped noticeably at my touch.

"Not here," I said softly. "Not now. I want this to be in our own bed, in our own home. Okay?"

"Yes," Nick answered.

"Good. Then move over. I need to lie down." I stretched out on my side facing Nick, resting my hand on his side, his skin warm under my fingers. I didn't realize that my shirt had fallen open until I heard Nick gasp, and felt his fingers on my chest.

"Steven, what is this?" he asked, sounding really upset. I touched my chest, and felt the ridge of a scar.

"Huh?" I answered, running one finger the length of the scar. It started just over my left nipple and ran diagonally down to my right side. "He broke through my shields and cut me pretty badly. Siana didn't say anything when she helped me get dressed."

"You fought him? How? Steven, I thought you beat him with magic!"

"I did. But... come here, Nick. Let me tell you the whole thing." I settled onto my back, and drew Nick to me. Once he was settled with his head on my shoulder and my arm around him, I took a long breath and began, "I need to say this all at once, so don't interrupt me, okay? When they took you, I didn't know what to do..."

I have no idea how long I talked, how long he listened. I told him everything, starting with my insane teleport to Fergus's grove. I left nothing out, not even my creation of the death fetch and where it was now, and when I finally stopped, he said nothing. We lay there, and the only thing I could hear other than Nick's breathing was the soft buzz of conversation outside the room.

The quiet quickly grew too much for me to bear. "Nick?" I murmured. "You still awake?"

"Yes."

"Oh," I said, then groped around for something else to say. "I was starting to think I'd bored you to sleep."

"You did all that. For me," he said, wonder mingling with something else in his voice.

"I love you," I answered. "I wasn't going to let you go. You... you're mine. And I'm yours. I told you that in the car. I'm not leaving you. Ever."

I felt his cheek against my shoulder as he nodded. Then he shifted, and when he spoke again, he was leaning over me, and I could feel his breath on my face. "Say that again?" he asked.

"Which part? The I love you, the you're mine and I'm yours, or the not ever leaving?"

"All of it," he said.

I smiled and reached up, sliding one hand up his neck and into his hair. "I love you. You are mine, and I am yours. And neither of us is ever leaving the other." I pulled his hair as I tugged his head down to kiss him, and he moaned against my lips. We shifted together until we were lying chest to chest, kissing and touching each other. Neither of us was in any shape for anything more, and the last thing I remember as I fell asleep was Nick's breath, warm on my chest as he slept in my arms.

Chapter Fifteen
Homeward Bound

I woke up abruptly when the door opened, rolling upright and shielding the bed while I drew on my still-depleted magic to defend Nick... and stopped when I heard Liam laugh.

"Good reflexes, my brother. It's mid-morning. Do you intend to sleep another day away?"

"Another day?" I repeated, noticing as I pulled my shields back in that I was alone in the bed. "Where's Nick?"

"In the sitting room, visiting with Siana. She came to check on you both, and found Nick awake and you completely unconscious. We decided to let you sleep, but Nick will not eat without you. Something about not wanting to spend eternity in the Elvenlands? I don't know what he means."

I scrubbed my face and groaned. "He's been reading too many fairy tales. Tell him his name is not Persephone, and to eat something. I'll wash up and be out in a minute."

"Should I know who this Persephone person is?" Liam asked, making me laugh.

"No. It's a story reference. Nick will get it. Go on, I'll be right out."

I came out into the sitting room to hear a most wonderful sound—Nick laughing. I walked towards the sound, and nearly got bowled over by Mirage, who jumped up on me in her excitement.

"Steven!" Siana called out. "How do you feel?"

"Fine," I answered, going to my knees to wrestle with Mirage, who pressed up against me and started to rewash my face. "Not as raw, I don't think. My tanks are still low, though."

"That is perfectly understandable," Siana said. "You haven't eaten in over a day. You have to eat and rest, and your power will restore itself. Mirage, let him up."

Mirage whuffed slightly and backed off, making me laugh.

"You get her to listen better than I do," I said as I got back to my feet. "What do we have to eat? Nick, how are you feeling?"

"I am fine. Still somewhat confused. I met someone named... Siana, who was he?"

"He met Aodh this morning, Steven," Siana supplied. "Who wanted to know everything Nick could possibly tell him about your world."

"Really? Aodh never asked me about anything." I came over to the table and was met by Nick, who had apparently gotten up to greet me. He ran his hands up my arms, slowly, as if where checking to make sure I was real. I smiled and reached up to grab his hair, pulling him down for a kiss. "Love you, Kolya. And I'm starving."

"Sit. Eat," Liam said, clapping me on the back. "Barra was here as well this morning. He wanted to extend his invitation to the both of you. You are welcome to remain in the court for as long as you like."

"It would be a chance to rest and heal, to come back to your full power before returning to your home," Siana added.

I considered it while I started to eat, listening to the conversation that picked up where it left off. Liam was telling them something that Siana found amusing. When he mentioned Donal, I set down my cup.

"Liam, what were the losses from that assault?" I asked.

"Surprisingly light, Steven. Thanks to you. We had fifteen dead, and twice that injured."

I winced. Fifteen dead, because I hadn't done my job well enough.

"Steven, that's over four hundred alive, because of your protections," Siana said gently. "Mourn the dead, but do not blame yourself."

"And Donal?" I asked. "He's okay?"

"Fine, and full of himself," Liam answered with a long-suffering sigh. "I'm about to kick him back out from under my roof, and he doesn't even live with me anymore!"

"Donal... that is your son, no?" Nick asked. "I have a daughter..." He stopped, and I turned towards him, starting to ask if he was all right. He stopped me with a single question. "Steven, how long have we been here? In the Elvenlands?"

I frowned, thinking, then shook my head. "I've lost track. A few days?"

"And how long is that in our world?" Nick asked. "Weeks?"

I slowly shook my head. "I don't know. Liam? What's the time difference? Do you know?"

"At first, the days march in step," Siana answered, much to my surprise. "They start to diverge after three days. Or is it four? I don't remember, truly."

"How do you know that?" I asked.

"My mother was something of a historian. She charted out the time differences once, to amuse herself. The amount of time you've been here, I should think it would be no more than a week in your world."

"A week?" Nick asked. "Steven, how are we going to explain being missing for a week?"

I shook my head. "I don't know. But I don't think we should stay here any longer, Nick. I want to go home."

"Then we shall send you home," Liam said, his voice firm. "Oh, I was also going to tell you that I am going to be taking up my father's place as Gatekeeper."

"You'll be in the grove?" I asked. The idea made me ridiculously happy—having the grove be empty the next time we went would have been heartbreaking.

"Yes. He told me how much he valued your visits, and I hope that you will continue to do so? I can work with you on your sword-play."

"I need a teacher, too," I reminded him. "Someone to help me with my magic. So I can learn Si magic and maybe find a way to get rid of this thing in my head."

"I will find you that teacher," Liam promised. "And Aodh says he will contact his mother in Eire, see if she is willing to come across the seas to train you herself. We will do whatever we can to help you, Steven. We owe you a great debt."

"You know I'm the one who owes you. All of you," I said. I reached over and found Nick's hand. "I'd never have been able to do this without all of you."

I heard a chair scrape on the floor, then someone—Siana—was hugging me from behind. "You are our friend, Steven. We will help you, regardless. There are no debts between us."

I touched her arm, then turned my head and kissed her cheek. "Thank you, Siana. Now, who gets to send us home?"

"A plan, first, I think?" Liam suggested.

"All right," I agreed as Siana moved away. I picked my cup back up and took a sip of wine. "Who has an idea?"

We decided to first check the clearing where Nick and I had stopped that night. After a week, I didn't think there was any chance that the car was still there, but it would at least give us a place to start. Liam took the location from my mind, and he cast the spell to open the way, showing me how to do it so that I could return to the Elvenlands whenever I wished.

"I've embedded the location of the Court into your stone, Steven," he told me. "Use that as your guide, and you'll come back here, to the courtyard."

Once he opened the door, we walked out of the Elvenlands, and onto the shoulder of the highway. I couldn't hear any traffic, and Nick confirmed what I was thinking when he said, "It's the middle of the night."

"Do you see the car?" I asked.

"I cannot see much... yes!" I heard Nick moving away, then the sound of a car starting. "Steven, you left the keys in the ignition?"

"Nick, we were kind of distracted!"

"No, it is a good thing! My wallet, my phone, those are all gone. If you had taken the keys, we'd be no closer to home."

"Then let's go home," I said, smothering a yawn. I turned, and smiled as Liam hugged me hard.

"You did very well, High Wizard," he said. "I will see you soon, my brother?"

"It will take us a few days to get things ironed out here. Soon. Not sure when, but soon."

"Good. I will see you both at the grove."

"Thanks. Tell Donal that if he hurts Siana, I'm going to kick his ass, okay?"

Liam coughed, and sounded shocked when he gasped. "Donal? And Siana?"

I laughed and clapped him on the shoulder. "Make sure I'm invited to the wedding."

"Wedding?" Liam squeaked. "He... no! He's but a boy!" I left Liam sputtering more in that vein as Mirage and I got into the car. I closed the door, clipped the belt around me and sighed as Nick started to drive.

We didn't talk about much on the way home. There didn't seem to be much to say. Mentally, I made a list of what we'd need to do—cancel Nick's credit cards, get him a new driver's license. Get him a new cell phone, and get one for me. Contact the coven, and sit them down and tell them what had really happened.

"Penny for your thoughts?" Nick murmured.

"Just thinking about what we have to do when we get home," I answered. I reached out and rested my hand on Nick's thigh, smiling at the feel of the silken leggings under my fingers. "Wish I could see you. I'd love to see how you look like this."

"I look like a fool," he muttered. "You, however, look marvelous in these clothes."

"Do you still want—"

"Yes," Nick answered before I'd finished asking the question. I felt his leg tense under my hand, and ran my fingers up his thigh towards his crotch, finding him already half-hard.

"If you do that, we will have to stop," Nick said firmly. "And I do not think we want to do that again."

"Right," I pulled my hand back rested it in my own lap, pressing hard against my own erection. I heard Nick laugh, and knew that he must have seen me.

"I will want that, later," Nick said softly.

"Oh, trust me. You'll have it. Soon as we get home. The bags and the laundry can wait until morning. Can we go any faster?"

"Only if you can be sure that we will not be pulled over for speeding," Nick answered. "But I think that would be a waste of magic, and I want you fully awake when we get home."

"Yes, sir," I answered, and heard him snort. That set me off, and we laughed for miles, just from the sheer relief of being on our way home.

Finally, we got off the highway and made our way through the silent Catonsville side streets to our house. Nick pulled the car into the garage and stopped it, and we all got out and walked inside. The air was warm and stale, and I heard Nick moving around for a moment before the hum of the air compressor started, and the air conditioning kicked on.

"The answering machine is flashing. Should I listen to the messages now?" he asked.

"Go ahead. We can deal with anything important in the morning," I answered, stripping off my belt and doublet and sitting down on the couch, leaning my head back and letting Mirage jump up and rest her head on my lap. It was good to be home.

The messages started to play—Mary, calling to check in on us. Another from Mary. A third from Mary, demanding that we call her. One from Nick's lawyer, telling us that the results of the tests were in, and that Nick needed to call him. Yet another call from Mary, who now sounded frantic. Then...

"Is that Harry?" I asked, sitting up.

"Yes," Nick answered. I heard the message stop, then start over from the beginning.

Hi, Nick. It's Harry. Just... wanted to apologize again, and see how your... how Steven was doing. Look, I'm really sorry. And... you're not going to have to worry about Trevor any more. I just got the news. His boy found him on the floor in his apartment yesterday morning. Looks like he has a seizure of some kind, fell and hit his head. He's dead, Nick. Give me a call, will you? The number hasn't changed. Bye.

"Dead?" I repeated as the message ended. "Trevor's dead?"

"From a seizure," Nick said softly. "A seizure... like Joey?"

I blinked, not making the connection that Nick had. Then it hit me. "They were both used by Vikentiy. Nick, do you think..."

"That it was Vikentiy's magic that destroyed them? Perhaps," Nick answered as he came around and sat down next to me. "We will never know."

"I could probably tell. But I don't think the people at the morgue will let me check. So we'll leave it alone," I said. "So, first thing in the morning, we need to call Mary, George, and Celia. And the coven."

"I will probably need to go to Pennsylvania," Nick said. "If the tests show what I already know, then I will need to face Grace in court."

"We."

"What?"

"I'm going with you. This time, and every time after you need to go until we get Natalie back." I turned to face him. "Kolya, when we do get her back, we need to talk to George about how I go about adopting her."

Nick went absolutely silent. I couldn't even hear him breathing. Then he whispered, "You would do that?"

"She's going to be my daughter, too, right?" I asked. "I'm going to be her step-father? Then I should do it all the way." I felt a shiver down my spine, and got worried. "Unless you don't want me to do that?"

"Steven..." Nick started to say. He stopped, and the next thing I knew, he had pulled me into his arms and was holding on as if he were afraid I'd run away. I wasn't sure if he was happy or sad or upset or what—he'd lost his English again, and I just held him and waited for him to remember to repeat himself so I could understand. Before that happened, he pulled back, then caught my face between his hands and kissed me hard enough to loosen my teeth. I gave back as good as I got, and ended up straddling Nick's lap, pulling open his shirt as he struggled with mine. Then I remembered what the plan was supposed to be; I hooked my finger underneath the chain that I'd sealed around Nick's throat and tugged gently. His whimper of need went right to my cock. "Go into the bedroom. Pull out anything you want me to use on you. Keep it simple. Then strip, and wait for me," I told him as I slid off his lap and stood up. I heard him stand, heard his unsteady footsteps as he walked away, towards the bedroom. I turned then, and headed into the kitchen. I fed Mirage, made sure she had fresh water, and told her she was the best girl, then went and fetched my new bodhran from out of the car. I took it into the house and brought it to my room, settling it and the tipper onto the top of the shelves. I'd find a proper place for it later. But for now, Nick was probably ready for me. I ran my fingers over the drum, then hesitated.

"You need a name," I murmured to the drum. "Magic weapons get names, right?" I frowned, thinking. I didn't know much Irish, but for some reason, I knew this word. "Anfa. Your name is Anfa," I said. The word meant *tempest*—an appropriate name, I thought. I trailed my fingers over her again, nodded, then headed off to the bedroom.

I closed the door behind me and leaned against it for a moment, closing my eyes and letting soft tendrils of magic flow through the room until I found Nick. He was on his knees next to the bed, and I could feel his need, as rich as good chocolate.

"What did you choose?" I asked, almost not recognizing my own voice. Where had this dom in my head come from?

"You said to keep it simple," Nick answered. "There are straps laid out. And the cuffs. I was not sure which you would prefer."

"Fair enough," I said, coming towards the bed. I ran my fingers over the blanket until I found one of the straps, picked it up and turned around. "Stand up. Wrists behind your back, and stay still."

I heard him moving, and when I reached forward, I felt his

back; I ran one hand down his spine and found his crossed wrists. "Very nice," I murmured, using the strap to secure his hands behind his back. I ran my hands up his arms, down his sides, listening to him gasp and moan as he tried to do what I'd told him and not move. It was about this time that I realized I really had no idea what to do with him now that I had him like this. Nick was always so inventive. All I could think of to do to him was bend him over and fuck him.

Or maybe not. There was one thing that Joey had done to me, back before he'd gone off the deep end... I smiled slightly, picking up the rest of the straps and moving the cuffs off of the bed "On your knees on the bed," I told Nick. "Need help?"

"Yes, thank you," he answered, and I steadied him while he got onto the bed and into position. Once he was kneeling, I used my hands to put him into the position I wanted him—essentially, sitting on his heels. Then I picked up the straps and got to work, tying his ankles to his thighs, trying to avoid touching his cock while I did so, since I was afraid he'd go off.

"Well?" I asked when I finished tying off the last strap. "Can you move?"

I heard Nick grunt, felt the bed shifting, then rocking. Then I heard a soft whump, and laughed as I realized Nick had tipped over. When I touched him again, he was lying on his side, still squirming against the straps.

"Very nice," I said again, running my hands down his body, enjoying his moans of pleasure. "I wish I could see you. You must be so amazing like this. Now, did you pull out everything you wanted me to use on you?"

Nick whimpered, then answered, "... I think so."

"Lube?"

"On your nightstand. With a glove and condoms."

I smiled and patted his ass. "Good. Now, let's get you where I want you." I concentrated, wrapping Nick in magic and lifting him, holding him in mid-air as I pulled our big wedge cushion out from under the bed and set it up. Once it was where I wanted it, I lowered Nick down onto it, putting him into just the right position—ass in the air, helplessly waiting for me. I pulled on a glove, picked up the lube and knelt behind him, setting the tube down next to my knee and starting to massage Nick's ass. He struggled, gasping softly as his movements pressed his cock into the cushion, then louder when I momentarily pinned him in place.

"Stop that," I murmured. "I don't want you coming yet." I picked up the lube and licked my lips, suddenly nervous. I'd always been the bottom. I'd never topped anyone before. "Ummm... safeword?" I asked. I knew it, but I wanted to be sure.

"Tolstoy," Nick murmured.

"All right." I squirted some lube into my hand, considered how long it might have been since Nick was last fucked, then added some more. Without saying another word, I slowly slid a single slick, gloved finger into Nick's ass. He was tight, and I was glad of the extra lube as I teased and tormented him, opening him slowly as he whimpered and struggled and begged for more. Finally, I couldn't take any more—I stripped off the glove and fumbled for a condom, then poured still more lube into my hand, greasing my cock up and wiping the excess off on Nick's hip. I held my breath as I pressed up against his ass, then slowly started to push, feeling his sphincters pushing back against me until they finally relaxed and I slid into Nick's incredibly tight ass. I never knew it was like this, and I knew I wasn't going to last long, especially not when Nick yowled as I started to move against him, squirming under me as I grabbed into his bound wrists for leverage.

It was too new, too much sensation, entirely too heady, and I was done way too fast, gasping and shouting, then folding down over Nick's back, panting, exhausted, and completely sated. I could feel Nick under me, shivering, whining softly, and I realized that he hadn't come yet.

"Kolya?" I whispered.

"... please? Styopa? Please?"

At that moment, I couldn't have done magic if my life

depended on it, so I checked and made sure that what I was about to do wouldn't send Nick falling off the edge of the bed, then rolled him off of the cushion so that he landed on his side. The cushion got shoved onto the floor, and I pulled my struggling and moaning lover into my arms and laughed. "Now what are you going to do?" I teased him gently, running my hand up and down his side. I caught his hair in my other hand, combing my fingers through it a few times before catching it tight and pulling his head to mine.

I had planned to tease him, play with him for a little while before letting him come, but I couldn't do it. It was too much of a turn on to put him on his back, to explore his chest and belly with my tongue while I jerked him off hard and fast. He came hard, then went completely limp, panting and whining softly as I ran my fingers through the puddles on his stomach.

"You okay like this?" I asked. "I need to go get a towel, but I don't want you leave you like this if it hurts."

Nick mumbled something in Russian, and sighed happily, which I took to mean that he was fine. So I got up and fetched a washcloth from the closet, soaked it in warm water, then came back and found Nick snoring slightly. He woke up as I started to wash him off.

"You okay?" I repeated.

"I am fine. This... is very good," he answered. "I like this."

"Something that was done to me once," I said. "I'm going to roll you over and untie you. Then you can put the cushion away."

"Yes, sir," Nick said with a deep chuckle. I smiled as I pulled him towards me, then started picking out the knots in the straps. Once Nick was free, I lay back on the bed and thought about what we'd just done. It had been really hot... and something had been missing.

"You are thinking?" Nick asked as he got back on the bed and curled up with me. "What are you thinking?"

"That I'm not really a top. Not yet," I answered. "That... God, Nick, that was amazing. And... yeah, I can do that, but I don't know enough. I need to learn more. I really had no idea what to do with you, other than fuck you silly and make you come."

"That is the important part," Nick said, laughing. He hummed softly, then slid one arm over my stomach and pulled me closer to him. "I can understand how you feel. And I can accept that. I will ask you, when I need to be taken in hand. And I will help you to learn, if that is what you want."

"Great. More lessons," I teased. "Only I don't think I'll mind these all that much. Pull up the covers, will you?"

I heard Nick grunt as the bed shifted, then the covers settled down over us both as he lay back down.

"You will do fine, once you know what you are doing," he said, pulling me into his arms. I shifted around until we were spooned together, then turned slightly.

"With what?"

"With everything. You will do fine. We will be fine. And together."

I smiled and settled down to sleep. He was right. I'd learn, and we'd do fine. Together.

Heart's Master Playlist

(in order of mention)

Ain't Even Done with the Night. John Mellencamp.
Nothin' Matters and What If It Did

Bend Over, Greek Sailor.
traditional

Jingle Bells. James Pierpont
traditional

Mary Mac. Off Kilter
Etched in Stone*

Whiskey in the Jar. Off Kilter
Kick It*

Coal Quay Market. Cherish the Ladies
The Back Door*

Put Your Shoulder Next to Mine and Pump Away
traditional

Lost Forever. Van Canto
Tribe of Force

John O'Dreams. Clam Chowder.
Salvaged*
(Lyrics by Bill Caddick. Music by Pyotr Ilyich Tchaikovsky)

Magic Taborea. Van Canto
Tribe of Force

*The author's preferred version.

About the Author

Elizabeth Schechter has been called one of the top erotica and alternative sexuality writers in the world. Her writing credits include the award-winning steampunk erotic romance House of Sable Locks and the Celtic fantasy *Princes of Air*. Her shorter work has appeared in anthologies edited by D.L King (*Carnal Machines*), Laura Antoniou (*No Safewords*), and Cecilia Tan (*Jingle Balls; Like a Prince*). Elizabeth Schechter was born in New York at some point in the past. She is officially old enough to know better, but refuses to grow up. She lives in Central Florida with her husband and son, and a most accepting circle of friends who are both very amused and very proud of the pervy, fetish writer in their midst. Elizabeth can be found online at http://elizabethschechterwrites.com or at https://www.facebook.com/Elizabeth.A.Schechter.

Also by Elizabeth Schechter

House of Sable Locks

A steampunk novel of dark passion. In a respectable neighborhood, on the top floor of a beautiful house, crouches the Succubus; by design, and by temperament, she is all that men crave and fear. To the wealthy and privileged men of London, the Succubus is a test they must pass to gain access to the House of Sable Locks, the most exclusive brothel in town. However, to William, a wealthy young man born and raised in India, she is the very essence of his desires.

William is recovering from the loss of everything he knows and loves when he first meets the Succubus. With great care she tears him apart… and he falls in love again. But their idyll cannot last: there is a killer loose in London, and the darkness of William's past is about to collide with the terror of his present.

Tales from the Arena

New Editions Forthcoming in 2017

The Ishkarin were created to be the perfect soldiers. The perfect predators. The perfect sadists. But what happens to the perfect soldiers when the war they were created to fight is over? In the Arena, the Ishkarin find an outlet for their natural instincts. Populated by the Collared, the sexual submissives who live to kneel before the predators, the Arena guarantees that the Ishkarin will not prey on the people they have sworn to protect.

Princes of Air

Long ago, the Raven-Goddess Morrigan bore nine sons; each of them was gifted by their mother with the ability to change their shape and fly as ravens. Their mother charged them with the task of protecting the people of Eire, and gave them each another gift — the ability to recognize their one true mate. Niall, the youngest of the nine, believes his mate lost forever, and discovers how wrong he is when he is taken captive by Arlaith, a power-mad woman who seeks to overthrow the High King. Arlaith's plans unleash an ancient evil that threatens the people, the land itself, and what hope of happiness Niall and his brothers hold.

Gay Romance
from Clasp Editions and Circlet Press

Simulacrum by Rian Darcy
In the virtual world of Simulnet, no one knows who you really are, making it the perfect playground for the imagination… and for a serial killer. Shaun's world turns upside down when a police detective asks for his help finding a murderer somewhere in the cyberspace sex clubs, ramen shops, and massage parlors of Simulnet. His partner on the case will be a prickly and enigmatic programmer known only as Lore. Combining romance, mystery, and cyberpunk, Rian Darcy creates a world for the reader every bit as engrossing and heart-stopping as Simulnet itself.

Chocolatiers of the High Winds by H.B. Kurtzwilde
This gay steampunk romance follows the globe-trotting adventures of young Mayport Titus, the sole scion of the Titus Chocolate fortune. Mayport's father, an adventurer and entrepreneur, established the intercontinental chocolate trade before he and his wife were lost when their airship went down over the ocean and left Mayport orphaned. Now determined to make his own way in the world, Mayport rebuilds his father's old airship, The Dutch Process, and revives the business with the help of Thiervy, an intimate school friend. But their partnership will be tested. Love between men is not sanctioned in society, punishable by death for airshipmen, and kept behind closed doors. Chocolatiers of the High Winds is a rollicking romance in classic adventuring style, punctuated with passion and sweetened with chocolate.

The Prince's Boy by Cecilia Tan
In a fantasy world where the lust of male for male fuels Night Magic, Prince Kenet lives a sheltered life. Isolated from the war that threatens the kingdom, he and his whipping boy Jorin are of age, but still sneak forbidden pleasures in their bed at night. When a dark mage tries to bespell Kenet into sexual submission, the prince and his boy are thrust into the world of intrigue, sex, and war. Drawing on complex themes of dominance and submission, Tan weaves a complex, sex-filled adventure that is part "Three Musketeers" and part "Claiming of Sleeping Beauty."

Circlet Press
Erotica for Geeks

Celebrating the Erotic Imagination Since 1992

Receive books like this one for joining the
Circlet Press, Inc. Patreon supporters!

http://patreon.com/circletpress

Circlet
Press

Join the Circlet Press email list to find out about
new releases, special sales and discounts,
and what our authors are up to:

http://www.circlet.com/contact-us/email-newsletter/